Dear Reader,

Scarlet is now two months old and I was delighted by your response to last month's launch. From your reaction, it seems that *Scarlet* is just what you've been waiting for, so I hope that you'll enjoy the four books I've chosen specially for you this month.

There's a questionnaire at the back of this book and, if you didn't complete and return one last month, I'd be delighted if you'd do so as soon as possible. When we receive your completed questionnaire, we'll be happy to send you a surprise free gift.

This month, *Scarlet* is offering you a book set deep in the heart of Texas, another which takes place in Canada and two with English backgrounds. Do you like this mixture of locations? What's *your* favourite setting? And how do you like our covers?

Because we want you to remain a *Scarlet* woman, we'd like your views on what you like best about our new list, so do drop me a line.

Till next month,
Best wishes,

Sally Cooper

SALLY COOPER,
Editor-in-Chief – *Scarlet*

About the Author

Kay Gregory was born and educated in England. Shortly after moving to Victoria, Canada, she met her husband in the unromantic setting of a dog club banquet. Since 1961, Kay and her husband have lived in the Vancouver area, and they have two grown sons who frequently return home to commune with the contents of the family fridge!

At various times, Kay has cohabited, more or less willingly, with dogs, hamsters gerbils, rats and ferrets . . . currently down to one neurotic dog. Over the years Kay has had more jobs than she can count: everything from packaging paper bags (the bags won and she lost the job!) to running a health food bar, cleaning offices and working as a not-very-efficient secretary. Kay says: 'Writing books is definitely the best job I've ever had, and one I don't plan to change. Selling my first long contemporary novel to *Scarlet* is one of the most exciting things that has happened to me.'

*Other **Scarlet** titles available this month:*

A QUESTION OF TRUST – Margaret Callaghan
IT TAKES TWO – Tina Leonard
DECEPTION – Sophie Weston

Marry Me Stranger

KAY GREGORY

MARRY ME STRANGER

Enquiries to:
Robinson Publishing Ltd
7 Kensington Church Court
London W8 4SP

First published in the UK by Scarlet, 1996

A copy of the British Library Cataloguing in
Publication data is available from the British Library

ISBN 1-85487-483-7

Printed and bound in the EC

10 9 8 7 6 5 4 3 2 1

To my husband, BOB, without whose love, support computer skills and cooking I would never have completed this book. To **Judy McAnerin** for having the courage to read it before it was one. To **Catherine Spencer** for being a true friend. To **Bob and Graeme Lindsay** for their South American inspiration, and to everyone (you know who you are) who helped my dreams become a reality.

PROLOGUE

No. Oh, no. *No!* Brand slammed his fist into the pillow. It wasn't possible. He swore, silently and with passion. He couldn't have, *wouldn't* have . . .

The woman who lay beside him in the bed wrinkled her nose in her sleep. Brand inhaled a long draught of air. He *had* to stay in control. This square attic room with its sweating walls *must* stay in focus. He couldn't allow it to turn upside-down.

Slowly the room – or was it his head? – came to rest the way it was meant to be. He forced himself to keep calm as he lay on his side and gazed at his companion of the night. If that was what she was. He supposed she must be. Her long, dark hair was spread out on his pillow and her chest rose and fell steadily, as if she had been asleep for some hours.

Brand dashed a hand across his eyes. Surely to heaven he must be dreaming. Just as he had been dreaming last night that his Mary was once again beside him. Although Mary had been merely pretty, and this woman with the heart-shaped face, impossibly long eyelashes and soft, sensuous lips was beautiful. Breathtakingly beautiful.

And she couldn't be more than – sixteen?

He groaned and flung himself onto his back, staring, without seeing it, at the single, unshaded lightbulb.

That dream – had it not been a dream after all?

Slowly, with profound reluctance, he dragged himself up to take another look at the girl who was sharing his bed. In the pale light from the fly-spattered window he saw her eyebrows draw together, as if she sensed that her waking would be troubled.

A memory caught at his mind, hazy and without conclusion. Last night, as he had been heading for forgetfulness in a bar, a young girl had run up to him, calling out as though he was her friend. She had begged him to stay with her until the man who was chasing her had gone. He hadn't recognized her, hadn't cared. But she had been frightened and in trouble. He had probably said yes. All he knew now was that he had spent the evening in the bar with someone who didn't talk much, drinking himself into oblivion. If he was not mistaken, they were now in a room over that bar.

Who was she? She didn't look like a lady of the night. There was something innocent and patrician about her face, and the dress that lay crumpled on the floor was made of expensive material.

4

But if she wasn't for hire . . .

Dear God, what had he done? He closed his eyes for a few seconds, and then, very carefully, so as not to disturb her, he drew the sheet down from her neck.

She was naked, with a soft feminine body that curved in all the right places. A tightness constricted Brand's chest. Mary had had a body like that. Was that why, last night, he had dreamed . . .?

But this ripe young creature was not Mary. And in the dream hadn't he wondered how their wedding night could be happening again – but with a subtle, intoxicating difference?

No! Surely it wasn't possible . . .

Or was it?

Crushing the sheet in his fist, he made himself draw it down to her knees. Yes, there it was. A small, reddish-brown stain that before it had dried had been a truer, deeper red.

It had been real, then, the dream.

A sob caught in his throat and the girl stirred, smiled in her sleep, and placed a trusting hand on his chest.

A shudder ran through him, followed by a wash of tenderness that took him by surprise. She looked so soft, so vulnerable, so – young. And she had been so giving . . .

Oh, yes, the dream had been real. How could he possibly have thought otherwise? Brand pressed his fists against his eyelids, seeking to still the pounding in his temples as memory stirred, prodded to life the knowledge his mind had sought to blot out.

This innocent angel of his dreams had given him a gift that could only be given once. A gift most gently reared women in her country of rigid tradition chose to keep for the man they would marry. As his lost love had kept it for him . . .

Mary. He threw his head back and the words that rasped from his throat were an anguished groan of grief, torment and remorse.

'Mary. Forgive me!'

There was no answer, as he had known there couldn't be. Yet, for the first time since he had lost his Mary, Brand knew he would survive the lonely years that lay ahead.

His companion's eyelids fluttered upwards, and he looked down into the deepest, widest, loveliest dark eyes he had ever seen.

'Hi,' he said, wondering at the softness of her skin, the symmetry of her delicate features and the way her small hand reached confidently for his. 'Did you sleep well?'

Asinine question! She had slept like the baby she was. It was what had gone before that mattered.

She inclined her head solemnly. 'Yes. Did you?'

Brand closed his eyes. 'Apparently.'

He felt her hand tighten around his fingers, and he made himself look at her again. 'Who are you?' he asked.

6

'I am Isabella. And you . . .?'

'Me? I'm just a stranger you kissed in the night.' Bitter irony. But the truth. He smoothed a lock of hair gently off her forehead.

She smiled, fixed the big, serious eyes on his face. 'Then marry me, stranger,' she said.

Brand swallowed. Her smile was sunlight blotting out the darkness, the age-old message that Eve had sent to Adam.

And he nodded. His Mary was gone. This beautiful, trusting woman-child was in his bed. She had asked him to marry her, and how could he deny her that protection? After what he had unwittingly done, he owed her more than a casual kiss and dismissal to the tender mercies of the streets.

Yes, he would marry her. It didn't matter.

And what else was there to do?

CHAPTER 1

The house was in sore need of a fresh coat of paint. That was the first thing Isabella noticed as Brand helped her out of the ancient Volkswagen Beetle he had driven from the airport. Shabby house, shabby green car with a case of incurable rust . . . She glanced doubtfully at her husband, who was busy swinging luggage onto the sidewalk.

He didn't look battered and run-down. Just sad. So why were the car and the house in such startling contrast to his appearance? This virile, darkly compelling man she had married ought to be driving something fast and expensive, like the planes he flew for a living, and she had expected his home to be either large and imposing or a penthouse.

Brand returned her look with one that practically dared her to complain, so she gave him a brave smile and went back to studying the house.

How tall and narrow and *grey* it was compared to the welcoming, white-walled haciendas she was accustomed to in her South American homeland.

9

Her family's principal residence, in particular, had been large and sprawling and surrounded by a spacious brick courtyard that trapped the sun. Here, there was no courtyard, and even the weather was grey – as damp and cold and depressing as she had read that the west coast of Canada was *not* supposed to be.

Isabella shivered, and pulled up the collar of the navy blue raincoat Brand had bought for her just before they boarded the plane. She had wanted red, but he had said red was too flashy for the wife of a man who was in mourning. She had stifled an immediate impulse to argue. His mourning was too obviously real.

'Cold?' Brand asked, shouldering two suitcases and striding ahead of her up the cracked flagstone path.

'Yes, a little,' she admitted, skipping to keep up with him. 'Is Vancouver always this gloomy?'

'There's a saying here on the coast that we don't tan – we rust. But, no, it's not entirely true. See, there's a crocus blooming over there.' He pointed at a solitary purple flower poking through a patch of neglected lawn. 'Spring will be here before long.'

Isabella heard the way he said spring – as if it were a season of despair – and she guessed springtime meant nothing to him this year. Would it ever? What had she done, marrying this stranger with the dark, tormented eyes? This stranger about whom all she

10

really knew was that he was out of his mind with grief over the loss of his bride of six days. Her name had been Mary, and she had been killed in a landslide on their honeymoon.

Yet Brand had been kind to the frightened girl he had picked up on the teeming city streets, and even in his drunken, anguished stupor he had made love to her with tenderness and passion. She had experienced no doubts that morning three days ago when she had awoken in his bed above the bar and seen him leaning over her as if he didn't want to believe what his eyes were showing him.

She had known at once he was destined to be hers.

It wasn't until they had found a priest to marry them, and were safely on the plane, that practical doubts had begun to penetrate her euphoria.

Brand had looked so desperate and so sad – and he had hardly spoken a word to her on the long flight back to Vancouver . . .

Now, gazing up at her tall, dark-haired husband as she followed him up the path to the dilapidated house, it wasn't only the damp that made Isabella shiver.

'Why are we going this way?' she asked. Brand was heading round the side of the house instead of climbing the wooden steps to the rickety old-fashioned porch.

'Our entrance is at the back.'

'But why?'

11

'We live in the basement, Isabella.'

'In the basement? But there's a whole house up there.' Had she married a beautiful crazy man?

'Another tenant lives in that part. Some woman with a baby. Mary and I decided we didn't want to blow all the money we earned on rent. We planned to live cheaply until we'd saved enough to buy a house of our own. That was Mary's big dream – a house of her own.'

There was that devastating bleakness again. Lord, what had she let herself in for?

'So you – that is, we – are going to live in a cellar?' She couldn't, *wouldn't* believe this.

Brand stopped by a narrow door with more peeling paint. Something that might have become a smile if he had allowed it to develop flickered across his lips and disappeared. 'Not a cellar, exactly. The advertisement called it a "deluxe basement suite".'

Deluxe? That meant luxurious, didn't it? Maybe their home wouldn't be so bad after all. Her spirits lifted a little.

But as soon as Brand opened the door, and rusty hinges whined in protest, she knew it was going to be worse. Worse than her most pessimistic nightmares.

Steep, uncarpeted stairs led down to a dungeon-like passage with a concrete floor that felt cold beneath her feet. Two unmatched doors, set across from each other in flimsy, particle-board walls, looked as though they had been rescued from a dump. Which they probably had, she reflected morosely.

'This is ours,' Brand said, throwing open the door on the right.

'What's behind the other one?'

'Who, not what. His name's Gary Roseboy. He's a security guard for one of the shipyards. Or so he says. It's true enough he works unusual hours.'

'Don't you believe him?'

Brand shrugged. 'Sure. Why not? It's his extra-curricular activities I have a problem with.'

Isabella didn't know what extra-curricular meant, but Brand looked so grim she decided not to ask. He had spoken of their neighbour as if he were mouthing profanities.

She glanced doubtfully at the open doorway and wondered why two apartments had been squeezed into such a small space. There were plenty of squalid shanty towns in her own country – but surely Brand didn't expect *her* to live like that? As she crossed the threshold she closed her eyes, afraid of what she would see.

When she opened them again, reluctantly, the first thing she saw was the slime-green linoleum covering the floor. She shuddered, and it was several seconds before she found the courage to lift her head.

They were standing in a cramped kitchen with a chipped white sink, a small, once-white fridge and a stove that could have been purchased in the bargain department of a turn-of-the-century antiques shop. It even had legs. The remaining floor space was taken up by a scratched wooden table with two square-backed chairs and a green and red tartan loveseat.

'It's very small,' said Isabella. 'Dark. And it smells of mould. Why is there just that one little window?'

'Because this is a basement.' Brand switched on the light. 'There. Better?'

It wasn't. Now she could see the cracks in the walls. And with the light on Brand seemed larger and the room even smaller. 'The floor is very dirty,' she said. 'And that looks like grease on the stove. It is a stove, isn't it?' She forced back a rising tide of panic.

'Yes. It comes with the apartment.' Brand's voice was clipped.

Was he angry? Angry that she didn't admire this terrible little hole? 'Where is the drawing room?' she asked. 'And the bathroom? And the – the bedroom?'

'Drawing room?' Brand laughed. It was the first time she had ever heard him laugh, but it wasn't a sound calculated to cheer her. '*Drawing* room?' he repeated. 'There isn't one. The bathroom's through there, although I'm afraid the plumbing tends to be unpredictable, and the bedroom is this way.' He opened a door without looking at her, and she walked past him into another tiny room.

It contained a brass double bed, two small, un-painted chests of drawers and an equally small but surprisingly new-looking steel desk. The pale blue walls and carpet were almost clean. This was better. Isabella started to say so, but Brand interrupted her tersely.

'I'll have the bed taken out, of course.'

'Taken out? But . . .'

'And have two single ones put in. I'm sorry, but there's only the one bedroom.'

'Oh, but there is no need. I mean, are we not . . .?' She stumbled to a halt.

'No,' Brand said. 'We're not.'

'But – we are married.'

'I'm aware of that. But you needn't worry. I've already taken advantage of you once. I don't plan to do it again.'

'You would not be taking advantage.' She held herself stiffly, unwilling to betray her hurt.

'Of course I would. You're scarcely more than a child.'

'That is not what you thought three nights ago.'

Brand put a hand over his eyes. 'Isabella, you have to understand. Three nights ago I had only just lost my wife. I didn't know what I was doing, and you offered comfort. For which I was grateful.'

'Comfort? That was all?'

'No, of course it wasn't all. You know that as well as I do. But it didn't mean anything, Isabella. Other than that I'd temporarily lost my sanity – along with the wife I had waited four years to marry.'

Oh. Yes, of course. Brand was still in love with that

15

fluffy blonde Mary – which was as it should be. All
the same, she couldn't help regretting it. She thrust
her tongue pensively into her cheek. No. No, it
wasn't sensible to expect him to feel anything for
another woman yet. But soon, once he'd had time to
get over his grief, she would find a way to make him
love her – more than he had ever loved that timid,
insipid little Mary.

Isabella squared her shoulders. Except for that
once, when she had run away from home, she was
used to getting what she wanted. Certainly any dress
or piece of jewellery she coveted. So why should it be
any different now, just because what she wanted this
time was a man? She *would* make him love her. She
would. For now, though, perhaps it would be better
to appear sweet and sympathetic.

'I understand,' she said, touching Brand on the
arm. 'Of course you are not yet ready to forget your
other wife. I would not expect it.'

'I'll never forget her.' Brand spoke with such
finality that Isabella was tempted to believe him –
until she remembered that she almost always got her
way. In the end.

'Of course you won't,' she said softly. 'I do understand. Come, we had better unpack.'

That night Brand slept in a sleeping bag on the floor.
When Isabella woke early in the morning she saw
him lying there, and remembered the cracked walls

16

and the grease – and the grey skies and all the people with their heads down scurrying from the rain – and she put her hands over her face and began to cry.

Brand grunted and turned over. 'Shut up,' he said.

'What?' Isabella gasped and stopped crying. 'What did you say?'

'Mm? I said, shut up.'

Her shocked silence must have got through to him, because all at once he came fully awake. She watched as he rolled over and propped himself up on one elbow. He didn't look particularly contrite. 'Listen, there's no point in crying, Isabella. I know this apartment isn't much . . .'

'It's horrible. Quite horrible.'

It was too. But it was the sight of Brand lying there on the threadbare blue carpet, all rumpled and sexy and sleepy, and refusing to join her on the bed that had made her cry.

'You could have found a cleaner place.' She wasn't about to tell him the truth. It was too humiliating.

'Mary said she'd fix it up herself,' Brand replied with a hint of impatience. 'It's only dirt.'

Hearing the impatience, Isabella let out a howl like a wolf cub that had lost its mother, and allowed the tears to continue unabated.

Brand swore quietly, extricated himself from the sleeping bag and stalked off into the bathroom. Isabella glared balefully at his back and thumped the pillow with her fist. A second later she heard the pipes begin to knock as Brand turned on the water for his shower.

Damn him anyway. He had no right to tell her to shut up, no right to bring her to this dump, no right – no right not to love her at least a little.

She was still crying when he emerged from the bathroom, but more from temper than genuine distress.

Brand scowled at the dark-eyed and nearly naked nymph flooding his bed with her tears. 'Look,' he said, 'I know all this is a shock – '

'It is worse than a shock.' Isabella rubbed her knuckles over her eyes. 'And you don't even care.'

'I do care.'

He stood in the doorway with a towel draped around his hips and his thick hair wet and dark across his forehead. She could just see the tops of his funny, curled-over ears. The first time she'd noticed them she had laughed, but Brand had told her almost proudly that those were the Ryder ears. Now they seemed a part of him, and she loved them.

Isabella pulled the sheet over her head. He looked so desirable, and so unfairly unavailable standing there all wet and warm from his shower, that she wanted to scream in frustration.

'Can't you even apologize?' she snapped from beneath the covers.

'Apologize for what?'

'For bringing me here – to this place.'

'You wanted to come,' he said wearily. 'You asked me to marry you. Remember?'

She pushed the sheet down and sat up. 'Yes, but I had no idea – '

'That flying planes hasn't yet made me rich? That's not my fault, Isabella. In a few years . . .

'You should have told me.'

'Somehow I think I did.'

'Yes, but I didn't know – '

'All right,' he interrupted. 'So you didn't know, or didn't understand, how little money we would have to start out with. Wouldn't you have married me, then, if you had known?'

He didn't care either way. She could tell. The question was purely clinical. And of course she would have married him. What choice had she had? Besides, she'd wanted to.

Not that she was about to admit that to this scowling, towel-clad Adonis who was currently blocking her exit from the room.

'You owe me an apology,' she insisted.

'Not any more, I don't. I married you. That's apology enough. Now get up out of that bed and stop snivelling.'

Isabella, who had never been spoken to so roughly in her life, was so astonished that she did as she was told.

That evening, as Brand trudged wearily around the

19

side of the house and down the stairs, his nose was assaulted by the unusual smell of polish and disinfectant. What on earth had Isabella been up to? He wasn't in the mood for surprises.

It hadn't been a particularly good day. But then, how could it have been? Without Mary, no day was good, and Isabella's presence only made him more aware of what he'd lost. His old woman of a boss hadn't helped much either, with his insistence that Brand see a doctor instead of flying those two prospectors to Yellowknife. There was nothing wrong with him. Nothing he couldn't handle on his own, without the aid of needles or pills.

He sniffed. The smell seeping under the basement door was not unpleasant. Better than the odour of mould and rancid grease that had been the most potent aroma when he'd left the apartment that morning.

Poor little Isabella. No wonder she'd cried. He should have been kinder to her. But, dammit, what in hell had she expected? This was the home he had planned to share with Mary. It wasn't easy listening to his child-bride run it down – however justified she was in her complaints. Perhaps he should have realized how the place was likely to affect her. But he hadn't. His surroundings had never mattered to him much. They mattered even less now.

He sniffed again and unlocked the door. Something was cooking on that apology for a stove. Stew?

Burned, if he wasn't mistaken. He hurried over to pull the heavy cast-iron pot off the element. Just as he did so Isabella came out of the bedroom.

She was wearing the sweater and green wool skirt he had bought for her along with the navy raincoat – and she filled them remarkably well. Only a smudge of black grime across her nose detracted from the image of Domesticated Little Woman she was so obviously striving to create.

'Hello,' she said. 'I've been cleaning.'

'Yes, so I see. It's on your nose.'

'What is?' Isabella hurried into the bathroom to inspect her face, and Brand took the opportunity to look around the kitchen.

The linoleum was polished and shining, the walls clean, and the stove and the fridge were both white now, instead of grey. The tartan loveseat was still damp from a scrubbing and the table, set for two with place-mats and paper napkins, had been pushed against the wall to give an illusion of space. No lacy doilies or feminine frills, he noted with relief. Just a sensible, practical rearrangement. He raked a hand through his hair. Who would have thought his spoiled South American brat could be so capably domestic?

'It looks much better,' he said, smiling at Isabella as she came out of the bathroom with a clean face and a well-washed nose. 'You've done wonders.'

The smile she gave him back was radiant. It would

21

have warmed his heart if he'd been capable of warmth.

'Do you like it?' she asked eagerly. 'Are you sure?'

'I like it very much. What else have you been doing?'

'Oh.' She put a hand to her mouth. 'I started to cook dinner, but – '

'It's all right. I think I caught it in time.' Brand lifted the lid off the pot – and gazed doubtfully at the congealed brown mess that simmered like primordial mud in the bottom. He didn't give a damn what he ate, but Isabella had made such an effort to please him that he hated to see her disappointed. Besides, she was likely to turn on the waterworks again, and he had enough tears of his own left to cry.

She came up behind him and peered into the pot. 'I have killed it, haven't I?' she moaned.

'I think it was already dead.' Brand was taken aback to find himself wanting to put his arm around her, to offer comfort as, not long ago, she had tried to comfort him. Poor child, she looked so forlorn standing there gazing into the remains of what might have been their supper.

'Don't worry,' he said. 'You're not the only woman who can't cook. Now, fetch your coat. There's a pizza place down the road. We'll eat there, and then I'll take you on a tour of Vancouver in the rain.'

'Pizza!' Her eyes lit up. 'I've never had pizza. Is it good?'

22

'Very good.' He took her hand, and she gave him a smile as sweet and trusting as the one she had turned on him that first morning.

Lord, she was beautiful. He had recognized that from the moment he had laid eyes on her. But when she smiled she was Cleopatra, Helen of Troy and Aphrodite rolled into one – an innocent, but almost lethal package.

Yet she was still a child. Easily upset and at the same time so ready to be placated with a treat. He shook his head. Children were a responsibility as well as a delight. Pray God he would be able to handle this one, because if the mutterings of that old fool of a doctor turned out to have any substance, he wasn't sure he'd be able to cope with a mosquito – let alone this gorgeous teenager masquerading as a woman.

He gave her hand a squeeze, and told her again to fetch her coat.

As they headed up the stairs together he wished for the thousandth time that the past six days had been but a dream – that Mary was still alive and Isabella no more than a fantasy of the night who would vanish with the revealing light of day.

But when he woke in the morning she was still there, serene, alive, and breathing softly in his bed.

CHAPTER 2

Isabella was in the bathroom trying to unplug the washbasin when the thumping sound started up in the passageway.

Dear heaven, what was happening out there? Had Gary Roseboy and one of his assignations fallen down the stairs in their eagerness to get to his bedroom? She had found out what extra-curricular meant by now.

Brandishing the chopstick that she had been using to poke at the drain, Isabella hurried out to investigate the disturbance.

Two beefy young men in back-to-front baseball caps were standing just outside her door, holding what looked like a pile of old fenceposts wrapped in used pyjamas.

'Ryder?' said the shorter of the two.

'Um – yes, I am Mrs Ryder,' Isabella admitted.

'Right.' He glanced at a crumpled square of blue paper. 'Delivering two beds with mattresses. Where d'you want 'em, ma'am?'

Oh. So that was what was in the pyjamas. Beds. Isabella felt a coldness in her stomach. 'I *don't* want them,' she said.

Brand might have spent the last week sleeping on the floor, but that was his problem. She had no intention of encouraging his militant celibacy. There was always a chance that if he became sufficiently uncomfortable he might actually consider joining her in their bed.

The man who had spoken scratched his head. 'Already signed and paid for, ma'am. Nothing here about returning for refund.'

'I don't care,' said Isabella. 'You'll have to take them back.'

'Can't do that, ma'am. Like I said, signed and – '

'I know. Paid for,' she interrupted. 'But you can't bring them in if I refuse them.' She tapped her foot impatiently on the concrete, and the man stared at his paper and began to scowl.

'Isabella? What's going on?' a familiar voice demanded from the top of the stairs.

She looked up in time to see a pair of black leather boots appear in her line of vision, followed by a seductive pair of masculine legs in jeans. Eventually the whole of a stern-visaged Brand emerged into the passageway to demand again, 'Well? I asked what's going on.'

She waved her chopstick at the pyjama-clad fenceposts. 'I'm trying to explain to these men that we don't need any new beds.'

'Then you're explaining wrong. I told you I was having the double taken out.'

'Yes, but I didn't think . . . Brand, we are married. This is ridiculous.'

'No,' said Brand. 'It's sheer self-preservation. And a damn sight more comfortable than the floor.'

'But –'

'This isn't open to debate, Isabella. Now, get out of the way and let the men do their job.'

The two delivery men exchanged smirks. She felt her cheeks turning pink.

'Brand, please . . .' She searched his face for some sign of softening, and didn't find it. He was standing with his legs apart and both hands on his hips, looking like the Rock of Gibralter on a power trip. This was one battle she wasn't going to win.

The delivery men's smirks grew broader. Her face grew pinker. Biting her lip, Isabella turned her back on Brand and his accomplices and stalked back into the bathroom.

'Damn,' she muttered, stabbing viciously at the drain. 'Damn, damn, *damn*!' All at once the backed-up water in the basin gave a triumphant gurgle and disappeared. She gave the now unobstructed outlet a final stab for good measure and marched back out to the kitchen.

Brand was just closing the door on the delivery

men. When she glanced at the bedroom she saw that the fenceposts and pyjamas had miraculously been transformed into two narrow wooden beds with striped mattresses.

'We have no sheets that will fit them,' she said sullenly.

'I'll pick some up later.'

'But there was no need . . .' She allowed her voice to trail off. What was the use? Brand wouldn't listen. She might as well talk to the fridge.

He was standing against the door with his arms crossed. There was a hint of wry amusement in his eyes. 'Don't look so wounded,' he said. 'One day you'll understand. And be grateful.'

'You sound just like my father,' she snapped.

'Do I? Perhaps that should tell you something,' he said drily.

'Oh! How could you? You know you liked it when we – when we . . .'

'Shared the same bed?' he suggested. 'Yes, you're right, I did. It's not something I'm proud of.' He uncrossed his arms and came towards her. 'Don't sulk, Isabella. It won't do any good.'

She opened her mouth to tell him exactly what she thought of husbands who wouldn't sleep with their wives, but Brand put two fingers across her lips and said softly, 'Don't. You know you'll regret it.'

Isabella resisted an impulse to bite him. His fingers smelled of strong soap. When she took them

27

away, she said, 'Oh, very well. *I* don't care. Why should I want you snoring in my bed?'

To her fury, instead of insisting indignantly that he didn't snore – which as a matter of fact he didn't – Brand only laughed. 'That's better,' he said. 'Now then, I have an appointment I have to keep. But I'll be home after that. Would you like to go out to a movie?'

'What's this? A bribe so I'll be a good little girl?'

Irritation replaced the amusement in Brand's eyes. 'If you like. That's up to you. It wasn't intended as a bribe.' With that he turned on his heel and vanished through the door so rapidly that it was a few seconds before she took in that he'd gone.

Isabella, with her eyes firmly averted from the new beds, walked across to the loveseat and slumped down. If only she was better at being patient. The business of his dear departed Mary was bad enough. But if Brand persisted in thinking of himself as El Cid protecting her lost virtue, then breaking down his resistance was going to take much longer than she'd thought. She rubbed her eyes, picked up a cushion and threw it in the direction of the bedroom.

In the evening, when Brand came home, he was carrying a small red box. 'Here,' he said, handing it to Isabella. 'And it's a peace-offering, not a bribe. Do you suppose we can call a truce? At least for the moment?'

'How long is a moment?' asked Isabella.

'Open the box,' Brand said tersely.

She opened the box. It contained a thin silver bracelet with a design of intertwined leaves. Her father had given her one very like it, only more expensive, not long before she ran away.

When Brand clasped it gently around her wrist Isabella gulped, dropped her head onto his shoulder and said, 'Thank you,' in a voice so muffled he could hardly hear it.

He stared over the top of her head, breathing in the sweet, fresh scent of her hair. Hell. This beautiful sprite he had married was turning out to be more of a handful than he'd expected. And more of a temptation.

'Come on,' he said abruptly. 'Let's go and find something to eat. Then you get to choose the movie.'

As he might have guessed she would, Isabella chose a sentimental love story. It was a gentle tale, with the happy ending he had been denied in reality. When they came out afterwards into the rain, she clung to his arm and smiled up at him with stars in her eyes.

'It has been a beautiful evening,' she said.

Seeing her smile, just for a minute and until he remembered, Brand was inclined to agree with her.

Isabella hugged her arms around her chest. This time her surprise wouldn't turn into an overcooked disaster. This time Brand would be impressed. What, after all, could go wrong with a soufflé? It was just a matter of beating up eggs and adding a bit of cheese. Mariette, her family's French cook, had made them often. She glanced at her watch, a dainty silver one that seemed too expensive for this mousehole of a kitchen, and hoped Brand wouldn't be much longer.

He wasn't flying today, although he had gone out to the airport as usual. It was odd that he hadn't flown at all during the three weeks they had been in Vancouver. When she had asked him if he was still on holiday he'd said, no, that the flight schedules were being rearranged but he expected to be back in the air any day now.

Isabella didn't want him in the air. She wanted him on the ground and in her bed. But there was no point telling him that. She hadn't believed he was altogether serious before, but the humiliating scene over the delivery of the two single beds had convinced her. Well, almost convinced her. She had tried once more to change Brand's mind, but that time, instead of responding, the moment she had brought the subject up he had turned his back on her and gone all taciturn and brooding.

Apart from that, she had to admit that most of the time he was good to her, in a distracted sort of way – and thank heaven he had stopped tossing and turning all night on his solitary bed next to hers. She hadn't heard him call out Mary's name since that first week.

Isabella stole another look at her watch, and

sighed. Brand still looked desperately tired a lot of the time. But his dark eyes were less cavernous now, and they no longer appeared to have sunk into his head. That was something.

Oh, yes, surely if she waited, and was patient, he would have to love her in the end. Why, only the other day he had taken both her hands in his and said, 'Good for you,' when she'd told him that Judy, the young mother upstairs who had become her friend, was helping her to polish up her English. Not that it needed much polishing. She and her sisters had shared a British governess.

Isabella gave the eggbeater a final swirl, and was just putting the baking dish in the oven when a tentative knock sounded on the door. She hurried to open it, wearing a smile of welcome that would have made her hospitable mother proud.

A young man with brown curly hair and dimples stood on the threshold looking sheepish.

'Hello, Gary,' said Isabella. 'What have you run out of this time?'

'Milk,' said Gary. 'Can you spare some? I'd go to the store, but I only need a cup . . .'

'And it's raining,' Isabella finished for him. 'It always is. Yes, I can spare you a cup. Come in.' She pulled a carton out of the fridge and poured milk into the oversized mug Gary held out to her.

'Thanks,' he said. 'You're a doll, Isabella. If you ever get tired of old Brand, just let me know.'

'He's not old. He's twenty-six. And I won't get tired of him – ' Isabella broke off as the lock clicked open and Brand's formidable figure loomed in the doorway.

He raised his eyebrows, glancing incuriously from Gary to Isabella.

Gary grinned nervously. 'Just joking,' he said, and sidled out into the passage.

'What did he want this time?' Brand asked. 'Apart from you?'

'Milk,' said Isabella. 'And he was only teasing. He knows we're married.'

'That small detail has never troubled him before.' Brand spoke over his shoulder as he took off his coat and disappeared into the bedroom.

Isabella watched him go with her lips pursed. Soon she would make him look at her when he spoke. She was tired of being almost invisible. Not that Brand was unkind, quite the contrary, but he was so abstracted she sometimes felt as if he thought of her as a kind of household pet, to be kept happy with the occasional scratch or pat on the head.

'Did you have a pleasant day?' she asked when he came back into the kitchen wearing jeans, and with the sleeves of his white shirt rolled back to just below his elbows.

'Mm?' He glanced her way as if he had temporarily forgotten her existence. 'No, as a matter of fact I didn't.'

'Oh. I'm sorry.' She knew better by now than to ask him what was wrong. He would only grunt and say he was going out to buy a paper.

'Not your fault.' He pulled out a chair and sat down at the table, his eyes staring through her as they did so often. She guessed he was thinking of Mary – and yet his expression was tough and hard, where surely it ought to be tender and filled with regret . . .

Impulsively, Isabella took the other chair and leaned towards him. 'Brand,' she said, reaching across the table to touch his hand, 'why can't you talk to me? I am your wife.'

He shook his head and pulled away from her as if her touch repelled him. 'I've given you all I can, Isabella. I'm sorry if it isn't enough.'

Isabella bit the corner of her lip. 'It is enough,' she said, trying to sound as if she meant it.

It was too soon. Of course it was. She had been expecting too much. Mary had only been dead a few weeks. Brand had said he had waited four years for her – though why any red-blooded man, which Brand definitely was, would wait four years for a creature like Mary . . .

She took a deep breath and fixed her gaze on the solid strength of his muscular forearms. They had been bare like that on the day she had first laid eyes on Brand and his first wife. The two of them had come to her father's hacienda, asking for directions to one of the mountain trails. Brand, absorbed with his pretty bride, hadn't noticed the young girl devouring him with her eyes from behind a trellis. She had thought him the most romantically handsome man she had ever seen – and his wife the silliest.

Mary had had a round, soft face surrounded by fluffy blonde hair. It had made Isabella think of a sugar pudding.

'Brand, it's getting late,' she complained, after Diego Sanchez had given them directions and offered tea. 'What if it gets dark and I fall?'

Brand smiled down at her with a fondness Isabella found nauseating. 'No problem. You're as light as a kitten. But you're not going to fall. I won't let you.' He looped a possessive arm around her waist.

Mary's answering smile was a masterpiece of wistful martyrdom. 'Oh, very well. But we *have* been walking for ages.'

Brand touched her cheek. 'No, we haven't. An hour isn't ages – and you said you liked walking.'

'I do, but . . .'

'Are you really tired, sweetheart?'

'Exhausted.' Mary sighed.

'We'll go back to the hotel, then,' Brand said – but Isabella could tell he was disappointed.

'Weakling,' she muttered at Mary, as she and her husband passed the concealing trellis. But she spoke in Spanish, so, although Mary looked around, when she saw no one there she only shrugged and gazed adoringly up at Brand.

Less than a week later there was a landslide on the other side of the mountains, and the news eventually reached the hacienda that a Canadian tourist had been killed.

The following day, Isabella ran away from home.

That fateful morning started out normally enough, with the maid, Juanita, bringing in her morning tea and drawing back the curtains. But as soon as Isabella finished her breakfast of cheese and rolls, which the family ate on a glassed-in veranda facing the mountains, her father asked her to come along to his office. Surprised, she followed him.

What could this be about? She hadn't committed any really heinous offence since her thirteenth birthday, which she had elected to celebrate by releasing all her father's prized horses from their paddock. The repercussions of that escapade had been too painful for her to consider trying it again.

On the other hand, when she *could* get away with it she rarely did anything she was told unless it suited her. Her father said she was responsible for most of his grey hairs. He was used to being obeyed, yet she guessed he was privately amused by his youngest daughter's small rebellions. Certainly most of the time he ignored them – perhaps because when he really wanted her obedience, he got it. Over the years, Isabella had spent a number of hours locked in her room, and in the end she always became so bored with her own company that she gave in and did as her father ordered. Usually it was a matter of completing the lessons set by her governess, or apologizing to a guest whose manners she had audibly criticized – or to a sister whose property she had borrowed without asking.

But there had been no guests at the hacienda for two weeks, she no longer had to do lessons and her sisters were all married. So why was her father putting on that oh, so serious, important face.

'Sit down, Isabella.' Diego Sanchez took the massive leather chair behind his desk and began stroking his small, black moustache.

Isabella sat. 'What is it, Father?' she asked.

Diego cleared his throat. 'In the matter of your marriage – ' he began.

'What marriage?' She gripped the arms of her chair, her mouth open in an O of astonishment. 'I'm not getting married. All the men I know are married to my sisters.'

'Not José Velasquez,' Diego said.

'José Velasquez? That old groper! But he's at least fifty, and he has bad breath and he's always pawing at me when he thinks nobody's looking.'

'He has offered for you, Isabella, and he is our neighbour. When you marry him, our family holdings will be joined. Your children will inherit a great deal of land.'

'I don't have any children. And we don't need any more land.' Isabella heard her voice rising in panic.

36

Her father had an obsession with expanding his estates. In his youth, he had been a middle-class salesman, but over the years he had gradually built up his holdings until now he was a very wealthy man – a man the country's leading families could no longer ignore. He *didn't* need more land, but he thought he did. He said it was to provide security for his wife and six daughters, but Isabella knew that *he* was the one who needed to feel secure.

'You will have children with José,' Diego explained, as if he were talking to a child who thought babies were mailed special delivery from the baby factory.

'Ugh! But I can't bear him near me. Father, please. I don't love him. I don't even like him – '

'Enough.' Diego held up his hand. 'Love, my child, is for storytellers and dreamers. So you will do as you are told, just as your sisters did. It's for your own good, you see. José will look after you. He's a good man – '

'He's not. He's a horrible man. I won't marry him, Father, I *won't*.'

Diego closed his eyes as if in prayer. 'Isabella, you are my youngest child. All your sisters married the men I chose for them, and not one of them has complained about my choice.'

'But I'm not my sisters. Father, please understand.' She couldn't believe this. The father who had loved and indulged her all her life *couldn't* mean to marry her off to that awful old man. He *must* see it just wasn't possible.

But Diego had never been one to see what he didn't want to see. The sunlight streaming through the window glinted off the gold of his signet ring as he leaned towards her and said heavily, 'I understand that you are very young. And you must accept that I know what is best for you. Now, go and find your mother. She will help you decide on dresses and food and flowers and – oh, all those details you women so enjoy.' When Isabella didn't move, he flapped his hand at her and said impatiently, 'Go on, go on. I have work to do.'

Isabella held her ground. 'If you try to make me marry him, Father, I'll run away.'

Diego was more used to getting his own way than Isabella was. But even he must see that allowing herself to be married off to José was quite different from submitting to some casual parental whim. He *couldn't* expect her to give in to him this time. And if he did, he didn't know her very well.

Diego puffed out his cheeks. 'What did you say?' he asked, frowning.

'I said I'd run away.'

'I see. In that case, we'll have to see to it that you don't get the opportunity.' He strummed his fingers on the desk. 'Yes. No doubt the wedding can be organized for next week. That way you will only need to be kept in your room for a few days. After that you will be the responsibility of my good friend, José.'

'No! You can't.'

'I will not have my wishes thwarted, Isabella. Not this time. I'm sorry, but you'll thank me in the end.'

Her father's pride and self-esteem were at issue now. Too late, Isabella saw that by opposing him so boldly she had made a grave tactical error. She should have wept and begged and pleaded, and appealed to his fatherly affection. Now he would never back down.

She made to stand up, but her father picked up a small silver bell and rang it briskly. At once a man with a thin face and big hands came bustling in from an adjoining office.

'Take Señorita Isabella to her room. And lock the door behind her,' Diego ordered.

The man blinked. 'Lock the door?' he repeated.

'That's what I said.'

'*Sí, señor.*'

Isabella found her elbow gripped in the man's big, bony hand as she was hustled out of the office and up the stairs.

'Miguel, please . . .' She tried to protest. 'You can't mean to do what Father says. He has no right – '

'Certainly he has the right.' Miguel's tone was dismissive. 'I need my job, *señorita*. I cannot go against your father's orders.'

It was true. Isabella had known her father's downtrodden secretary for years. There was no point in looking to him for help.

When they reached the top of the stairs, Miguel pushed her firmly into her room, muttered something about regretting the necessity, and slammed the door loudly so her father would hear. After that she heard the key turn in the lock and the sound of his footsteps returning down the stairs. Shaking with anger as much as with fear, Isabella crossed to the window.

There must be some way to escape. If she could only think of it.

'Isabella?' Her mother's soft knock and timid voice came to her through a mist of angry tears. A moment later she was clasped tight against Constanza Sanchez's ample bosom.

'There, there,' said Constanza, patting her daughter helplessly on the shoulder. 'There, there. It won't be so bad. José is a good man, and he loves you.'

'No, he doesn't. He just wants to get me into his bed. Mother, please, can't you make Father understand?'

'No, my little one. I cannot. You will have to accept that he's doing this for the best. You are very dear to him, you know.'

She might have known her mother would be no more help than Miguel. Sweet, gentle Constanza had long ago subjugated her will to that of her husband. And she, Isabella, might be very dear to her father, but where land was involved he was incapable of seeing any point of view but his own.

Constanza looked as if she was about to burst into tears, so Isabella kissed her and told her not to worry.

When her mother left, she turned back to the window to plan her escape. Behind her, she heard a quiet click. Her mother was dutifully locking her in.

The drop down to the courtyard was sheer. If she tried it she was sure to break a leg. As for climbing down her bedsheets as they did in books – it might work. More likely the bedsheets would tear. In any case they weren't nearly long enough.

Steaming with frustration and nearly desperate, Isabella flung herself onto her bed and buried her face in the pillows. She didn't move again until Juanita found her there when she arrived with lunch.

'Please, you must help me,' Isabella cried, rolling onto her back when the young maid touched her on the shoulder. 'Juanita, could *you* bear being married to that man?'

Juanita shook her head. 'No, *señorita*. He is old, and not very nice.'

'Then you will help me?'

Juanita twisted her apron around her hands. 'I could forget to lock the door, but . . .'

'But you would get into trouble. I know.' Isabella wrinkled her forehead. 'Listen, if you give me your key and leave the door open just before siesta, I can

41

slip out, lock it behind me and slide the key back under *your* door while they're all resting. No one will see me, and I can make it look as though I climbed out the window.'

'They will never believe – '

'Yes, they will.' Isabella swung her feet to the floor, seized with sudden hope. 'It won't occur to them that you would dare to defy Father. Nobody but me ever does. I could hang my sheets out the window. They won't reach, but they'll think I dropped off the end. Juanita, please . . .'

Juanita nodded. 'Yes. Perhaps in your place I would do the same. I will help you.'

Isabella jumped off the bed and hugged her. 'You're a good friend. Oh, Juanita, I promise I'll never, ever forget you. And once I'm safe and have enough money I'll send you – I'll send you a reward. I promise.'

'There is no need.'

But Isabella knew there was a need. Like so many in her country, Juanita's family was desperately poor, which made the slight risk she was taking doubly courageous. She deserved a reward, and some day, somehow, she would get it.

Later that afternoon, when everyone was resting or asleep, Isabella packed a beadwork shopping bag with a few family photographs, some of the frivolous, lacy underwear she favoured and all the pocket money she hadn't yet spent. Then, very cautiously, she opened the door, locked it behind her and crept quietly up the stairs to Juanita's room.

Nobody saw her leave except Juanita, who waved goodbye from a balcony as her young mistress hurried across the courtyard and down the long, winding driveway to the road.

Looking back on that day now, already Isabella wondered at her own audacity. Just seventeen and gently bred, she had had no idea how to look after herself on the streets of the big, dirty city where she had headed with the aid of an elderly truck driver who, in return for most of her money, had picked her up with no questions asked.

Later, alone in the city, unbelievably, she had caught sight of José. He had looked furious and a little drunk. As she had stared frantically around for a hiding place she'd seen Brand, and, recognizing him as the romantic prince of her recent daydreams, she knew at once that she had found the refuge she sought.

It had proved a fortunate decision.

Brand had smiled at her without really seeming to see her, but he had taken her arm and led her into the bar. She had spent the evening with him, grateful for his protection and desperately affected by his grief. Later he had said he was going upstairs, and hadn't objected when she'd followed him – had perhaps not even noticed. By the time she had climbed into the bed beside him, partly because she wanted to offer comfort and partly because there was nowhere else to lie down, he had fallen into a drunken sleep.

In the small hours of the morning he had awoken and made love to her most tenderly. He had called her Mary.

When dawn had come, Isabella knew, with the naïve confidence of her seventeen years, that Brand was the man she would marry.

José hadn't found her, and the next day, at Brand's insistence, they had mailed a brief note to her parents, informing them that she was well and in good hands. When that was done they had gone to find the priest.

Brand shifted in his chair. Isabella, her gaze on the wide leather strap of his watch, saw his fists clench slowly, then equally slowly relax. What was the matter with him? Did he regret their marriage so very much? Perhaps that was why he was always so withdrawn, why he sometimes behaved as though he scarcely knew who she was. Or did he feel that any affection he showed to his new wife would be a betrayal of the old one?

She raised her eyes. He was still sitting with his head bowed and his arms resting on the wooden table that no amount of polish could restore – but as she watched him all at once his shoulder muscles stiffened.

'What's that smell?' he asked, turning to glare at

44

the stove. 'You haven't been cooking again, have you?'

Since the fiasco of the burned stew, which had been followed by burnt chicken and rock-solid fish, Brand had insisted on doing all the cooking for the two of them. He was a competent, if uninspired cook, having learned to cope in his bachelor days, he said, when in between flights he had come to roost in a succession of studio apartments.

Isabella lifted her nose and sniffed. 'It's just a soufflé,' she said. 'Mariette, our cook, used to make them all the time. I don't think much can go wrong with eggs and cheese.'

Brand groaned. 'I told you to leave the cooking to me. Couldn't you, just for once, do what you're told?'

'That's not fair. I – ' She broke off as Brand rose to his feet and went to check the oven. When he didn't say anything, she asked, 'Is it all right?'

'Only if you like pancakes with the consistency of dried sponge,' Brand replied. He removed the dish from the oven and placed it on top of the stove.

Isabella got up and went to see for herself. 'But . . . it was supposed to rise,' she protested. 'I don't understand . . .'

'All you have to understand,' he said grimly, 'is that from now on *I* will do the cooking. We can't afford to keep throwing out food.'

Isabella was furious to feel tears swimming into her eyes.

Brand turned from the stove to see his wife standing in the middle of the floor with her hands clasped in front of her and her lower lip quivering like a child's. Sighing, he put down the fork he had been about to poke at the ruined soufflé and pulled her into his arms.

'It's OK. It doesn't matter,' he said soothingly. 'I know you meant it for the best.'

She was soft and yielding as a baby – yet his reaction to her softness was the reaction of a man to his mate. It was a sensation he hadn't expected and didn't welcome.

'Don't,' he said gruffly as she began to make whimpering noises against his shoulder. 'Don't cry. We'll go out for pizza again.'

Immediately he felt her arms began to steal around his neck.

'No,' he said, grabbing her hands and holding her away.

They went out for pizza – again – but this time Brand was taciturn and Isabella sulked.

When they got home, Isabella gave him a woebegone look and asked what she had done to make him angry.

'Nothing,' he said. 'You haven't done anything.'

'Then why won't you speak to me?'

Brand sighed and sat down on the loveseat. 'What do you want to talk about?' he asked.

Isabella frowned. 'I don't know. Nothing special.'

'Good,' said Brand, getting up again. 'In that case why don't we discuss the weather? I believe it's raining.'

Isabella glared at him and flounced off into the bedroom, expecting him to follow with apologies. When he didn't, she flung her clothes on the floor and went to bed.

The following day, Brand came home looking almost as glazed and distraught as he had on the night they first met.

Her pique forgotten, and not knowing what else to do, Isabella ran to him and threw her arms around his waist.

'What is it?' she cried. 'Brand, what's happened?'

'Nothing.' He detached her quite gently, dumped a brown paper bag onto the table and pulled out a bottle of rye whisky.

'But there must be something. Please – let me help you.'

'You? Help me?' It wasn't the unconscious cruelty of his words but the parody of a laugh that followed which chilled her bones.

'I'd like to,' she whispered. 'If you would *please* tell me what's the matter . . .'

'You want to know what's the matter? All right, I'll tell you what's the matter. I lost my pilot's licence, that's all.' He unscrewed the top of the bottle and stood up. 'And that, my privileged little wife, apart

47

from depriving me of the only work I know, means that you and I may soon be unable to live in this luxury to which we've become accustomed.'

He waved an arm at the cracked walls and the dilapidated fixtures and went to the cupboard to pull out a glass.

CHAPTER 3

Isabella moved slowly across to the table and sat down. What was he talking about, this man who was her rock of security in a strange land? He couldn't have lost their only means of support. He couldn't. Surely he had to be joking.

Brand closed the cupboard and turned around, and his ravaged face told her what, in her heart, she had known from the moment he walked through the door. In his softer moments Brand sometimes teased her. But he would never joke about his job.

His father had been a pilot too, and the younger Ryder had practically grown up in an airport. He had told her once that it had never crossed his mind to do anything but walk in his father's flight boots. Flying loggers and prospectors to their jobs, and ferrying much needed supplies to the people who lived and worked in isolated communities around the province was his life. The small planes he piloted had been his first, if not his only love. Isabella knew that he even relished the occasional hair-raising flights in appalling weather conditions to pick up passengers in need of emergency medical help.

He would never voluntarily give up the life he loved. That had been brought home to her forcefully when she had made the mistake of suggesting he look for a ground job.

'Mary would never have asked that of me,' she had been told.

No, Mary probably wouldn't have. Nor would Mary have had the courage to fly with him. Isabella would have, but Brand had only laughed when she'd asked if she could accompany him on the job.

He wasn't laughing now. He was splashing a strong shot of whisky into the glass.

'Brand? Why? What did you do?' she whispered, fearful of his reaction if she spoke too loudly.

Brand pulled out a chair, turned its back to the wall, and sat down with his long legs extended in front of him. 'Do? I didn't *do* anything.'

'Oh.' She ran hands which suddenly felt clammy down her skirt. 'Then why – what . . .?'

'Why can't I fly any more? That's what I'd like to know.' He glared at the contents of the glass then set it on the table with a smack. The brown liquid swirled around the rim, but it didn't spill.

'Brand, please . . .'

He raised his head, scowled at her, and went back to contemplating the glass.

Isabella, not knowing what to say or where to go, picked up the kettle and began to fill it.

Usually when Brand saw her doing anything in the kitchen he told her not to. Today he didn't say a word, but continued to sit at the table glaring at the whisky he wouldn't drink.

In the end, Isabella edged over to the tartan loveseat and sat down quietly, with her hands folded in her lap and her anxious gaze fixed on his face.

Whatever had happened to make Brand lose his licence had seemingly caught him off-guard and without defences. But if he wouldn't speak to her, wouldn't accept her sympathy or acknowledge that this catastrophe was her problem as well as his, she had no idea what she ought to do.

Around midnight, Brand suddenly stood up and went to bed.

Isabella followed him.

'Brand?' she whispered uncertainly to the still form hunched beneath the covers. 'Brand, are you all right? Can I do anything?'

'Yes,' he growled. 'You can shut up and go to sleep.'

With unshed tears stinging at her eyes, Isabella crawled into her bed and shut up. But she didn't go to sleep. Hours later she was still wide awake, listening to his breathing. In the morning, when she woke up, Brand had already left the apartment.

That evening he returned home well after seven,

carrying an armful of books on business and accounting. He laid them on the table without a word. Then, and still without speaking, he began to read.

Watching him, for the first time since he'd delivered the bombshell Isabella felt the stirrings of indignation. Damn it, he had no right to shut her out. She was his wife, not the household cat – and it wasn't *her* fault her name wasn't Mary.

'Brand,' she said, planting her fists on the table and leaning over him, 'you are not being fair. I have a right to know what happened. I am – I am . . .'

'My wife,' he finished for her, slamming his book shut and looking up. 'Yes. So you are.' He held her gaze, and for a moment she saw behind his forced composure to the battle he was fighting with himself. Then he ran a hand through his hair and she caught a glimpse of his oddly shaped ears. 'I'm sorry,' he said stiffly. 'You're right, of course. I had no business taking my frustrations out on you. Unfortunately, you happened to be there. The reason I lost my licence is that according to every damn doctor who's looked at me I have developed something they explained as "an inner ear problem". A mild one, but it makes no difference. Do you know what that means?'

'It means you can't fly planes,' Isabella said.

'Bingo.' He smiled crookedly. 'Directly to the point, as usual. That's what I like about you, Isabella. You know how to say what you mean.'

'I'm glad there's something you like about me.' She straightened and turned her head away, so he wouldn't see the sudden dampness about her eyes.

'Oh, Belleza.' The low voice coming from behind her was husky now, softer than it had been. 'Have I been such a brute?'

Isabella stood perfectly still. She felt something tug at her hair, and when she looked round she saw that Brand had curled a lock of it around his knuckles and was pulling her gently towards him.

'Belleza?' she repeated, surprised and touched. Belleza? Beauty? Brand's Spanish was dubious, but he certainly knew how to use it to effect. 'No, you haven't been a brute,' she assured him. 'I know life hasn't been easy for you since – ' She broke off. Mary was *not* going to worm her way into this conversation. Not when, for once, Brand was noticing *her*, and even seemed to like her. 'What are you going to do?' she asked him, hoping the question wouldn't shatter this softer mood.

'Do?' He shrugged. 'There's only one thing I can do. Since I've reached the end of one career, I may as well get started on another. I've always thought I'd like to run my own airline – that when I couldn't fly any longer myself I'd employ others to do the job for me. I just didn't expect it to happen quite this soon.'

'You're going to run an airline?' She gasped. 'But – how can you? Won't it take money we don't have? And if it fails . . .'

53

'It won't fail. Trust me.'

'But where will you get the money?' Had losing his licence scrambled the wires in Brand's brain?

'I have connections in the business. And I plan to start out small. Just a few planes and tried and true runs. Nothing exotic at first. The bank seems to think I'm a good risk.' He grinned for the first time in days. 'Besides, the manager was a good friend of my father's. You don't need to worry, I promise.'

Isabella took him at his word. Why shouldn't she? Brand might be moody, distant and at times downright dictatorial, but he was also her prince and her protector. She knew he wouldn't let her down.

In the weeks that followed, Brand worked like a demon to get Ryder Airlines off the ground. He rarely stopped moving long enough to talk to Isabella any more, but as time passed she supposed he must be having some success.

When he was at home he was either cooking something fast and more or less edible, talking on the phone, or punching keys on the portable computer he had set up on the desk in the bedroom. He made no move to change their sleeping arrangements, and when he fell into bed at the end of each long day he was almost always instantly asleep.

If it hadn't been for her friendship with Judy, the

young mother upstairs, Isabella was sure she would have gone crazy with loneliness in this strange, unfamiliar city. The people all talked too fast, and she hadn't yet got used to the weather, let alone the fact that nobody, not even Brand, seemed to think she needed looking after. She wasn't used to so much independence. At home, her family had always taken it as their right, as well as their obligation, to run her life.

She had almost reached the point of thinking she couldn't bear this frustrating and mostly solitary existence one day longer, when Brand's widowed mother phoned from her home in Kelowna to say she was coming for a visit.

Isabella had only met her mother-in-law once, at the memorial service for Mary – a strange, awkward occasion where she had felt she didn't belong. Mairead Ryder had left immediately following the service.

Now, in mid-April, she was coming back.

A frenzy of cleaning followed, as Isabella tried to turn their squalid basement into something like a home. It wasn't possible, of course, and when Brand's mother erupted into their small kitchen almost an hour before she was expected, for a few seconds Isabella was speechless.

Mairead, sharp-eyed, diminutive, and trailing clouds of purple and pink silk, was in her early sixties. With untidy white hair pinned around her

55

head like wisps of smoke, she seemed to Isabella like a brighter and fluffier species of one of the more flamboyant tropical birds from her own native land.

'I thought I'd better let you two get used to each other before I stuck my nose in,' Mairead announced breezily the instant she arrived. Her button-black gaze took in the postage-stamp kitchen. 'Hmm.' She bustled across to inspect the equally cramped bedroom quarters. 'Not that you have room for an extra nose; I do see that. Just as well I booked myself into the Sheraton.'

Brand grinned. 'Very wise, Mother. You might otherwise have been forced to endure my cooking first thing in the morning.'

Mairead gave an exaggerated shudder and darted a quick glance at Isabella.

Isabella coloured. 'Brand says my cooking is worse than his,' she explained defensively.

'Brand's a fool.' Mairead dismissed her son's opinion with a wave of her dainty hand. 'Very well, it sounds as though I'd better take the two of you out to dinner. There's a restaurant I want to try at Van Dusen Gardens. They have rhododendrons there, so I've been told. I'm fond of rhododendrons.'

'They're not on the menu,' Brand said drily. 'I'm sorry, Mother, but I'm expecting a call from a client. I have to stay near the phone.'

'Good.' Mairead picked up her handbag. 'That

will give me a nice chance to get to know Isabella. Come along, my dear. My son obviously prefers his own company to ours.'

'Not at all.' Brand was less blunt than his mother. 'Unfortunately, I don't have a choice.'

'Nonsense,' said Mairead.

Isabella thought of protesting, but Brand was smiling for a change, so there didn't seem much point. Besides, Mairead, who apparently doubled as bulldozer, was already calling for a taxi.

The restaurant overlooked the gardens and was filled with light and colour on this soft spring evening. At first Isabella was nervous, but after they had been shown to a quiet table next to one of the long windows she soon found herself falling under her mother-in-law's spell. Mairead, although forthright and perceptive, was not the critical gorgon she had feared, but a source of endless charm and wisdom.

'Don't you let that boy of mine have everything his own way,' she advised as she buttered a roll. 'He's been through a lot, I know. But he's tough. Just like his father. Stubborn too. He'll pull through, don't you worry. And *you* must take care of yourself. Let's have some champagne.'

'I do try to take care of myself.' Isabella ran a finger along the edge of the laquered table. 'But . . .' She stopped. Her mother-in-law was busy ordering champagne from a pretty blonde waitress.

The transaction completed, she turned back to Isabella. 'Do you?' Her dark eyes were filled with sympathetic perception. 'Are you sure?'

'Yes, I . . .' Mairead smiled, and all at once Isabella's guard crumbled to dust. 'I do. But he's still in love with Mary.'

'Mary? Ah, yes. A sweet thing, if a little pampered. But then so were you, I imagine. You can't expect a man to recover from that sort of loss in only three months. Wouldn't be decent – quite apart from the rest of it.'

'No, but he's always so busy, and he never seems to have time to talk – '

'He hasn't much choice about that, my dear. Not if he's going to provide for you and a family.'

'A family?' Isabella's laugh was hollow. 'No chance of that, Mrs Ryder. You've seen the bedroom.'

'Yes, but that doesn't mean . . . Oh. Hmm. I see.' Mairead tapped her fingers on the table. 'You'll have to be patient then, won't you? Not easy, I know. But you're very young. Trust me, my dear, one day you'll make my only son a wonderful wife.'

'And will he make me a wonderful husband?' Isabella twisted her green napkin in her lap and pinned her gaze on the kiwi vine trailing across the trellis outside the windows.

Mairead laughed. 'That's the spirit. You'll do. Yes, he'll be a good husband to you. If he isn't, I'll have something to say about it. Now, then, let's finish our meal and have a look at those famous rhododendrons before it's dark.'

They finished their meal in companionable accord, and fifteen minutes later, feeling relaxed and mellow with champagne, they left the dining room to inspect Mairead's rhodendrons.

As they walked along the sloping, petal-strewn path, through a glorious gauntlet of rhododendrons and azaleas, in every shade from crimson to palest ivory, Isabella was reminded of the sunshine and bright sunsets of her home. She breathed in the scented air and smiled.

Brand's mother thought she would do. Maybe there was hope for her yet.

The next few days were the happiest Isabella had known since she married Brand. She and Mairead shopped and talked and explored Vancouver together, and laughed when Brand raised his impressive eyebrows and accused his mother of leading his wife astray.

'Hah,' said Mairead. 'Isn't that a case of the pot casting aspersions at the kettle?'

Isabella wasn't sure what aspersions were, but she smiled when Brand's skin turned the colour of dull bronze and he grunted and refused to meet his mother's eye.

Her mother-in-law was different in every way from her own quietly traditional mother. But it didn't matter. In no time at all the two of them had developed a mutual and very real affection.

Once Mairead left, the basement felt even quieter and emptier than it had before. Deeply involved in his new venture, Brand still had little time left over for his wife.

Often she visited Judy, who had started to teach her cooking as well as English, but she couldn't spend all her time upstairs. Judy had a baby, a family and her own circle of friends. Isabella, used to being surrounded by people, often found her own company desperately hard to endure.

Then one day she bumped into Gary in the narrow passage between their doors.

'Haven't seen much of Brand lately,' he remarked.

'No. He's been very busy,' she agreed. 'I haven't seen much of him either.'

After that, Gary began to appear at her door almost every day on one pretext or another. When Isabella found herself looking forward to his visits she decided it was time to stop waiting for her husband to make the next move and form her own plan of action.

'Isabella?' Brand, arriving home early for once, paused in the doorway when an unusually enticing smell drifted across the room and up his nose.

'Yes?' All smiling innocence, his wife looked up from whatever it was she was fussing with on the stove. 'You do look glamorous in that suit. I didn't expect you so soon.'

Good God. Brand closed his eyes. She had the face of an angel when she smiled at him like that. If only she wasn't so damn young. If only she didn't want so much more than he had to give . . . He swallowed a groan.

If only Isabella were Mary.

'I can see you didn't expect me,' he said. 'You're cooking. Isabella, I thought I told you – '

She held up a slender white hand. 'Wait. Don't say anything until you've tried it.'

He sighed. Even in those tight jeans with the bright red blouse she looked like a kid. A kid with a secret she was just bursting to tell. No doubt it was connected with whatever abomination she was brewing on the stove. In spite of his suspicions, Brand allowed himself a small smile. 'Do I have to?' he asked. 'Try it, that is?'

'Yes. Yes, you do.' She pulled out a chair. 'Sit down.'

'Not just yet. I'd like to change first.'

Isabella shook her head. 'There is no need. You look beautiful just the way you are.'

'Not beautiful, Belleza. Men aren't beautiful.'

'You are,' she said simply, once again knocking him dead with the guileless loveliness of her smile – the smile that had unhinged him from the moment he had first looked on her face.

He rubbed a hand over the back of his neck. 'Nevertheless, I wish to change. Be careful not to burn yourself, won't you?'

As he went into the bedroom Brand heard a noise that sounded like a giggle. He stood still. Did that little nymph he had married have any idea what she did to him? For the past months he had buried himself in work – not only because it needed to be done, but because it was the only thing that kept him from compounding the harm he had done her already. That he must avoid at all costs. He owed it not only to her but to the memory of Mary.

'Why, Mary, why?' he muttered as he threw off his jacket. 'Damn it, you had no right to die, no right to leave me at the mercy of that juvenile temptress in there. Four months is too damn long to wear a halo – and God knows, I'm no saint . . .'

You have to be, Ryder, he answered himself. She's a child. A beautiful child who deserves a chance to grow up. If you lay a hand on her now you'll be the biggest bastard who ever married a woman he didn't love. And you've done enough damage already.

When he went back into the kitchen, Isabella was serving up soup.

He tasted it. It was good. He told her so.

Her face lit up like a star. 'Do you really like it?'

'I wouldn't have said so if I didn't. You know that.'

She made a face. 'Yes. That is true. The last time I

62

cooked, you said it looked like cheese-flavoured sponge.'

'There you are, then.'

He watched her take a deep breath. 'There is more. You do like fish, don't you?'

'That depends.' Her face fell, and he added quickly, 'On whether it's cooked properly.'

He doubted if any fish Isabella had got her hands on would be anything but dry and tasteless. But she *had* tried to please him – even though he'd told her not to. It wouldn't hurt him to be kind – provided he could find a way to discourage her from doing it again.

But, to his astonishment, the sea bass she placed in front of him was not dry. It was moist and flaky and covered in some kind of sauce. The baby carrots and the peas and potatoes that went with it were crisp and tangy in his mouth. The dessert that followed was a creamy, canary-coloured dream.

'That was great,' Brand said, laying down his knife and fork when he had finished. 'Isabella, you amaze me. Where – how . . .?'

'Judy showed me. I asked her to teach me. She said that once I got the idea, I was a natural.'

'A natural what?'

'Cook,' said Isabella, with a smugness that made him want to laugh. But he didn't dare laugh at Isabella's cooking. Not now. Not ever again. She took it too seriously.

'You are indeed a natural,' he assured her gravely.

'Do you mean it?'

'Of course I mean it. Come here.' He held out his hand and she bounced up and came over to him, seizing his outstretched hand as if it were some kind of prize.

Now that she was this close to him, he wasn't sure what he ought to do with her, but Isabella made the decision for him. Without asking, she settled onto his lap and wound her arms around his neck.

Fire sliced through his belly and up into his lungs. He couldn't breathe; he was choking on the scent of her hair, her incredible body ... 'Isabella,' he gasped. 'Isabella, for God's sake. Get off.'

When she only smiled at him like a cat with a saucer of cream, he took her by the shoulders and stood up, lifting her bodily until her feet left the floor. 'Don't ever do that again,' he said, putting her down and turning his back on her while he fought to regain his self-control.

'Didn't you like it?' she asked, in a voice so small it made him feel like a heel. He wanted to turn round and crush her in his arms.

Instead he made himself speak calmly, as if he hadn't been on the point of laying her down on the table amidst the plates and the fishbones and the forks. 'It doesn't matter whether I liked it. Just – don't do it again, OK?'

When she didn't answer, he made himself look at

her. 'Oh, Lord,' he groaned. 'You look like a baby bird who's missed out on the last of the crumbs. I'm sorry, Isabella, but . . .' He gestured helplessly at the remains of their meal, unable to finish.

She blinked rapidly, then said in a stiff, reedy voice, 'Don't be sorry. I wasn't looking for crumbs.'

No, Brand thought, making an effort to batten down his cynicism. You were looking for the whole damned meal. And, so help me, you very nearly got it.

From now on he would have to be a lot more guarded in his dealings with Isabella Ryder.

'Come on,' he said. 'What we need – what *I* need, anyway – is fresh air. Let's go for a walk.'

She nodded without enthusiasm and went to fetch a sweater she didn't need.

Outside, the May breeze was gentle, the air warm and cherry-scented, and the trees across the street were heavy with pink and white blossoms. As they walked, companionably now, Brand's pulse-rate returned slowly to normal.

When Isabella slipped her hand into his, he didn't pull it away.

Isabella did all the cooking after that. She enjoyed it, in spite of the antiquated state of the kitchen. For one thing, it gave her something to do – for another, Brand seemed to like it. Judy had been one hundred percent right. She *was* a natural once she'd learned how to follow a recipe and, eventually, how to experiment on her own. One day, she decided, she would like the opportunity to expand her repertoire, to cook for a roomful of people instead of just the two of them. But that was in the future.

The present was her main concern now, and the present was not proving satisfactory.

Brand was spending even less time at home than he had before, and, although he usually came home for meals, he was rarely on time. Often he continued to work while he was eating – scribbling notes to himself or staring into space as if he were planning the birth of an empire instead of one medium-sized airline.

She supposed she ought to be thankful that he never failed to compliment her politely on the meals she cooked – as if she were the hired help, Isabella sometimes felt. She wasn't thankful, though, because as often as not he would go out again as soon as he had helped her clear the table, and not return until the small hours of the morning. If he found Isabella waiting up for him, as he frequently did, he would frown and tell her she ought to be in bed.

'I don't want to be in bed,' she snapped at him one evening, after he had been out three nights in a row and come back smelling, not unpleasantly, of whisky. 'Not by myself. And I'm sorry you find my company so dull.'

'I don't find you dull,' he said tiredly. 'Now, run along.'

'I will not run along.' Isabella jumped up from the table to stamp her foot. 'This is my house too. I don't have to go to bed if I don't want to.'

'Spoken like a spoilt little girl.' Brand shook his head at her. 'All right, stay up if you want to, but I'm afraid I haven't time to entertain you. After an entire day spent wining and dining customers, I have a lot of work left to do.' He put his briefcase on the table and sat down.

'Pig!' shouted Isabella, too tired and too confused to hang onto what was left of her temper and good sense. 'If I were Mary you'd find time to entertain me. Wouldn't you?'

Brand raised his head. There was a world of emptiness in his eyes. 'Mary? Mary wouldn't have asked it of me. I told you that. She would have understood that if I don't work my butt off I can't expect Ryder Airlines to succeed. And if it doesn't succeed, how in hell do you think we're going to eat? Life's been too easy for you, Isabella. You've always had someone on hand ready to pick you up when you fall down. But in my world a comfortable existence is earned only by hard work and effort.'

He pulled a pen out of his breast pocket, tapped it on the table, and went on in a marginally less grating tone, 'I suggest you stop glaring at me as if you'd like to have my head on a pole, and go on and get yourself some rest. Or, if that doesn't suit your ladyship, be a good girl and read a book. I'd buy you a TV, but we can't afford it yet. Now, if you don't mind, I have to get on with these figures.'

With mounting fury, Isabella watched him take a stack of files out of his briefcase and start to organize them into neatly labelled piles. How dared he treat her as if she were no more than a burdensome responsibility he had somehow brought home by mistake? How *dared* he? If she wanted to, she could be just as sweet and docile as that simpering Mary he thought so much of. But who wanted to be like her? So all right, he had to work hard. She accepted that in a way. But working hard didn't mean he had to treat her like the maid.

'Pig,' she said again. 'You're a pig, Brandon Ryder. A mean, boring old pig.'

'Good,' said Brand without looking up. 'In that case I promise not to bore you any longer – provided you promise not to bore me.'

'Oh!' Isabella raised her foot to stamp it again, but just in time she remembered that stamping her feet would only reinforce Brand's belief that she was no more than a spoiled, annoying child who kept getting in the way of the important business of her elders.

All at once the fight went out of her. Shoulders drooping, she turned to go into the bedroom.

'Isabella.' Brand's voice, weary but commanding, stopped her in her tracks.

'Yes?' she said with her back to him.

'Isabella, I know it must be hard for you some-times, living in a strange country, isolated from everyone you love, everything you're used to. And I realize I'm not as patient as I should be, that I don't spend as much time with you as I should – '

'Not everyone I love,' said Isabella.

'What?'

'I am not isolated from everyone I love.'

'What do you . . .? Oh. I see. Oh, my God!'

The note of outraged alarm in his voice made her whirl around. He was leaning back in his chair gazing at her with what she could only interpret as con-sternation. In the corner of the kitchen, the fridge began to hum. It would need repairing soon.

'It's all right,' Isabella said. 'I know you don't love me.'

With a certain detachment, she watched the mus-cles in his chest expand as he drew in his breath. 'I'm very fond of you. Sometimes. And I know you're fond of me – or at any rate that you need me. But you're not yet eighteen, Isabella. You have no idea what love means.'

'And I suppose Mary had?'

'Yes. I certainly hope so, since she was married to me.'

'*I'm* married to you.'

'That's different. We had no choice. You might have had a child.'

'That had nothing to do with it.'

'It had as far as I was concerned.' Brand tipped his chair back and for a long moment gazed silently at the damp-stains on the ceiling. When he looked at her again he asked, as if he were suggesting a cup of tea, 'Do you want to go home, Isabella?'

Her heart did a weird little tango and turned over. 'I can't. I'm married to you.'

'That needn't be a life sentence. You're not pregnant. Your parents would take you back. Wouldn't they?'

'Yes, but I don't want them to. Father would expect me to do everything he said.'

Brand smiled as though he didn't want to but couldn't help himself. 'And isn't that just about what I expect?'

She returned the smile warily. 'Women have more freedom here. In my country we have to do exactly as men tell us. Well – most of the time. If I went back now, my father would think I'd given in to him. He'd still want me to marry José Velasquez once my marriage to you was annulled.

'Annulled?' The fridge stopped humming abruptly.

'It would be arranged.'

'I see. Therefore, mean and boring as I am, I'm the lesser of two evils? Is that it?'

Did he think this situation was funny? And no, that wasn't it. Wouldn't he ever understand that her feelings for him were anything but shallow? That they were not merely the feelings of a child who was used to getting her own way? She sighed. Probably her constant complaints about his lateness and lack of attention hadn't helped much to change his opinion. But it was too late to do anything about that now. Somehow she would have to think of a way to make him see her as a woman. A desirable woman.

But first she must convince him not to send her home. Her heart did another dance – a tarantella this time – at the very thought.

'Please don't send me home.' She widened her eyes and sent him her softest, most appealing smile – the one that had so enchanted José. 'I want to stay here with you.'

Brand closed his eyes, and she heard the faint rasp of his breath. 'Very well. I won't send you home.' His chair scraped the floor as he turned back to his papers.

Isabella gripped her hands at her waist and breathed a heartfelt prayer of thanks to the Deity. What if she had pushed Brand too far? What if he *had* sent her home?

If he had, she couldn't have borne it. Even the thought was bringing tears to her eyes.

She turned round and hurried into the bedroom. If she was going to cry, at least she could spare herself the humiliation of doing it in front of Brand.

Closing the door quietly behind her, she lay down

fully clothed on the bed. And in the end she didn't cry. The fridge started humming again, and its persistent monotone sang her to sleep.

When she woke, all the lights in the apartment were out, and someone was tucking a blanket around her neck.

'Brand?' she whispered sleepily.

'Hush, now.' His hand brushed against her cheek. 'Yes, it's me. Go to sleep.'

She wasn't sure, but she thought she felt the touch of cool lips on her forehead. Then the bed beside hers creaked once, and a minute later she heard the sound of Brand's deep, regular breathing.

She smiled dreamily into the darkness. It was some time before she fell asleep again.

'Bella, can you take the baby for me? Just for about an hour? He's got one of those summer colds and I don't want to drag him out in the rain. Otherwise I'd take him over to my mother's.'

Isabella blinked at the freckled, pixie-faced young woman leaning in the doorway with a bulky blue bundle in her arms. 'Take the baby?' she repeated. 'But Judy, I don't know anything about babies.'

'Doesn't matter. He's asleep. Just get him out of here if the house catches fire. I had a call from the agency and there's a chance of a job.'

Isabella took in the fact that her friend was dressed in a neat skirt and blouse instead of her usual milk-stained T-shirt and jeans. Judy's ex-husband sent regular support payments, but she was desperately anxious to begin supporting herself.

'And who will look after Billy if you get the job?' Isabella asked with serious suspicion.

Judy laughed. 'Don't worry, Mom will. Really, it's just for an hour. Please?'

How could she say no? Judy, not Brand, had helped her with her English, shown her where to shop and how to cook – and Judy was the one who had listened when she'd complained about Brand's long hours and absorption with his work. She was the only real friend Isabella had.

'Yes, of course,' she agreed, holding out her arms to accept the blanket-wrapped bundle. 'What shall I do with it?'

'Billy is a he, not an it. Bella, are you sure it's all right?' Judy suddenly looked worried.

'Of course. We'll be fine.' She gave Billy what she hoped Judy would believe was a maternal smile. Luckily Billy didn't see it. 'I'll put him on the bed, shall I?'

Judy's face cleared. 'Yes, do that. I'm sure he won't wake up. Thanks a million, Bella.'

Isabella smiled and wished her luck.

She was sitting in the kitchen being very quiet when, ten minutes later, somebody knocked loudly on the door. Isabella jumped, and the baby started to grizzle.

Whoever was at the door knocked again.

Muttering under her breath, Isabella put her finger to her lip and hurried over to quiet her unwelcome visitor. As she pulled open the door her eyes were signalling, Be quiet.

Gary stood on the threshold holding an armful of pink carnations. 'Thought you could do with some cheering up.' He beamed. 'Brand's still not around much, is he?'

'He's been busy.' Isabella was automatically defensive. As Billy's grizzles rose to full-throated protest she added irritably, 'You've woken the baby.'

'You don't have a baby,' Gary pointed out.

'Oh?' She put her hand on her hip. 'What's that noise, then?'

'Judy's baby?' he suggested. 'Can I come in? These ought to be put in water.'

'Oh. Yes, of course. Thank you. It's kind of you.' She knew her thanks sounded tepid, but at this stage she was more concerned with the wails coming from the bedroom than with Gary's doubtful sensibilities.

As he puttered about the kitchen looking for a suitable container Isabella returned to the bedroom to see what could be done about Billy.

It didn't take long for her to realize nothing could be done. The moment he saw she wasn't his mother, Billy knew that all was not right with his world. And said so.

Gary came to the door of the bedroom. 'What's he yelling about?' he asked.

'I don't know. Do *you* know anything about babies?'

'Not a damn . . .' He paused as Isabella bent over Billy, the V of her white blouse exposing a delicious glimpse of cleavage. 'Here, let me have a look.' He was across the room in seconds, his gaze directed dutifully downwards.

When Isabella became aware that Gary wasn't actually looking at the baby, she shifted sideways and picked the child up in her arms. His blanket felt damp, and the smell assaulting her nostrils was definitely not powder and sweetness.

'I think he's done something,' she said helplessly.

'Probably.' Gary sounded gloomy. 'Maybe if you put him down he'll go to sleep.'

'He was asleep. If you hadn't knocked – '

'I came to bring you the flowers.'

He looked so hurt that Isabella wished she hadn't complained. Gary liked her, wanted her company – which was more than could be said of her husband. 'Yes, of course you did,' she said. 'They're lovely.' Billy turned up the volume, and she winced. 'Gary, what do you suppose I should do?'

'Change him, I expect. Then maybe he'll shut up and we can – talk.'

'Yes. I suppose Judy must have left a clean diaper

somewhere.' She pulled at a corner of the blanket. 'Oh, dear. Everything's soaked, including my bedspread. Gary, go into the bathroom and fetch a towel. Please.'

While he was gone Isabella removed the blanket and dropped it onto the floor. The bed's red-faced, howling inhabitant let out another roar, and she took a deep breath and began to unbutton his terry-towelling sleeper. As she worked she wrinkled her nose.

'Remind me never to have one of these,' she muttered as Gary came back with two towels.

'I'll try to remember,' he replied. 'Just give me the chance.'

Isabella didn't look at him, but she knew he was leering. She wished she hadn't spoken.

The sleeper joined the blanket on the floor. She groaned as she looked at what was left, and sat down heavily on the bed. Billy objected, loudly, and Gary promptly sat down beside her. She could feel his breath tickling her ear, and his upper arm rubbing against her back. 'Oh, dear,' she said again, her gaze on the suspiciously stained diaper. 'Gary, I don't know what to do.'

'Maybe I do,' Gary said, leaning over her so that both arms were around her shoulders and one of them was pressed against her breast. 'For you, pretty lady, I'll do anything.'

'I'd say you've done enough,' observed a caustic

voice from the doorway. 'What do you think, Isabella?'

Isabella, who was making a tentative attempt to peel back the nearest diaper tab, straightened so fast that the back of her head hit Gary smartly on the chin.

CHAPTER 4

Gary rubbed his chin and turned to face the door.

'Brand! Hi. I was just giving your charming wife a hand with the little one, here.'

'So I see. Why don't you finish the job, then? I don't think babies are Isabella's specialty, so if you'd like to help – '

'No, no.' Gary stumbled hastily to his feet. 'Just doing what I could, but – um – since you're here to take over . . .' He cleared his throat. 'Time I was on my way.'

Brand nodded and stepped politely aside. 'Suit yourself.'

Gary shuffled past him looking as if he expected bloody retribution to descend on his head at any moment. Brand smiled cynically and watched him go.

He had been acquainted with Gary Roseboy long enough to know that the only reason his over-sexed neighbour had offered to help with young Billy was the fact that the help involved a bed and Isabella.

What his wife's feelings were on the subject, he wasn't sure. Her back was to him, and he had an idea she was deliberately ignoring him while appearing to concentrate on the damp, screaming object flailing its small fists on her bed.

Brand leaned against the doorjamb, observing Isabella's reluctant fumblings with disbelief. She was doing her best, he supposed. But could she really be that ineffectual?

She went on fumbling, and the baby went on screaming. Brand shook his head and, shoving his hands into his pockets, tried to figure out just what it was that was bothering him about this gentle, domestic scene – apart, of course, from Isabella's astonishing ineptitude.

Ah. He nodded. Yes, that was it. Gary Roseboy was at the root of his unease. His neighbour's none-too-subtle campaign to seduce his wife was supposed to be arousing all kinds of atavistic urges in his manly breast. Wasn't he supposed to want to challenge the young Romeo to a duel or slit his throat?

The trouble was, he had no desire to do either. What he actually wanted was to shake some sense into Isabella, who didn't seem to see what was going on.

Yet he couldn't fault her. While she was always civil to Gary, and welcomed him as a good neighbour should, she never actively encouraged him. Not that he could tell, anyway. Even so, she should have known better than to let him into their bedroom – with its two chaste single beds.

'What on earth do you think you're doing?' he asked, as Isabella continued to fiddle with the tabs on the diaper. 'You have to take the damn thing off if you expect to change it. And he's not going to stop yelling until you do.'

'I don't know how to change it,' she admitted. 'And anyway, Judy didn't leave me a clean one. She told me he wouldn't wake up.'

Brand detected a faint note of panic in her voice. God, she was helpless sometimes. Maybe she hadn't been around babies much, but surely any half-intelligent woman – any half-intelligent *person* – could change a diaper. Even Gary had seemed inclined to try.

The thought of Gary stirred him to action. 'Here,' he said, sliding his hands under Isabella's arms and shifting her to the end of the bed. 'You watch. I'll take care of it.'

Billy, startled by the sudden change of face, and relieved by the touch of businesslike hands that seemed to know what they were doing, reduced his protests to a couple of routine sobs.

'There we are, young man.' Brand removed the offending diaper and replaced it with one of the towels. 'Isabella, find me a couple of pins.'

When, a minute later, she came back holding two straight pins, Brand finally lost patience. 'For heaven's sake, woman,' he snapped. 'Do you want to kill the kid? There are safety pins in a box in my top drawer.'

Isabella went to fetch them, and as her arm brushed against his shoulder he thought he heard a subdued sniff that didn't come from Billy.

Hell, she wasn't going to start crying on him, was she? He hadn't meant to make her cry, but, dammit, no one, not even Isabella, could be stupid enough to attempt to fasten a diaper with regular pins.

She handed him the safety pins without a word, and he inserted them deftly into the towel and picked up the child in his arms. 'Fetch another towel – a large one,' he ordered. 'We don't have any blankets small enough for this little fellow.'

He waited, listening to Isabella thumping about in the bathroom. When she came back, carrying a pale green rectangle embroidered with yellow daisies, her eyes looked suspiciously moist.

Good grief. As if the day hadn't gone badly enough, was he about to have a weeping Isabella on his hands?

'Hey,' he said, wrapping the towel around the baby. 'Don't look at me as if I'd just kicked you in the teeth. I guess you don't know much about babies because your sisters' children all have nannies.' He forced a smile to his lips. 'It's just that we don't go around sticking pins in them. They seem not to like it.'

Isabella returned a watery version of his smile. 'I wasn't thinking. At least – I thought the pins I brought you would do the job – that you could tape over them – or something.'

'That's not the way it works,' he said, with what he felt was admirable restraint. 'Here, do you want to hold him?'

He could tell she didn't, but she took the child anyway. To please him? he wondered. She did quite often try to please him. Now he could see her eyeing the baby as if she expected Billy to burst into a howling aria at any moment. When all he did was favour her with a toothless smile, she brightened, and carried him out to the kitchen.

Brand took the soiled clothing and bedspread into the bathroom. When he came back, Isabella was sitting in a corner of the loveseat with Billy cradled in her arms. He couldn't see her eyes because her long hair had fallen across her face, but she seemed to be examining the baby's toes.

'Madonna with Child,' he murmured. A pain, for which there was no reason, twisted unexpectedly in his gut.

Isabella looked up. 'What did you say?'

'Nothing. I – ' Whatever he had meant to say was cut off by a brisk tap on the door.

'Judy!' Isabella, with obvious relief, jumped up to hand a gurgling Billy back to his apologetic mother.

'Oh, dear. I was sure he wouldn't wake up,'

exclaimed Judy when she saw the green towel wrapped around her son. 'I can't think what happened. He always sleeps in the afternoon.'

'Gary happened, I expect,' Brand murmured. 'He usually does.'

Judy giggled uncomfortably, and Isabella gave him a sharp look and asked her friend if she had managed to get the job.

'Yes! I did. Isn't it great? Just entering data, but it's a start. Listen, thanks again, Bella. I have to run. Mom's waiting to hear how I made out.'

Isabella nodded. 'Of course.'

'I notice you didn't say, "Drop him off any time,"' Brand observed as his wife shut the door behind Judy.

Isabella tossed her head. 'No. You said yourself that babies aren't my specialty.'

'So I did.'

'*You* seemed to know what you were doing, though.' She sounded accusing, almost as if she resented his competence with Billy.

'I ought to.' He hitched his hip onto a corner of the table. 'I've flown enough babies to hospital and back. Helped to deliver one once. It was quite an experience.'

'It must have been.' She stuck out her lower lip, and he knew he had somehow annoyed her. 'I suppose you like babies,' she muttered.

'Yes, as a matter of fact I do.'

'I don't see why.'

'That's because you're still a baby yourself.'

'I am not! You have no right to say that. Just because – '

'OK, OK.' He held up his hand. 'I'm sorry. I take it back. Listen, Isabella, I've had a long day – '

'You haven't. You're home early.'

'All right, a *bad* day, then.'

'Not that bad.' She leaned towards him and made a production out of screwing up her nose. 'You've been drinking. I can smell it.'

'Yes. I took a potential client out to lunch. He ate everything on the menu, then turned me down. What is this? The third degree?'

She didn't answer directly. 'Do you always drink when you take your clients to lunch?'

'Only if they do. Why?'

'Sometimes I smell it on you. I don't like it.'

'Isabella . . .' He crossed his arms and looked her severely in the eye. 'Just at this moment, I don't much care what you like. But, if it matters to you, I drink as little as possible. Let's face it, even if I wanted to we couldn't afford it. Now, do you suppose you could start supper? I'm hungry, and that's something you *are* good at.'

'You mean it's the *only* thing I'm good at, don't you?' Her voice rose indignantly.

Brand winced. 'No. I meant it as a compliment.'

84

It was more or less true. Not that he was in any mood to hand out compliments at this moment.

Isabella glared at him. Glaring was another thing she was good at. It made her look wild, passionate, torrid – and incredibly sexy.

He ran a hand over the nape of his neck, levered himself off the table and said abruptly, 'It's hot in here. I'm going out for some air.'

Isabella clenched her fists as the door slammed shut behind him and she heard him running up the stairs.

Why was it that every time she opened her mouth around Brand he made her feel like a juvenile idiot? If she could only persuade him to stop thinking of her as just another burden he had to bear, if he could learn to see her as a woman – a woman who wanted desperately to be his wife in all the ways that counted – then maybe he would realize she was more, much more, than just a cook.

Muttering words she had heard Brand use when he thought she wasn't listening, Isabella crossed to the cupboard and pulled down a package of rigatoni.

So he liked babies, did he? Well, if he hoped to have any of his own he'd have to do something about his sleeping habits. Even she knew that much, despite her mother's embarrassed reticence on the subject of the birds and the bees.

What would it be like to have a baby? Brand's baby? Briefly, the thought made her feel all soft and womanly inside. But the sensation passed almost at once, leaving her with a vague feeling of discontent.

She began to run water into a saucepan. Hot droplets splashed up against her arm. Ouch. Wrong tap. She grimaced. The point, of course, was that any babies she managed to produce would *not* be Brand's. Not if he refused to share her bed.

The pan hit the bottom of the sink with a thud as the implications of that conclusion sank in. Oh, dear Lord. If Brand wanted children, and he didn't want them with her, that meant . . . No. She wouldn't even think it. She *had* to find a way to make him love her. Because if she didn't, sooner or later she would find herself alone in a land that wasn't hers. And she wouldn't be able to bear it. Brand was everything – her life, her security . . . her heart . . .

Slowly, Isabella drew herself up and squared her shoulders. 'I will find a way,' she said to an unresponsive cupboard. 'I will, I will, I – ' She broke off as the door opened and Brand walked back in.

'Who the hell are you talking to?' he asked, looking around as if he expected to find the kitchen filled with people he didn't want to see. 'Have you hidden our friend Gary under the bed?'

'I was talking to myself.' She slanted a cautious glance at his face. He had asked the question as if he were merely curious, not as if he particularly cared.

That was because he *didn't* care, she decided, after a brief appraisal of his mockingly arched eyebrows.

86

He wasn't worried about Gary. Not a bit. His gaze was directed hopefully at the stove. All the same, just to test him, she said, 'Gary likes me, but he isn't serious. He only comes to see me because he's bored.'

'Don't be an idiot.'

Isabella put a hand to her throat. 'I'm not. He knows I'm married.'

Brand ignored that and gestured at the carnations which Gary had stuffed into a plastic water jug and left sitting on the table. 'Where did the flowers come from?'

'Oh. Gary brought them. To cheer me up.'

Brand shook his head at her and rolled his eyes at the ceiling.

Isabella frowned. 'You don't *mind* him visiting me, do you?'

'Why should I?' He crossed to the sink and began to wash his hands. 'Just be careful, that's all. Where women are concerned, Gary Roseboy knows exactly what he's about.'

'And you think I don't?'

He turned off the tap and picked up a bleached white teatowel. 'I think you're very young. And more than a little gullible.'

'What's gullible?' Isabella asked.

Brand stopped drying his hands, observed her bewildered frown, and after a pause snapped, 'Pretty,' before he went to take off his jacket.

Isabella didn't believe him.

The next morning, when he'd left for work, she took out the dictionary and looked the word up.

' "Gullible", ' she read out loud, forming the syllables carefully with her lips. ' "Innocent, naïve, trusting." So that's what he thinks of me.' But she wasn't naïve. She knew quite well what Gary had in mind. José had looked at her like that. She had only told Brand their neighbour was harmless because as far as she was concerned he *was* harmless. Why would any woman be interested in Gary when she had Brand?

If she had Brand. Hmm. Isabella put her elbows on the table and cupped her chin in her hands. He had, several times, told her she ought to be careful around Gary. *Could* that possibly mean he cared . . .? Even a little . . .?

She was frowning reflectively as she closed the dictionary and carried it back into the bedroom. Everyone kept telling her she was young. First her family, then Brand – even Mairead. But, young or not, something had to be done about her relationship with her husband. She had known that for some time. The question all along had been *what*.

Now, maybe – just maybe – she had her answer.

The cool, unsettled days of July melted into a hot, sizzling August. Brand, seemingly oblivious to the heat, continued to work like a fiend. Isabella continued to resent his involvement with the airline and lack of attention to her. Then one day he came home with his hair dishevelled, his tie askew and an unusual glitter in his eye.

'Brand! What's the matter? Is your business not doing – I mean, it's not in trouble – is it?' she asked him, anxiety making her stumble over her words.

To her amazement, instead of brushing off the question, Brand grinned and put his hands on her waist. A second later he was swinging her in a dizzying arc around the kitchen. When her feet caught the back of a chair and knocked it over, he put her down.

'No,' he said. 'No, my Belleza, Ryder Airlines is *not* in trouble. On the contrary, we are running in the black. A few months from now you and I will be able to leave this godforsaken dump behind us.'

'Good.' Isabella, breathless and laughing, was instantly filled with hope. 'That means you'll be able to spend more time at home with me. Doesn't it?'

Brand's grin faded, and he looked as deflated as if she had somehow plunged a needle into his dreams when he wasn't looking.

'I wouldn't count on it,' he said, and vanished into the bedroom.

In that moment Isabella knew, without further doubt, that it was time to put her plan into action.

Brand watched the small float plane disappear into the clouds and reluctantly looked at his watch. Six o'clock. He couldn't put off going home much longer.

Isabella had been angry with him yesterday, and he wasn't sure whether he'd be met with smiles, accusations, or sulks. She hadn't said much, but he knew he had offended her by refusing to commit his time to her once they moved. Not that he'd meant to hurt her. Dammit, surely she had to understand . . . No. On second thoughts, why should she? He wasn't certain he understood himself. All he knew for sure was that the more he saw of Isabella, the more he had to keep reminding himself that she was only seventeen.

He shrugged irritably and began to stuff papers into a banker's box. One of these days, very soon, he was going to have a real filing cabinet and an office which allowed him room to turn around.

Half an hour later, with a firm smile plastered on his face, Brand threw open the door to the apartment. He was met not with sulks or accusations, but by the smell of something hot and spicy simmering on the stove – and the sight of Gary Roseboy simmering on the loveseat next to Isabella.

She was smirking at him like a dizzy Southern Belle. The ultra-sweet smile on her lovely lips and the fluttering sweep of her dark eyelashes might have made Brand laugh if he hadn't wanted so badly to haul her into his arms, swat her on the behind and kiss the silly smirk off her face.

Gary's pupils were noticeably dilated – and his knees were touching Isabella's.

'Good evening, Gary,' Brand said, ruthlessly tamping down his Neanderthal urges. 'What have you come to borrow this time?'

As he waited for an answer it occurred to him that this was something new. His wife appeared to be responding to Gary's blandishments. Up until now she had always kept him at a distance, with casual smiles and a seemingly naïve unawareness of his intentions.

Brand strummed his fingers on his thigh as he watched Gary fidget with the buttons on his shirt-cuffs while Isabella feigned a sudden interest in the slime-green linoleum. The pot on the stove was burbling merrily as he crossed to the table, set down his briefcase and began to shrug off his jacket.

Gary leaped up as if he'd been propelled by a spring. 'Er – just being neighbourly,' he mumbled. 'Thought Isabella might be feeling lonely.'

'Thoughtful of you,' Brand murmured. 'Wasn't it, Isabella?'

'Oh, yes, very thoughtful,' she agreed, abandoning her inspection of the linoleum. 'Gary is always so kind.'

'Isn't he?' Brand opened the door politely as their neighbour scuttled to make his escape. Not that there was any reason for the little creep to behave like Peter Rabbit on the hop from Mr McGregor. The worst he need expect was a well-placed boot in the backside if he kept up his pursuit of Isabella. Gary Roseboy wasn't worth going to gaol for. Isabella, on the other hand . . .

He ran an appraising eye over her youthfully curvaceous figure. She was seated demurely on the loveseat wearing a pale blue dress and looking as if butter had turned to sugar in her mouth. She was nothing like Mary. But, God, she was gorgeous. And when she looked at him with those unbelievable eyes, sometimes, just lately, he had half-forgotten how much he missed Mary . . .

But he mustn't forget. While she'd lived Mary had been everything to him. No one could take her place, even though – and there was no use denying it – even though that adolescent siren in angel's clothing sitting over there on the loveseat might one day be well worth going to gaol for.

The thought startled him unpleasantly. Isabella was very beautiful. But she wasn't yet a woman. And when she was she would still be a self-centred, spoiled little madam who expected him to cater to her whims.

It was odd, though. The sight of her batting those long eyelashes at Gary had made him want to do all sorts of things to her that wouldn't – and shouldn't – be tolerated by the courts. Odd, because it really shouldn't matter to him. Their marriage had not miraculously become a real one just because on one incredible, agonizing night he had held Isabella Sanchez in his arms and dreamed she was his wife.

'Why are you glaring at the bread board?' Isabella's voice, soft and innocent as a kitten's, cut into his thoughts and made him turn his head. 'Isn't it clean?'

'Was I glaring? I wasn't aware of it.' And why did he have a feeling that this particular kitten had cat's claws?

Isabella didn't answer him, only smiled wistfully and got up to stir the big pot bubbling on the stove.

Was her plan working? she wondered. It was impossible to tell. Brand hadn't *seemed* to mind her flirting with Gary. Next time she would have to be more obvious. Then maybe he would remember she was his wife and do something to make sure she remained his. In her country no man would stand by and allow his wife to make eyes at another man. Isabella squashed a potato viciously against the side of the pot. The problem was, this *wasn't* her country – and Brand hadn't seemed to notice she was flirting.

It was very puzzling.

Over the next five days the temperature outside rose steadily, and one afternoon, when the heat in the basement became unbearable, Gary knocked on the door and asked if Isabella would like to come out for a drive.

'We could go to Queen Elizabeth Park,' he suggested. 'It'll be cooler on the grass under the trees. Smell a lot better too. It's stuffy down here.'

He was right. It was stuffy. Somehow the heat had managed to concentrate the smell of age and mould until it made her almost physically ill.

'I *would* like to go out,' she told Gary. 'But Brand – '

'Leave him a note.'

'Oh.' Isabella stroked her lip thoughtfully. Yes, she could leave Brand a note letting him know she had gone to the park with Gary to escape the heat. The irony might not be lost on him. And perhaps it would finally convince him that other men saw his wife as an attractive, desirable woman – even if the 'other men' were only Gary. He was all she had to work with, so there was nothing to be done but make the best of him.

'All right,' she agreed. 'Let's go.'

The air in the park was fresh and cool, and the drone of traffic only a distant background to the peace of the summer afternoon.

They strolled around the park for a while, admiring the view of Vancouver and the mountains and visiting the quarry garden, which Isabella said reminded her a little of home. Then Gary said it was too hot to walk any more, and they returned to the grassy slopes below the summit. Isabella, spotting a likely shade tree, promptly sat down on the grass. Then she propped her back against the trunk and closed her eyes.

'You look like a dryad – a wood-nymph – in that pretty green sundress,' Gary said as he sat down beside her. 'I hope old Brand appreciates what he's got.'

Isabella pretended not to hear him.

'You're not going to sleep on me, are you?' he protested.

'Maybe. For a little while.'

'But I want to talk to you.'

'What about?'

'About how beautiful you are.'

She opened her eyes. 'Thank you. Gary . . .?'

'Yes, pretty lady?'

'Don't you have a proper girlfriend of your own? Apart from those women you keep – ' She broke off awkwardly. 'I mean, you're nice-looking and . . .' She stopped again. Soft fingers were stroking her arm.

'Do you think so?' Gary continued to stroke. 'Yes, I've had lots of proper girlfriends. But none of them as beautiful as you.'

'Oh.' She didn't know what to say to that. He wasn't the first man to tell her she was beautiful, but so far her beauty hadn't done her much good. Brand didn't notice it and it was her looks that had attracted José. If only she had been ordinary-looking, like other girls . . .

No, that wouldn't have helped. If she had been ordinary-looking she never would have met Brand.

95

Brand . . . Isabella narrowed her eyes and squinted against the sun. Was she seeing things? That purposeful figure striding across the grass looked disturbingly familiar. But . . . surely he hadn't followed her to the park? Finding her gone, wouldn't he have started making supper? Or settled down to work as he always did?

No. Apparently he wouldn't. The man standing over her with the flat mouth and eyes like a one-way mirror was most definitely Brand.

'Hello,' she said, blinking up at him. 'You must have got my note.'

'I did.' He put a hand on the tree trunk and stared down at her.

Isabella was just beginning to wonder if he planned to stand there for the rest of the day when he lowered himself onto the grass beside her, stretched out his never-ending legs and said, 'And when were you thinking of coming home?'

'I don't know. When Gary is ready, I suppose.'

'Yes.' He looped an arm around her shoulders. 'Well, now *I'm* here, so you can come home when I'm ready instead.' He spoke as if Gary, seated on his wife's left, was invisible as well as profoundly deaf.

'Yes, of course.' Isabella's flesh tingled at his touch. His closeness was exhilarating and a little frightening, the possessiveness of his arm an aphrodisiac that once more gave her hope.

Did the fact that Brand had come after her mean

that he was beginning, at last, to look on her as a possible bedmate instead of a rather bothersome china doll?

Gary cleared his throat and mumbled something about having to get back.

'Don't let us keep you,' Brand said.

'No. Thank you.' Gary scrambled to his feet and began to jog across the grass towards his car.

The corner of Brand's mouth turned down. 'Your friend is in a hurry all of a sudden.'

'You scared him away,' Isabella said boldly. 'He'll be back.'

'No doubt. To borrow plum jam, I imagine. He seems unusually partial to plum jam.'

Damn Brand. Wasn't there *anything* she could do to get through to him? She knew he didn't find her repulsive. The one night they had shared proved that – even if he *had* believed she was Mary . . .

On the drive home in Brand's new Jetta – the Beetle had been traded in a month ago – Isabella made a point of singing Gary's praises. 'He's so kind and attentive,' she effused. 'Always ready to lend a helping hand.'

'I'm sure he is,' Brand said evenly. 'Depending, of course, on where you want him to put that hand – and assuming that's the kind of attention you're after.'

Isabella wasn't in the habit of grinding her teeth, but if, at that moment, she could have sunk them into

Brand without running the car off the road, she would have done it.

When they got home she made supper as usual, and as usual Brand told her it was good.

'Are you going out?' she asked him when they were finished.

'No. Any business I have can be done at home. No clients who need amusing tonight.'

'No,' said Isabella. 'Just a wife.'

Brand sighed. 'Isabella, I've done my best. I bought you a TV only last week. In a few months, when we move, perhaps you can take some courses or something – and by then, as you said yourself, I may have more time to take you out. But for now can't you understand that Ryder Airlines must come first?'

'Yes,' said Isabella. 'I understand.' This time she succeeded in biting her tongue instead of asking if Mary still came first too. Damn it, that gutless little blonde had been dead for seven months. He couldn't still be grieving over her. Could he?

As the months passed, she began to believe he could. Because nothing changed.

Gary continued to turn up at every opportunity, but now Isabella only let him in when she knew Brand would shortly be home.

She guessed that Gary knew exactly what she was up to but went along with it in the hope that his persistence would pay off. She had now become not just a girl he hoped to lure into his bed but a full-blown challenge. Even so, he continued to find urgent business elsewhere the moment he heard Brand's key turn in the lock.

Isabella waited hopefully, but Brand said not a word. She was sure he noticed, so maybe he didn't care about the frequency of their amorous neighbour's visits.

Eventually she went to Judy for advice. 'He doesn't love me,' she wailed. 'I think he's still in love with that silly Mary.'

Judy looked doubtful. 'He may be. But now he has you, and he can't carry a torch for her for ever.' She bent to pick up Billy, who had just learned to crawl and was heading for a box of kitty litter. 'They say the way to a man's heart is supposed to be through his stomach. Not that I've ever believed it. All my ex ever ate was overcooked meat and two veg. Still, you could try fancy puddings or something. You never know what'll turn a man on.'

Isabella doubted if it was puddings, but she tried them anyway.

Brand ate everything she prepared for him, and made a point of praising all the rich concoctions she lovingly produced. Sometimes he even rewarded her with a perfunctory kiss on the cheek. It meant nothing. Beyond these casual demonstrations of approval he continued to treat her as an engaging but troublesome younger sister.

'It's not to be borne,' Isabella muttered to herself

99

one particularly frustrating morning as she stood at the sink washing up after breakfast. 'He's a passionate, warm-blooded man. I know he is. And the way we're living isn't natural. If he keeps it up much longer I'll go mad.' She placed the last plate in the rack and jerked the plug out of its hole.

'Brand,' she groaned, bowing her head over the dirty, swirling water. 'What can I do to make you want me?'

Only that morning, as he had brushed past her on his way to the door, he had smelled so irresistibly of soap and aftershave, and looked so deliciously sexy in his smartly cut suit, that she had caught him by the wrist and cried, 'Brand, please. Don't go. You forgot something.'

For a moment he had frowned and looked annoyed. Then his face had cleared, and he'd bent down to brush his lips across hers. Without warning her stomach had rolled over, her body had begun to quiver – and Brand had lifted his head as if someone had grabbed him by the hair. As he'd towered above her, frowning, for one breathless moment she'd thought he meant to stay, that at last he would take her in his arms and carry her off to bed.

She should have known better.

He'd said, 'Goodbye, Isabella,' and made briskly for the door. 'I may be a little late this evening,' he'd added over his shoulder.

He was always 'a little late'. Hurt, resentful and

still trembling with a raging and unsatisfied desire, Isabella had stuck out her tongue at his back and looked for something to throw.

There had been nothing except a velvet cushion given them by Mairead. Besides, it would have been a futile gesture when what she'd really longed to do was grab him around the waist, drag him into the bedroom and *force* him to give her what she wanted. Unfortunately, he was much too large to drag. Damn him.

She glared at the door, which he'd closed behind him with a snap, and shoved her thumbs into the belt of her jeans.

The business with Gary wasn't working. And it had surely gone on long enough.

The time had come to try more drastic measures.

Brand paused outside the door to the apartment. God, he was tired. It had been a gruelling day. He felt as if he'd been run through a mangle and hung out to dry in the rain. But at least his struggles had been fruitful. The bank manager had been persuaded to extend a loan for the expansion of the airline, the two pilots who had threated to quit had been persuaded not to, and a lucrative mining company contract he'd thought he'd lost had been pulled out of the bag at the last minute.

He swiped a hand over his forehead, counted to ten, and made an effort to erase all signs of strain from his features. If Isabella detected a chink in his armour, a hint of vulnerability, she would use it to further her own ends. Just what her own ends were he wasn't sure, but he guessed they involved bed and a commitment he wasn't willing to make. A commitment he had no *right* to make.

Footsteps sounded on the other side of the door, and he thought he heard the faint creak of springs. Bracing himself, he stepped into the kitchen.

No savour smells greeted him this evening – and no demurely domestic figure stood beside the stove, stirring and tasting and prodding busily with forks. Brand let his gaze roam slowly around the drab little room that Isabella had done so much to brighten. The table was set, the appliances scrubbed clean, and the red apron she sometimes wore was hanging on a peg beside the door. Yet he could have sworn he'd heard her moving about a moment before he came in.

'Isabella?' he called. 'Where are you? Are you all right?'

'I'm in here,' replied her low voice from the bedroom.

She must be ill. That was all he needed tonight.

Don't be a bastard, Ryder, he admonished himself as he moved towards the bedroom. The poor kid can't help it if she's sick. She . . .

Oh, no! No. He slammed to a stop. *No!* She wasn't, couldn't be . . . Not tonight. Please. He raised his eyes in supplication, but no bolt of illumination descended from on high to solve his problem. And what a problem this was! One which, as usual, he would have to solve without divine assistance.

'Isabella,' he said, 'get up at once. You look like a teenage hooker.'

She was stretched out on her bed wearing a black transparent negligee that made imagination gloriously redundant. Not that he had ever lacked imagination where Isabella was concerned. He closed his eyes, hoping that when he opened them again the unlikely vision would turn out to be a trick of the light.

But of course it wasn't.

His very young wife had propped herself up on one elbow and was languidly drawing up the hem of her negligee to expose a tempting length of smoothly delectable thigh. His stomach muscles clenched, and sweat began to bead on his forehead.

'I said get up,' he repeated, reining in his temper – and a susceptible part of his anatomy – with enormous effort.

Isabella batted her eyelashes and arched her neck so that her hair swung like a heavy curtain over her shoulders. She looked like a bad parody of a Delilah setting out to seduce an unwary Samson.

'*Get – up*,' Brand said through his teeth.

Isabella gave him what he could only suppose she imagined was her best Delilah smile. 'Brand, darling,' she drawled, 'that's not very loving. Come to bed. You look tired.'

'That,' Brand said, 'is very possibly because I *am* tired. Now, are you going to do as you're told, or do I have to – ?'

'Come and get me?' Isabella suggested, giggling and holding out her hand.

Lord, give him patience – and a double dose of self-control. Brand swallowed the unexpected surge of bile that rose up in his throat.

A sudden burst of wind rattled the small window above the beds. Isabella jumped.

Ah. So she wasn't as sure of herself as she wanted him to think. And she was nervous. Good. Damn it, couldn't the beautiful little idiot get it into her head that he had no taste for silly games, no time for her juvenile manipulations?

'I'll come and get you,' he said. 'But if I have to, you may not like it.'

'But I'm tired too.' Isabella pouted.

Anger, as well as the frustration he had been holding at bay for weeks, began a slow burn deep in his belly. Did Isabella *have* to pull this stunt today, of all the days she could have chosen? He'd had enough – more than enough. More than he intended to take.

'Fine,' he said. 'Have it your way, Isabella. Don't say I didn't warn you.'

Allowing himself no time to think, Brand closed

the gap between them, took Isabella's outstretched hand and hauled her roughly off the bed and onto the floor.

When she stumbled he attempted to pull her upright, and her free hand brushed against his thigh.

He sucked in his breath.

'What is it? What are you doing?' Isabella moaned. 'Brand, you're a man. I'm your wife. Please . . . come to bed.' She reached for his belt.

With an oath, Brand released her and stepped back.

He had heard the note of desperation, seen the bewilderment in her eyes as she'd begun to accept the finality of his rejection. It only served to madden him further.

'I don't bed teenage tramps in black negligees,' he growled.

Isabella's beautiful, flower-like face seemed to fade and lose its youthful glow in front of his eyes. Ruthlessly, he ignored an immediate knife-blade of guilt. He was tired of feeling guilty around this demanding, incomprehensible creature he had married. All he needed now was peace. She had to be made to understand that their marriage could only work if she accepted its limitations – at least for the next several years. And if, in order to make her grasp that unpalatable reality, he had to hurt her – well, so be it.

He loosened his tie. Did she have to look at him

with those sad, enormous eyes of hers, and make him feel like the world's biggest heel?

'Go and get dressed,' he said wearily.

'I hate you,' said Isabella.

Deliberately she slipped the straps of her negligee over her shoulders, allowing it to fall to her waist. Then she gave the flimsy material a little shove, and the entire diaphanous garment tumbled softly down around her ankles.

Brand watched it fall.

Isabella waited for him to look up, and when he did she held his gaze for a long, challenging moment, daring him to react. But all he did was put his hands in his pockets and meet her look with one of stern-lipped censure. Suppressing a sigh, she bent to pick up her property. After that she turned her back on him and began to dress with as much dignity as was possible in the circumstances.

Her only grain of consolation was that just before Brand shut the door on her she thought she heard him groan.

But it might have been her imagination.

She stared at his neatly made bed, just an arm-length away from her rumpled one. This was the end, then. The end of hope. She had no other tricks up her sleeve. Unless . . . No, that wouldn't help.

Perhaps, some day in the future, time and its famous power to heal would succeed in dimming Brand's memories of Mary and Ryder Airlines would become less of an obsession. When – if – that day ever came, maybe he would turn at last to the woman he had married not out of love, but out of guilt.

She would probably be old by then. Old and ugly. But at least he wouldn't be able to accuse her of being too young.

With a cry that was part despair, part helpless frustration, Isabella threw herself onto the bed. She lay there with her face pressed into the pillow until Brand came in and told her he'd made soup, and that if she was hungry she had better get up.

She wasn't hungry, but Isabella did as he suggested. Brand made good soup, and there was nothing to be gained by antagonizing him further.

It wasn't true what she had told him. She didn't hate him. She wished she could. But since that wasn't possible, the only thing left for her to do was wait.

But Isabella wasn't good at waiting.

Three weeks later, while Brand was sleeping, she clasped the silver bracelet he had given her around her wrist, then packed her one suitcase and left him.

CHAPTER 5

'Veronica! What have you done with my briefcase?'

Isabella held the phone away from her ear as a forceful and impatient male voice cut off her caller's speech in mid-sentence.

'Excuse me. Could you hold on a moment?' The woman on the end of the line sounded brisk, efficient and resigned. She didn't wait for an answer, which was just as well.

In the small office set up in one bedroom of her rented apartment, Isabella sat holding the receiver in a death grip. Her gaze was fixed on the earpiece as if she expected it to burst into flames. With her free hand, she wiped unexpected moisture off her forehead.

She would have known that male voice anywhere, anyhow, any century – even though she hadn't heard it in five years. Those deep, melting-molasses tones were carved on her heart as deeply as the passion she had once shared with their owner.

But this was not how she had dreamed of hearing that rich baritone again.

As the hot mist cleared from in front of her eyes she could still hear him shouting instructions about his briefcase. And any moment now Veronica would return to the phone to pick up the threads of their conversation.

Veronica. Who was she? Girlfriend, mistress, employee? And why had she phoned Capable Catering? Isabella twisted a lock of her hair into a corkscrew.

'Sorry to keep you waiting. Is this Capable Catering?' Veronica sounded brusque now, but at least she was back on the line.

'Yes,' said Isabella, surprising herself with her calm. 'I'm Isabella Sanchez, the owner. Can I help you, Ms –?'

'Dubois. Veronica Dubois. I work for Mr Ryder of Ryder Airlines. He's looking for someone to cater a pre-Christmas dinner. In his home – '

'How large a party?' Isabella interrupted crisply.

She didn't believe this. She was actually managing to sound as pleasantly businesslike as usual, and she didn't think her voice so much as hinted that Spanish, not English, had been her first-spoken tongue.

'About twenty, I believe. It's for some of his company contacts and their wives. Do you think you can handle it, Mrs Sanchez? I've had good reports of your service, but I understand you haven't been in the business for long . . .'

'A year in Edmonton, four months in Vancouver,' said Isabella.

'Yes?'

A brief silence followed, and she realized Ms Dubois was waiting for an answer. *Could* she handle it? This wasn't the way she had meant Brand to find out she was back in Vancouver, but . . . maybe fate was finally taking a hand in her affairs. Or did she detect the more mundane influence of her well-meaning patrons in Edmonton? Not that it mattered. In the next few seconds she would have to make up her mind . . .

The door opened, and a small girl trailed into the makeshift office clutching a pink stuffed hippopotamus with purple eyes.

Isabella took a deep breath. She had never in her life suffered from indecision, and she wasn't about to start suffering from it now just because Brandon Ryder's voice had caused her heart to start running on empty and knocked most of the air out of her lungs. For Connie's sake she must seize this opportunity.

'Yes, certainly I can handle it,' she said. 'Would you like to discuss menus, Ms Dubois?'

There. She had done it. The die was cast. And although she didn't admit it to Veronica, she knew in her heart that she would have catered this particular party even if she'd been asked to do it for free. She would have had no choice, because until the bonds of the past were either loosened or made strong enough to last, her life would remain for ever in limbo.

For Connie's sake, as well as her own, it was time to stop drifting and make things happen.

Brand's house was in Richmond, only a few miles from the airport. It was hidden from the road by a line of fir trees, but as his was the only driveway leading onto the winding stretch of road Isabella had no trouble finding it. She did, however, have trouble keeping her mouth from gaping in amazement when she pulled her van up in a swirl of gravel by the back door.

The house was huge, a Mediterranean-style mansion set down in a landscaper's dream of a garden. Its clean white lines and flat roof reminded her of the house she had grown up in, far away under the hot skies of her South American homeland. But it was bigger and more impressive than any of the dwellings her family owned.

Isabella shook her head. Who would have guessed that the man she had lived with in that dreary little basement on the east side would, only five years later, be the owner of a rich man's showplace like Marshlands?

But then Brand had always said Ryder Airlines would succeed.

He deserved his success. She, of all people, knew just how hard he had worked to achieve it.

Still feeling dazed, she was just starting to unload the first cooler when she heard a door open behind her. She stopped moving. There was someone there, waiting to let her in. Every muscle in her body tightened in the cold December air.

'Mrs Sanchez?'

It was a woman's voice greeting her. Isabella slowly unfroze. Of course she couldn't expect Brand to open his own back door. Not any more.

'Yes,' she said, lifting down a box of supplies and turning around. 'I'm Isabella Sanchez. I do hope I've come to the right entrance.'

'You have.' For a moment the beautifully groomed woman in her forties, with the short, boyishly cut red hair, seemed as frozen as Isabella had been. Then she inclined her head in gracious acknowledgement and said coolly, 'Excuse me. I had no idea you would be so – young. I'm Veronica Dubois, Mr Ryder's housekeeper and general factotum. Welcome to Marshlands, Mrs Sanchez.'

Housekeeper? thought Isabella as she continued to unload containers. This woman in the smartly cut grey silk dress didn't look much like her idea of a housekeeper. Or a factotum. She made herself smile politely as she wondered just what kind of house-keeping Veronica Dubois was expected to perform. It *had* been five years. Brand was a man, albeit a man with extraordinary will-power. It wasn't likely . . .

She stiffened her spine. In all her almost twenty-three years, she had only encountered one situation she couldn't change. There was no reason to allow this to be another.

For the first half-hour in Brand's house, as Isabella moved efficiently about the huge, white, modern kitchen, she kept glancing anxiously at the door. But the only person who came through it was Veronica who, as soon as she saw that work was progressing smoothly, left the caterer to get on with her business.

At eight o'clock two young maids arrived to carry the meal through to the guests. Isabella started to relax. It was beginning to look as though she wasn't even going to catch a glimpse of the man who had disturbed her dreams for so many years. Her lips curved wryly. Had all her apprehension been for nothing?

Feeling hot, thirsty and a little foolish, she sank down at the spotless white table. But she had to swallow a whole glassful of water before the knot that had twisted her intestines all evening at last began to unwind.

How different this clean, sparkling kitchen was from that other kitchen. The one with the green linoleum and the cracked walls where, on rare occasions, she had known a happiness greater than any she had found in the challenging years that came after.

'Excuse me.'

Isabella jumped. How long had she been sitting here, dreaming and remembering?

One of the maids stood in the doorway, fidgeting with the corner of her apron. 'Mrs Sanchez, Ms Dubois sent me. She said to tell you the dinner was excellent, and would you please come through to the dining room so they can thank you.'

The knot twisted tighter than ever. 'Yes, of course.' She took a last gulp of water and stood up, smoothing down the skirt of the sensible black dress she always wore on the job. 'Will you show me the way?'

She followed the girl out into the hall, past a huge, old-fashioned Christmas tree with glittery, store-wrapped presents underneath and through endless wide passageways with hardwood floors polished to a glossy chestnut sheen. By the time they came to a pair of solid glass doors framed in oak, Isabella's eyes were so glazed with tension that she couldn't distinguish any of the people in the room, let alone the one man who had brought her to this pass.

'Mrs Sanchez,' announced the girl in a squeaky voice, and the hum of conversation stopped at once.

Vaguely, Isabella was conscious of someone standing up, coming towards her. Veronica Dubois, of course.

'Brand, this is the lady we owe our thanks to. Mrs Sanchez, who created the delicious meal we've just enjoyed. Mrs Sanchez, Mr Ryder insisted on thanking you in person.'

Veronica's hand was on her elbow, guiding her across the floor towards a shadowy figure standing at the head of the table. 'Brandon Ryder, president of Ryder Airlines,' announced the housekeeper, as if she were introducing a crowned head of state.

For an instant the silence was deafening. Then that never-to-be-forgotten voice said with chilling clarity, 'Yes. Mrs *Sanchez* and I have met. Good evening, Isabella. You've scarcely changed at all since last we met.'

Abruptly the room came into focus, and Isabella looked up to see the wide, black-coated shoulders of the man whose existence had lured her back to Vancouver as inevitably as the swallows returned to Capistrano. She raised her eyes higher, and her gaze fastened on full lips that exposed a bare glimpse of white teeth. From the corners of those well-remembered lips thin grooves made a line to flared nostrils. Finally she tilted her head back to stare boldly into deep, furious black eyes.

Brand had changed. He looked older, and maturity made him even more savagely attractive than she remembered. His dark hair was longer now too, hiding the unusual shape of his ears and curling enticingly on the back of his neck. But from the rage she could see him battling to control Isabella knew that enticing her was not what the president of Ryder Airlines had in mind.

Nor had it ever been, really, she remembered with a sharp pang of regret.

'I *have* changed, Brand,' she said quietly.

'I doubt it.' The words were spoken under his breath, but even so the guests sitting closest could hear.

Veronica, seeming to sense imminent disaster, took Isabella's arm and said brightly, 'Well, isn't that nice? Mrs Sanchez, thank you so much for the meal. We did enjoy it. Didn't we?' She turned to beam at the guests, who all looked expectant, as if they were anticipating a titillating after-dinner drama. They murmured dutiful and disappointed assent as the lovely caterer was led from the room.

'So you and Brand are, um, friends?' Veronica was delicately feeling her way. 'I didn't realize that when I made the arrangements.'

'No. No, I know you didn't.' Isabella stared at the thin line of the other woman's mouth.

The housekeeper stood hesitating in the doorway of the kitchen. 'You should have told me. Because I doubt very much if Brand will have time to talk to you this evening – '

'Oh, yes, Brand will,' came a hard, clipped voice from right behind them. 'In fact he wouldn't miss the opportunity for the world. Veronica, go and look after my guests. Mrs *Sanchez* and I have some unfinished business to discuss.'

116

Veronica, with a veiled glance at her employer and a suspicious one at Isabella, lifted her chin and went obediently to do as she was told. Brand took Isabella none too gently by the arm, hustled her into the kitchen and shut the door.

'Now,' he said, 'tell me what in hell you think you're up to. What the devil do you mean by creating a scene in front of my guests?'

Isabella rubbed her arm and sat down at the scrubbed kitchen table. Her legs felt too weak to support her. 'I'm not up to anything,' she said, not looking at him because she couldn't bear to see the condemnation in his eyes. 'And I had no intention of creating a scene.'

'Don't give me that. When have you ever not been attempting to manipulate something or someone? And I can tell you right now, miss, you're through with manipulating me.'

'I'm not miss,' said Isabella. 'I'm still a Mrs Brand.' When she looked up to find him glowering at her, it dawned on her just how irrelevant that must sound. She tried again. 'Brand,' will you please stop standing over me breathing fire. If you want to talk to me you can sit down like a civilized human being. Then maybe we can have a civilized conversation.'

'What I've got to say won't take long,' said Brand, pressing his fists onto the table and leaning over her. 'And when it comes to you, I've long since ceased trying to be civilized. You'll remember how little good it did me the last time. Now, do you plan on telling me why you're here? Because if you don't, I have guests to look after.'

Isabella ran her tongue across her lips and felt her heart drop down to her stomach. This wasn't how she had dreamed of their reunion. And now, with Brand glaring down at her as if she were an insect he'd like to crush beneath his feet, she knew it was neither the time nor the place to set things straight. She should have trusted her instincts and phoned him first, given him some warning. But the opportunity to show him to his face that she had become an independent and capable woman of business had, at the time, seemed too good to pass up.

'I do have something to tell you,' she said, holding her voice steady with an effort. 'But not now. You're right that I shouldn't have come. I'm sorry I did. So please, when you're ready to talk, will you phone me? Miss Dubois has my number on file.'

The look on Brand's face made her want to dive under the table. But long ago she had run away from a very different man, who had frightened her a lot more than Brand did – and she had vowed then and there never to let fear rule her actions again. Now, when anyone tried to bully her, she always stood her ground and fought back.

But this time there was nothing to fight. Brand continued to glare at her for a few seconds, started to say, 'What you need, Isabella, is – ' and then broke off, growling something about not wanting to be had up for murder. After that he turned his back on her and strode from the room.

As she watched his broad black shoulders disappear down the passageway Isabella was furious to feel tears pricking at her eyes. She choked them back ruthlessly. She hadn't cried in almost five years, and there was no point whatever in starting now. Tears wouldn't help settle her current dilemma. Only a cool head and unclouded thinking might.

Stiffening her spine, she stood up and began to pack away her supplies. The best thing she could do now was get on with her work and wait for Brand to make the next move. If he was still the man she remembered, he would do so in his own good time.

He would feel he had to.

The air outside was cold, with a dampness that hinted at snow. Isabella shivered as she opened the back of her van and hurried to stow away the implements of her trade. No one came to help her, and by the time the last box was safely in its place her fingers were numb and her nose felt as if Jack Frost had claimed it as his own. Slamming the van door behind her, she turned on the engine and waited for its warmth to thaw the frozen blocks that had been her feet.

Knowing it would take a while for the heat to do its work, she turned up the collar of her coat. This was a different cold from the cold she had become used to in Edmonton. Damper, more penetrating . . .

It had been on a night very like this one that her last scene with Brand had been played out.

She remembered the cold hitting her face as she had shut the door to the apartment they had shared. It had made her hesitate briefly, looking, perhaps, for a reason not to leave. But a car horn had blasted her out of her moment of indecision, and with a courage born mainly of youthful ignorance of the dangers of Vancouver streets at night, she had walked the two blocks to the bus depot.

There had been an old tramp asleep in front of the entrance. She had stepped over him, but he hadn't woken up.

Isabella's hands curled tightly around the wheel as she stared at the huge house looming over her in the darkness.

Brand's house.

Such a long time ago it all seemed now. Almost a lifetime . . .

The van's engine purred and began to belch forth warmth, and Isabella stopped trying to force the torrent of memories back. As they poured into her consciousness, unstoppable now, she was seventeen again, moving blindly towards the end of her marriage.

It had all been so unexpected. Just three weeks earlier she had vowed to wait patiently for Brand to recover from his loss and learn to love her.

Fate, and Gary Roseboy, had changed all that.

Brand, as usual, had been working late on that last fateful night when Isabella, dressed in a prim cotton nightgown and robe, had opened the door in answer to a knock. She had hoped to find her husband waiting on the threshold to be admitted. He did knock sometimes – usually with a boot – when his arms were full and he didn't feel like juggling with his key.

But it had been Gary who stood grinning in the dimly lit passageway.

'Hi,' he said. 'Can I borrow a cup of sugar?'

'Yes. All right.' Isabella knew that what he actually wanted to borrow was his neighbour's wife, but she decided to let him in anyway, confident of her ability to keep him at arm's length. He had been alone with her many times before – and tonight, with Christmas coming, she was feeling especially lonely and neglected. It would be pleasant to be noticed and admired.

She was just pouring the sugar when she heard Brand's key in the lock. Gary didn't hear it. He was too busy ogling his hostess. Isabella thought quickly, too quickly, and on the spur of the moment she put down the sugar bowl and flung her arms around his neck. Gary, predictably, obliged with a passionate kiss on her parted lips.

Brand came to a halt with his hand on the doorknob. It was obvious at once that his day had not gone well. He looked tired, and there were heavy, bruised-looking shadows under his eyes. But when his gaze fell on the entwined figures of his wife and his neighbour Isabella saw weariness change to an icy, unforgiving fury.

Horrified, she bit back a gasp. Brand's head swung briefly towards her, and she saw his lips curve in contempt. But by the time he turned back to Gary he had his emotions well under control.

'I hate to seem unneighbourly,' he drawled, 'but I'd be obliged if in future, Gary, you would confine your attentions to the contents of my fridge. I can accept occasional shortages of milk, sugar or plum jam. But I'm damned if I'm lending you my wife.'

Isabella took a quick step backwards. On the surface, Brand didn't sound dangerous. But she didn't miss the fire beneath the ice – or the way his fists were bunched against his thighs.

Gary didn't miss that either. She saw him swallow. 'Sorry, didn't mean – heat of the moment, you know . . .' He began to sidle towards the door.

Brand held it open, and when Gary came abreast of him he took him by the collar, put his boot on the young man's backside and propelled him out into the corridor with such force that his body connected with the opposite wall. They watched him pick himself up and stumble the few feet to his apartment.

Brand closed the door and turned to Isabella.

'It wasn't what it seemed, Brand,' she said quickly.

'I didn't know he was going to – um – kiss me . . .'
Her voice trailed off. Brand was looking her up and
down as if she were a mare of dubious parentage up
for auction.

'Didn't you, my dear?' His reply was pure Rhett
Butler. Then he went into the bedroom and slammed
the door.

Isabella stood with both hands clasped in front of
her, watching the flimsy panels shudder beneath the
impact and wondering if the rickety frame would
hold.

It did.

'Brand!' she cried after him. 'Brand, please listen . . .'

There was no answer. She glanced at the small
Christmas tree perched on a corner of the table,
muttered, 'Merry Christmas,' under her breath,
and marched across the room.

He was lying on his black-quilted single bed
staring up at the ceiling. 'Get out,' he said, when
he heard her come in.

'Brand – '

'I said get out.'

'No. I won't get out. I'm your wife.'

'Is that so?' He swung his legs to the floor and was
upon her with such speed that she scarcely knew he'd
moved until she felt his hands grip her shoulders.
'And I thought you'd forgotten that boring little
detail.' He stepped back, took in her demure white

robe and the old-fashioned, high-collared night-gown. 'So innocent-looking,' he murmured. 'No wonder I was so easily deluded.'

Isabella held her ground. 'You weren't deluded,' she said. 'I don't even like Gary. And I didn't . . .' She hesitated. 'I didn't really mean him to kiss me.'

'Kiss you? Are you trying to tell me that's as far as it went?'

'Brand! How could you?' Isabella felt anger well up inside her and boil over. Not because Brand had read more into the scene with Gary than was there. She couldn't blame him for that. But because the scene would never have happened if he had taken the trouble to show her that she mattered to him at all.

'Yes, that's as far as he went,' she shouted. 'And it's further than you've gone in eleven months. We're married, Brand. Or hadn't *you* noticed that boring little detail?'

'Oh, yes.' Brand was still arctic. 'I'd noticed. I also noticed you batting those come-hither eyelashes at our hormone-crazed neighbour. And, as I seem to remember telling you before, I don't bed teenage tramps wearing negligees – or touch-me-not night-gowns.' He flicked the decorous ruffle at her neck. 'So if you think . . .'

Isabella *had* stopped thinking. All she knew was that suddenly she wanted this beautiful man who had just rejected her so coldly more than she'd ever wanted anything in her life. And she wanted to make him swallow his cruel words.

She moistened her lips, and with a smile that showed him just a glimpse of small teeth she drew back her arm and aimed a hard slap at his face.

He stepped aside, and her flailing fingers encountered only air. She stumbled, and turned furiously to take another shot. But when he caught her arms and held them at her sides she found herself pressed intimately against his lean and powerful frame – and felt something she hadn't expected. Brand *wasn't* altogether indifferent to her charms.

Lifting her head, laughing a little wildly, she began to revolve her hips in a slow, erotic motion that she could see from the sudden flaring of his nostrils was at last beginning to shake his iron control.

'Stop it, Isabella,' he said harshly.

For answer she laughed again, and began to undo the buttons on his shirt.

Then suddenly, frighteningly, she was no longer the one orchestrating the scene.

Brand, his eyes glazed more with anger than with desire, put his hands on her waist and growled, 'All right, Isabella. If that's what you want . . .'

Before she had time to draw breath she found herself lifted against his chest, and a few seconds later she was sprawled on her back across his bed.

He had taken her then. There was no other word for it. But because it *was* what she wanted she gave as much as he took, and in the end the fury of their mutual passion brought them together in a conflagration of such blazing intensity that for a few brilliant moments it was as if the whole room had erupted into flames.

Afterwards Brand was quiet. Frighteningly quiet. Then he said he was sorry. Isabella wasn't sorry, and she told him so.

'Nevertheless, I shouldn't have done it,' he replied, as if he had been the only one involved. 'You could turn out to be pregnant.'

'But that would be . . . Oh.' Suddenly she understood what was on his mind. If she turned out to be pregnant, he wouldn't be convinced the baby was his. Isabella felt her heart shrivel up like a wilted autumn leaf. 'Nothing happened with Gary,' she said, fighting an urge to pound Brand with her fists. 'Nothing. Brand, you have to believe me.'

He nodded, and patted her shoulder. 'It doesn't matter whether I believe you or not. You're still a child, Isabella. A lovely, immature child. You've always been catered to and taken care of, and I'm afraid that means you'll always be dependent on some gullible fool of a man – like me – to look after you. So you needn't worry. Since I happen to be your husband, I suppose that man might as well be me.'

Oh! How *could* he? Was that really all she was to him? A child? After what they had just shared, that was *it*?

126

'No,' she replied dully, unable to look at him now. 'I wouldn't think of imposing such a burden on you, Brand. *You* needn't worry. I can look after myself.'

'Nonsense. Whatever comes of this is obviously my responsibility.'

She hadn't answered him, hadn't trusted herself to speak, and after a few minutes Brand had turned on his side. Isabella had thought he was probably only pretending to be asleep, especially when he'd started to talk to himself. But much later, when his breathing had become regular, she'd got up and begun to pack her clothes.

He hadn't woken up, and long before morning she was gone.

When she'd reached Edmonton she'd written a letter to Brand, with no return address, telling him not to bother trying to find her. She'd assured him she was well, and had a job she liked very much. Then she'd thanked him politely for having married her, hoped his life would be a happy one and assured him there wouldn't be a child.

When, a month later, she discovered there would be, she knew it was too late to go back.

CHAPTER 6

'Whatsa matter, Mommy? You look sad.'

Isabella smiled at the dark-haired child skipping along the street beside her. 'I'm not sad, Connie,' she said quickly, adjusting the big box of soap in her arms. 'Just a bit tired. The party I catered last night ran very late. Did you have a nice time with Edwina?'

'Mmm. She let me eat a whole bag of toffees.'

She would, thought Isabella, noting the artfully ingenuous look in her daughter's eyes.

Edwina was the retired pastry cook who looked after Connie for her whenever she had a catering job to do. She was devoted to the little girl, but, having parted happily with her own teeth at the age of twenty, she didn't see any particular advantage to healthy molars. Isabella did, and she intended her point of view to prevail. Eventually. She sighed. Edwina was unlikely to stop cultivating cavities for the benefit of the dental profession without a struggle.

Connie gave her mother a sharp look. 'You're cross *and* sad,' she insisted.

128

'Yes, I *am* cross about the toffee,' Isabella admitted. 'But why should I be sad on a beautiful windy day when the sun is shining, my shopping is finished for the week, and I've had a wonderful walk on the beach with my favourite daughter?'

'I don't know. But you are.'

Isabella shook her head. Connie was far too perceptive for a four-year-old.

Was she sad? On edge, certainly, and suffering from an all-too-familiar irritation with the president of Ryder Airlines.

Brand hadn't called. Christmas, spent peacefully with Edwina's large family, had come and gone. Now it was the middle of February, and she refused to go on waiting for him for ever. He had been given his chance to make a move towards her on his own terms. Now it was up to her. So she would see him just one more time, and after that she would make up her mind to forget him and get on with her life. A life that could conceivably include Felix Napier, who was willing to be a father to Connie.

She tossed her windblown hair back from her eyes. Yes, Brand had been given his chance. She had always meant to come back to him when the time was right, not because she held much hope that things would change, but because she owed it to both of them – as well as to Connie – to find out. And now she had no choice but to face the truth.

Brand's feelings for her were exactly the same as they had been on the night she left him.

He didn't want her. It was that simple. And she was no longer at all sure she wanted him. Why *should* she want a man who, in the past, had looked on her as a frightened child who happened to have the body of a woman – he had been more than half right about that – and now seemed to regard her as some kind of scheming black witch? He had only married her because he believed it to be his duty. And she supposed she couldn't really blame him for resenting the juvenile albatross he had been forced to bring home from the tragedy of his South American honeymoon.

But Brand was strong, and even in the midst of his grief she had to concede that most of the time he had tried to be kind to his very young bride.

Isabella bit the corner of her lip, knowing that she had been the cause of many of their problems. She had been so crazily, immaturely in love with him that her impatient teenage heart had refused to accept that he needed time to recover from the loss of his Mary.

She shifted the box of soap to her other arm. Yes, and her teenage brain must have been out of order too, or she would have known better than to expect a recently widowed man of twenty-six to fall passionately for a seventeen-year-old fan club of one who sat waiting for the crumbs of his attention like a baby bird waiting to be fed.

Remembering that eager baby bird, Isabella grimaced. But when she and Connie rounded the corner onto the quiet Point Grey street where they lived, a gust of wind blew them both backwards and she began to smile.

Connie laughed, and Isabella grabbed for her hand. 'Come on,' she said. 'Let's make a run for it, before we're blown all the way back to the beach.'

Connie started to run with her, and then all of a sudden she pulled back. 'Mommy? Who's that man standing by our door? He's looking at us in a real funny way.'

Isabella lifted her head, which had been bowed against the wind. They were almost home now. And there was indeed a man standing on the steps of their ground floor apartment.

She opened her mouth, felt the blood leave her face, and just for a moment she couldn't see.

That was when Isabella Sanchez, who had never fainted in her life, tripped over a crack in the pavement, dropped her soap, and landed in an undignified heap at the feet of the man who was still her lawfully wedded husband.

Brand rested his shoulders against the grey brick of the apartment entranceway and propped one booted foot on the opposite wall.

He had watched them running towards him, the

slim young woman and the child, as an unexpected pain jabbed him in the ribs.

She was still as lovely as ever, but the years had brought a cool radiance to her beauty, a composure that hadn't been there before. Had his wild South American temptress finally grown up? It seemed so to him as she ran gaily down the street with the laughing child.

For a brief, surprising moment he had felt like moving out of the shadows to take her in his arms. But the impulse faded almost at once. Isabella as a teenage siren had been trouble enough. As a mature, confident woman, there was no telling what havoc she might wreak.

Brand stood his ground. He hadn't spent the last six weeks making up his mind to see her – or, more accurately, to see what she was up to – only to give her the upper hand the instant he laid eyes on her again.

Oh, yes, Isabella had been trouble. He gazed bleakly at the determined tilt of her softly rounded chin. Trouble from the moment when, all those years ago, he had woken up to find her in his bed. And he had learned the hard way that Isabella was a problem it was always best to face with his armour on. If, now, for some devious reason of her own, she had decided she wanted something from him again, he had to convince her she wasn't going to get it. Because there was no doubt in his mind that, unless he did, sooner or later she would turn up in the wrong place and at the worst possible time yet again. It seemed to be a habit of hers.

A gust of wind shrieked round the corner, and he turned up the collar of his jacket. Why had she come back? His life was going as smoothly as it ever did, business was good, and he didn't need her beautiful, disruptive presence in his life. If he'd had any sense, and hadn't been so involved with Ryder Airlines, he would have seen to it that the connection between them was severed long ago.

Brand shoved his hands into the pockets of black jeans. They were almost upon him now. He felt a flicker of irritation that she had a child with her. Who was she? In the old days, Isabella hadn't been the type to go soft-eyed over other people's children. Her ineptitude with young Billy had been ludicrous. His mouth twisted. He hadn't thought of that particular incident in years. Not that it mattered. The point was that unless this little girl was about to be returned to a waiting parent, she was definitely going to be in the way.

Brand was just thinking that he might have to postpone this confrontation, because he didn't approve of forming battle lines in front of children, when Isabella looked up and met his eyes.

He watched in disbelief, stifling an unlikely urge to laugh, as she collapsed like an ungainly rag doll at his feet.

133

'Just where I always wanted you,' he murmured, after a few seconds of astonished silence during which he saw her skin turn from golden olive to a soft dusty rose. 'Too bad you didn't think of it before.'

'Bastard,' said Isabella.

Brand raised his eyebrows and allowed a malignant grin to light his features. 'At a loss for words, Isabella? How unlike you.' This was turning out better than he'd expected. He held out a hand, which she ignored.

With a shrug, he bent to pick up her purse, and as soon as he'd found a key, and without further ado, he scooped her up in his arms. Immediately she started to squirm, so he asked amiably, 'Want me to toss you over my shoulder?' and wasn't sure whether he was relieved or sorry when she settled down at once. After that he carried her unusually limp and yielding form into the neat but sparsely furnished apartment which these days she apparently called home. Shaking his head, he deposited her on a plain brown sofa that angled across a corner of the room.

His arms, all of a sudden, felt empty.

When he straightened, he discovered her gaze fastened on him with such concentrated speculation that he began to feel as if his body were up for grabs.

The small girl was clinging to his ankle. 'It's all right,' he assured her. 'There's nothing wrong with your friend that a few minutes' rest won't put right.' Turning to Isabella, he added under his breath, 'Keep looking at me like that and I may also recommend a cold shower.'

She started. 'Oh! You conceited – '

'Bastard?' suggested Brand helpfully. 'You know, you really should do something about improving that limited vocabulary of yours. Although, come to think of it, I don't believe that particular word used to be part of your repertoire. Am I right?'

He could hear Isabella drawing in air to deliver a blistering response as he strolled back out to the street to collect the box of soap that had flown from her arms when she'd hit the sidewalk.

His triumphant one-upmanship was short-lived.

'She's not my friend,' announced the child the moment he returned to the apartment. 'She's my mommy.'

Oh. Game, set and match to Isabella. Shock hit Brand like a baseball in the stomach as, without breaking stride, he walked over to the counter that divided the small cupboard of a kitchen from the living room and laid down the box of soap with measured deliberation.

Isabella stared at his back, trying to read his reaction from the set of his shoulders. But he continued to hold them with the natural confidence she had always admired. When he turned around, his features revealed a polite, carefully controlled blankness. Nothing more. It was as if shutters had closed over his face.

'Your mother?' he said to Connie. 'I didn't know that.' He smiled then, and if the smile was an effort, it didn't show. 'I guess I *should* have known, shouldn't I? You look very like her.' He turned to Isabella, who sat up at once and began to unbutton her coat. 'You've been busy since last I saw you, Mrs Sanchez.'

Isabella noted that this time he pronounced her last name without emphasis, as if it meant nothing to him. She put a hand to her head, wondering why it seemed to be revolving. It couldn't be the fall. All *that* had hurt was her dignity. So of course it had to be Brand. He had always had the power to make her feel light-headed. But at least he wasn't blazing mad at her today. Obviously the shock of her reappearance had worn off. That was something. His casual mockery she could cope with and even laugh at.

She shifted slightly on the sofa, wishing he had warned her he was coming. Because she had another, more shattering revelation in store for Brand. And how could she explain to him about Connie with the child standing there all big-eyed and listening – the child who had been told that the father who loved her was far away, but that he would one day come back to meet his cherished daughter?

She had been so sure Brand *would* love his daughter. He was good with children and genuinely liked them. She would never forget how he had come to her rescue that disastrous day when Judy had left her to take care of baby Billy. Yet all she could read in his eyes now was an aloof, almost clinical detachment.

Which meant he had no idea Connie was his.

'Yes,' said Isabella, swallowing hard and forcing herself to sound as cool and detached as he did. 'I have been busy. Would you like a cup of coffee? Or something stronger?'

He nodded. 'Coffee. I'll make it. You'd better take your coat off and wash that mud off your face.'

Isabella didn't argue, but got up to do as he suggested. She had reason to know Brand was competent in a kitchen. He could certainly be trusted with the coffee.

Thank heaven for a few minutes' respite. Going into the bathroom, she bent forward to rest her forehead against the cool, flat glass of the mirror. And immediately, inevitably, her mind returned again to the night five years ago when her marriage to Brand had finally come apart.

It had been her own fault. She should have known better than to give Gary an opening, better than to encourage a man whose intentions had been so transparently dishonourable. Oh, yes, she had asked for all the trouble she had got. But she hadn't meant to. God knows, she hadn't meant to.

Isabella picked up a facecloth, then let it drop from her fingers. She had loved Brand so much. And he *had* been good to her when he'd had the time. Especially at first. Why, oh, why, had she been such a fool? How could she have repaid him so unkindly? And had five years really passed since that devastating night?

It didn't seem so. For all her recent business success, at this moment Isabella felt like the nervous, excited young girl she had been the day she had followed a man she hardly knew to an unknown land.

As she stood there, remembering, gradually Isabella became aware that Connie was giggling in the next room. Slowly, almost reluctantly, she returned to the present and her surroundings. Her head was still pressed to the bathroom mirror. It felt cold. She straightened and turned on the tap. Brand was here, on the other side of the door. He no longer belonged to the past.

And it was time he learned the truth about Connie.

Isabella took a deep breath and pulled her thick mauve sweater down over tight black trousers. Edwina would look after Connie for a while. She could explain to the child that Mommy had important business to discuss with the nice man. Connie understood about business.

Oh, yes, Connie would understand. What was less certain was that Brand would behave like a nice man.

Isabella scrubbed the mud off her face, touched her wrists with the scent of gardenias and squared her shoulders. When she returned to the living room she was smiling a small, brittle smile.

Brand had coffee ready on the table beside the sofa. He was sitting in the only armchair, a solid brown tweed wingback, holding Connie on his knee while the two of them studied a book about a pink hippopotamus.

He looked up briefly when Isabella entered, and went on talking to Connie.

'Connie,' said Isabella, taking a seat on the sofa, 'I think you'd better go up to see Edwina for a while. I'll just give her a call to say you're coming – '

'I want to stay with Brand.' Connie's expression was mutinous, and without quite meaning to she kicked Brand sharply in the leg.

'Hey,' he said. 'Watch it, young lady. It's a bad idea to go around kicking people. You never know when they're going to kick you back.' He threw a significant glance at Isabella, who looked away.

Connie gazed up at him anxiously, and started to scramble off his knee. '*You* won't kick me, will you?' she asked as her feet hit the floor.

Brand shook his head. 'I promise I won't. If you promise not to do it again.'

'I promise.' Connie nodded solemnly, and the stern planes of Brand's features softened. He reached out to smooth back a length of the glossy brown hair that had fallen in front of her face.

Isabella, watching him and the child with a growing ache in her chest, saw his big body suddenly go rigid. Something arced across the room and struck her with the force of a bolt of lightning. But when Brand looked up, and she saw his eyes, she realized that what she had felt was the overwhelming power of a rage he could just barely control.

Dear heaven. She moistened her lips. What could she say? It had happened so swiftly, so unexpectedly. She had never meant him to learn the truth like this.

'What's the matter, Brand? Are you cross with me?' Connie, child-like, immediately assumed *she* had transgressed.

With an obvious and extraordinary effort, Brand produced a smile. 'No, I'm not cross with you,' he said, in a voice that was almost but not quite steady. 'I'm surprised, that's all. Did you know you've got ears just like mine? They curl over at the top like little handles.'

'Like yours?' Connie climbed back onto his knee, and, putting both hands beside his head, pushed the thick hair behind his ears. Then she wriggled round to face her mother and announced delightedly, 'Mommy, he has. Brand has got ears just like mine.'

Isabella opened her mouth, tried to speak, but at first the words wouldn't come. Then, when she could see her silence was beginning to worry Connie, she managed to choke, 'Yes, darling, I know he has. It – it happens sometimes.'

Brand looked directly at her for the first time since

140

he'd caught sight of Connie's ears. 'It does, doesn't it?' he said, in a tone so clipped and cold it froze her blood. 'Especially to people whose last name happens to be Ryder.'

'My last name's Ryder,' said Connie. 'Mommy's is too, but she uses Sanchez for business.'

'Only for business, Isabella?' Brand spoke in the same icy tone.

She shook her head. 'No. I'll explain later.'

'Yes, you will,' he agreed. 'Connie, I'm afraid Mommy's right. I do need to talk . . . *business* with her. But when we're finished I'll take you out for a pizza if you're good.'

'Mommy too?'

Isabella watched Brand draw air into his lungs. 'If you like,' he said. She knew what it had cost him to say that, and the knowledge hurt.

'I'll call Edwina,' she murmured.

A few minutes later Connie left the apartment hand in hand with Edwina. They sat listening, not looking at each other, as two pairs of feet clattered up the outside stairs leading to the second floor apartments.

It wasn't until a door slammed up above that Isabella turned to face the man in the black jeans and the black shirt, whose blazing black eyes were filled with such pain and rage that, insanely, she longed to throw herself into his arms and beg forgiveness.

She didn't do it because she knew that forgiveness wouldn't follow. The way he was looking at her now, she was more likely to find herself hurled across the room. So she sat down again on the sofa and said quietly, 'I was beginning to think you weren't coming. Why didn't you phone me first, Brand?'

Brand stood up and walked across to the window. When he turned to face her, she saw that he had himself under control.

'I believe in the element of surprise.' The edges of his lips curled downwards. 'For obvious reasons.'

'Yes. You always did.' She studied the harsh lines beside his mouth, and added softly, 'I'm sorry, Brand.'

'Really? And I suppose you think that makes up for all the lies, the years of deception and concealment?'

His words cut. As they were intended to. Isabella stared down at the worn, dun-coloured carpet, not wanting to see the accusation in his eyes. 'I never meant to deceive you,' she said stiffly. 'And I didn't want you to learn the truth like this. I thought you'd come sooner. I was going to explain – '

'I've been up north on business. In part because I needed time to decide if there was any reason why I ought to see you again. Now tell me – what kind of *explaining* did you have in mind? There's a hell of a difference between explanations and excuses, Isabella. That's my daughter up there.' He pointed at the ceiling. 'What did you plan to tell me? That she was

142

Gary's? Or the result of a one-night stand with some other poor fool you picked out to use and throw away?'

When she heard his fist crack down on the windowsill, Isabella looked up from the carpet. She didn't want to. She was too afraid of what she would see. Brand sounded like an enraged bull about to tear apart her small apartment.

But when she made herself face him she found that he was standing quite still, with folded arms and his dark head bowed between his shoulders. She couldn't see his eyes.

Her heart lurched painfully. However much he might be trying to hide it by going on the offensive, Brand was hurting. Not because of her. He didn't care about her. She swallowed hard. But because of Connie.

'There has never been anyone but you.' She pressed her knees together and sat ramrod-straight on the sofa. 'I planned to tell you she was yours.'

'You expect me to believe that?' He lifted his head and hooked his thumbs into his belt.

Isabella gazed up at him. He looked like some avenging black devil, poised there against the window with his lips twisted into a sneer. But still she had to try to get through to him, to get past his anger and hostility. She understood the anger. But the truth he didn't know, and she knew he wouldn't accept it, was that if he had loved her all those years ago she would never in a million years have left him.

'Yes,' she said. 'You may as well believe it, because it's true. I always meant you to know. That's partly why I came back to Vancouver.'

'To introduce Connie to the father she'd never met?' His voice was harsh with disbelief.

'Yes. That was one reason. I decided it was time.'

'Time? Oh, I see.' He slapped his palm – hard – against his thigh. 'You mean before I noticed that life was passing me by and made the move I should have made at the beginning? Before I married again, and produced some other child with a more immediate claim to my assets – which, as you have no doubt discovered by now, are considerable? What happened, Isabella? Did whoever was supporting you in your accustomed style – a style I wasn't able to provide for you before – get tired of being played for a patsy?'

Isabella pushed her hands between her knees, trapping them so tightly that they hurt. She had to. Otherwise she would have leaped up in a futile attempt to claw Brand's handsome face. Which wouldn't have done a thing for the daughter whose welfare had to be her primary concern.

'I told you,' she said frozenly. 'There has been no one since you, Brand. And my "accustomed style" has become hard work, making the best of what I have, and doing whatever needs to be done. As you

144

ought to be able to see with your own eyes.' She gestured at the predominantly brown room with its functional, unadorned furniture.

Brand gave it a perfunctory glance. 'Interior design was never one of your interests. Your talents in that line were strictly practical. And I see perfectly serviceable things and a damn good address.'

'The damn good address is essential for my business,' said Isabella, damping down an urge to scream at this magnificent, ungiving man who was her husband. 'How much confidence do you imagine my customers would have in a company that worked out of a packing crate beside the railway, which was about all I could afford when I came to town?'

She had the sour satisfaction of seeing him frown, and knew she had momentarily shaken his conviction that she was purposely concealing her prosperity. But not, of course, his conviction that she was a scheming little witch.

'All right,' he said. 'So maybe you have fallen on hard times – a problem I have no doubt you'll find a way to resolve. But not through me.'

'I don't need you to solve my problems, Brand. My business is beginning to do quite well.' Isabella spoke wearily, but with pride. Somehow the urge to scream had left her, and all she felt now was a determination to show Brand that she could manage very well without his help. As she had, indeed, managed for five years. 'I just need to do what's best for Connie. She – she deserves something I haven't been able to give her. Something I thought you might be able to provide – '

'*Money?*'

She flinched at the scorn in his voice, and without meaning to she jumped to her feet. '*No! Not* money, Brand. Connie doesn't need money. She needs – she needs the love of her father.'

Brand's face had been sternly composed, but suddenly it was suffused with livid colour.

'*You* have the gall to tell me that? You, who wrote me a letter assuring me there wasn't going to be any baby. You, who have raised my daughter for the past four years without letting me know she existed. My God, Isabella – ' He broke off, and she watched him ram his fists into his pockets, his jaw clenched so hard she expected it to crack.

Then he turned his back and strode towards the door.

She knew he was leaving because he was afraid that if he didn't he would hit her. But she still ran after him and touched her hand to his shoulder. The muscles beneath his shirt tensed up at once like corded rope.

'Brand, I'm sorry.' She spoke quietly, trying not to betray her agitation. 'Please understand. I didn't want to keep her from you. But I *couldn't* tell you. You despised me. That's why I left you. Because, in a way, I *had* manipulated you into marriage. And after that last night, when you said you would take responsibility for a baby even though you wouldn't believe it was yours, I knew I had to give you a chance to live your life free of obligation to a woman you neither loved nor cared for – '

'What?' Brand swung round at that, brushing her hand from his shoulder. 'Is that what you thought? That I'd look on my own wife and child as an *obligation*?' His eyes turned dark with scepticism – and something deeper that made her pulses quicken. 'Isabella, children are a privilege, not a bargaining chip in some high-stakes marriage contract. You had no right to hide her existence from me.'

His hand was gripping her arm now, pressing into it. 'I didn't intend to hide anything,' Isabella said, standing her ground stoically. 'When I wrote to you I honestly didn't think I was pregnant. When I found out I was, I – I thought it was the wrong time to tell you. You wouldn't have believed the baby was yours. And I was very young. Only just eighteen. If you'd known, you would have made me come back – '

'Damn right I would.'

Isabella closed her eyes. 'I know. But I *couldn't* go back, Brand. I couldn't live where I wasn't wanted, bring up my child in an atmosphere of hate and suspicion.'

'I never hated you, Isabella.' Suddenly Brand looked very tired.

'Maybe not, but you often told me I was a spoiled little brat.'

'Because you *were* a spoiled brat.' He shook his head, and she was astounded to see the beginnings of a bleak-looking smile. 'A brat with guts, though. You wrestled the English language to the ground with amazing speed.'

Praise? From Brand? 'I had an English governess,' she reminded him. 'I already spoke English well.' When his eyes narrowed pointedly, she added, 'All right, not as a Canadian would speak it. But I learned fast. I could have managed on my own within three months.'

'You didn't, though. We were together for more than *ten* months, as I remember.'

Isabella became aware that the pressure of Brand's fingers on her wrist was beginning to send unwelcome shivers up her arm. Unwelcome and disturbingly seductive. A quiver of heat ran down her spine.

But she didn't ask him to let her go.

'Yes,' she agreed, not quite steadily. 'We were. I didn't leave because – I was grateful to you. And I was still young enough and foolish enough to believe I could help you to forget.' Well, at least that was part of the truth.

'Forget?' He frowned. 'Forget what, Isabella?'

She didn't want to answer. He was wounded already.

148

Why open up another old scar? But she could tell from the grim line of his mouth that he wouldn't accept an evasion.

'I was talking about your honeymoon,' she said, lowering her head so she wouldn't have to see that long-ago grief reflected in his eyes. 'About Mary being killed . . .'

'Thank you for reminding me.'

His sarcasm sliced through her like a razor. She rooted her gaze firmly on the floor.

After almost a minute had passed, he asked, 'Did you really imagine you could make me forget?'

He spoke with an odd, rasping inflection, unlike his usual low baritone, but she supposed all it meant was that he was deliberately rubbing salt in the cut.

'I told you I was young and foolish,' she said, hating the break in her voice.

To her surprise, Brand let go of her arm, and she felt his knuckles touch her chin. 'Look at me, Isabella.' His tone was commanding but unexpectedly gentle.

Isabella lifted her head. Even when his features were twisted with anger, it was no hardship to look at Brandon Ryder. He was a beautiful man. But she looked without expectation. Brand had never loved her. He never would. It wasn't his fault, but she could no longer afford to succumb to the undeniable pull of his sexuality.

'Isabella . . .' He seemed to be having trouble

speaking. 'Isabella, at twenty-six I wasn't all that mature myself. I know I kept comparing you to Mary. It wasn't fair of me. And, yes, it's possible I misjudged you. If so, I regret it. But that doesn't alter the fact that Connie is my daughter, and that you kept her from me quite cold-bloodedly and knowing full well that I'd want to be a part of her life.' He stopped, took a long breath and produced what she supposed was meant to be a smile. 'I realize that when we were together I was often distracted by the demands of my business, impatient with you – '

'Yes. You were.' Isabella drew herself upright. 'You also told me I was a lovely, immature child who was so used to being catered to that I would always be dependent on some gullible fool of a man like yourself. And that since you happened to be my husband, you supposed it might as well be you.'

Brand raked a hand through his hair. 'Did I say that?' To Isabella's amazement, she saw a genuine smile touch his lips. 'Not tactful, but I suppose it made a certain amount of sense.'

'Not to me it didn't.' She tugged at the hem of her mauve sweater. 'To me, when I was forced to think about it, there at the end, it meant that if there was ever to be any hope for us I had to prove to you that I *wasn't* a child. That I could stand on my own feet, make my own living . . . become a woman you would be able to respect. And if, while I was doing it, you found someone else – then I owed it to you to let you be free.' She took a quick breath. 'You haven't met anyone else. Have you?'

'No.' Brand ran a hand round the inside of his collar. 'I suppose it didn't occur to you that my two attempts at marriage might have left me a bit . . . shall we say gun-shy of that particular institution? And as for brief encounters . . .' He shuddered. 'I learned my lesson.'

Was he teasing her? Actually teasing? 'Has it?' she asked, responding to this astonishing change of mood. 'Left you gun-shy, I mean?'

'No,' he admitted. 'Merely cautious. Apart from which, for the most part I've been too damn busy to worry about romantic entanglements. Also, I happen to be married.'

Oh. So that was why he had never bothered to track her down and demand a divorce. Apart from being cautious, he had been too involved with his burgeoning business to take the time. But now – now he was successful, settled . . .

If he wanted it, he had all the time in the world to deal with lawyers. As she had. If she wanted it.

Yes. For Connie's sake it was time to make decisions. That was what Felix had said, and Felix was right. Funny, she couldn't quite remember what he looked like . . .

Isabella studied the rugged planes of Brand's face. He didn't look so dangerous any more – but – would he ever be able to forgive her? Would it matter if he didn't?

She had no answer to that. But, whatever the case, she had to try to make him understand.

'Brand – I've told you I'm sorry about Connie,' she began. 'Truly I am. But if I'd told you before, when I was having so much trouble making ends meet, you might have tried to take her away from me. Oh, not to be cruel,' she added quickly, seeing the look on his face, 'but because you would have thought it the best thing for Connie.'

Brand dragged a hand wearily across his forehead. 'I don't know what I'd have thought. I wasn't given the chance to think, was I? But I'm not a monster, Isabella.' He tipped his head back, gazed at the ceiling as if for inspiration, then said abruptly, 'All right, what's done is done. It's too late to change the past. But not, I warn you, too late to change the future. What I mean to do now is get to know my daughter. Will you phone Edwina, please, and tell her to send Connie down?'

He didn't look at Isabella again, but brushed past her and threw himself back into the chair. From the corner of her eye she saw him communing with a brown spot on the wall.

With a feeling that was something like dread, she went to pick up the phone.

★ ★ ★

'Brand, how come you didn't have sugary on your ears when you were little?' Connie asked through a mouthful of pineapple pizza.

'Sugary?' Brand gave her a puzzled smile.

'She means surgery,' explained Isabella, laying a crust of pizza carefully back on her plate.

'I see.' He glanced at her sharply before turning back to Connie. 'Why should I have surgery? Don't you think I'm pretty just the way I am? You certainly are.' He grinned at the little girl, who giggled back.

'Silly. Boys aren't supposed to be pretty.'

No, and Brand is no boy, thought Isabella wistfully. He's a man, and as unattainably desirable as ever.

So far the meal had gone smoothly. Brand had been polite to Isabella, charming to Connie, and the undercurrents that could so easily have spoiled the occasion for the child had been kept firmly under control by both adults. Isabella wished this tenuous truce would continue, but she wasn't under any illusions.

'*I'm* having sugary,' said Connie. 'Next week. Aren't I, Mommy?'

Isabella nodded.

'What?' Brand put his fork down and glared at her. 'For heaven's sake, why?'

Isabella didn't answer, but Connie, reacting to his tone, hung her head. ''Cos the kids in kindergarten laugh at me. They say I must come from another planet. And I don't.'

'Of course you don't.' Brand looked so belligerant that Isabella was glad Connie's schoolmates were well out of his reach. 'Besides, people can't even see your ears,' he objected. 'They're covered by your beautiful hair.'

'They're not when I run,' said Connie. 'Why don't you want me to have sugary, Brand?'

Brand took a long breath. 'I didn't say I don't want you to. But I like you exactly the way you are.'

'' 'Cos I'm like you?' Connie had always had a habit of going straight for the jugular.

Brand smiled wryly. 'I suppose so. Partly.'

Isabella didn't like the sound of that 'partly', and she knew she hadn't heard the last of Connie's 'sugary'. But for now, if Brand would just go back to playing the kindly companion to his daughter, the rest of the evening might still pass without further dissension. With a little luck.

Luck, in Connie's forthright hands, was not with her.

Isabella was gazing pensively at the tiffany lamp suspended above their table, and half-listening to Brand telling Connie about a dog he had owned as a boy, when she heard her daughter laugh and say confidently, 'When my daddy comes back I'm going to ask him to buy me a dog. Mommy can't afford one right now.'

'You want a dog? I'll buy you a dog,' Brand said promptly.

Isabella was about to remonstrate when Connie said, 'Oh! Will you really?' She put down the slice of pizza that was halfway to her mouth and added matter-of-factly, 'I guess that means you're my daddy. I thought you might be.'

CHAPTER 7

The tiffany lamp tilted, seemed to explode into a thousand fragments of light. Isabella closed her eyes, then opened them again when she heard what sounded like somebody choking.

It was Brand, hastily lowering his glass and with his gaze fixed on Connie in surprise, disbelief and – was that elation she read in the deep-set black eyes? Yes, it had to be. Brand was *pleased* that Connie had guessed he was her father.

But all he said, in a deadpan voice that gave away nothing, was, 'What makes you think that, Connie?'

'Well, your ears are the same as mine. And you said you'd buy me a dog.' When Brand gave her a lopsided smile, she added with a shade of anxiety, 'You *are* my daddy, aren't you?'

Brand switched his gaze to Isabella, and his look told her he that wasn't asking a question but was *telling* her, with no ifs, ands or buts, that he was about to tell Connie the truth. And that if she had any

156

objections they would be summarily and promptly overruled.

Isabella shifted in her chair. It wasn't the way she had planned to tell her daughter. But there was a hardness about Brand these days, a ruthlessness that hadn't been there of old. It would do no good to oppose him. Nor was there any point in lying to her child.

She gave Brand a small, almost imperceptible nod.

'Yes,' he said, turning back to Connie. 'I am your daddy. And I feel proud and lucky to have you for my daughter.'

'Then why did you go away?' Connie's gaze was direct and accusing.

Brand glanced back at Isabella, and when she saw him take a breath and open his mouth to answer she said quickly, 'Connie, Brand – your daddy, I mean – couldn't help it. You see, something happened, and *I* was the one who went away . . .'

'I get it.' Connie nodded sagely. 'You mean you got mad at each other and got divorced. Like Jimmy Prentiss' mom and dad. And Louella Chomniak's, and Maggie and John's, and Annabelle Maki's – '

'No, not quite like that,' said Isabella, interrupting her daughter's phlegmatic recital of modern-day marital failures. 'Your father and I never got divorced.'

'Oh.' Connie thought about that for a moment and then gave each of them a bright and beatific beam.

'Good. Then you can be married again like a proper mommy and daddy. And I can have a dog.'

Brand growled something under his breath, and refused to look at Isabella. But when he caught sight of his daughter's anxious face he said hastily, 'It may not be quite that easy, sweetheart. We'll talk about it later. But I promise you I won't go away. Mommy won't either. OK?'

There was something about Brand's 'OK' that brooked no argument. From his daughter or from his wife. And when Isabella threw him a cautious glance she saw that the easy confidence she had long ago come to expect of him had been strengthened by an air of resolute authority. It would not be easy to escape from Brand again – if he wanted to hold her. Which, of course, he wouldn't. There wasn't much hope of Connie's dream coming true. She could tell from the way he rolled his eyes at the lampshade that the thought of the two of them becoming 'proper' parents didn't fill him with instant elation – any more than the thought of being a 'proper' husband had done in the old days.

She licked a smear of tomato sauce thoughtfully off her middle finger, by no means convinced that her own dreams of a happy and contented future included life with this hardheaded man. Not any more.

Two hours later, after they had returned to the apartment and Connie had retired reluctantly to bed,

158

Brand appropriated the armchair again and abruptly ordered Isabella to sit down.

She was long past the stage of refusing to do as he said for no other reason than to assert her independence, so she lowered herself on to the sofa and clutched a gold and brown tweed cushion to her chest. The feel of its rough bulk in her arms provided much needed support.

'Right,' said Brand, stretching his legs and resting his palms loosely on his thighs. 'You and I have a few matters to set straight. First, what's this nonsense about Connie having surgery on her ears?'

'It's not nonsense. The other children tease her. It's made her self-conscious.'

'She seems happy enough. The kids used to tease me too.'

'Mm-hm. And what did you do about it?'

Brand's twisted smile wasn't even sheepish. 'I'm afraid I used to see to it that *their* features became a little out of the ordinary as well. Temporarily.'

'And that's how you want Connie to handle it? By flattening some other little girl's nose?'

Brand's black eyes gleamed with sudden provocation. 'Why not? It worked for me.'

'I don't doubt it,' Isabella said. 'But I'm not raising Connie to be a prizefighter. Or a bully.'

Brand inclined his head. 'Thank you,' he said gravely.

Isabella eyed him sceptically. Was he deliberately

mistaking her meaning in order to get under her skin? If so, he was doing a fine job of it.

'Connie's heart is set on the operation,' she insisted.

'Is it?' Brand smiled blandly. 'All right. I'll agree to the surgery.'

Isabella repressed a sarcastic rejoinder. It wasn't up to Brand to agree to anything. And she had a feeling he'd never really intended to oppose Connie's operation. He was just flexing his parenting muscles.

This opinion was confirmed a moment later when Brand leaned forward and said peremptorily, 'Right. Second and most important point. Connie's my daughter. From now on I intend to be a part of her life.'

'Yes,' agreed Isabella, hearing the regret for lost years that simmered beneath the dictatorial words. She wasn't going to argue with him about that. Connie needed a father. Brand had that right. And Felix – Felix, as yet, had no rights.

'Yes,' said Brand. 'And that means I expect to pay for her education, her upkeep and any extras she may need. I do not expect to pay one damn penny for you.'

Isabella tried not to grind her teeth. 'I'm not for sale,' she said, pulling the cushion tightly against her chest.

Something that might have been surprise – or even amusement – flickered briefly across Brand's features, before being replaced by his more usual rock-jawed impassiveness. 'And if you were, I wouldn't be buying,' he assured her. 'As I said, I'll pay for all Connie's needs.' He glanced round the spartan apartment. 'This will do – with a bit more furniture, of course. It's a good neighbourhood. But I'll expect to see her on a regular basis. Have her at my house on weekends.' He paused long enough to give the room another critical once-over. 'What arrangements do you make for her when you're working?'

'Edwina looks after her. She's reliable, she's kind, she's devoted. And she's upstairs.' Isabella laid the cushion on her knees. 'Brand, Connie is *my* daughter first. I've brought her up so far. I'm not going to let you run her life, and I don't want or expect you to support her altogether.'

'May I reminded you that you've kept her from me for four years? Now that I know I have a child, I mean to play a part in her upbringing. A large part. Whether you like it or not.'

'You're not taking Connie away from me.' Isabella heard her voice come out high and hard, like a knife-blade scratched across glass. Had she made a terrible mistake? Should she have stayed safely in Edmonton, out of Brand's autocratic reach? Oh, but she had so needed to get away, had needed to be sure before she made a commitment to Felix. Needed, once and for all, to settle the matter of her marriage.

161

And now she was more unsure than ever.

'No. I'm not taking Connie away,' Brand agreed. 'For her sake. She . . .' He hesitated, then went on in a battened-down voice, 'She obviously loves you. One day I hope she'll love me as well. But in the meantime I've no wish to hurt her.'

'You won't get the chance, Brand.' Isabella spoke with a brittle composure.

'That remains to be seen.' He stood up suddenly, and she was at once conscious of his height and of the way he seemed to dominate the room. Nothing had changed there.

'I guess that's it, then,' he said. 'For the moment. We can iron out the details later – once I've had a chance to think things through.' His mouth curved cynically. 'Paternity takes a bit of getting used to. Tell Connie I'll see her tomorrow.'

Isabella, still clasping the cushion, stood up and took a quick step towards him.

'What's the matter?' he gibed. 'Want me to stay? We've already been there, Isabella. It wasn't a success.'

But it *had* been a success, if only for a few fleeting moments of passion. And Brand knew it, remembered as well as she did. He would never admit it, though. Not now that he knew about Connie.

She turned away from the mockery in his eyes. 'No, I don't want you to stay,' she said, staring at a fly on the window.

162

She didn't either. Not when his lips were flattened into an unyielding line and his body was rigid with rejection.

His body . . . Why did it have to be as hypnotically seductive as ever? And did those full lips *have* to hold the irresistible invitation they always had? Oh, if only things could have been different . . .

She pulled herself together abruptly. Things weren't different. They never would be. And the sooner she accepted that the better.

Isabella lifted her chin and was already on her way back to the sofa when she felt Brand's hand touch her shoulder.

'Connie,' he said, in a voice that held no warmth but was no longer deliberately cutting. 'You called our daughter Connie. What sort of a name is that? Is it short for Constance?'

'No, for Constanza. After my mother. Her full name is Constanza Mairead Ryder.'

'Mairead? You called her Mairead?' He spun her around so that she was facing him again, and his touch was like a flame through her sweater. '*My* mother's name?'

'Yes. She was kind to me.'

'Unlike her son,' Brand said drily.

She made an effort to smile. 'You tried,' she told him. 'At the beginning I think perhaps you tried too hard – trying not to let me see how much you were grieving for Mary, being nice when I made such a terrible mess of the cooking and – oh, everything. But later you were so busy, and I was – difficult.'

'That's one way of putting it,' he agreed.

Isabella ignored the interruption. 'And your mother, she said I was very young, but that in a few years I'd probably make you a good wife. She told me I had to be patient.'

Brand let out a crack of disbelieving laughter. 'That's what she said to me too. But in those days I had no time for patience. Not that it was ever one of my more notable virtues.'

'No,' said Isabella. 'I remember.'

She did. Vividly. His determination to turn Ryder Airlines into a paying proposition, the long hours, the indifference to his own needs or the needs of anyone around him . . .

Yet his dedication and vision had worked. His charter service was one of the most successful in the business, or so she had been told by some of her customers who knew about such things.

'It's not surprising you had no time or patience for a wife,' she murmured, not really realizing she was speaking out loud. 'Especially for a wife who wasn't Perfect Mary.'

For a few seconds the silence was black and absolute. Then, as she heard Brand draw a harsh, inward breath, it dawned on her exactly what she'd said.

He broke the silence coldly. 'I had no time for a

164

wife who demanded more attention than I could give her, who pouted when she didn't get it and who went around wriggling her delectable bottom at susceptible neighbours. And as you say, I had no patience for a wife who wasn't Mary.'

Isabella gazed up at him, stunned, stricken and momentarily bereft of words.

Brand pivoted on his heel and made swiftly for the door.

She stared after him, her initial contrition for taunting him with Mary lost in a white-hot haze of resentment. Every word he had uttered might be true, but that didn't give him the right to speak to her as if she were still the thoughtless, troublesome teenager he had married in haste and obviously repented of at leisure.

She was a woman now, and the mother of his child. Just as he was a man. A hard, uncompromising man, whose superior backside she would at this moment very much like to kick.

She contented herself with running after him and grabbing him by the arm.

Brand whirled round, his face as dark and enigmatic as she had ever seen it. 'What is it, Isabella?' he demanded. 'Waiting for me to kiss you goodnight?'

She gasped, frozen into unbelieving silence. No, she wasn't waiting for that. In another time, another place, she had waited night after night for a kiss that had only occasionally been bestowed. And then it had been no more than a hurried peck on the cheek before Brand had dismissed her to her solitary bed and returned to his computer and his maps and his books.

But then, in retrospect, and considering the way they had married, why had she expected anything else?

Her anger drained away and she shook her head. 'No. I'm not waiting. I'm not as desperate as I used to be, Brand.'

'I see.' His eyes narrowed. 'No, I suppose you wouldn't be. No doubt you're now able to pick and choose. Who is it, Isabella? Some rich client looking for a bit of action on the side – ?'

'*No!* Brand, I don't have to put up with your – your inexcusable innuendoes. Yes, there *is* a man I've been seeing. He wants to marry me. But our friendship has always been just that. Friendship.'

A shadow, so fleeting she wasn't even sure she had seen it, passed over Brand's face and was gone. As Isabella stared up at him, angry and resentful, suddenly he caught her face between his hands and tilted it upwards. His lips parted in a parody of a smile, and he seemed to be studying each feature as if he wanted to imprint it on his brain.

At least he'll have no trouble identifying the remains, she thought wildly, forcing herself to stifle a near-hysterical giggle.

She ran the tip of her tongue along her upper lip – not to entice, but because her mouth had gone dry.

Watching her, Brand swore softly. 'What the hell?' he said. 'Why not? If it's *friendship* you want, I'm just the man to oblige.'

She had no time to grasp his meaning before he had dragged the protective cushion from her arms and tossed it over his shoulder. Then his mouth was on hers – and the dream that had haunted her nights for five years was, incredibly, starting to come true.

But not in the way she had dreamed it.

Brand had kissed her before – twice with passion, more often in dutiful abstraction. But he wasn't abstracted now. He was kissing her as though he had a job to do, one which he meant to carry out with bloodless efficiency, conscientiously, and with meticulous attention to detail.

Knowing his heart wasn't involved, Isabella refused to let herself raise her arms to him when she felt his tongue part her lips with expert insistence.

After a while, when she didn't respond, he moved his hands from her face and slid them in slow motion down her sides.

Isabella felt the old, familiar heat stirring and liquefying her loins. In that moment her longing for him was so great that, if her mouth hadn't been inescapably trapped, she might have cried out to him to take her, right here on the dun-coloured carpet. Instead, she stood stiff as a soldier being inspected by his general, and forced herself to hide her needs from this man she had come back to for her daughter's sake – and in the hope and expectation that she would find her passion for him had long since run its course.

Only it hadn't. And when, suddenly, he wrapped an arm around her waist and hauled her against the length of his body, she gave no resistance. Nor did she resist when he moved his left hand erotically over her rear, arousing and inflaming unbearably, until he caught her below the hips and lifted her feet off the floor.

That was when she finally gave in, with a moan of surrender, and wound her arms tightly around his neck. And that was when the nature of Brand's embrace changed subtly – when, just for an instant, she felt him respond to her, not as an obliging machine, but tenderly and with passion, as a man might respond to his woman.

But almost at once he let her go, and she wondered if she had only dreamed the passion.

As she staggered backwards, dizzy and off balance, she saw Brand's brooding dark eyes fixed on her with a kind of angry incredulity, as if he couldn't quite believe he had touched her.

'Don't worry, Brand,' she said, once she had regained her ability to breathe. 'I haven't cast a spell on you. And now that you've dealt with that bit of business, don't you think you ought to go home?'

Brand wiped the back of his arm across his forehead. It was beaded with sweat. 'Yes,' he agreed. 'That's what I plan to do. Goodnight, Isabella.'

He reached behind him, pulled open the door and then turned his back, pausing for less than a second to slam it closed. His footsteps rang out sharp and stacatto on the steps before they faded into the stillness of the night.

This time Isabella didn't follow. Instead she drifted in a daze into the kitchen and pulled a coffee mug out of the cupboard. When she discovered it contained the mouldering remains of last week's home-made pea soup, she knew that the damage wrought by Brand on her peace of mind was deeper and far more dangerous than she had thought.

She bent over the sink and watched the green sludge trickle down the drain – and all the while she kept thinking of the look of stunned scepticism on Brand's face when he'd finished kissing her.

That settled it, surely. Brand might be Connie's father, but it was obvious he would never again accept her, Isabella, as his wife. Six years ago she had coaxed him into a marriage he didn't want and had never really accepted. Later, she had flirted with another man until he had kissed her. And finally – in Brand's eyes the most unforgivable of all – she had neglected to tell him he had a daughter. It was hardly surprising he didn't trust her.

Isabella thumped herself down on a hard kitchen

chair and fixed her gaze on the moonlight glinting through a gap in the curtains.

Oh, yes, that kiss settled it. She had come back to Vancouver for three reasons that were inextricably linked in her mind. One was the need to put time and distance between herself and Felix in order to come to a decision. Another was to give Connie the chance to know her father. And the third, but not the least important, was to find out if her girlish passion for Brand had ever been more than a starry-eyed adolescent infatuation.

She had always known she would come back, and Felix, bless him, had said he understood. So why did she still have doubts about him? He was a good man, he was fond of Connie, and he seemed to accept that if Isabella was ever to give herself to him with a whole heart she would first have to exorcise the ghosts of her past.

Brand had certainly done that for her tonight. With a vengeance, and without compunction, he had shattered any illusions that remained.

She watched the lights of a car passing in the street and shivered suddenly, although there was nothing wrong with the heating in the room. Then, briefly, she was a young girl again, running from José, and Brandon Ryder was again the young man with the haunted eyes and hollow, grief-stricken features whom she had seen walking down a street in the capital city of the country that was no longer her home.

So long ago . . . Or so it seemed. She was a woman now – a woman who would never again hold that wild-eyed young man in her arms. Isabella reached for a cup of coffee she hadn't made, then put her elbows on the table and propped her chin in her hands.

'It serves you right, Isabella,' she said out loud. 'How else could you expect him to take the news he has a four-year-old child he's never met? Did you really expect him to thank you for keeping her a secret?'

The sound of her own voice made her start and, half laughing at herself, she stood up and marched into the kitchen to start the coffee.

The past was done with. Tonight had been a fiasco. And in a couple of weeks, when Connie was over her operation, she would call Felix.

When a hard little lump began to form in her chest she doused it with scalding hot coffee. Except that it turned out to be scalding hot water, because she'd forgotten to put the coffee-grounds in the pot.

Brand stood in the doorway of the private hospital room he had insisted on arranging for Connie, and watched Isabella bend over his daughter's bed.

By rights, Connie should have been out of hospital the same day she went in, but there had been some problem with the anaesthetic and they were keeping her in for observation.

He felt something lodge in his throat as, unnoticed by the other occupants of the room, he gazed at the slender figure of the mother of his child. She looked so young, so vulnerable as she smiled tenderly down at her daughter, her soft eyes wide and concerned. It was hard to remember that she was a deceitful little witch when she had the appearance of a ministering angel. At this moment she even reminded him of Mary.

Mary had always been gentle with children.

He watched, stone-faced, as Isabella smoothed the hair from Connie's forehead and whispered, 'It's all right, darling. Don't be frightened. Everything's fine – and you have the world's prettiest ears.'

Connie smiled sleepily, and Brand saw Isabella's shoulders sag with relief. He realized then how tired she was, and knew that she had been waiting anxiously at the hospital all day. But instead of feeling sympathy he felt irritation. Damn it, *he* should have been here to share the waiting – just as he should have been beside her the day Connie was born. She had denied him that privilege. Now, all these years later, it seemed as if nothing had changed. She hadn't even troubled to let him know that a cancellation had caused the operation to be rescheduled. He had only found out when he'd called at the apartment to see Connie and been met by an agitated Edwina.

Brand scowled at the top of Isabella's head. She had shut him out again, just as she had shut him out before. Damn her anyway. Involuntarily, his hands curled into fists.

What in hell had possessed him a week ago? It had been an act of insanity to kiss her. He had known that even as he'd tasted the remembered sweetness of her lips and allowed his fingers to tantalize the ripe body that had always held the power to drive him mad – even when he hadn't known what he was doing.

He should never have touched her. Because now that he had it would be next to impossible to keep from doing it again. But he must. What was it she had said? Something about casting a spell? But Isabella was more than just than a spellbinder. She was an aphrodisiac dipped in black magic. And if he swallowed that magic potion he would be lost.

A bell sounded somewhere down the hall, and Brand forced his clenched fingers to relax.

Something, some added electricity in the air, must have touched her then, because she lifted her head and raised smudged dark eyes to his.

God, she was beautiful. Brand's jaw tightened as he remembered how she had felt in his arms, how she had responded to him with reluctant abandon. But of course she had always responded. Probably not only to him. He remembered she had mentioned a 'friend'. A 'friend' who wanted to marry her. His lip curved down in a sneer, and, seeing it, she lowered her eyes.

'How is she?' he asked abruptly, gesturing at the drowsy little girl.

'She's fine.' Isabella looked up at him and smiled coolly, and he felt a renewed stab of resentment that she hadn't taken the trouble to let him know Connie was in hospital.

'Good,' he replied, vowing that he would find a way to shake that maddening composure of hers before this evening was over. In truth, he had a notion he'd been shaking it all week, every time he had shown up at the apartment to visit Connie. But Isabella had become adept at concealing her feelings – when she wanted to conceal them.

He smiled back at her with a coolness that equalled hers, and thought how much he was going to enjoy making her squirm.

Ignoring her now, he walked over to the bed. Connie held out her hand. He took it and said softly, 'Your mother's right. Your ears are much prettier than mine.'

Connie giggled. 'You're funny,' she said. And then, as her eyes began to droop closed, 'Are you going to take Mommy home now? I think you'd better, 'cos she's awful tired. But you can come back and fetch me in the morning.'

'Thank you. I will.' Brand swallowed an unlikely urge to laugh. His daughter was as much of an autocrat as he was.

'And will you look after Mommy?'

Little schemer. In her childish, unsubtle way Connie was trying to play matchmaker to her parents. And who could blame her?

'All right.' He smiled and tried to sound neutral. He must have succeeded, because Connie nodded contentedly, and in only a few seconds she was sound asleep.

Brand picked up Isabella's black coat, which was lying across a chair, and held it out to her. 'Unlike you, I keep my promises,' he said. 'Let's get going.'

'Thank you, but I don't need looking after. I can take a taxi.'

Her voice and her eyes were weary, but he could see that she didn't mean to give an inch. Lord, couldn't she just, for once, make things easy for him? 'Maybe you don't,' he snapped. 'But I have one or two things I want to say to you, so a taxi's out. Have you eaten?'

'No, but – '

'Good. Neither have I. Put your coat on.' When she didn't move, he draped the coat over her shoulders and turned her in the direction of the door.

'Brand, I'm not leaving. Connie – '

'Connie is asleep. And she asked me to take you home. Which I will do, but not until you've put some food inside you. You look like the ghost of last week's washing, and it doesn't suit you.'

In fact, he thought that pale, translucent look suited Isabella very well. It made her look ethereal

175

and lovelier than ever. But she had apparently forgotten to eat, and he felt the stirrings of an old obligation to take care of her. It had been simpler in the old days, though, when she had been his youthful dependant. Now she was a self-possessed and impossibly obstinate woman – who was going to eat a full meal whether she liked it or not.

'Let's get going,' he said again, ignoring her murmurs of protest. 'My car is just round the corner.'

To his surprise, and exasperated relief, Isabella made no further objections and allowed him to steer her into the corridor.

Brand drove his car – a sleek blue Jaguar – rather too fast out of town. Isabella sat on the seat beside him and remembered with a kind of nostalgia that he had always driven as if he were behind the controls of a plane. She leaned her head back, and almost at once the bright glow of passing streetlights became a single blurred yellow line seen from under half-closed eyelids. Then everything turned dark, and the next thing she knew Brand was pulling the car up outside a small restaurant with a heavy oak door.

'Where are we?' she asked, struggling to stay awake. 'I'm not dressed properly – '

'You look very beguiling in those black trousers. And the red blouse sets off your eyes.' Brand's voice was without expression, but when she glanced up at him, startled, a spark of something white-hot passed between them, and before he turned away she saw the sudden dilation of his pupils, and knew that her presence was affecting him more than he wanted her to know.

She felt a quick surge of triumph, and suddenly she wasn't sleepy any more.

'Where are we?' she asked again as Brand helped her out of the Jag. 'I don't recognize – '

'I'd be surprised if you did. The Warren is for members only. It has the advantage of being quiet, private and discreet.'

'A good place to bring wives you don't want the rest of the world to see,' said Isabella, not bothering to pretend she wasn't hurt.

'Or mistresses,' he said, patting her on the rear in what she was sure was a deliberate attempt to annoy her. 'But in fact I thought you'd prefer to eat somewhere quiet. You've had a rough day. Once I've said what I have to say to you I've no particular wish to make it rougher.'

'Thank you,' said Isabella, not sure how to take this casually possessive yet passionless Brand. She had expected him to be angry that he hadn't been notified in time about Connie's surgery. But he seemed not to care.

In that, she soon realized, she was wrong.

Brand steered her down a few steps into a dimly lit room with a highly polished wooden floor and only a few judiciously placed tables. Conversations in this establishment would indeed be private. A bright fire was burning in an enormous stone fireplace, and some good brasses hung on the panelled walls along with a selection of Victorian art.

The maitre d' led them at once to a table by the fire, and as Isabella sat down all of a sudden she felt warm, cosseted and unexpectedly content – which was odd, because contentment was the last thing she had felt all week.

Brand had taken his new responsibilities as a father to heart, and even though she had tried to persuade him to make his visits coincide with the evenings when she was working, he had sabotaged her efforts at every turn, showing up whenever and wherever it happened to suit him.

She had found his presence disturbing, unsettling and embarrassingly electric, charged as it was with the memory of his kiss.

Now, though, in this warm and firelit room, she felt almost happy. And why not? She was about to spend an intimate evening with her husband, as she had once or twice done in the past, when Brand had taken extra trouble to be nice to her. On those occasions, though, their meal had invariably featured pizza.

Isabella smiled and began to relax.

Not for long. Only minutes later she was jolted out of her euphoria.

'Why didn't you call me about Connie's operation?' Brand demanded brusquely, the instant the waiter had departed with their orders.

Isabella twisted her fingers in her lap. Brand was becoming altogether too bossy. He was Connie's father, of course, but he would do well to remember that *she* was Connie's mother – the one who had the final say in all matters pertaining to her daughter.

'I did call you,' she said finally. 'Veronica said you were at work.'

'I see. And is there some reason you didn't contact me at my office?'

Isabella wasn't deceived by the mildness of the enquiry. 'Yes, as a matter of fact there is. Ms Dubois also told me you had left orders you were not to be disturbed.'

'I had. And I suppose it didn't occur to you that I might make an exception in the matter of my daughter's welfare?' His voice grated unpleasantly, and the firelight flickering over his face and severely cut suit made him look like some dark and sexy devil. Isabella felt a quick twinge of alarm that she recognized was part sheer physical excitement. Oh, Lord. The last thing she needed now was a renewal of that old and unproductive hunger.

'Of course it occurred to me,' she said. 'But there was nothing you could do. I knew I wouldn't get through to you right away, and I hadn't a lot of time before we had to leave for the hospital. So I decided

I'd phone you tonight.' She spoke hurriedly, conscious of a rising tension in the atmosphere between them.

'Did you?' He reached across the table and took her wrist. 'Isabella, I want to make something crystal-clear to you. From now on, when anything as major as an operation happens in Connie's life, I expect you to make sure I'm informed of it. At once.'

'And if I don't?' she asked defiantly, sympathizing, in a way, with his request that was in reality an order, but incensed that he assumed he had a right to give it.

'If you don't, I promise you I can make life unpleasant for you. Or have you forgotten?'

No, she hadn't forgotten. How could she? Brand had no patience with defiance for the sake of defiance. He had always seen childish behaviour as exactly what it was, and treated it accordingly. Never with violence, but with a kind of cutting detachment that hurt more.

'I doubt if there's much you can do to make my life any more difficult than it is,' she said quietly. 'Except, I suppose, start a campaign to undermine my business. And you wouldn't do that.'

'Wouldn't I? What makes you so sure?'

He was still holding her wrist, and she felt heat spiral up her arm and settle in a fiery coil in her stomach. She swallowed. 'You – you're not like that. You've never been vindictive.'

'You have no idea what I'm like, Isabella. You never had.'

'Yes, I did. I always knew you were kind, and honourable enough to take responsibility for your actions. If you hadn't been, you wouldn't have married me.'

Brand's mouth twisted, but his grip on her wrist loosened a fraction. 'Is that so? You amaze me, Mrs Sanchez.'

'I don't see why.'

'Kind? Honourable? Responsible? How could you bear to part with such a paragon?' Still holding her wrist, he turned over her hand and began to rub his thumb across her palm.

Isabella tried to pull away as the heat sizzling up her arm lit a small, curling flame deep in her belly. Did he have any idea what he was doing to her? She looked into his eyes, saw their sudden glitter, and knew that he knew exactly what he was doing. Tormenting her, and enjoying every second of it.

Resentment struggled with desire and threatened to choke her. 'You – you . . .' she began, searching for a way to express her feelings.

'Bastard? Jerk? Pig?' he suggested. 'Changed your mind about me, have you, Mrs Sanchez?'

Oh, God. She should never have come back to Vancouver. No, she hadn't changed her mind about him. She wanted him as much as she always had. And at this moment she also wanted to throw half a dozen of the delicate blue plates at his head.

Instead, incredibly, she heard herself saying, 'My name isn't Mrs Sanchez, Brand. It's Mrs Ryder.

The glitter in his eyes became brighter, more disturbing. 'Then why don't you use it, Mrs *Ryder*?'

'I . . .' She hesitated, hating him, as she had in the past, for the power he still had to hurt her, to make her *feel*. But that was no reason not to tell him the truth. 'Because I'm not sure I have that right any more. It's Connie's name, but I stopped using it after I left you because . . . I used to think that if ever you tried to find me, you would search for me as the Isabella Ryder who was – no, not was – *is* your wife. And I didn't want to be found.'

Brand ground out a word she had never heard him use before and hoped she wouldn't hear again. He dropped her wrist so abruptly that her forearm landed on the table with a crash, shaking glasses and rattling the knives and forks. Disapproving heads swivelled in their direction. Plucked eyebrows rose in civilized censure.

Isabella turned away to stare into the bright flames leaping in the fireplace. After a while, when she realized Brand wasn't speaking, she forced herself to look up. He was staring at her as if she had just announced that she was Dracula's mistress come for her nightly snack.

'What's the matter?' she demanded. 'I haven't said

anything you didn't know already. And please, stop looking at me as if you expect me to sink my fangs into your neck.'

Brand lifted his wine glass and leaned slowly back in his chair. 'You did that long ago,' he murmured, with just the barest flicker of a smile. 'And very pretty little fangs they were too. Efficient as well. You drew blood.'

Isabella frowned. He did look almost edible, lounging there in his dark suit, and with his dark eyes sending a message she was almost afraid to interpret. 'What do you mean?' she demanded.

'That I did search for you.' He straightened, all clipped and businesslike again. 'But not necessarily because you were my wife.'

Something in the way he spoke convinced her that she ought to get up and leave – now, before he drew his own draught of blood.

But she didn't leave.

Instead she sat very still, and asked in a voice that sounded as though it had been strained through a colander, 'Why, then? Why did you search for me, Brand?'

A waiter came to light a candle in a glass bowl in the centre of the table, and the shadows on Brand's face shifted and seemed to deepen. 'Because,' he replied, 'you were an aggravating, exasperating, bothersome and impossibly charming little fiend, for whom, in a moment of madness, I happened to have made myself responsible. So I hired a detective.'

'You – you did? He didn't find me.'

'Oh, yes – *she* did. Your trail wasn't at all hard to follow.'

'But – you didn't come.'

'No. Did you expect me to?' He turned sideways, apparently smitten by a sudden fascination with a still-life of armour and crossed swords.

'Expect? No. But I think, in my weaker moments . . . I hoped.'

'Weaker moments? You?'

'Oh, Brand.' If only he would look at her, give her some indication that he had feelings under that rock-like exterior. 'Yes. Me. I missed you.'

'Did you? I'd never have guessed it from your letter. It arrived just as I was about to make the trip to Edmonton to collect you.'

'Oh. And it changed your mind?'

'Not at first. I still felt responsible. But it did convince me to get my detective to dig a bit deeper. She was very efficient.'

'I see. And after that you decided not to come?' She wasn't sure why it mattered. Yet somehow it did.

Brand shrugged, and Isabella followed the fluid movement of muscles across his chest. 'I'm no masochist, my dear. You had made it abundantly clear that you were doing very nicely without me. According to my source, your address was that of a

184

provincial cabinet minister. So, as she assured me you looked healthy and contented, and I'd never caught you in an outright lie before, I assumed you'd found some other dupe to support you.'

CHAPTER 8

Isabella drew back as if he'd struck her. She tried to smile, to match the cutting lightness of his words with equal lightness. But the smile wouldn't stay on her face when she remembered that Brand had always spoken in that clipped, dispassionate way when he was hurting and felt the need to hurt back. Which meant he hadn't forgiven her for anything. Perhaps she shouldn't have reminded him that she was still his wife. Not that she was asking any favours on that score . . .

'You were never a dupe,' she said finally, refusing to respond to his gibe and giving up all attempts to solve the enigma that was Brand. 'Only a man of principle with a strongly developed sense of right and wrong. And no, I found no one else. Somewhere between leaving you and giving birth to Connie I learned to stand on my own two feet. In my country girls often grow up fast. It just took me a little longer than most.'

'Hmm.' Brand switched his gaze from the picture to the fire, but still she couldn't see his eyes. 'I see. So

I was a man of principle.' For several endless seconds he was silent, watching the flames dance across the logs. When he looked up, the expression on his face had changed, become softer, less cynical. 'You're right. I must have been. Because I frequently wanted to do things to you that civilized men are not supposed to do with teenage girls. I was also, at times, tempted to put you on a plane and ship you back to your long-suffering parents – especially when you began to work your wiles on Gary. But I never did any of those things. Did I?'

Isabella gaped at him, not sure whether she wanted to laugh, kick him, or ask him what civilized men didn't do with teenage girls. In the end she only said mildly, 'You did offer to ship me home once. I didn't realize I was meant to accept.'

He shrugged. 'I'm not sure you were.'

Now, what did he mean by that? Isabella was about to tell him that in any case it was a good thing he hadn't tried to ship her anywhere, because she wouldn't have gone, when he spoke again.

'Well, Isabella, it seems we've come full circle. And, since you have apparently decided I've been deprived of my family long enough, what, exactly, do you have in mind? Because if you expect me to go on as I've been doing this past week – visiting my daughter at your convenience – '

'You haven't so far,' said Isabella. 'You've been visiting her at *your* convenience.'

He shifted his gaze from the fire and met her eyes, the corner of his mouth tipping up briefly in acknowledgement. 'So I have. But, I repeat, what, exactly, do you have in mind?'

Isabella looked down at the snowy white cloth covering the table. She didn't know what she had in mind. She had come back to Vancouver undecided, but suspecting that her marriage to Brand would turn out to be irrevocably over. If that had been so, it would have been a relatively simple matter to arrange for him to have generous access to Connie even if she lived in Edmonton with Felix. But nothing had been simple since that moment two months ago when she had answered the phone and heard her husband's well-remembered voice shouting at Veronica Dubois.

So what *did* she have in mind? Brand's eyes, the tension in his jaw, even the way his hand lay curled on the table, all demanded an answer to that question.

As the waiter placed a salad plate in front of her Isabella tried to decide if this was the right time to tell him the truth – or the truth as she saw it now. He certainly wasn't in an accommodating mood, and he was angry that she hadn't got in touch with him about Connie's surgery. He also seemed to think he had a right to take control . . .

'What I was thinking,' she said slowly, picking up a fork and stabbing it at a mushroom, 'was that you should get to know Connie better – '

'Fine. And in order for that to happen she'll need to spend time with me at Marshlands.'

'Oh.' Isabella saw that his jaw now looked ready to take on an army, instead of one small and slender woman. Yet she had no desire to fight him. 'Yes. All right,' she agreed. 'For a few days.' She took a deep breath. 'But where Connie goes, I go too.'

'There's no need. Veronica will look after her.'

'No,' said Isabella, her voice sounding overloud in the small room. 'Veronica will not.'

Brand picked up his wine glass and twirled the stem between his fingers. 'Why not? What do you have against Veronica?'

'Nothing.' She forced herself to stay calm. 'Is she your mistress?'

'What a delightfully old-fashioned term. No, my dear, she is not. It may have escaped your notice, but I'm married.'

'That never stopped anyone before. Especially a man as handsome and – and virile as you.'

His eyes gleamed at her in the firelight with sudden and unmistakable meaning. 'Thank you. Or a woman as beautiful and provocative as you. None the less, Veronica is not my *mistress*.'

'And I haven't provoked anyone since you.' Isabella crushed her napkin between her fingers, still reeling from the impact of that look.

'Haven't you? That's hard to believe. Your friend

in Edmonton must have mineral water in his veins instead of blood.'

She smiled, determined not to let him see he'd rattled her. 'I could take that as a compliment, I suppose. But considering the source – '

'Considering the source, it's unlikely,' Brand agreed.

'And Felix is a gentleman,' Isabella finished loftily.

'Felix? Ah. Your latest conquest. He sounds a very dull fellow. Having a dreary time of it, were you?' Thought you'd liven things up by stirring up old husbands?'

Isabella had an impression that Brand's barbs were not remotely directed at Felix. But if they weren't that would mean he actually *cared* that she had a friendship with another man. And of course that was nonsense. If he cared at all, it was only for his right of possession.

'No,' she said acidly. 'I was having a very agreeable, peaceful time with Felix. I felt loved, Brand. It made a nice change.'

Brand's eyes darkened to smoke, and he let out a harsh bark of laughter. It played havoc with her nerve-ends and she had to force herself to steady her voice and say neutrally, 'But I believe we were discussing Connie's visit to Marshlands. Not my private life.'

'So we were.' Brand's response was also neutral. He waited for Isabella to go on.

She took a deep breath. 'I won't send Connie to

stay with you on her own. She's too young. And she's used to having me with her.

'I see.' Brand laid down his knife. 'In other words, you're part of the package.'

'If you want to put it like that.'

'I don't. But it seems I haven't much choice. This time. Very well, then, I'll pick the two of you up from the hospital tomorrow.' He speared a tomato and a piece of lettuce and went on eating his salad.

'Tomorrow? But I thought – '

'Don't. Just be ready.'

'Brand, I refuse to be bullied.' Isabella clanged her fork against her plate, causing a bespectacled gentleman in the far corner of the room to clear his throat and glare at her over the top of his glasses.

'I'm not bullying. I'm just telling you.' She was still gaping at him when, suddenly and surprisingly, he grinned. 'Besides, my mother is coming down from Kelowna on the weekend. To meet her only granddaughter. And if you think *I'm* bullying, just wait till you see Mother on the warpath.'

Isabella made a face, and felt an unexpected lifting of her heart. 'I *have* seen your mother on the warpath. Remember? And I know what you mean.' To her confusion, she found herself grinning back. 'I love your mother, Brand, but she always had a mind of her own.'

'She did. And she hasn't changed any.' Brand's tone was dry. 'I assume that settles it, then?'

Isabella nodded reluctantly. Mairead wasn't the only Ryder who had a mind of her own. But she couldn't keep her mother-in-law from her only grandchild purely to get the better of Brand. Besides, it was unlikely Mairead would let her. That redoubtable lady had a way of organizing the world to suit herself. Her son had come by his take-over personality quite naturally.

'Good. And now you and I have some catching up to do.' Brand leaned back in his chair. He looked deceptively relaxed.

'Catching up?' Isabella eyed him doubtfully.

'Mmm. You told me your life hasn't been easy, and I think I'm beginning to believe you. So how have you managed to look after yourself and my daughter since the night you stormed out of my house?' His voice sounded even enough, but Isabella detected a note of reserve. Or was it mistrust?

Perhaps Brand didn't like the idea that Connie might once have been in need.

'I didn't storm,' she reminded him. 'I walked out the door while you were talking in your sleep. You were muttering about a place called Bella Bella. You used to fly up there, didn't you?'

Brand smiled, the kind of sexy smile that made her go hot and cold all over. 'I did. But more likely I was talking about *Isabella*,' he said softly. 'You had a talent for disturbing my dreams.'

'You didn't let it show. Sometimes when I looked

192

at you in the morning you used to turn your back on me and stare at your chest of drawers – as if you found it a lot more fascinating than your wife.'

'Did I? Probably in an attempt to save my sanity.' He looked at her without expression. 'Go on. Tell me how you've managed to survive.'

He was determined to have an answer. With a rush of indignation, Isabella realized he still half thought she had found some man to support her. Or a series of men, perhaps. Well, all right, then. He wanted to know. There was no reason not to tell him.

'You always made sure I had money for small expenses,' she reminded him, in a voice that was as flat and unrevealing as she could make it. 'It was enough to get me to Edmonton on the bus.'

'Why Edmonton?'

'It's the capital of Alberta. As I speak Spanish I had an idea there might be a consulate there that I could work for. And it was far enough, but not too far, from Vancouver.'

Brand swept a hand through his hair. It fell across his forehead, making him look rakish and unbearably appealing. 'I suppose that makes a crazy kind of sense.'

'I thought so. But there wasn't any work at the consulates. I spent the first few days in a hostel for homeless teens.'

'Appropriate,' Brand muttered, refilling his wine

glass but not even glancing at hers. 'Just the place for the wife of an up and coming airline executive.'

She had hit a nerve. Unintentionally this time. 'I didn't stay there long,' she hastened to assure him. 'The woman who ran the hostel had friends in high places, and I was taken on by Mr Brownson-Wing and his wife.'

'As a translator?'

'No. As a nanny to their two little boys.'

Brand put his wine glass down with a thump. 'A nanny? Good grief. What did you do with them? You couldn't change a diaper in those days, for heaven's sake.'

'They weren't babies. I didn't have to change diapers. We got along very well.'

'Well I'm damned.' Brand shook his head. 'And did you teach them Spanish?'

Isabella smiled ruefully. 'No. Their father spoke French, English and Cantonese. He seemed to think that was enough.'

'I see. And when it became obvious that you were pregnant? What happened then?'

She crumbled a piece of flax bread and kept her eyes on her plate. 'The Brownson-Wings were very kind. They let me stay on, and when I had Connie they stood by me. I went on looking after the boys, and later they encouraged me to take courses – in business management and gourmet cooking, mostly. I was already a good cook, thanks to Judy. And then, once I was ready to start my own business, they helped by recommending me to their friends.'

'Did you never think of getting in touch with your parents?' Brand sounded as if he didn't at all approve of what he was hearing – because of Connie, of course.

'Yes. Yes, I did. Not because I wanted their help, but because I missed them.' She reduced the remainder of the flax bread to a pile of crumbs, remembering how difficult it had been to summon up the courage and the forgiveness to write. 'They came at once to take me home. And Connie too, of course. I should have expected that, but I didn't. And of course I wouldn't go. So my father shouted a lot, and my mother cried. But in the end they went home again without me.'

'I don't blame them,' muttered Brand. '*I* should have had as much sense.'

Isabella glared. 'They didn't *want* to leave me.'

'No?' Brand raised his eyebrows and grinned annoyingly.

'No.' She tossed her head, making her long hair fly around her face. 'Besides, it was all right in the end. My mother stopped crying, and when my father saw I meant it he stopped shouting. I think he was proud of me in a way. Now we keep in touch regularly by mail and phone, and next year there's going to be a big family reunion. All my sisters and their families will be there, and a lot of long-lost cousins and people

I haven't seen for years. And Juanita, who used to be my maid.' Isabella smiled. 'She's married now. I was able to help them buy a small house. That's partly why it's taken me so long to build up a bank account.'

Brand frowned. 'That's all very well. But what about before that? When you were in no position to help anyone? Surely before that your parents did something for you financially?'

'No. I wouldn't let them. I wanted to succeed on my own.'

'Hmm.' He shook his head. 'And it seems you did. Without much assistance from the rest of us.' His voice was abstracted, as if he wasn't sure whether he regretted that she had been without support or admired her for her independence. 'Are you telling me you were never in need?'

She shrugged. 'I didn't have a lot of money. But I managed. Why? Did you want me to be starving in an attic or something?'

'Don't be ridiculous. Naturally I'm concerned for Connie.'

Naturally. Isabella stifled a sigh, and smiled winningly at the waiter as he placed their main course in front of them. Brand fixed her with a stern eye which she ignored. 'Connie was always fed and clothed,' she went on with outward serenity. 'And we had a solid roof over our heads. I rented a small apartment as soon as I started up my business.'

'By which time I owned a rather large apartment,' Brand said tersely.

'Did you? Yes, you were starting to do well even before I left.'

'But not well enough for Ms Isabella Sanchez, the rich landowner's spoiled youngest daughter.' He drew his knife through the swordfish on his plate as if he were dealing with her neck.

Isabella thought about how it would feel to curl her fingers around *his* neck, and came up with an unexpectedly physical reaction. Brand had a nice neck – strong – and his hair stroked it in just the right way. He had nice hair too . . .

Stop it, Isabella. She made herself think about what he'd said, and sat up ramrod-straight.

'Brand, that's not fair. That wasn't why I left you, and you know it. Of course I was shocked when you brought me back to a dark basement suite with cracked walls, no servants and plumbing that only worked sometimes. I know I cried – '

'For two days.'

'No, just one.' She smiled wryly. 'And that was sheer temper because you wouldn't apologize and pamper me and shower me with sympathy and attention.'

'Very remiss of me,' he said drily. 'Unfortunately there were other, more pressing matters on my mind.'

'I know. Mary. And the problem with your ears.

197

And after that Ryder Airlines. I understood all that in a way, you know. So I stopped crying and tried to make the best of it.'

Brand's lips quirked, and if she hadn't known better she would have sworn she heard laughter in his voice. 'Yes. You did. You went through that cramped little suite like a pint-sized tornado. Tidied it, scrubbed it, rearranged it, and actually managed to make it look liveable. Not pretty – that wasn't your style – but more like the apartment – ' He broke off abruptly and frowned.

'More like the apartment you'd planned to share with Mary,' Isabella finished for him without acrimony.

He lifted his head and flashed her a sharp glance. 'Yes,' he agreed. 'More like that. You did a good job, Isabella.'

Isabella tried to conquer an improbable urge to purr like a cat who had been handed a saucer of rich cream, but Brand, noticing her struggle, shattered her pleasure at once by adding flatly, 'At the same time you were a beautiful, demanding encumbrance who wanted more attention than I could give.'

Isabella stopped wanting to purr.

Brand leaned forward suddenly, resting his forearms on the table. She saw a flicker of something that might have been warmth in his eyes. 'We had some interesting times, didn't we, Mrs Ryder?'

'Yes.' She responded to the warmth at once. 'We did. You made me laugh. Sometimes.'

Brand nodded. 'Yes. And when you laughed – sometimes – I used to wonder if maybe you wouldn't suit me after all. Once I had you straightened out and smartened up, of course.' His warm, seductive baritone belied the calculated provocation of the words.

Isabella felt her heart jump and miss too many beats.

'I wouldn't have suited you at all,' she said quickly, knowing she couldn't afford to succumb to the dictates of her much too susceptible hormones. Brand was only amusing himself at her expense. Getting his own back perhaps. 'And I don't take kindly to being – did you say straightened out?' She took a sip of wine and laid her glass carefully down on the table. Then out of the blue she heard herself blurting, 'Did you know you just called me Mrs Ryder?'

Brand picked up his knife again and buttered a piece of bread, taking his time about it. 'Did I? Perhaps that has something to do with the fact that when you married me you elected to take my name.' Taking her by surprise, he reached across the table for her hand. 'I see you still wear the wedding ring I gave you.'

Isabella glanced at him doubtfully, but heavy lids shielded his eyes, and only a slight stiffening of his jawline made her wonder if maybe – just maybe – he wasn't as indifferent as he seemed to be to the fact that she was still his wedded wife.

'Do you want me to give it back to you? And change my name officially and forever to Sanchez – or something else?' The words were out before she had a chance to suppress them.

For a long time Brand didn't reply, but continued to eat as if she hadn't spoken. After a while, Isabella began to push vegetables around her plate in a futile attempt to convince herself that his answer didn't matter. But when, finally, he put his knife and fork together, he replied, 'Something else? No. Sanchez? Not necessarily. It's less confusing that my daughter's mother bears my name.'

His daughter's mother. Not 'my wife'. On the other hand, he hadn't demanded a divorce. Which left her – where? She smoothed a hand over her hair in an irrational attempt to settle the seething confusion in her brain.

When she looked at Brand again she saw that his lips were parted, showing white, even teeth – and his eyes were sending her a message. A message she wasn't ready for. That told her more than she was anxious to know.

Isabella's chest constricted. Brand might not want her for his wife. But he surely wanted her in his bed as much as – and there was no sense denying it – as much as she wanted him in hers. Or was it possible he was only playing cruel games? To pay her back for the games she had played with him?

She picked up a grape from the fruit bowl and bit into it, trying to concentrate on its juicy sweetness. Brand watched her, and after a moment he too picked up a grape and put it between his teeth.

'As you wish, then,' she said, feeling the juice trickle down her throat as her stomach turned an unexpected cartwheel. 'I'll remain Mrs Ryder till further notice.'

'Yours or mine?' asked Brand, snapping off another grape.

'Yours or mine what?'

'Who gets to give their notice first?'

'That depends on circumstances, doesn't it?' she replied lightly, and was surprised to see two small lines forming on either side of his mouth. Had he imagined the decision would be all his?

After that, to her relief, the conversation changed to less personal matters. Brand spoke of the airline's expansion, the building of his house and the changes that had taken place in Vancouver since she'd left. In her turn, Isabella told him of the triumphs and disasters of the catering business, and of how she had once emptied chocolate sauce over an especially deserving diplomatic head.

By the end of the evening they were laughing.

At least they were until Brand delivered her to her door.

As Isabella fitted the key in the lock she could feel

him standing right behind her, his breath gently teasing her hair. When she stepped inside, he was still with her.

'It's late,' she said over her shoulder.

'I assume that means you don't mean to offer me coffee?'

'Or anything else.'

'Did I ask for anything else?' They were standing in the doorway, and all of a sudden Brand put his hands on her shoulders and spun her around.

She gasped, all her senses throbbing at his touch. 'No. No, you didn't,' she said.

'And I'm not going to.' He spoke as if the wary comradeship of the last few hours had never happened. 'Don't waste your wiles on me, Isabella. No one makes a fool of me more than once.'

'No. They never did. And you were never a fool.' She shrugged away from him and held out her hand. 'Goodnight, Brand.'

He looked at her extended palm as if he expected it to turn into a snake, but eventually he took it briefly and said, 'Goodnight. I'll pick you and Connie up at check-out time.'

Isabella nodded dumbly as he turned away. She was still standing in the middle of the floor, gazing at an empty cup and a half-eaten biscuit on the table, when she heard his car start up and growl off into the night.

★ ★ ★

'Good afternoon, Mrs Sanchez. How nice to see you again.' Veronica's carefully modulated tones gave away nothing of the chagrin Isabella was sure she must be feeling at the intrusion of another woman – and a wife at that – into the house she considered her personal domain.

Brand had assured her that Veronica was not and never had been his mistress, and she believed him. But the svelte redhead in the tailored grey suit was an attractive woman who showed no signs of suffering from a sexual neurosis – and Brand exuded sexuality just by breathing. Surely it would be impossible to live under his roof for over two years and *not* harbour dreams of mixing business with pleasure?

On the other hand, maybe she was just ascribing her own yearnings to the other woman. Maybe Veronica preferred small men with twinkling blue eyes, and her possessiveness over Brand was strictly related to the job.

Isabella remembered one of the more useful expressions Brand had taught her. In a pig's eye!

'Mrs Sanchez?' Veronica's raised eyebrows reminded her that she hadn't responded to the housekeeper's practised welcome.

'Good afternoon. It's nice to be back.' Her reply was equally practised and restrained.

She stepped into the sunlit, airy hallway of Marshlands, and Brand, with Connie clinging tightly to his hand, moved up from behind to take her by the elbow.

Veronica frowned, and Isabella said, 'I do hope we aren't causing you too much inconvenience, Ms Dubois.'

'Of course not. It's my job to be inconvenienced.' Veronica's smile was as ambiguous as her words.

Isabella looked up in time to see Brand brush a hasty hand across his mouth, and decided not to provide him with further entertainment. 'Come along, Connie,' she said. 'I'm sure Ms Dubois would like to show us to our rooms.'

She had a suspicion that what Ms Dubois would actually have liked to do was show them out of the house and into the muddy waters of the Fraser. But she guessed Veronica would do anything to maintain her aura of elegant efficiency.

She was right. The housekeeper touched a hand to her hair and said, 'Of course. Please come this way.'

After they had climbed to the top of a gracefully curved wrought-iron staircase, she and Connie were shown to adjoining bedrooms looking across the flat plains of Richmond to the North Shore Mountains and the white snow saucer of Cypress Bowl.

'Oh, I love my pink and white bed,' Connie cried, ignoring the view and patting the luxurious quilted cover. 'And the pink flowered curtains, and – oh look, Mommy, I've got my own bathroom. It's got a sink shaped like a shell. And gold taps.'

'Yes,' said Isabella, with a sinking feeling. 'It's very pretty.' It was exceptionally pretty, but it was going to be hard to wean Connie from all this luxury when it came time for them both to go home.

Her own room was more sophisticated, with pale green draperies and soft primrose-yellow walls. And the bed was much bigger than Connie's. More than enough room for two people. She walked over to the window and stared wistfully at the snow-covered mountains. Why was she wasting her time with thoughts like that? Brand might want her, but he had made up his mind not to have her – and his will power was considerable, as she knew all too well.

So was hers.

She shrugged irritably and turned back into the room to begin unpacking.

When she went downstairs with Connie half an hour later, it was with a mixture of relief and disappointment that she learned Brand was no longer in the house

'He had some business to attend to at the airport,' Veronica said. 'Mr Ryder is a very busy man.'

Who can't afford to waste his valuable time on riff-raff like Connie and me, thought Isabella, noting the smug lift to the other woman's voice. She didn't think she much liked Veronica.

'Yes,' she said sweetly. 'My husband has always been active.'

She was rewarded by Veronica's quick frown, and after that she and Connie were left to their own devices. They heard the housekeeper's heels tapping smartly on the floor as she made her way along one of the polished hardwood corridors.

They spent the rest of the afternoon exploring the extensive grounds, which, to Connie's delight, included a fishpond, natural woods and a swimming pool.

By the time they returned to the house, dusty, dishevelled and laughing, it was almost time to clean up for dinner.

Veronica met them by the back door. 'Mr Ryder phoned to say he'd be late,' she informed Isabella. 'So I took the liberty of ordering an early meal in her room for the little girl.'

Connie opened her mouth to protest, but Isabella, suspecting that Veronica hoped to provoke a scene, said calmly, 'Perhaps that would be best. Tell me something, Ms Dubois. The last time I was here I was called in specifically to do the cooking and catering. Who normally handles it?'

'Cook does. Mrs O'Brien. But she doesn't do large parties. She says it disagrees with her constitution.'

And if eyebrows could sneer, thought Isabella, yours would be doing it.

'Mommy, I don't want to eat in my room –' Connie began.

'Just for tonight,' Isabella said briskly. 'And, as your father means to be late, I'll have *my* supper sent up as well. We'll eat together.' She smiled brightly at Veronica, who bore a sudden surprising resemblance

206

to a goldfish, and hurried her daughter upstairs.

'I don't like Ms Dubois,' said Connie sulkily. 'And I don't want to eat in my room.'

'No,' agreed Isabella with deliberate ambiguity. 'Never mind, tomorrow we'll be eating downstairs.'

In that she was to be proved right.

Tonight, however, supper was served to them on black lacquered trays with red linen. Connie, pleased with the colour, stopped complaining and started eating instead.

They were just finishing a mouthwatering Belgian chocolate truffle dessert when the front door slammed. A few minutes after that Isabella heard the sound of Brand's voice raised in what sounded like wrath. It was answered by a quieter, woman's voice, obviously placating.

Isabella smiled, picked a book from the shelf beside the bed, and settled herself in a green and white striped armchair by the window. She had read just one paragraph of *Wildflowers of Southern B.C.* when peremptory knuckles cracked against the door.

She raised her head and one eyebrow as, without waiting for a response, the owner of the knuckles stalked into the room. He looked powerful and a little intimidating in a charcoal-grey pinstripe suit and crimson tie.

'What in hell is going on?' Brand demanded, kicking the door shut and leaning against it as if he were the Grand Inquisitor and she a prisoner up for interrogation. 'When I invite my family to stay, I damn well expect them to take their meals with me. Veronica tells me you chose to eat in your room.'

His family? Isabella bent forward, gripping the arms of her chair. Then she sank back again. Of course. By his family, what he really meant was Connie. And she was damned if she would tell him that it had been Veronica's idea to get his daughter out of the way as fast as possible. The decision to acquiesce had been her own. And she wasn't in the habit of telling tales.

'I'm sorry,' she said coolly. 'I assumed you would be dining with Veronica as usual. Connie is only a child, Brand. She's used to eating at six. And, in case you've forgotten, she just came out of hospital and she's tired.' She nodded at the adjoining door. 'Right now she's trying to keep her eyes open until you've been in to wish her goodnight.'

Brand glared at her. 'Of course I hadn't forgotten. And for the record, Veronica is my housekeeper and occasional hostess. We rarely take our meals together. So from now on you and Connie will eat in the dining room with me. Is that understood?'

'Yes, sir. At six,' agreed Isabella, saluting.

Brand shot her a murderous look, muttered an uncomplimentary name under his breath and strode across the carpet to Connie's door. Smiling sourly, Isabella eyed his expressive back. Damn him, even when he was angry he moved with such a smooth, feral grace that just watching him made her mouth turn dry. He paused for a moment before entering Connie's room, and she saw his shoulders relax as he made an effort to get his temper under control.

Then he disappeared, closing the door behind him, and she heard Connie give a sleepy, contented laugh.

When Brand came back he no longer looked like the Grand Inquisitor. His features had softened and his mouth was tipped up in a smile.

'She's asleep,' he said. 'She asked me if I minded that her ears won't look like mine any more.'

'What did you say?'

'I told her that as far as I was concerned she was beautiful with or without the Ryder ears.'

'And did that satisfy her?'

'I think it must have done. She held up her arms, and the moment I kissed her goodnight she fell asleep.'

Isabella heard the tenderness in his voice, saw the unusually soft light in his eyes and, just for a moment, she wished she could change places with her daughter.

'You do like children, don't you?' she said, turning her head away so he wouldn't see the unexpected wetness on her cheeks.

'Yes. You know I always have.' To her confusion he came up behind her and placed a hand on her shoulder. 'What's the matter, Isabella? You're not crying because I lost my temper, surely? As I remember, my disposition was a matter of supreme indifference to you in the days when we used to share a home.'

Oh, no. Never indifference. But most of the time it had been a matter of pride not to let him know that he could hurt her. Pride, and sometimes concern for his feelings. She had known from the first that he bore a terrible load of guilt for what had happened in that room above the bar, and in her more selfless moments she had had no wish to add to that burden.

'I'm not crying,' she said, blinking rapidly. 'You're imagining things.'

'Am I?' He bent over and brushed his thumb across her cheek. She could smell the clean, masculine scent of his skin.

'Of course.' She gulped. 'Doesn't Cypress look lovely with the fairylights all around the bowl? Like a giant flying saucer hanging on the side of the mountain.'

'Very lovely. But not as lovely as you.' His voice was warm and deep, like the rich, sweet chocolate they had eaten for dessert.

Isabella swallowed her breath, and, without stopping to think, she raised her eyes to look up at him.

He was frowning at her, his full lips slightly compressed. 'I thought so,' he murmured, touching her cheek again. 'Now, tell me what's the matter, Isabella. Has something upset you? Besides me, that is?'

'No. Just you,' she replied lightly. 'But that's normal.'

'So it seems.' His voice was dry as dead leaves. 'But tears, coming from you, are not.'

'I'm all right.' She tried to sniff discreetly, and ended up sounding like a mouse with an exceptionally bad cold.

'Hmm.' Brand's frown deepened, then he said bluntly, 'I apologize for losing my temper. I had one too many problems at work, and then, when I came home, expecting to be greeted by my daughter, and discovered my house was being treated as a luxury hotel with room service laid on, I – '

'Erupted,' said Isabella. 'I heard you.'

He smiled wryly. 'Did you? Yes, I erupted. I shouldn't have. Of course Connie is used to eating earlier. The problem, I suppose, is that I'm not.'

'No,' agreed Isabella with a sigh. 'You always kept horribly irregular hours.'

'And you used to wait for me, and throw tantrums when I didn't show up.' His smile took the sting out of the words.

'Only at first,' she said defensively. 'And now the situation seems to have been reversed.'

'Are you accusing me of throwing tantrums?' There was more amusement than indignation in his voice.

Isabella found herself smiling too. 'Well, I didn't

hear you stamp your feet,' she admitted. 'But you *were* shouting.'

'Guilty as charged,' he agreed. 'All the same, I didn't mean to make you cry.'

'You didn't,' Isabella said truthfully. 'At least not because you were shouting.'

'Why, then?' He put a finger under her chin and tilted her face up. 'I don't want you crying, Belleza. As long as we're together under one roof, we might as well try to get along.'

Belleza. Beauty. The name Brand had called her on those rare occasions in the past when she had pleased him – when she had hoped, briefly, that underneath the impatience he couldn't always hide he had actually felt a kind of affection for his burdensome and often aggravating young wife.

Infuriatingly, once again she felt her eyes fill with tears. Damn it, how was it this man could always reduce her to a mindless lump of blubbering insecurity? She drew in a long, bracing breath and took a firm grip on herself. 'Of course,' she said brightly. 'For Connie's sake, we *have* to get along.'

He nodded, and the softness died out of his face. 'Yes. For Connie's sake. So from now on you will be ready to eat with me in the dining room. At six – '

'And you will be home,' finished Isabella. She stood up because his legs were brushing tantalizingly against her thighs and she felt an overpowering need to put a reasonable distance between herself and

212

the sexual magnetism he exuded without even trying. She stepped back and held out her hand. 'Let's shake on it.'

Brand took the outstretched hand.

But they didn't shake on it.

The moment their fingers touched, electricity forked and sizzled like wildfire through her veins. Heat, searing and inescapable, melted the lower half of her body, leaving her powerless to resist when Brand, with a muffled expletive, began to draw her slowly towards him. His grip was strong, his arm taut as whipcord, as if he knew exactly what he was doing. But his eyes were as she knew her own must be. Stunned, disbelieving, and dark with passion.

When his lips covered hers she stopped breathing.

CHAPTER 9

Brand tasted the velvet-soft sweetness of her mouth, breathed in the scent of her hair, and as his need grew memories of other years, other embraces, filtered through his mind, fuelling and heightening his desire.

Isabella, dreaming and innocent beside him, that first horrific morning above the bar. And later, Isabella, ripe mouth laughing at him, taunting him with her youthful woman's body, luring him on until he could control his passion no longer.

Isabella. Damn her beguiling little heart. As he slid his hands over the full curve of her hips to shift her up against him he knew that at this moment it no longer mattered to him what she was, or what she might have done. Later, no doubt, would come a reckoning, but for now all he wanted was this woman he had wanted almost from the beginning. This woman who had never been like Mary, and who, at last, was no longer forbidden fruit.

He curved his fingers over the roundness of her

denim-covered bottom, felt her flesh quiver at his touch, and desire merged with a kind of savage triumph as she wrapped her arms around him and let out a small, incoherent moan. He deepened his kiss, refusing even to let her pause for breath as he swung her off the floor and bore her over to the bed.

'Brand,' she whispered, tearing her lips away. 'Brand . . .'

'Shut up,' he growled, lowering her onto the green and white quilt.

His mastery of the moment lasted only a few seconds.

'Mommy! Mommy, don't let it get me. No! No, don't, please don't . . .' Connie's scream penetrated the wall like a crazed alarm bell. Brand swore, and his hand froze on the waistband of Isabella's jeans. Then he straightened, and was off the bed and at the door of the adjoining room so fast he wasn't sure how he got there.

He switched on the light. Connie was sitting up in bed, her face the colour of fresh-frozen bread dough. She was clutching the pink flowered quilt as if she expected it to be ripped from her fingers.

'It's OK, sweetheart,' he said. 'Nobody's going to get you. I won't let them.' He crossed the room in two strides and sat down on the edge of the bed. 'Did you have a bad dream?'

Connie nodded, rubbing her fists across her eyes. 'I – I guess so. There was this big yellow-eyed monster – with ears like mine used to be. And it wanted to steal my new ears – '

'Hush, sweetheart.' Brand put his arm around the narrow shoulders as Connie's childish treble rose in renewed panic. 'There's nothing to be afraid of.'

'She'll be all right in a minute.' Isabella's soft voice spoke from right behind him. 'Won't you, Connie? I'll just make her a mug of warm milk – '

'Mrs O'Brien will do it,' Brand said shortly. He pushed his fingers through the hair that had fallen in a dark wing across his forehead. 'I'm afraid she's still waiting to serve my dinner.' He paused for a second, breathing deeply, then smiled down at Connie and asked gently, 'OK with you if I go eat now?'

'Yes.' Connie nodded. 'Mommy will stay. She always does.'

Brand threw Isabella a hard look. 'This is a regular occurrence? We'll discuss that later.' He gave Connie a quick hug and stood up, his eyes still fixed on his wife. 'Among other things.'

Other things, he thought as he took the stairs two at time, like the fact that I can't keep my hands of your damn body. And the fact that you don't want me to keep them off, in spite of your 'friend' called Felix. It's got to stop. I will not have my life disrupted again by the most conniving, beautiful, seductive little bitch I have ever had the doubtful privilege of taking into my bed. He slammed his fist on the banister, bruised his knuckles and swore.

The problem, he acknowledged grimly as put his head round the kitchen door, was that if he didn't take her into it again soon, he was likely to go out of his mind – or at the very least give her a chance to make a fool of him again. And he was damned if he meant to do that. One kick at the can was all his lovely wife was going to get.

He told Mrs O'Brien about the milk, apologized gruffly for his lateness, and went into the dining room to eat. Alone.

He'd had all he could take of Isabella Sanchez Ryder for one day.

It was surprisingly warm for February, and Isabella was sitting on a bench by the fishpond when Brand came home from work the following day. Connie, quite recovered from her nightmare, was in the kitchen entertaining Mrs O'Brien.

'You're early,' said Isabella, putting a surreptitious hand to her breast to conceal the sudden pounding of her heart. Her husband's formidable figure was advancing down the flagstoned path in an intimidatingly purposeful way. 'It's only four o'clock.'

'I know what time it is.' Brand sat down at the far end of the bench and rested an ankle on his knee. 'Isabella, you and I have one or two matters to set straight.'

She saw that his gaze was riveted on the still waters of the pond, and knew his failure to look at her boded ill.

217

'Yes,' she agreed. 'Connie went right back to sleep after you had the milk sent up to her last night.'

The corner of Brand's lip curled sceptically. 'If that's your oblique way of asking why I didn't come back to finish what I started, the answer is that I came to my senses. That particular mission was aborted. If Connie hadn't had a nightmare, God knows what would have happened.'

'*I* know what would have happened,' Isabella said quietly.

He nodded. 'Yes. I guess you do. And I've learned my lesson. I won't be put in that position again.'

'I liked the position you were in.' Isabella gazed innocently at an orange-tinted cloud.

Brand made a sound that was a cross between a growl and a reluctant chuckle. 'I don't doubt it. But what you're after, Isabella, I'm afraid you are not going to get. So you may as well get used to the idea.'

'I am used to it. I should be after five years.' She swivelled round on the bench and pulled her red knitted jacket tightly across her chest. 'And you, Brand? Are you used to it? It didn't seem so last night.'

Brand's hard profile gave nothing away. 'I admit I find the lack of your lovely body a discomfort and a considerable inconvenience,' he conceded, turning towards her and fixing his gaze on the soft swell of her breasts beneath the jacket. He paused. 'Am I to understand you're making me an offer?'

218

'I don't know.' She stared at the big hands curled loosely on his thighs, remembered how they had curled around her . . . *Was* she making him an offer? Was there any point in trying to mend the fragile fabric of a tenuous affection she wasn't sure had ever really existed? Yes. Yes, maybe there was. For Connie's sake. And – oh, who did she think she was fooling? She might not love Brand any more. He didn't make loving him easy. But she wanted him with a hunger she could barely control. And he was, after all, her husband . . .

Swallowing her pride, she asked, 'If I *was* making you an offer, I suppose – would you take pleasure in refusing it?'

'Pleasure?' A spasm passed over his face, and was replaced, gradually, by a guarded smile. 'Yes, I believe I would. You see, I fell into that trap once before. And look what it got me.'

'It got you Connie. Among other things.'

The smile disappeared and a small muscle in his neck began to throb. 'Yes. Connie – whose existence I wasn't aware of because her mother didn't choose to let me know.'

'I told you why, Brand.' She put out a hand to touch him, then drew it back. 'You said yourself that what's done is done.'

As the orange cloud lost its fire and turned to purple he continued to regard her steadily and without warmth. Isabella waited, willing him to speak, and when he didn't she exclaimed with rising frustration, 'All right, so you can't forgive me for the past. I suppose I have no right to blame you.'

'No right at all,' he agreed. 'And you can forget the tears, Isabella. They no longer fool me.'

'I'm not crying.' She was almost shouting now. 'And, Brand, can't you get it through your head? I've never tried to fool you. Nothing *happened* between me and Gary – '

'Maybe not. But he wouldn't have made a play for you if you hadn't led him on.'

'Yes, he would. That's the way he was. Not that it matters. Brand, how often do I have to tell you . . .?' Her voice dropped to just above a whisper. 'There was never anyone but you.'

'There was Connie,' he said, so harshly that she winced. 'Quite apart from Gary, and Felix, and whoever else you've managed to notch up. Connie is the reason you and I can never – ' He broke off, and a series of emotions moved darkly across his face. First, very briefly, there was pain, and she saw him struggle with it and suppress it. Then bitterness and the desire for retribution. Then desire alone. But that was followed almost at once by a black, malevolent glitter that made her grip her hands tightly in her lap. She would *not* let him see how defenceless she was against his anger. He might enjoy that. And she had already given enough of herself away.

She made to stand up, but Brand stretched a long

arm along the back of the bench and pressed her shoulder down.

'I haven't finished yet,' he said.

'Oh, haven't you?' She wriggled indignantly away from him, but decided to stay after all. Sooner or later they would have to finish this conversation. It might as well be now. 'And what other crime are you planning to lay at my door?'

'No crime. Just poor judgement. I assume Connie has nightmares because you allow her to watch too much TV.'

Isabella experienced a burning sensation behind her eyes. How dared this arrogant man, who was her husband in name but not in reality, presume to criticize the way she raised her daughter?

'Then you assume wrong. Connie has no more nightmares than other children,' she said coldly, and then couldn't resist adding, 'Last night's episode was a rare, but *opportune* occurrence.'

Brand ignored the deliberate barb. 'And I suppose you'd like me to believe that TV has nothing to do with it. Do you monitor her viewing by telepathy?'

Isabella stiffened. 'What's that supposed to mean?'

'You're out several nights a week. How can you possibly provide adequate supervision?'

Could blood really boil over? Hers felt as if it was about to in this crisp February air. 'Brand, I understand that you're just trying to prove you're a responsible parent, but my arrangements for Connie

221

when I'm working are *my* business. They are also entirely satisfactory . . .' She paused, remembering Edwina and the toffee, then went on firmly, 'Edwina is extremely careful of what Connie watches. As I am myself. Besides, if you must know, I haven't been able to afford a TV for her to watch until very recently.'

Brand's jawline became marginally less rigid, and she hurried on to press what she hoped might be an advantage. 'That reminds me – I'm catering a party tomorrow night. Will there be any problem leaving Connie with you? Or shall I call Edwina?'

Brand stretched like a large and dangerous cat flexing its limbs before pouncing on its prey. 'There would be no problem leaving her with me if you were, in fact, catering a party. But I'm afraid you'll have to cancel. My mother is arriving tomorrow night.'

'Oh. What a shame I won't be here to meet her,' Isabella replied sweetly, as she deliberately sat on hands that were just itching to scratch a certain autocratic face. 'There's no question of cancelling, of course. But don't worry. I'm sure to be back by the time your mother is up and about in the morning.'

Brand's eyebrows drew together. He leaned forward suddenly to take her chin between his forefinger and thumb. 'What do you mean, there's no question of cancelling? Mother is particularly anxious to see you – for some reason best known to herself. And since you're a guest in my house – '

A guest in his house? Was that all she was? Oh. Yes. Yes, of course it was.

'A guest, maybe, but not a prisoner.' She spoke with difficulty because his fingers were compressing the corners of her mouth. 'I still have a business to run, Brand. I can't afford to get a reputation for being unreliable. How would you have reacted if I'd cancelled my arrangement with *you*?'

He narrowed his eyes, but then, to her amazement, his lips parted in what might have been a grin. Or a grimace; she wasn't sure which. He dropped his hand and laid it on her knee. 'Badly,' he admitted. 'I'd have raised Cain. And you would have been given no opportunity to cancel on me again.'

Isabella wished he would move his hand. It was sending all kinds of erotic communications up her leg. 'That's what I mean,' she said, trying not to squirm.

Brand smoothed his fingers over the fabric of her jeans. She had an idea he knew exactly what he was doing to her and was enjoying himself immensely at her expense.

'So you see,' she said with a kind of desperation, 'I can't possibly cancel.'

'All right. I take your point.' He stopped stroking abruptly and stood up. 'How many more of these affairs do you have booked?'

'Nothing till next week. Your mother will have left

by then, won't she? So it shouldn't interfere with your schedule after tomorrow.'

'Hmm.' Brand didn't look particularly pleased. 'We'll see about that.' He held out a hand. 'Up you get, then. Maybe you haven't noticed, but it's almost dark. Mrs O'Brien will be serving dinner soon. No sense ruffling her feathers by being late.'

And whose fault would it be if we were? Isabella thought. But she didn't say it. Instead she slipped her hand into his where, in spite of everything, it seemed to belong, and walked with him up the path to the house.

'Isabella, my dear! How delightful to see you again. And how clever of you to produce my lovely grand-child. I always knew you'd make a wonderful mother. Some day.'

Isabella blinked. The party last night had run late, and she was still rubbing sleep from her eyes. But even so, how could she possibly have forgotten about Brand's mother?

Smiling, she stumbled down the last two stairs as a small figure in flowing orange swept regally across the hall to greet her.

Mairead Ryder, now in her mid-sixties, had chan-ged very little in five years. She had the same halo of white hair pinned around her head like wisps of smoke, the same button-black Irish eyes that missed nothing, and her skin, mapped by a fine disregard for the sun, was only a shade darker and more lined.

'Mrs Ryder.' Isabella held out her hands, which were immediately clasped in Mairead's veined ones. 'Oh, it is so good to see you too. But I couldn't have produced Connie on my own.'

'Hmm.' Mairead turned to glance up at her only son, who had just entered the hall and was standing beside her looking poker-faced. 'That may be true. But if you're talking about my boy, here, I can only say he took his time about giving me a grandchild. I've often felt he needed a good boot in a soft place.' She beamed complacently. 'And I've always thought you'd be the one to see he got it.'

'Oh, she did that all right,' muttered Brand. 'I'm still bearing the bruises.'

'My granddaughter is not a bruise,' said Mairead. 'Brandon, stop standing around being disagreeable. If you've got work to do, then get on with it. Go and impress a boardroom or something.'

Isabella tried not to choke at the quizzical gleam in Brand's eye as he looked down at his diminutive mother and murmured that as a matter of fact he did have a boardroom to impress. She watched his back as he strode smartly across the hall in his power pinstripes and thought, with admiration, that Mairead Ryder must be the only woman in the world who could tell Brand what to do and make him do it.

'Come and have breakfast with me,' said Mairead. 'I want to hear everything that's happened.'

At least, Isabella thought warily, her mother-in-law had not – yet – condemned her for depriving her of her grandchild for the past five years. But then Mairead had always been one to weigh the facts before making an irrevocable pronouncement.

'I have to see to Connie first,' she began. 'She's still in bed . . .'

'No, she isn't. You had a late night at your party, didn't you? Connie has been up for hours. Veronica gave her breakfast, and now she's helping Mrs O'Brien with the dishes.'

'Oh,' said Isabella, feeling a bit like Cinderella the morning after the ball. Except that she'd been working, not dancing, and her particular prince wasn't Charming. He was also more likely to turn up with a pair of flight boots than a glass slipper.

Mairead eyed her sharply. 'Don't worry. Between the two of us we'll get him licked into shape.'

Isabella was impressed anew by her mother-in-law's mind-reading skills, but she couldn't imagine herself licking – well, on second thoughts, maybe she could. She felt her face flush as she followed Mairead into the bright, sun-filled breakfast room, with its yellow curtains and red-maple table and chairs. Isabella sniffed blissfully as the invigorating smell of morning coffee drifted across the room to convince her life was worth getting up for after all.

'Now,' said Mairead, sitting down and helping herself to orange juice from a big, ice-cold jug, 'tell me what my boy did to make you run away with my only grandchild.'

Ouch. Isabella winced. Mairead had always been as direct and about as deadly as a missile.

'He – um – he didn't. That is . . .' She ground to a halt and made a frantic attempt to grab her elusive thoughts and get them into some sort of order.

'All right,' Mairead said briskly. 'None of my business, is that it?' She gave an impish grin. 'That's never stopped me yet.'

The grin was contagious, and Isabella had to smile back. 'It's not that it's none of your business – I mean Connie *is* partly your business. But you see, Brand and I had a – well, a difference of opinion – '

'I know that, my dear. Brand is a lot like his father was. A strong man, a hard worker, not overburdened with patience, and so full of principles it makes life very hard for us less scrupulous mortals. You're not above bending a few rules, are you, Isabella?'

Isabella laughed ruefully. 'I think I've bent them all,' she admitted, helping herself to toast and scrambled eggs from a covered stainless steel dish.

Mairead nodded. 'So have I. So now, tell me – why did you find it necessary to leave my son? His precious principles certainly extend to taking responsibility for a baby.'

'Oh, I know. It wasn't Brand's fault. At least – I mean, he didn't know I'd had the baby.'

'Knew you'd left him, though. Must have noticed that. Why didn't he have the sense to fetch you back?'

'He didn't really want me back,' said Isabella, fidgeting with her yellow-checked placemat. 'And – I expect he told you I wrote him a letter from Edmonton to let him know I was all right – that I didn't need his help . . .'

'Hmm. But you did need him, didn't you?' The Irish eyes were extra bright.

'Yes. Yes, I did. But you see, I had to learn to stand on my own feet.' She put her coffee cup down and leaned forward. 'Mrs Ryder, I'm sorry, so very sorry, that you and Brand missed Connie's early years. At the time I thought staying away was the best thing I could do. But now I'm not sure . . .' She lowered her eyes, afraid to look at the older woman. 'Maybe I was wrong to run away. I think Brand despises me for that.'

'He's hurting,' Mairead agreed gruffly. 'Can't expect him not to be. But I've no doubt it's partly his own fault.' Her voice softened. 'You know the best part of all this nonsense?'

Isabella shook her head.

'It's that we have Connie now. She's a lovely child, Isabella. You've done well.'

Isabella felt a vague twinge of alarm. Mairead hadn't meant to worry her, she knew, but that 'we have Connie now' could only have come from Brand. And Brand did not have Connie. He was her father, but she, Isabella, was the one who would care for her and raise her to adulthood.

She smiled uneasily at Mairead, who was busily buttering toast. 'Thank you,' she said. 'But I think Connie just came that way. Naturally.'

'Don't sell yourself short. It's not like you. Now, then . . .' Mairead took a neat bite of toast and, after a pause, went on firmly, 'First of all, there's no sense in blaming yourself for what's over and done with. Yes, I think you were wrong to run away. But my son can be difficult, I know. And you were deplorably young. Far too young to get married. Brandon should have known better.'

'I don't think he felt he had much choice.' Isabella sighed. 'Those principles, you know. And I did have him backed into a corner.'

'Yes, he told me how it happened. And of course he was in a state of shock. He'd just lost his wife of six days, and woken up to find you in his bed. He still should have waited.' Mairead shot a sharp glance across the table. 'He told me you were a clever little schemer, but that he was stuck with you.'

Isabella smiled wryly. 'He was right. Except that attaching myself to Brand was very much a spur-of-the-moment kind of scheme. I didn't set out to sleep with him, but when it happened I decided to make the most of the opportunity. I did ask him to marry me. And, yes, I suppose he was stuck. Although a lesser man would have refused to pay for his lapse.

Not Brand, though.' She dropped her gaze to the cold remains of her egg, and twisted another corner of her placemat. 'Mrs Ryder – it must have been a terrible shock for you as well – to see your son leave for his honeymoon with one woman and have him come back with another.'

'I survived,' said Mairead drily. 'Mary was a sweet thing in her way, but much too soft for Brandon. No backbone when it came right down to it. He'd have made her life hell without meaning to.'

'Oh, but he loved her so much. That night when I – when he rescued me – his hands were all bruised and raw from – from trying to reach her, I think. Although he never told me much about what happened.'

'He told me,' Mairead said. 'Damn foolishness, if you ask me.'

'It wasn't the wisest place to be hiking at that time of year,' Isabella agreed. 'There had been warnings posted, and I heard my father tell them to stay on the safe hiking trails. But the accident happened later, on a different mountain, so perhaps they forgot – or else didn't understand him. Brand's Spanish isn't very good.'

'Wouldn't have listened anyway. Young people always think they're immortal. Poor Mary wasn't.' Mairead shook her head. 'Brandon told me they would have been all right if they had kept going as he wanted, but Mary complained of being tired so they turned back.'

Isabella's attention was caught by two herons gliding past the window on their way towards the marsh. 'She was complaining of being tired the only time I saw her as well,' she murmured.

'I'm not surprised. Mary told Brandon she liked hiking, but if you ask me – not that anybody ever does – her idea of a hike was a gentle stroll around a duckpond. Or maybe a shopping mall.'

The herons vanished over the horizon. Isabella giggled, then felt guilty because Mary was dead. 'Perhaps she wanted to please Brand,' she suggested.

'Hmm. Wanted him to *think* she wanted to please him anyway. Not that I'm saying she didn't love him. She did. But she wasn't right for him. Ah, well . . .' Mairead swallowed the last of her orange juice. 'Perhaps it was meant to happen the way it did. With the best will in the world, Brandon could never have made her happy. I know. I'm his mother. He was hard enough to handle as a child. Impossible once his father died. He was only fourteen, you know, when that happened.'

'Yes. Brand told me his father's plane crashed while he was on a rescue flight. But I think that only made him more determined than ever to be a pilot.'

'Determined? Pig-headed, you mean.' Mairead waved a piece of toast at Isabella. 'Never mind. You're a match for him. Tough enough to give as good as you get. Much better for him than Mary, my dear. I saw that the moment I met you. Only trouble was you hadn't had a chance to grow up.'

'I know,' agreed Isabella. 'And now that I hope I *have* grown up it's too late.'

'Nonsense. You're still married to him, aren't you? He never made the effort to divorce you, which must count for something. You are also the mother of his child.'

'But that's just what he can't forgive me for,' groaned Isabella.

'Nonsense,' Mairead said again. 'Give him time. *I* can see you love him, even if he can't.'

'What?' Isabella's mouth fell open.

'Come, come. I'm not blind, my dear. Plain as those ridiculous Ryder ears.'

Oh, God. No. Isabella dropped her face into her hands. *Was* it as plain as that? She took a long, shuddering breath. And if it was, why, until this moment, had it not been plain to her?

Oh, Brand. She pressed her knuckles into her eyes. Dear bossy, upright, uncompromising Brand. The only man I've ever wanted. Why did it take your wise and wonderful mother to make me see what I should have seen for myself? Because she's right. I've loved you from the moment I first saw you. And I actually let myself believe it was over! Oh, *how* could I have been such a fool? How could I have thought even for a second that Felix could take your place in my heart . . .?

Isabella lifted her head, and as she did so the mists of self-delusion fell away and she accepted the truth it was no longer possible to escape.

'Yes,' she said unsteadily to Mairead. 'Yes, I do love him. But – oh, Mrs Ryder, he doesn't care – '

'Huh. Maybe he doesn't at the moment. Or maybe he does and doesn't know it. But in time I believe he will.' Mairead paused to concentrate on pouring coffee from a steaming pot, then said abruptly, 'You're going home at the end of next week, I understand?'

'Yes. I am.'

'Good. Don't change your mind.' Her smile was wickedly conspiratorial: 'Brandon has always wanted what he's told he can't have. And gone after it and got it in the end. It's the challenge that appeals to him, I think. So just keep your courage up, my dear. Now . . .' She stood up in a swirl of orange chiffon. '*You* can read the papers and finish your coffee. *I'm* off to get to know my grandchild – and give Veronica and Mrs O'Brien a chance to get on with their work.'

Isabella nodded wordlessly and watched her mother-in-law float out of the room in a sunset-coloured cloud. The day seemed darker and colder once she'd left.

After that Isabella sat amidst the remains of breakfast, not reading the papers but trying desperately to

233

make some kind of sense out of the chaos of her emotions.

She loved Brand. He wanted her, but wouldn't have her because he also despised her. Oh, heaven help her, it was going to take all the courage she possessed just to get herself through this coming week. Beyond that she wasn't even willing to think. Not yet. Thinking and decisions could come later.

Mairead stayed at Marshlands until the Sunday night, charming both Isabella and Connie with her wit and wisdom, and keeping Brand firmly in his place whenever he showed a tendency to act the part of master of his house.

'I'm too old to be bullied by my own son,' she'd told him tartly one day, when he had suggested she take an afternoon nap. 'And Connie and I are going shopping this afternoon, so we'll hear no more nonsense about children needing to rest after meals either. What do you know about children?'

Brand, with a pointed glance at Isabella, had murmured that he'd have known a lot more if he'd been given the opportunity, but that in any case he was learning. Fast.

Once Mairead had returned to her home in the Okanagan, life at Marshlands began to settle into a routine. Connie attended kindergarten during the day while Isabella caught up on her paperwork, collected the messages on her answering machine, read, explored the garden and generally managed to keep out of Veronica's way.

There was no sign of a thaw in that department. Veronica resented Isabella's presence in the house and made no secret of it except when Brand was around. But she ran the household with a terrifying efficiency, and Isabella had to admire her dedication to her employer.

Each day Brand arrived home punctually at five-thirty, ate dinner with his wife and daughter and spent the rest of the evening until Connie went to bed entertaining the little girl with stories of his flying adventures, or playing games which she invariably won.

Until the night before they were due to leave Marshlands, he avoided being alone with Isabella.

The wind had been gaining force all that day, and by nightfall it was whistling through the eaves and blowing gusts of noisy rain against the windows. Isabella lay wide awake in her bed. She was feeling restless anyway, because she knew that however much she accepted the need to get on with her life she was going to miss this house, which, in a strange way, had begun to feel like her home. And, oh, how she was going to miss Brand. She didn't want to miss him. She wanted to miss Felix. But Brand was in her blood, as he had been for the last six years.

She was desperately afraid he always would be.

When yet another blast of rain hit the window, and she knew sleep would continue to elude her, Isabella got up, pulled on a dark blue brushed cotton robe and made her way quietly down the stairs. If she wasn't going to sleep, she might as well make herself some tea.

She had forgotten to put on her slippers, and the wooden floor was cold beneath her feet. But just as she was about to turn back she heard voices. She glanced at the watch she had forgotten to take off. Two in the morning. Apparently she wasn't the only one who couldn't sleep.

'I'm sorry, Brand, but you must see that it puts me in an impossible position.' Veronica's voice, scissor-sharp and uncompromising, came from the other side of the closed kitchen door.

'I see nothing of the sort.'

Isabella paused with her hand on the doorknob.

A second later she staggered back as the door flew open and Veronica stalked out. She was wearing a high-necked green velvet robe that accentuated the startling pallor of her skin in the glare of the light from the kitchen. Her eyes looked unusually large and much too bright.

'My resignation stands,' she flung over her shoulder at Brand, and swept down the passage towards the hall.

CHAPTER 10

Isabella peeled herself off the wall and stood in the kitchen doorway, too stunned to move.

Brand muttered a string of words in which the phrase 'Damn fool of an addlebrained woman' figured prominently. Eventually he looked up and saw her hovering there.

'Isabella!' His features were as stormy as the wind besieging the windows, and his eyes raked over her blue robe with a look that was faintly insulting, as if he were seeing right through it to the body whose eager response to him no amount of deep breathing could control. Just the sight of his virile frame in skintight jeans and a black sweatshirt was an aphrodisiac that set her blood racing.

'Listening at keyholes, Isabella?' he enquired when he had finished his inspection. 'I might have guessed.'

'I came down to make tea,' she said, lifting a frostily disdainful chin. 'What's the matter, Brand? Veronica not proving a satisfactory slave? You'd better look out your whips and chains.'

Brand, obviously fighting to keep his temper, said, 'If there's any of that to be done, I can promise you you'll be the first to find out.'

He didn't mean it. Brand wasn't like that. But he did look as if he'd been sorely tried. 'What's the matter?' she repeated, less acidly.

'The matter, my dear, is that, thanks to you, Veronica has handed in her resignation.'

'Thanks to me? But – '

'There's no need to go all wide-eyed and innocent on me. She said she was resigning because of you. Therefore you must have done something to upset her.'

'Yes,' agreed Isabella, nettled. 'I made the mistake of existing.'

Brand put his hands in his pockets as if he needed to restrain them. 'Yes, that's a problem,' he agreed. 'Mine, not Veronica's.'

Isabella clasped her fingers behind her back, not trusting them to keep out of trouble while she wondered at the blindness of men in general, and this one in particular. 'Veronica was hoping to marry you,' she told him with what was left of her patience.

'Don't be ridiculous. Veronica is – was – my housekeeper. She's known from the start I was married.'

'In name only.'

'No. In the eyes of the law. That makes me off-limits.' Brand rammed his hands deeper into his pockets and pinned her with a look so uncompromising that she had to force herself not to recoil. 'You do realize,' he said, changing the subject with high-handed abruptness, 'that this means you'll have to stay on at Marshlands. At least for a while.'

Isabella stared at him. He was standing with his legs apart and his jaw aggressively squared, looking exactly as she imagined the master of a slave ship might have looked on a stormy night. And woe betide the slave who had attempted to cross him.

Well, she had never been known for her caution.

'No,' she said firmly. 'I can't do that, Brand. Connie and I are leaving in the morning.'

Brand took a step towards her, then thought better of it and sat down on a corner of the table. He folded his arms and angled his legs out in front of him.'

'You can't,' he said. 'Veronica has resigned. I need a housekeeper. You're my wife, as you've pointed out to me on more than one occasion. So for once, instead of causing me a problem, you can solve one for me.'

Just as if I'm some interchangeable cog in his well-oiled housekeeping machine, Isabella thought disbelievingly. Yet, in a way, she wished she *could* stay. Brand would manage without her very well. But it would please her to run his house for him, to act as if she were his wife in more than name . . .

No. She mustn't even think it. Brand didn't want her as his wife. He had made that abysmally clear.

'I'm sorry, Brand,' she said with quiet resolution.

'But you'll have to solve your problem some other way.'

When he only looked at her with his head lowered, as if he were a bull about to charge, she turned her back on him and started to leave the room.

'Stay where you are,' he said.

Isabella stopped, too startled to ignore him. Did he honestly think he had the right to tell her what to do? Frowning, she turned to face him, curiosity getting the better of her normally well-developed sense of personal preservation.

He was still sitting on the edge of the table looking inflexible, and when she raised her eyes he lifted a finger and beckoned.

'Come here,' he said when she didn't move.

Not wanting to, furious with herself for obeying, Isabella began to walk towards him. She couldn't do anything else. There was something so extraordinarily compelling about Brand's black-clad figure on the table, something so commanding in his eyes, that she found herself powerless to ignore him.

She walked warily, unsure of what was coming, and when she got close to him he put his hands on her waist and drew her in between his legs.

'I want you to stay,' he said, softly now.

Isabella swallowed, unnerved by this sudden change of tactic. 'No,' she said. 'No, I can't.'

Instead of arguing, Brand ran his hands down her hips. Isabella gasped, and he moved them slowly down the backs of her legs, then up again, over her rear and lower back, drawing her ever closer to his body until she was trapped by the lean, hard heat of his thighs.

'Don't, Brand,' she whispered. 'Stop.'

'And if I don't?'

'I . . .' Sanity returned as she looked up to meet the light of victory gleaming in his eyes. Brand might be the sexiest man in the world, but she wasn't that easily defeated.

'What are you offering me, Brand?' She reached behind her to put a stop to the intimate seduction of his fingers. 'The chance to look after your house for a while – in return for services rendered?'

Fleetingly, he smiled. 'I suppose you can put it that way.' He caught both her hands in his, holding them loosely against her sides.

Isabella shook her head. She had to get away from him. If she didn't, she would find herself agreeing to give him anything he wanted. 'You said – you said that was out of the question.'

'Mmm.' He nodded. 'But I've been thinking things over, and – '

'And you have this little housekeeping problem. So you've decided to be generous with your favours until a more amenable doormat comes along.'

To Isabella's fury, instead of admitting it, or even denying it, Brand laughed.

'It's not funny,' she told him, drawing herself up to

her full height before realizing, too late, that her full height was unlikely to impress.

'No,' he agreed, sobering at once. 'Of course it isn't.' To her further dismay, he leaned forward suddenly and kissed her lightly on the tip of her nose. 'Isabella,' he said softly, 'you're irresistible when you glare at me like that. You shouldn't do it. And you can't go away. I don't want you to.'

Was he serious? No, this was just a ploy to get him what he wanted. In other words, a temporary housekeeper with a nice bit of bed thrown in for old times' sake.

He smiled at her, that full, lazy smile that long ago had stolen her heart for ever. And, incredibly, ridiculously, she opened her mouth to say yes.

But out of nowhere, just in time, came a memory of the last time she had been alone in this kitchen with Brand. He hadn't been smiling then. His face had been cold with condemnation. And all at once she knew she couldn't give him what he wanted for no other reason than that he had a smile to die for. She just couldn't. But maybe when she'd had time to think, to understand what was happening . . .

'I – I'll think about it,' she said quickly. 'Brand, please let me go. Give me time . . .'

His face seemed to close up, and he released her immediately, shifting her away from him as if he had no idea how she had come to be in his arms in the first place.

'Time?' he said. 'You've had five years, Isabella. I'll give you till tomorrow evening.'

She nodded, wondering if it was pain she heard in his voice, or merely a familiar impatience. 'Yes, tomorrow,' she agreed. Turning from him, she practically ran out of the kitchen.

But just before she closed the door she glanced back – and caught a glimpse of his face. He looked tired and frustrated and, for a few seconds, almost as confused as she was.

She pulled the door shut, forgetting all about the tea she had come to make and half expecting Brand to fling it open again and order her to come back at once. But no furious bellow followed her down the passage to the hall, and when she paused at the bottom of the stairs all she heard was the voice of the wind howling for admittance.

Isabella shivered and hurried on up to her room. But her rumpled bed looked so cold and uninviting that she collapsed into the green and white chair instead.

That was when she remembered about the tea.

Damn. She put her hands over her ears to deaden the sound of the storm and wondered if she wanted to go back.

No. She would do without her tea. She couldn't risk another encounter with Brand. Not tonight. Nor did she wish to run into Veronica who, at two o'clock in the morning, had been prowling the house in a green velvet robe.

Isabella stroked the smooth arm of her chair. Strange, that. Most people gave notice in the morning, not in the middle of the night wearing a robe. What on earth had Veronica been up to? And why had she and Brand been together in the kitchen?

It didn't make sense. Particularly as Veronica loved her job at least as much as she loved Brand. Assuming she did love Brand, who was a catch any way you looked at it. Love wouldn't need to be a part of the equation – although it probably was.

Poor Veronica. For the first time, Isabella felt a certain sympathy for the efficient Ms Dubois. Brand wasn't an easy addiction to give up. She, of all people, should know that . . .

She sat up suddenly, frowning, as a sound that wasn't wind interrupted her disconnected musings. Was that Connie crying in the next room? She hurried to investigate.

But Connie was fast asleep, with one arm around her hippopotamus and the other around a pink elephant Brand had given her. Isabella bent over her little daughter, breathing in the scent of her favourite apple-blossom shampoo. She smiled, watching the gentle rise and fall of Connie's chest, the sweep of dark lashes on her cheek – and all at once it was as if a weight had been laid on her shoulders – not a heavy weight, but one that would be there for always.

She knew what that weight was. It was the knowledge that Connie would never again be hers alone. From now on Brand, who was her father, would always be a part of her life. In other circumstances she might have celebrated that knowledge. But not now. Sighing, Isabella turned away from the small bed and made her way back to her room.

The sound of sobbing was louder now. She frowned, and opened the door leading onto the corridor. Yes, somebody was definitely unhappy. Veronica? It had to be. Mrs O'Brien never stayed overnight.

Isabella hesitated. It wasn't her business. Veronica didn't even like her. On the other hand, if the housekeeper could be persuaded to stay on, she, Isabella, would be absolved of any perceived obligation to remain at Marshlands. That, surely, would be the ideal solution to all their problems. Why was she even hesitating?

Securing the belt of her robe firmly around her waist, Isabella marched towards the sound of the sobbing like a soldier setting out to do battle.

'Veronica?' She tapped on the housekeeper's door. 'Veronica, may I come in?'

All at once the house fell quiet. Even the wind was briefly silent. Then a muffled voice said, 'Who is it? What do you want?'

'It's me. Isabella. Mrs Ryder. Is there anything I can do?'

No answer. As Isabella hesitated, wondering if she

ought to knock again, the door was abruptly dragged open.

'What do you want?' Veronica repeated.

'I – I heard a noise, and I thought perhaps I could help.' Isabella tried not to stare.

Veronica, usually so sleek and well-groomed, looked as if she had been dragged out of a trashcan instead of her bed. Her boyish red hair was sticking up in spikes, her made-up eyes were smudged to a bruised-looking purple and her green robe was wrinkled like the skin of shopworn kale. Yet her face wasn't wet, or even damp . . .

Why, she couldn't have been crying after all! The sobbing noise must have been just that – noise. Or a venting of violent frustration.

'How can *you* help, Mrs Sanchez?' Veronica repeated ungraciously.

'It's Mrs Ryder. Can I come in? I'd like to talk to you, if you don't mind.'

'If it's about my decision to leave – '

'It is. I know Brand isn't the easiest man to get along with, but neither of us wants to lose you, Ms Dubois.' That wasn't strictly the truth, but it would do.

Veronica, regaining some of her poise, attempted to smooth down her hair. 'I have no choice,' she said glacially. The wind screamed and tossed a blast of rain against the window.

'I think you have. Please, can I come in? I *would* like to talk to you.'

'Oh, very well.' Looking more like her old self by the moment now that she sensed she had the upper hand, Veronica stood aside to let her pass.

'Your room is very pretty.' Isabella seized on the first conversational gambit she could think of. 'May I sit down?'

Veronica shrugged. 'Suit yourself.'

Not promising, Isabella decided. Veronica had no intention of meeting her halfway. In an attempt to regain control of the situation, she swept across the carpet and seated herself on the only chair in the room, a stiff little number in contrasting ice-green stripes. The walls were green too, as well as the bedspread, and the entire room had an air of cool, green, practical efficiency. Odd how rooms took on the personality of their owners, Isabella reflected as Veronica perched herself on the end of the bed and crossed her legs.

'Why were you – crying?' Isabella asked. Veronica hadn't been crying, but she couldn't very well ask her why she'd been making a noise like a banshee on heat.

The housekeeper didn't answer directly. 'I like my job, Mrs Sanchez. It will be a considerable wrench to give it up.'

'It's Mrs Ryder. Or Isabella, if you like. Why *did* you give it up, then?'

'Because there isn't room for two mistresses in this house.' Veronica sniffed, and her upper lip curved in a small, cat-like grimace.

No broken heart here, Isabella decided with relief. Those noises she had heard had undoubtedly been more temper than grief.

'I know you don't mean that literally,' she said.

Veronica only hesitated for a second. 'Of course not. I have rather more self-respect than that. Your husband is married, Mrs *Ryder*.'

'Yes, I had noticed.' Isabella curbed a childish urge to pile on even more sarcasm, and said instead, 'But there's no reason for you to leave Mr Ryder's employ on my account. If you like the job, why don't you keep it? Connie and I are going home tomorrow – as surely you must know?'

'Yes. But, according to the senior Mrs Ryder, you'll be back. I'm not fond of children, and I don't feel there are any permanent prospects for me here.'

What kind of prospects? Isabella wondered. She bit her lip to hide a smile. Apparently Mairead had been stirring things up behind the scenes. Trust her dear, unscrupulous mother-in-law.

'Mmm. I see.' She studied the other woman through her eyelashes. There were more lines on Veronica's face than she had thought. Lines that until tonight had always been covered by make-up.

The wind made a moaning sound in the eaves. 'Did you hope to marry Brand?' Isabella asked. 'Is that why you followed him down to the kitchen?'

Veronica gave an unconvincing laugh. 'You have a vivid imagination, Mrs Ryder.

'Have I? I'm glad. Because Brand's not an easy man to be in love with.'

Veronica winced, and again Isabella felt a flare of sympathy for the housekeeper. The two of them had more in common than she'd thought.

But Veronica wasn't looking for sympathy. She lifted an elegant shoulder and said, 'That's hardly my problem, Mrs Ryder.'

'No,' Isabella agreed. 'Of course it isn't. So would you please consider staying on as my husband's housekeeper? At least until he hires someone else.'

Veronica fixed her gaze on a collection of jars and bottles on the dresser. 'I can't do that, I'm afraid.'

'But why not?'

'That's my business, Mrs Ryder.'

'Yes. Yes, I suppose it is.' Isabella stood up. 'You won't reconsider, then?'

She knew Veronica wouldn't. But giving her the chance to refuse again would help to restore her pride. Isabella was feeling magnanimous. In her heart, she was *glad* the housekeeper wasn't going to stay. It was all too obvious now what she had been up to tonight in the kitchen, and if Veronica stayed – well, there was no telling what might happen. One day Brand might decide he could do a lot worse than his efficient, redheaded housekeeper. And who could blame him?

'I'm sorry you won't change your mind,' she said, hiding her true feelings behind a gracious, lady-of-the-manor smile. 'But naturally I respect your decision. Goodnight, Veronica. I'll see you in the morning.'

Veronica didn't answer, but as Isabella turned to leave from the corner of her eye she saw a change come over the other woman's face. One minute it had been composed and a little derisive. The next it was splotched with angry colour. Isabella hastened her pace and hurried out into the corridor.

She wasn't fast enough. As she turned to close the door, a tube of lipstick hit her in the face. She gasped, put a hand to her cheek and started angrily back into the bedroom. But she had only taken a step when a voice behind her said, 'Hell,' and a pair of muscular arms closed around her waist. She kicked out frantically as her back was clamped against a man's solid body – a body that was all too familiar, even though, at this moment, she couldn't see it.

'Brand!' Isabella exclaimed. 'What are you doing? Let me go this minute.'

For answer, Brand tightened his grip and swung her out of range of the bedroom door. A second later a jar of cold cream followed the lipstick.

'I'm keeping you out of the firing line,' Brand growled. Still holding her, he shouted, 'Veronica? What in hell is going on? Are you out of your mind?'

A tube of toothpaste narrowly missed his nose, but after that the missiles stopped coming.

Brand released Isabella and took a cautious step

forward. After one look at the livid face of his once imperturbable housekeeper, he asked again, 'Are you out of your mind?'

Isabella peered over his shoulder. Veronica was standing in the centre of the carpet with her shoulders heaving and her eyes blazing blue fire. No words came out of her mouth at first, but when they did, Brand put his hands over Isabella's ears.

For a few seconds all three of them stood there, frozen, then Brand removed his hands, said, 'Wait here,' to Isabella, and strode grimly into Veronica's bedroom. When Isabella made to follow, he muttered two succinct words below his breath and shut the door on her.

She thought about ignoring his instructions, but in the end curiosity kept her where she was. Imagine Veronica snapping like that. So much fire and fury beneath the ice. Isabella leaned against the wall and waited.

A minute or two later Brand, still looking grim, emerged from Veronica's bedroom and closed the door.

'What was *that* all about?' he demanded. 'For heaven's sake, woman — '

'Don't you start womaning me,' she snapped. 'I was trying to persuade her to stay on.'

'Were you, now? I gather you didn't succeed.'

'No. I didn't.'

'Good. Because I don't need any more aggravation

in my life than I already have.' He lowered his head aggressively. 'I hope you'll bear that in mind.'

Isabella said, 'Goodnight,' and turned away.

'Hold it. I haven't finished.' Brand caught her shoulders and pulled her back.

'But I *have* finished,' said Isabella. Then curiosity got the better of her again and she asked grumpily, 'What did you do to Veronica? She's very quiet.'

'I didn't strangle her, if that's what you mean.'

'You look as though you'd like to strangle both of us.'

To her astonishment, Brand's features relaxed and he started to laugh. 'The thought did cross my mind, I must admit. But you needn't worry. I offered Ms Dubois a generous settlement in return for her years of faithful service. It seemed to soothe her.'

'Oh,' said Isabella. 'A bribe in the interests of peace and quiet.'

'No,' said Brand. 'A token of my esteem in the interests of fairness. Now, if you'll just stay away from her for the remainder of the night, there's a chance we may all get some sleep. She was never the slightest problem before you came.' He shook his head, a man frankly bemused by the antics of womankind.

When a sudden gust of rain splattered the skylight above their heads, he saw Isabella's fingers twitch as if she itched to slap his face. She had tried that once before, a long time ago.

They were only a few inches apart. If he lifted his hand, curved it round the back of her neck, she would come to him in spite of her indignation. He could see it in her eyes. But he wasn't going to do it. Better she spend what was left of the night tossing and turning, burning up with need – as he had done earlier, before he'd given up and gone downstairs to be accosted by Veronica. Maybe a night like that would would help her make up her mind, so that by tomorrow she would agree to stay with him on his terms.

It was only a temporary solution, but it would have to do. These last few days he hadn't been able to think beyond temporary. He had Isabella Sanchez Ryder to thank for that.

He didn't lift his hand, didn't curl it around her neck or touch his mouth to her softly parted lips, although he wanted to. Instead he said, 'Goodnight, Isabella. Sleep well,' and left her leaning against the wall with her hand clutching the neck of her blue robe.

Isabella watched him go with a feeling of dreadful desolation. Then she shook her head hopelessly and trailed back to her bed.

She spent a sleepless night listening to the wind.

By morning the storm had died down. And Isabella had made up her mind.

She couldn't stay on at Marshlands. Brand didn't love her. That hadn't been love she had seen in his eyes last night. It had been knowledge of the power he had always had to melt her heart. And he only wanted a temporary convenience. So why prolong the agony? She should have seen that right away, of course, long before the scene with Veronica. But Brand's physical presence had a way of distorting reality, turning her to putty in his hands.

He had already left for work by the time she and Connie made their way down to breakfast, so she nibbled on a piece of cold toast, swallowed two cups of tea and sent Connie upstairs again to brush her teeth. Then she picked up the phone and began to dial.

'Yes?' snapped Brand's voice when he eventually came on the line.

She took a deep breath. 'It's me, Brand. And it's tomorrow. I've thought about what you said, and I have to tell you that – that I'm sorry, but I can't solve your problem for you. Connie and I are going home today as we planned – '

Brand gave an exclamation of frustration. 'Hold it right there. You agreed to wait until this evening – '

'No, *you* gave me until this evening. But it turns out I don't need that long.'

She heard something that sounded like a fist hitting wood. 'Isabella, you stay right where you are until I get there. I have a number of appointments I can't cancel, but after that – '

'No,' said Isabella. 'Brand, there isn't any point in my staying. Don't you see that if – '

He didn't wait for her to finish. She heard him growl something unfair and unprintable about the female sex before he slammed the phone down in her ear.

Isabella sighed and went to finish her packing.

As she climbed the stairs she met Veronica coming down, carrying two smart navy suitcases and a shoulder-bag. They nodded to each other and passed without speaking. The ex-housekeeper looked as cucumber-cool and in control as she had always done, and the satisfied smile on her lips made Isabella think Brand's 'generous settlement' must have been generous indeed.

By lunchtime she and Connie were back in the apartment in Point Grey.

'End of page, end of chapter,' Isabella muttered at a sink full of dishes. 'Now all I have to do is finish the book.'

She had a feeling that it might not be as easy as it sounded.

That evening, after Connie was safely tucked away in bed, Isabella went to her dresser and took out a battered red box. Inside it lay the silver bracelet Brand had given her so many years ago – the only gift she had ever received from him apart from the obligatory wedding ring. And the last time she had worn it was the night she'd left him.

She stood for some time staring at its delicate design, running her fingers over the smoothness of the silver. Then she put it back in the box. But as she started to close the lid she paused, lifted it out again and snapped it around her wrist.

'Oh, Brand,' she whispered as she settled herself in her well-worn armchair, switched on the television set and picked up a blouse she was mending. 'Oh, Brand. What have we done to each other?'

She didn't really see the flickering images on the screen. She was too busy remembering Brand's laughter, his come-hither voice telling her he wanted her to stay. But how could she have stayed? Mairead said Brand always wanted what he couldn't have. So did that mean he saw her as some unattainable nymph he could discard once his physical needs were met? No. No, that wasn't the man she had married. That man didn't make commitments he wasn't willing to keep, and if he said he wanted her with him . . .

She leaned her head against the back of the chair. Maybe he did need her to run his house. But he hadn't once told her he loved her. Because he didn't. Brand would never love a woman he didn't trust.

Carefully, with blank-eyed concentration, she mended a hole in her blouse that wasn't there.

When the knock came on the door, she jumped and stabbed her finger with the needle.

Brand? No, Brand had hung up on her. There was

no reason for her heart to be beating like a tom-tom as she went to see who was there.

No reason at all. Because when she drew back the bolt and pulled the door open a crack, it wasn't Brand who stood smiling on the threshold.

It was Felix.

Isabella stepped backwards. 'Felix! What – what are you doing here?' She tried to smile too, but only managed a half-hearted grimace.

'I missed you, Belle. The company owed me a couple of days' vacation, so I decided to put them to good use.' He put his hands on her upper arms and, before she could protest, dropped a wet and gentle kiss on her gaping mouth.

'Don't, Felix.' She swallowed hard and rubbed her knuckles across her lips.

Felix frowned, and pushed her, less gently, back into the apartment. 'Why not? Dammit, Belle, I want to marry you. You know that.'

Isabella waved him to a chair. She would feel less vulnerable once he was safely seated. 'Yes. Yes, I know.' She perched herself on the arm of the small sofa, eyeing him uneasily. 'I *am* grateful, Felix, and honoured, but – '

'But you're going to stick with that bastard you married?' Felix's voice, always a little nasal, rose irritably as he drew a quick breath into his barrel of a chest.

She saw that his hair was slightly greyer than it had

been the last time she had seen him. His mouth looked pinched in his fleshy face, and he sounded altogether more angry than anguished. For the first time in their acquaintance she wondered if perhaps Felix's desire for a speedy marriage was prompted more by his need to find a keeper for his three wildly out of control children than by affection for a woman who was eighteen years his junior.

'No,' she replied. 'No, I'm not going to stay with Brand. I can't – '

'Then for heaven's sakes, Belle, stop dithering and get a divorce. You said you needed to see him again just to be sure. And from the sounds of it you *have* seen him and it isn't going to work. So why not forget him? I need you. Don't you know that?'

Yes, she knew that. But Brand wasn't so easily forgotten. 'Felix,' she began, 'I – '

Crack!

Isabella stiffened, and glanced towards the door. Another visitor? One with no respect for his knuckles from the sound of it.

She went to answer this second knock with a sense that the evening wasn't real, that everything was happening in a dream. Any time now she would wake up.

'Who's there?' she demanded, not wanting any further surprises.

'Your friendly neighbourhood pervert,' a scathing voice rasped from the other side of the door.

Isabella closed her eyes. 'Oh, it's you, Brand.' She drew back the bolt to let him in. Astonishingly, her voice was quite steady.

'Thank you.' Brand's upper lip tipped in a caustic curl. 'Nice to know you haven't lost your talent for flattery, Mrs – ' He broke off as if he'd been punched in the stomach.

Felix, tight-lipped and glaring, was rising deliberately from his chair.

Isabella, following the direction of Brand's eyes, saw what he was glaring at, and groaned. Although she hadn't taken it in until this moment, the corner of Felix's mouth was lightly smeared with Coral Candy.

It was the only shade of lipstick she ever wore.

CHAPTER 11

Brand's stony gaze took in the presence of the other man and flicked to the unfortunate splash of colour on Felix's mouth. The music from the TV, soft and unobtrusive until now, roared to a thunderous crescendo as a cowboy on a white horse galloped onto the screen to sling the heroine over his saddle and ride off into a sickly pink sunset.

Perfect, thought Isabella. And with my luck Brand will ride off into the sunset with the remains of Felix slung across his saddle instead of me.

'I'm sorry, Brand,' she heard herself saying idiotically. 'Connie's already gone to bed.'

Brand, his gaze still riveted on Felix, said, 'I didn't come to see Connie. I came to see you.'

'Oh.' Isabella heard the tightness in his voice, and eyed his tall figure in casual trousers and a soft grey sweater with a mixture of yearning and apprehension. 'I – I left you a note after I phoned you. It's in your study. Didn't you see it?'

'I saw it.' He went on staring at Felix. 'And this, I

presume, is your friend.' He made it sound as though Felix was her pet snake.

'Yes,' said Isabella. 'Felix, this is Brand. My – er – my husband.'

The look Brand gave her made her want to sink through the dun-coloured carpet. If Felix was a snake she, apparently, came considerably further down the food chain.

'Good evening,' Brand said, bowing with over-played civility. 'I understand you want to marry my wife.'

Oh, dear heaven! Isabella forced herself to stand still instead of running from the room like a nervous rabbit. Felix was already swelling up like a vintage cockerel, and Brand-Brand reminded her more of a circling hawk.

'Yes,' replied Felix, holding his ground. 'I hope Belle will do me that honour.'

'*Belle*.' Brand managed to make Felix's nickname for her sound obscene.

'That's what I call her.' Felix puffed out his chest, looking pleased with himself.

Brand's mouth curved down as he turned to Isabella and drawled, 'Your suitor is obviously a man of imagination. I do see the appeal, of course, but don't you think he's a little old for you, *Belle*?

'Now, listen . . .' Felix began to bend his knees in a boxer's crouch. 'I'll have you know – '

'No,' said Brand. 'I'll have *you* know that Isabella

is still my wife and, as such, *my* responsibility – '

'I am not your responsibility,' Isabella interrupted hotly. 'I'm a grown woman and I'm responsible for myself.'

Just for a second, Brand looked almost nonplussed. Then he laughed softly and said, 'So you are. Sometimes I forget.'

When he turned back to Felix there was a look in his eye that Isabella had only seen there once before – and when she saw a fist begin to bunch at his thigh, she knew it was time to intervene.

'Felix,' she said. 'I'm sorry. It was sweet of you to come, and I *am* pleased to see you again, but – it's not going to work for us, you see. I know I said I'd think about it, but at the time I didn't realize – '

'You mean you're scared stiff of the Cro-magnon man, here. That's what this is all about, isn't it?' Felix's jeering response took her by surprise. 'Well, let me tell you, missy – '

'No need,' Brand cut in. 'You're wrong. She's not scared. Although she ought to be. And now, Isabella's friend, I think you should listen to the lady and get out.'

'What, and leave her alone with you? I most certainly will not get out. You can't – '

'He can,' said Isabella, remembering all too vividly the sight of Gary's rather presentable backside hurtling through the door of their old apartment. 'You'd better go, Felix. I'm sorry, truly I am. And I – that is,

262

I do hope you'll find someone – someone who . . .'
She fumbled for the right words with which to tell
Felix she wished him happiness with somebody else.

Brand took a step towards the other man. Isabella
immediately stepped between them. No way did she
mean to tolerate masculine pugilism in her living
room. Her body sagged with relief when, after a
moment's hesitation, Felix shrugged and said dis-
agreeably, 'OK, if that's how you feel, Belle, I'll leave
you to the caveman here. Annie Belinda will be glad
to have me back.'

With that parting shot he made his way past a
glacial-looking Brand, opened the door, and
slammed it so hard behind him that Isabella's five
framed prints of her sisters' weddings began to dance
a cha-cha-cha on the wall.

'Annie Belinda?' she muttered, staring after him.
'Annie Belinda!' Had Felix been keeping another
woman as back-up all along? In case his first choice
didn't work out, perhaps?

'He's been seeing Annie Belinda,' she said out
loud, still too startled to think straight. 'She was
Mr Brownson-Wing's secretary – '

'And you,' Brand interrupted grimly, 'are seeing
me. Couldn't you do better than that, *Belle*?'

Someone on the TV fired a gun. Isabella started.
Why did she always find herself taking deep breaths
around Brand?

As soon as she turned to face him she had her

answer. He looked magnificent. With the grey wool stretched across his chest and the firm line of his thighs moulded by dark, perfectly cut trousers, he could have been some pagan god descended from Olympus to cause trouble. His eyes, deep shafts of velvet fire, were mysterious and mythical too.

But the steam she could all but see emerging from his ears was entirely mortal.

'Better than what?' she asked.

'Than that ageing old goat with the leer.'

'He's only forty-one. And he's not a goat.' She moistened her lips. 'Brand, what are you doing here? I said in my note – '

'You said in your note – quite graphically – that you couldn't see yourself in the role of temporary *mistress* of Marshlands.'

'Yes. I mean no. No, I couldn't.'

'I see. And so you decided to finish what you'd started with Felix?' He spoke as if something sharp had unaccountably lodged in his throat.

'I never started anything with Felix.' Isabella stepped back from him and reached for the support of a chair. She began to talk much too fast.

'He – Felix – was a client of mine back in Edmonton. He works for an oil company and I met him through the Brownson-Wings. Then I catered a party for him and met his children. He's a widower. They're very wild, but I managed to keep them in order and out of the kitchen. More or less.

Felix noticed, and started asking me over to his house. He said the children liked me. After that he took me out a few times. But when he asked me if I would get a divorce so I could marry him, I – well, I couldn't believe it. We hardly knew each other – '

Brand held up a peremptory hand. 'As I remember, that didn't trouble you much when you married *me*.' He flung himself onto the sofa and waved at the tweed chair she was clinging to like an insecure octopus. 'Sit down.'

Warily, Isabella released her hold and sat.

'So,' Brand said without inflection. 'You hardly knew each other. I suppose that shouldn't surprise me.'

Isabella frowned. 'Why not?'

'Well, it's nothing new, is it? Apparently you still go around kissing strangers.'

'Oh!' It was as if he'd kicked her in the ribs. She had no breath to respond so she closed her eyes, and after a while the sickness passed. When she opened them again, it was only to be overwhelmed by a swift and appalling sense of *déjà vu*.

'I did not kiss Felix,' she said. 'He kissed me.' She clenched her fingers round the arm of the chair so she wouldn't be tempted to throw herself at Brand in a blind fury. 'It's the same old story, isn't it? You ignore me, treat me as if I only exist when it happens to suit you, and then when someone else so much as looks at me you act as though I've committed high treason.'

'*Looks* at you? I'm familiar with that lipstick of yours, you know. It tastes like – ' Brand broke off and brushed the back of his hand across his eyes. 'Isabella, I'm not a fool,' he finished in a flatter, less cuttingly hard-edged tone.

'I know you're not.' She pushed herself to her feet, unable to sit still under his unfair accusations any longer. 'Brand, I told you, Felix kissed *me*, not the other way around. And he asked me to be his wife, not a housekeeper with duties on the side.' She tossed her head. 'In any case why should you care? It's not as though you love me, is it? You never did.'

Brand's face went very still. His eyes were alive, though, and briefly she thought she saw in them uncertainty – and something else she couldn't interpret. 'Didn't I?' he asked.

Isabella gripped her hands at her waist. 'Why did you come here?' Her voice was so low she could scarcely hear it herself.

Brand was a long time answering. 'I read your note,' he said finally, not looking at her but staring at a point above her head. 'It got me thinking.'

'Thinking – about what?'

'About us. About you and me, Isabella. And Connie too.'

'What about Connie?' Isabella was immediately on the defensive.

'I want her to live with me.'

'No! I won't – '

266

'Wait.' Brand held up his hand. His features were still carved in granite, but she had an idea he was having a struggle to keep them that way. 'I also had to face the fact that there are other things I want besides Connie – want so badly I can't sleep at night.'

He waited for her to respond. When she didn't, he said harshly, 'I'm tired of sleeping alone, Isabella.'

Isabella still said nothing, because there didn't seem to be anything to say. At least nothing that wouldn't come out as a howl of near-hysterical laughter.

Brand threw her a sharp glance, then went on, almost as if were discussing his grocery list. 'You had reservations about a temporary arrangement, and I don't altogether blame you. I wasn't thinking clearly. I often don't around you.' He smiled obliquely and strummed his fingers abstractedly on a cushion. 'But you *are* my wife, Isabella. I've noticed you don't find me repulsive, and I came to the conclusion that if you could see your way clear to reserving that charmingly sexy body for your husband, I was, God help me, going to ask you to come back to my bed. On a permanent basis.'

Isabella twisted the ring on her finger. She felt numb. Unable to react. Brand had said he *was* going to ask her to come back. But then he'd come here and found her with Felix . . .

It couldn't make any difference, but she had to know.

'And now?' she asked. 'What is it you want of me now, Brand?'

His answer was a long time coming. 'I suppose,' he said at last, in a voice as neutral as tofu, 'that nothing has changed radically. I still want you.'

Isabella stared at him, curiosity slowly replacing her self-protective lethargy. Did he mean it? He sounded as if he did but wished he didn't. And his eyes reflected the strangest combination of hunger and reluctance she had ever seen.

That was when she realized that the man lounging on her sofa had become a total stranger – just as he had been on that other fateful night. She took in the carved set of his jaw, the easy sprawl of his long body. Could he really have spoken the words she had just imagined coming from his lips? Had he, in all seriousness, but casually and a little grudgingly, invited her to sign on as his bed-warmer?

No. She couldn't, *wouldn't* believe it.

'What did you say?' she asked shakily.

'I said I wanted you back in my bed. I'm talking about a marriage, Isabella. A real one. Not just playing house, as we did before.' He spoke roughly, but beneath the blunt words she detected a note of unease, or perhaps anger. It was as if he was being compelled to speak against his will.

Dazed, Isabella shook her head. So she *hadn't* been hearing things. She fixed her gaze, not on Brand's face, but on the thick hair falling across his forehead.

His appearance wasn't as businesslike as usual – but, oh, heaven help her, it was twice as sexy.

She knew she would have to answer him. But now he was leaning back, crossing his legs as casually as if he had invited her out on a date.

In the end, all she managed was a doubtful, 'Oh.'

Brand linked his hands behind his head. "'Oh' isn't much of an answer,' he pointed out.

A raucous laugh came from the TV set, bringing Isabella out of her disbelieving trance. Brand was serious. He meant exactly what he said.

'It wasn't much of a question,' she said, not looking at him, but at a drop of dried blood where she'd pricked her finger.

'Meaning?'

She raised her head. His gaze was guarded, watchful.

'Meaning that I'm not interested in the current vacancy in your bed.' She made her voice firm and bitingly clear. 'I already have a job, thank you.'

'I'm not asking you to give up your damn job.'

'No. Just my self-respect.'

'Your wh – ?' Brand caught back his words. She could see the veins standing out in his neck. 'Are you trying to tell me that sharing my bed again *would* be repulsive to you? That wasn't the impression I had – '

'No. Not repulsive.' She stared at the grey wool clinging to his chest, watched it rise and fall with his breathing. Illogically, she longed to bend down to stroke its softness.

Oh, no, making love to Brand wouldn't be repulsive. It was what she wanted more than anything else. But surely Mairead had been right. He only wanted her now because she'd turned him down. To him she would always be the devious little temptress he had felt obliged to marry in a strange land. Not a woman truly worthy of being his wife. That honour had been reserved for the sweet and spineless Mary. But now that the choice was no longer his, he had discovered he wanted Isabella back . . .

'Isabella? I hate to interrupt your musings, but is it too much to ask for a reply? Or are you dreaming of the dear departed Felix?' Brand's sarcastic rasp cracked across her thoughts.

Isabella jumped and glanced at him quickly, hoping for some sign that he was joking. She saw at once that he wasn't, so she shook her head and collapsed slowly back into her chair. 'No, Brand. I can't live with you again. Not on those terms.'

'What terms, then?'

As if they were negotiating the price of a prime piece of real estate. Or a prize cow. Isabella tugged at the sleeve of her heavy black sweater, stretching it mindlessly over her knuckles. 'I mean,' she said, staring at a worn patch on her jeans, 'that I can't live with a man who doesn't – care for me. Who only wants me as a body in his bed – '

Brand made an impatient movement with his head. 'I want you for more than that.'

'Yes, as Connie's mother, perhaps. And as someone to run your house and be your hostess.'

'You expect more than that? You weren't so particular when I married you.' He was looking at her as if she were asking for the moon, with Venus and Neptune thrown in. And yet – there was something, a kind of baffled frustration . . .

Isabella sighed. It meant nothing. Brand didn't really care – didn't even particularly like her. 'No. I don't expect more. But I was a child when you married me, Brand. A naïve child. I thought . . .' She took a long breath. 'I thought I could make you love me.'

There. She had admitted it. So much for dignity and pride. She lifted her chin defiantly.

Brand was watching her, but his eyes were hooded and she couldn't tell what he was thinking. After a while she went on in a flat, unemotional tone, 'I know now that won't happen. Because I no longer believe I can make you trust me. And without trust – how can there ever be love?'

'What reason have you given me to trust you? You want it all, don't you, Isabella?' Brand's voice vibrating across the room was low, gravelly, giving her no hint that she had ever touched his heart.

She closed her eyes so she wouldn't have to see the scorn she was certain would be written all over his

271

face. When she opened them again he was standing up, and on the television a moon-faced cowboy was wailing a lament for lost love. As usual, Brand's body seemed much too big for the small room.

'Yes.' She kept her voice level with a superhuman effort. 'Yes, I want it all, Brand.'

'Well, you're not going to get it,' he said, almost conversationally. 'You ask too much of me, Isabella.'

She didn't answer, but went on gazing at the point where his belt buckle bulged slightly beneath his sweater. The next thing she knew, his hands had closed over her wrists.

'What's this?' he asked, his voice suddenly distorted, as if there was some further obstruction in his throat.

'What's – oh.' She followed the direction of his eyes and saw that he was staring at the silver bracelet she had forgotten she was wearing.

'It's the one you gave me,' she said, swallowing. 'I know I shouldn't have kept it, but – '

'Why not? It's yours. Not that it's worth anything.' He had his voice under control, and now it merely sounded harsh.

'That isn't why I kept it. Not for the money.'

'Why, then?'

Isabella tried to look away but he wouldn't let her, trapping her chin firmly between his fingers.

'Why, Isabella? Why did you keep my peace offering?'

'Perhaps because I wanted peace?' she suggested.

He shook his head. 'Tell me the real reason.'

She didn't want to tell him the real reason. It would be one more arrow in his belt. Besides, she was fairly sure he already knew the answer. 'I never wore it until today,' she replied evasively. 'I'm sorry. Here.' Her hand went to her wrist, but Brand caught it before she could pull the bracelet off.

'I don't want it back,' he said gruffly. 'What would I do with a bracelet?'

'I don't know.' She smiled nervously. His hands were on her arms again and he was pulling her onto her feet. 'Wh – what are you doing? I don't want – '

'What don't you want?' He slipped a warm hand under her sweater, then over the flimsy fabric covering her breasts. 'Me?'

'I – ' She couldn't say it, couldn't pretend she didn't want him when his hips were moving against hers and his hands were playing her body like a harp.

'Well?' He held her away, and she longed for him to take her back into the shelter of his arms.

'Of course I want you,' she said. 'Surely you've always known that?'

'To be honest, my lovely Isabella, I've never been sure of anything about you.' He put his hands on her shoulders, and added with an unexpected and disturbingly crooked smile, 'Never mind. Now that we've established our mutual lust, I'm sure we can come up with something to meet our needs.' His tone was flippant, teasing, but his thumbs were pressing into her flesh, and she wondered, briefly, if there was a chance she might matter to him more than he wanted her to know.

Even so, she shook her head. She had to. 'No, I don't think we can. You see, to me, you're not just an itch that will go away the moment I give it a good scratch.'

Brand's eyebrows shot up, and to further confuse her he laughed. 'An itch? Isabella, I promise you I've never thought of you as an itch. As you say, itches eventually go away.' His lips twitched. 'You seem not to.'

'I did. For five years.'

'So you did.' He wasn't laughing any more. 'But you were always there under my skin.'

Like a burr, Isabella thought glumly. She tried to pull away, but he only tightened his grip and dragged her into his arms.

When his lips were almost touching her hair, he said meaningfully, 'Isabella, I mean to do a lot more than scratch you. And I mean you to do a lot more to me. So – '

'I don't doubt it,' she interrupted, swallowing hard in order to suppress a host of deliciously erotic imaginings. 'But I can't, Brand. I can't do what you want.'

He wound his hand through her hair, tilting her head back so she couldn't look away. 'Can't you?' he asked softly. 'We'll see.' He let her go then, looking her up and down as if he had never truly seen her before. 'All right. We'll leave it at that for the moment, then. I'll be in touch shortly about my daughter. Who, in case it hasn't occurred to you, would benefit enormously from a home with both a mother and a father in it.'

Oh. Of course that was what this was really all about. Connie. How could she, for one moment, have thought anything else? And he wasn't going to give up.

Isabella felt a sharp stab of fear.

Brand gave her a small, grim smile, and started to leave. Then he changed his mind and she watched his lithe body swing towards her. 'Before I go, maybe I should leave you something to think about,' he suggested.

'What do you mean?' She didn't trust that glitter in his eye.

'I mean this,' he replied, and scooped her back into his arms.

She was still gazing up at him with her mouth open when he closed it with a deep, hungry kiss.

Isabella didn't even try to escape. She didn't want to. Because although she knew in her heart that Brand was only exacting the payment he believed she owed him, the old, sensuous languor had immediately invaded her body, weakening her power to resist. So she returned his kiss, giving love where he delivered judgement, tenderness where he looked for retribution – and in the end his mouth softened, became warm and tender against her own. When he released her, it was with an oath and a low groan.

She stood in the centre of the floor, scarcely breathing, with both fists pressed against her heart. Then, as in a dream, she saw Brand move away, cross the room, and pause for a moment to rest his hands on the doorframe. He bowed his head and, as she watched in bewilderment, thumped it twice against the painted brown panels. But he said nothing further, and a few seconds later he was gone.

For a while Isabella remained frozen as a sculpture made of ice, staring at the door as if Brand still stood there. But eventually warmth began to creep back into her limbs. She touched her lips. The lips that Brand had claimed, telling her he would leave her with something to think about. As if she needed any reminder to think about her husband. And *why* had he kissed her? He was ruthless in business, she knew, but it wasn't like him to inflict hurt for no reason.

She put her hands over her face and flopped down onto the corner of the sofa where Brand had sat. It still held the heat of his body. She wondered if she was going to cry, but in the end she didn't. The tears wouldn't come. And anyway what was the sense in crying? She could have chosen Brand and a loveless marriage. Instead she had elected to carry on as she had done for the past five years, without a partner, but with a daughter who brought joy and laughter to her life. And if she had to fight Brand for Connie as he had hinted – well, she had always been a fighter. She would find a way to survive.

Isabella gave a little nod to convince herself, then picked up a pair of scissors and began methodically to repair the damage to her blouse. When that was done she turned to the TV. On the screen a young couple were embracing madly on a jade-green carpet. She watched them for a moment, then snapped the set off and went to get ready for bed.

The sheets felt cold, and as she lay there, sleepless, waiting for her body to warm them, she went over Brand's impossible offer again and again. It was like an endless disc revolving in her head.

Should she, could she change her mind?

No. She had made her bed – in more ways than one – and she would never again live with a man who didn't love her.

Not even if that man was Brandon Ryder.

CHAPTER 12

The phone was ringing. Isabella, emerging from the bathroom with a towel wrapped around her hair, hurried to answer it. But as she reached to pick it up somehow she knew instinctively that the caller was Brand, and she handed the receiver to Connie without a word.

She hadn't spoken to Brand in the three days that had passed since she had refused to move into his house, and she wasn't anxious to speak to him now. His kiss had shaken her more than she wanted to admit – and there had been something equally disturbing about the way he had informed her that he would shortly be in touch about Connie.

'Mommy! Daddy wants me to go to Marshlands again next weekend. Can I? Can I, Mommy?' Connie turned to her mother with shining eyes. 'Grandma Mairead's going to be there.'

Isabella's heart sank into her red fuzzy slippers. How could she possibly say no? 'Let me talk to your father,' she replied, accepting the receiver from the bouncing little girl as if it were an unexploded grenade.

'What's the problem?' Brand demanded. 'You want to come with her, I suppose. On your terms.' He sounded exceptionally short-tempered. She imagined him grinding his teeth.

'No,' she said, holding the phone away from her ear. 'The problem is that I *don't* want to come.' She didn't add that she couldn't face the thought of living in close quarters with him again in the house that might have been her home – if only things had been different. Or that she wasn't all that anxious for another encounter with Mairead. She had a feeling her mother-in-law would tell her she was a fool not to accept Brand's offer of a marriage of sexual convenience. Because sex, Mairead was certain to say, could lead to love. Except that in this case it wouldn't.

'Well?' Dimly she was aware that Brand was asking her a question.

'Yes,' she replied. 'Yes, all right. I suppose Connie can go to you on her own. She's used to Marshlands now, and as long as your mother will be there – '

'Fine,' Brand interrupted. 'I have an early meeting on Saturday. So if it's not too much trouble, perhaps you can bring her out to the house.'

'No, I . . .' She stopped. There was no reason she couldn't oblige Brand. But she didn't want to go to Marshlands. Didn't, if the truth were told, want to face Mairead at this time. But the truth wasn't going to be told.

'I can meet you somewhere, if you like,' she said. 'In the mall, perhaps.'

Brand heaved an exasperated sigh. 'All right. But let's say Minoru Lakes, around ten. I'll pick Connie up there when I'm through. Better for her than hanging around the mall, and you ought to be able to find it without getting lost. OK?'

It wasn't OK – the mall would be closer – but he made it sound as though she was an imbecile who wouldn't be able to find the buttons on her coat. So, just to show him, she said, 'Yes.'

On Saturday, as she happened to have an excellent sense of direction, they arrived at the lakes at ten o'clock on the nose. Brand was nowhere in sight.

Isabella smiled smugly at a heron perched atop a willow tree on an island in the larger of the two man-made lakes.

'Look, Mommy. Ducks,' Connie cried, running to the edge of the water. 'And – and – '

'Pigeons,' said Isabella, as a swarm of the rainbow-breasted birds landed at her feet.

But Connie was off again, running along the paved walkway that wound its way around the lakes, in pursuit of a quacking procession of mallards. Isabella hurried after her, wishing she could stop to enjoy the fresh, spring-green smell of the trees and shrubs.

'You mustn't bother the ducks,' she called. 'Connie, look at the waterfall.'

'Waterfall?' Connie was temporarily distracted from the birdlife.

'Over there.' Isabella pointed to curtain of emerald-coloured water cascading like mermaid's hair down a wall of rocks at the far end of the nearest lake.

'Oh, it's pretty. So are those purple flowers growing in the grass. What are they?'

'Crocuses. They're called crocuses.'

There had been a crocus in the grass the day Brand had brought her to their first and only home. He had pointed it out especially to cheer her. Isabella brushed a hand over her eyes. When she lowered it, Connie was already on her way across the wooden bridge separating the two sheets of water.

'Watch out!' Isabella shouted, as the eager little girl hurled herself after another feathered procession waddling in step towards the water. 'Connie, you'll fall in – '

She was too late. Connie, practically bursting with excitement, was intent on catching up with the ducks, who were launching themselves into the lake with a cacophony of indignant quacks and splashes.

At the last moment Connie remembered she wasn't a duck and frantically tried to pull back. But she couldn't stop. Her momentum carried her right to the edge of the lake, and as she began a relentless slide down the rocky bank, still fighting to maintain her balance, she let out a small, frightened scream.

Isabella, practically flying off the end of the bridge, made a grab for her daughter and missed. Fear that she couldn't allow to turn into panic froze her body for less than a second. Then she was kicking off her shoes, flinging herself forward, reaching out for Connie's padded jacket. But, unbelievably, as she teetered on the bank a man's arm shot out of nowhere from behind her, and a black leather driving glove closed around Connie's pink collar and held on. Small feet scrabbled to a stop just inches above the water.

Isabella, gasping, started to turn around, but her balance was already precarious and she lost her footing. Flinging up her arms, she too began to slide over the edge.

Connie was safe. That was all that mattered. She closed her eyes, waiting for the shock of cold water to steal her breath.

But instead something brushed against her neck. Then a masculine arm closed around her waist, and somehow she was back on the path.

The arm stayed there briefly, strong and comforting, before its owner turned to Connie and said sternly, 'Watch what you're doing, young lady. What do you think Grandma will say if I bring you home looking like something uliginous picked up by the cat? And as for you, Mrs Ryder – '

Brand. She might have known. 'I was trying to

catch her,' Isabella said, annoyed to find herself shivering now that the crisis was over.

'I know. Nice try. You'd have had her if I hadn't beaten you to it.'

Isabella couldn't believe her ears. Surely that wasn't amused admiration she'd heard in the voice that so often lately had been filled with recrimination? And his eyes – why, they were almost, but not quite, smiling.

In spite of her determination not to give Brand an inch, Isabella caught herself smiling too.

'Daddy,' said Connie, frowning, 'you don't have a cat. And what's – what's ul – uliginous?'

'Growing in muddy and swampy places. Which would have described you nicely if I hadn't caught you. Now see here, Miss Ryder – '

But Connie wasn't listening. Instead her big dark eyes were fixed on a fluffy white puffball nestled in an inside pocket of Brand's jacket. When the puffball started to squirm, and extended a black button nose, she let out a howl of delight that caused a passing and presumably deaf old gentleman to smile benignly, and his female companion to wince.

'You've got a puppy!' she cried. 'Oh, he's so cute. Daddy, is he for me? Is he really?'

Isabella's heart sank, and she felt a familiar urge to give a Brand a good hard kick. Not that it was entirely his fault. She had meant to tell him a dog was impossible the first time the subject came up. But she hadn't done so because so much had happened that day, and she'd been distracted. Just the same, he should have asked her first . . .

'Yes, he's for you,' she heard him telling Connie. 'Provided you give me a rock-bound promise that you won't go jumping into any more lakes.'

'Oh, I won't, I won't,' Connie assured him. 'Daddy, what's his name?'

'He doesn't have one yet. He's just a baby.' Brand bent over to put the little dog down on the path. 'You're his mother now, so you get to name him.'

'Fluffy, of course. Because he is,' said Connie.

'Brand.' Isabella finally managed to get a word in. 'Brand, we have to talk about this – '

'Oh, Mommy, don't say we can't keep him. We *have* to keep him.' Connie knelt down on the path and buried her face in the puppy's fur.

'Why don't you go and play with him on the grass,' Brand suggested, after a quick look at Isabella's stricken face. 'Your mother and I will work something out.'

'OK.' Connie threw him a look of worshipful adoration that made Isabella's insides go cold. How could she compete with a father who came bearing puppies, who owned a big house with a garden fit for a fairy princess? Did Brand have any idea what he was doing?

Yes, of course he did. Brand always knew what he was doing. It was one of his most irritating traits. She glanced up at him, shivering a little in the chilly spring air. But he was watching Connie trot across to the grass.

As soon as she was out of earshot, but not out of sight, Brand turned to Isabella and drawled, 'Is there some problem, my dear? You look as though you'd like to grind me up with plenty of salt and onions and stuff me into one of your excellent fish pies.'

'Oh, I wouldn't go that far. But I would like to knock some sense into your head.'

'That used to be my line,' Brand observed. 'You can't use it.'

'Brand,' Isabella said warningly as she slipped into her cold shoes and planted her hands on her hips, 'you should have checked with me first about the dog. Do you have any idea what you've just done?'

'As far as I know,' said Brand, taking her arm and marching her onto the bridge, 'I have just rescued my daughter from a dunking and given her a dog which I'm not sure she deserves.'

'It doesn't matter whether she deserves it or not. She can't keep it.' Isabella tugged her hand away and clenched her fist on the rail.

'Of course she can. Don't be obstructive.'

'I'm not being – obstructive . . .' She hesitated. 'At least, I'm not if by that you mean unfair and unreasonable.'

'Something like that,' admitted Brand. 'So tell me why it's fair and reasonable to deprive our daughter of a dog she so obviously wants. Caring for a pet will help to teach her responsibility.'

'Maybe. But Connie has always understood she can't have everything she wants, Brand. You'll do her no favours by letting her think she can.'

'I agree. She can, however, have a dog. In fact she has one.'

'*Brand!* Don't you understand?' Isabella dug her nails into her palms through the practical black wool of her gloves. 'I've already asked my landlord. He said, 'No pets.' Besides, I have a business to run. It wouldn't be fair to the dog.'

'Oh?' Brand settled himself beside her and rested his elbows on the rail. 'If that's the case, may I ask where you find the time to fit in a child?'

Isabella clamped her teeth down on her lip. I will not stamp my feet, she told herself. I will *not* stamp my feet. I couldn't anyway. They're frozen stiff. She counted to twenty. In English. Then started all over again in Spanish. By the time she was through she had herself under control.

'Connie is in kindergarten in the afternoons,' she explained, slowly and carefully, as if she were talking to a child. 'In the evenings, if I'm out, there's Edwina. But I can't expect Edwina to take care of a new dog as well.' When Brand continued to look at her as if he didn't believe a word she was saying, she added furiously, 'What difference does it make? We're not allowed to keep dogs in our building.'

'There's an easy solution to that, you know.' His eyes were suddenly very bright and hard. And this time Isabella knew exactly what he meant.

'No,' she said. 'I am not moving in with you.' She stood up straight, trying to give herself courage, but a sudden gust of wind made her flinch.

'I forgot,' said Brand, very softly. 'You're the lady who wants to have it all.'

Isabella swallowed. His voice, the way he was standing – all coiled strength against the backdrop of the bridge – and his eyes, appraising her with heavy-lidded cynicism, all contrived to send her an all too familiar message.

Brand wanted her as much as she wanted him. But he didn't like her.

'That's right,' she agreed, forcing a lightness into her voice she couldn't feel. 'But, just like Connie, I've always known I can't expect to get it.' To her annoyance, she began to shiver again.

'Ah, yes. Connie.' Brand gestured at the little girl who was running with Fluffy across the grass at a suitably safe distance from the lake. 'I get the feeling you're telling me she'll have to settle for a weekend-only dog. For the time being.'

'A weekend-only dog?'

'Mmm Mrs Crackitt, my new housekeeper, is devoted to dogs. She'll take care of Fluffy. Connie can visit him on weekends.'

'But I don't want – ' She broke off. What could

she say? That she didn't want Connie to spend every weekend at Marshlands getting used to its luxuries, and eventually learning to resent the time she had to spend at home with her mother?

Brand's answer to that, she knew, would be to repeat that there was a simple solution.

But his solution was anything but simple. She couldn't, *wouldn't* give up her independence for the dubious privilege of sharing her husband's bed. Not when she could never have his heart.

'I suppose,' she said doubtfully, 'that Connie could visit Marshlands once a month – ' She broke off again as all of a sudden the heron she had seen earlier left its perch in the willow tree and plunged towards the lake. When it surfaced, a plump silver carp was wriggling in its beak.

Isabella glanced at Brand. She had considerable sympathy for that carp. They had a lot in common.

Brand caught her look, but his mind was still on his daughter. 'Who would have thought it,' he said.

'Thought what?'

'That the helpless young girl who couldn't cope with a baby would turn into such a single-minded mother. Did you know maternity suits you?'

'Does it?' Why was he looking at her like that? His lips were smiling, but his eyes were flat.

'Yes.' Abruptly Brand turned away to watch the heron, which sat looking sated and a little bilious in its tree. 'What happened to Judy? Have you seen her since you came back to Vancouver?'

Oh. So he wanted to change the subject she hadn't brought up.

'No,' she said. 'Believe it or not, Judy moved to Calgary with her new husband just the week before I came back to Vancouver. I found out from her mother.'

'Ah. But you have other friends, I suppose?'

Isabella wanted to reply, Only you. But Brand wasn't a friend. He was the husband who wanted her daughter.

'No,' she said shortly. 'Not really. Brand, about the dog – '

'Yes. The dog. Do you think visiting Fluffy once a month will be enough to satisfy Connie?' It was almost as if he'd read her mind.

No, it wouldn't satisfy Connie. But it was the best she could do. Damn him anyway. He must have known exactly what would happen once he gave his daughter that dog.

'It will have to, won't it?' she said evenly. 'And, Brand, if you're trying to take Connie away from me, I promise you it's not going to work.'

'No?' He turned from her and propped a booted foot on the lower rail. 'But maybe that was never my intention.'

'Then what *was* your intention?'

'I thought I made myself clear. I don't just want

Connie, Isabella.' He paused to brush a leaf off his sleeve. 'You see, I too would like to have it all.'

His voice was low, gentle, dangerous – and the line of his jaw was about as yielding as pre-Cambrian rock. Isabella closed her eyes, because even now, when he was all hard angles, black leather and stern profile, she longed to put her arms around his neck.

'You don't want it all,' she retorted. 'All you want is a warm body in your bed.'

Briefly Brand's lips flattened. Then gradually they parted in what looked like the glimmer of a smile. 'You mean there's more?' he asked.

He knew there was more. Isabella studied him out of the corner of her eye, confused by the quick change of mood. He was staring down at the water rippling over the rocks, and studiously pretending to ignore her. But there was no doubt about it. That was a smug attempt at a smile she saw tugging at the edges of his mouth.

'Yes,' she said. 'I've been led to believe there's a lot more. What do you think?'

'Most of the time I try not to.'

Isabella could tell that wasn't true. The lines of the battle he was waging with himself were chasing each other back and forth across his face. Then all at once he seemed to come to a decision.

Abruptly he swung around, put his hands on her upper arms and shifted her up against the rail.

At first Isabella was too startled to do more than

blink. Then her voice came back. 'What do you think you're – '

'Figuratively speaking, I'm trying to back you up against a wall. Isabella, I have a reception I have to attend a week from Saturday. It's to be followed by a dinner and dance. I want you to come as my partner.'

'Partner?' Her eyes widened and she gazed at him in alarm. Was this a spur-of-the-moment invitation, or the next move in a carefully planned campaign?

'Wife, then,' he amended offhandedly. 'As a member of the board – it's a fund-raiser for the Children's Health Foundation – I'm expected to attend with my spouse. Last time I looked, that was you.'

'But – '

'Of course,' he added with a shrug, 'if you'd rather not, I can always ask Veronica to fill in. We had quite a talk the morning she left. There were no ill feelings. I'm sure she'll be glad to help out.'

Bastard, Isabella thought, catching the smirk he made no effort to conceal. But he was still holding her, and the inevitable warmth was steaming through her veins. He knew he had her backed against the wall – well, the bridge anyway – and that even though she didn't want to go to his reception she wouldn't be able to bear the thought of his attending with Veronica. She had given too much away that night at Marshlands.

It made no difference. She still had no choice but to refuse him.

She opened her mouth to say no, but heard herself saying instead, 'All right. I'll check my bookings, but I think I do happen to have that evening free. If I have, I'll go with you.'

When his eyes started to gleam, she added with a nonchalant shrug, 'After all, it is for a good cause.'

Brand's smile was Cheshire Cat smug. 'Oh, I'm a very good cause,' he agreed, releasing his hold and lounging back against the railing.

'I didn't mean *you*,' Isabella exclaimed. When she saw that he was laughing at her she looked around for Connie, who was sitting demurely on a bench hugging Fluffy. 'I have to go,' she told him stiffly. 'I'll just say goodbye to Connie, and – '

'No. First of all say goodbye to me.' He caught her wrist and held onto it.

'Goodbye, then,' she said, staring at the rare lines of humour around his mouth.

Brand shook his head. 'Properly. Kiss me.' He held his arms wide.

Isabella frowned. This was a Brand she didn't know. Bossy, arrogant, yet teasing in a hard sort of way. What was he trying to prove? That she didn't matter to him? Well, she knew that already. Just the same . . .

'Oh, very well,' she exclaimed. He looked so delectable standing there, with his jacket open to expose the dark green sweater stretched across his ribcage, that she found herself unable to resist him –

unable to resist the pleasure of once again being held in his arms.

With a sigh of resignation she walked into them. And with what might have been an answering sigh, or a groan of exasperation, she was immediately dragged against his chest. She lifted her chin and, standing on tiptoe, gave him a quick kiss on the cheek.

She'd half expected – half hoped? – that he would demand more. But he didn't. Instead he nodded and let her go at once. A small, indecipherable smile played at the edges of his mouth.

She backed away from him, hugging her arms to her chest and wishing she could tell what he was thinking. When she reached the end of the bridge she stumbled and almost fell.

Brand eyed her sardonically. 'You already have my attention,' he assured her. 'As for the ducks – they aren't likely to relish the competition if you were thinking of going for a swim.'

Isabella glared. Did he really imagine she had stumbled on purpose, in a bid to attract his attention? Just because, in the old days, it was exactly the sort of trick she might have pulled . . .

He responded to her glare with a grin so complacent it continued to irritate her all the way home.

The two days of the weekend seemed longer than usual, and lonely, and when Brand brought Connie back on Sunday night Isabella looked at him as if he'd brought her a priceless gift. As indeed, in a way, he had.

To her surprise he turned his head away, and she saw him clench his jaw as if he was in some kind of pain.

'Toothache?' she asked sympathetically.

He swung round to glare at her as if she had suggested he had fleas.

'I promised Fluffy I'd go back to visit him next weekend,' Connie announced, happily oblivious to the undercurrents seething around her.

'Oh. Did you, darling?' Isabella was horrified to find herself gulping back a sob.

Brand eyed her shrewdly but said nothing. A few minutes later he left.

As the week progressed Connie became more and more excited about the coming weekend, and Isabella, trying hard to suppress her hurt, knew that the lure of Marshlands and Fluffy was beginning to do Brand's work for him. She didn't have the heart to suggest that Connie should spend the weekend at home.

Early on Saturday morning Brand arrived to collect his small daughter, who was flitting about the room like a bee in rose bush. Without a word, he handed a long, flat box to Isabella and took Connie firmly by the hand. He refused to come in, and was at the door for less than a minute.

Isabella, feeling horribly bereft, trailed over to the kitchen counter to open the box.

Under layers of tissue paper lay a beautiful flame-red dress. It had a long, flounced skirt, cap sleeves and a deep, revealing vee at the front. She went into the bedroom to hold it up against her chest. In the long mirror behind the door it made her look striking and exciting, like some wild and exotic gypsy dancer. Was that how Brand saw her? As some wild and ungovernable wanton that it would be his privilege to tame? Ever since she had come back into his life there had been something strange and unfamiliar about Brand. It wasn't as if he wanted to hurt her exactly – that wasn't his way – but as if he had some purpose that he wasn't entirely sure of himself. Could the dress be part of that purpose?

She pirouetted in front of the mirror, watching the bright folds swirl and change colour in the light. It was truly a beautiful dress. But could she – should she – accept it? Brand was her husband. She had agreed to go to the reception and she certainly had nothing formal to wear. But . . .'

'But nothing,' said her reflection as she pirouetted again. 'Maybe you can't have his love. But that's no reason to turn down a magnificent dress that he's chosen specially for you. At least he remembered your size. And besides – it means he wants you to be beautiful just for him.'

Yes. In this dress anything had to be possible . . .

That night she went to bed burning with an excitement quite different from the dreary emptiness she had known the week before. Yes, of course anything was possible, if you hoped enough. And she had never quite given up hope.

The following Saturday, Isabella, wearing the dress and with a bright red carnation in her hair, was in the living room with Connie and Edwina when Brand's distinctive knock sounded on the door.

She was expecting it, but she jumped anyway.

'I'll get it,' said Connie, a little sulkily. She was still pouting because she hadn't been allowed to visit Fluffy this weekend. Isabella had tried to explain that Mrs Crackitt had the flu, but Connie, still not entirely sure of the father she had so recently met, considered that a very poor excuse.

The moment she opened the door Brand picked her up and gave her a hug, so it was several seconds before he noticed Isabella, who had risen gracefully and was standing beside the shabby brown sofa.

'Hello, Brand.' She bent to pick up her wrap. It was only as she straightened that she finally caught sight of his face. 'What's the matter?' she asked quickly. 'Is something wrong?'

Brand shook his head and lowered Connie to the floor. 'No,' he said, so curtly that she winced. 'Nothing's wrong. Shall we go?'

He held out his arm and Isabella moved slowly towards him. As he tucked her hand in his elbow she wondered if Bluebeard's wives had felt this way as they advanced, in fear and excitement, towards their first date with the man who was so briefly to be their husband.

CHAPTER 13

Brand handed Isabella into the waiting limousine and climbed in after her. He could smell the clean fragrance of her hair. Dammit, she had no right to smell so sweet and so desirable when they both knew . . . No, that wasn't true. He had no idea what Isabella knew or didn't know. But she had asked him if something was wrong, and surely to God she had to be aware that he wanted her so much it had become a savage pain in his gut. Wanted her right here, on the limo's supple seat. Wanted to pull her down and tear off that incredible dress that made her look like temptation incarnate – the sexiest woman in the world.

He must have been out of his mind to buy her that dress, Brand thought grimly, glaring at the neat black sandal peeping from under its hem. He had surely known what it would do to him. But then he had always been out of his mind around Isabella – with grief on the night she had first laid her lovely eyes on him and woven the inescapable web that had changed his life.

Not that it was grief he felt now. Far from it. Hell, he could scarcely recall Mary's hair colour, and his most urgent emotion at this moment was a raging agonizing desire – the like of which he hadn't known since that unforgettable night when Connie had been conceived.

He stared at the back of the chauffeur's head and thought of Isabella's smile, that soft, deceptive smile that could melt his bones. Just now, in her apartment, when she had stood up and moved across the room towards him with the dress clinging and swirling around her like dancing flames, he had come perilously close to losing all control. So he had snapped at her. Yet when he'd seen her bewilderment he had regretted even that brief unkindness.

He shifted on the seat so he could look at her. She was pressed into the corner of the limo as far away from him as she could get, and her beautiful dark eyes were wary, as if she thought he might indeed ravish her on the spot. Would she let him if he tried? The first time he had taken her he had been too drunk and too grief-stricken to know what he was doing. The second, too angry. And yet both times she had been a giving little wench. Which was more than he could say of himself. If it happened again – and if it didn't soon he would surely go insane – things would be different. He could promise her that much.

Except that the only promise she seemed to want was the unlikely affirmation of his love.

He let his gaze stray over the outline of her slender figure in the shadowed interior of the car, and involuntarily his lower lip turned down.

Isabella. Beautiful, bewitching Isabella. Every man's fantasy in scarlet. Isabella, who had taught him not to trust.

Briefly, very briefly, he considered turning his fantasy into reality at once, by offering her the promise she said she wanted. The less than honest promise of his love. But he didn't like liars. She had lied to him. He was damned if he would ever lie to her.

'Have I done something?' She broke into his thoughts with a voice that betrayed a nervousness he hadn't anticipated. 'Did you not mean me to wear the dress?'

Brand laughed without much mirth, and hit his forehead with the heel of his hand. 'No,' he said. 'You haven't done anything. Except drive me crazy. And, God help me, I did intend you to wear the dress. That's just the trouble.'

Isabella frowned. 'I don't understand.'

'I think you do. And if, by chance, you don't, you soon will once we get to the reception.'

'What are you talking about, Brand?'

He leaned towards her, pressing his fists into the soft leather of the seat. Good grief, she really was nervous. He *hadn't* imagined that quiver in her voice. And how on earth was he supposed to cope with a nervous Isabella? It was a facet of her personality he hadn't been aware of, certainly hadn't taken into account. She was always so resolute, so admirably assured . . .

'Don't worry, I won't hurt you,' he said gruffly.

She looked surprised. 'I know that. But what did you mean about – about once we get to the reception?'

Ah. So that was it. She was anxious about her first official appearance in public as his wife – or her first at anything more stylish than a pizza parlour or the malt-bar on the corner.

He smiled, feeling an unaccustomed protectiveness towards this beautiful young woman he more frequently caught himself wanting to chastise.

'I meant,' he said softly, 'that every man who sees you will be willing to give his teeth and all but his most crucial body parts in order to change places with me this evening. And that I won't let them.'

'Oh.' He saw her swallow. 'Does that mean you want . . .?' She hesitated, as if searching for words.

'I want you, Isabella. But you already know that.'

She nodded. 'Sometimes I'm not sure. But, yes, I – I know you *want* me.'

Brand heard the small break in her voice and guessed it was because she had asked for a lot more than wanting. Exasperation mingled with the desire he was still struggling to subdue. After all the deceit, all the betrayals, did she honestly imagine . . .?

He looked into her eyes. And saw a vulnerability he hadn't expected. Dear God. What had he done to her, and to himself, by inviting her to come with him tonight? He turned away with an inarticulate murmur of frustration.

Ten minutes later they arrived at the reception, which was being held in the ballroom of a majestic old hotel in the heart of downtown Vancouver. Brand helped Isabella out of the limo and took her hand. She wasn't wearing his bracelet tonight, he noted. But then whatever had made him think she would?

Her hand felt cold and small and defenceless, so he tucked it under his arm.

'It's all right,' he assured her as they climbed the steps. 'You, my lovely wife, are going to be a sensation.'

A sensation? Isabella thought wildly as she handed her wrap to the attendant in the cloakroom. I don't care about being a sensation. I just want to get through the rest of this evening without making a fool of myself. And not in the way Brand thinks either.

She had realized, after a while, that Brand imagined she was nervous about appearing beside him at one of Vancouver's more notable society events. He had obviously forgotten that she had moved in government circles for several years, and was used to catering for people who thought they were more important than they were.

No, she wasn't afraid of society's curiosity and questions. What terrified her was the thought of spending an evening being charming and polite to strangers, and all the while pretending that her relationship with Brand was of the normal, civilized variety – when what she had longed to do from the moment she first saw him this evening was throw herself into his arms and make passionate love to him on the nearest flat surface. It wasn't the first time she had been seized with that particular urge, but in full view of Connie and Edwina . . . She bit her lip. No. That wouldn't have won her any Mother of the Month award.

She heaved a rueful sigh. Did Brand have any conception of how impossibly desirable he looked in his black evening clothes, with that gleaming white shirt setting off the dark bronze of his skin? All she wanted was to touch him, to run her fingers over the deep lines etched into his face – some of which she guessed *she* had put there – to push her hands beneath his shirt, over his back, down to his hips and . . .

'Isabella, stop it at once,' she heard her own voice saying out loud.

The attendant glanced nervously at the phone. Isabella gave the woman a quick, confident smile, as if all the best people went around talking to themselves, and, after checking the flower in her hair, hurried out to find Brand.

He was standing beneath the chandelier in the vestibule, attracting surreptitious feminine attention. Isabella tilted her chin and sailed up to him wearing the most regal smile she could paste onto her face. He took her arm and returned the smile with one of his own. It made her gulp hard and stumble over her feet as she walked beside him into the glittering gold and white ballroom.

They were surrounded almost at once by an eager group of men all claiming Brand's acquaintance and demanding to be introduced to his charming partner. Brand, looking particularly craggy and unapproachable, obliged in a voice as dry as baked sand.

There were only a few raised eyebrows at the news that she was Brandon Ryder's long-lost wife, but Isabella noticed that most of the men seemed to moisten their lips a lot, and hold onto her hand for longer than mere politeness required. She also noticed that the majority of them were accompanied by svelte and sophisticated women in designer dresses, who looked palely green and disconcertingly hostile.

Brand guided her firmly through the throng towards the bar, and handed her a sherry without bothering to ask her what she wanted. After that he began to move her around the room, smoothly performing introductions and at the same time making sure she had no opportunity to stray from his side.

Once a man with a drooping moustache and long sideburns manoeuvred himself into a position where, by resting his elbow on another man's shoulder, he could allow his hand to trail with seeming innocence across Isabella's scarlet breast. Instantly Brand murmured something into Sideburns' ear that made the man turn pasty white and beat a retreat to the far side of the room.

At dinner they were seated at the head table. She saw that most of the board members sat next to other people's wives. Not Brand. When the foundation's chairman tried to shuffle her to the chair next to his, Brand, with a barely perceptible jerk of his head, indicated she was to sit beside him. Isabella did her best to look dignified, but she couldn't quite suppress a grin as she complied. Did he think she was some precious piece of property he couldn't afford to let out of his sight? Or a child who couldn't be trusted to behave? She didn't know whether to be grateful or resentful.

In the end she was neither. Just being next to Brand, feeling the occasional pressure of his thigh and once, when he bent to pick up the napkin she had dropped, his hand on her knee, was all the sensation she could handle. But she managed to smile and make conversation, and look delighted with the endless speeches that came after the meal. She supposed, when a waiter took away her empty plate, that she must also have managed to eat.

'Well done,' Brand whispered into her ear when it was over. 'You didn't fall asleep.' He straightened the carnation in her hair, and after that Isabella couldn't have said whether she was wide awake in a Vancouver ballroom or dreaming in some magical Shangri-La.

When the music started Brand took her elbow and drew her onto the dance floor. It wasn't until she was locked securely in his arms that she realized he hadn't asked her if she wanted to dance, and that it had never occurred to her to do anything but follow.

He held her firmly but correctly, one hard hand on her waist, the other curled not too tightly around her fingers. He was an average dancer, the kind who did what was expected of him with competence and grace but who avoided fancy footwork and show. By the time they had circled the floor twice Isabella was going mad with desire.

Instinctively she tried to press closer. Brand wouldn't let her. 'No,' he said drily. 'I asked you to come as my partner. Not as inspirational copy for the morning papers. Behave yourself, Isabella.'

How dared he? When she knew from the smouldering intensity of his eyes and the tension straining every muscle of his body that he too was aching with need. But then she had sensed from the moment he arrived at her apartment that his control was held in place by only the very finest of threads.

'You don't have to take out your frustrations on me,' she said, not caring much if the thread snapped right here on the dance floor. If it did, then she too could let go.

Brand's nostrils flared. 'Frustrations?' He spun her into a turn. 'What makes you think I'm frustrated?'

She gave him a sugar-coated smile. 'Aren't you?'

'Damn you, Isabella.' The words were a roughly growled caress, and in the same moment the band brought the number to a close. When it started up again with a faster, more overtly erotic beat, Brand led her back to their table.

No sooner were they seated than the ever-hopeful chairman came up to ask her to dance.

She glanced at Brand. The choice was hers, but she had no wish to provoke him further. He nodded curtly, as if he didn't much care, so she smiled and extended her hand. An instant later she was whirled into the eager businessman's arms. *He* had no qualms about holding her indiscreetly close, and soon she was struggling to maintain her distance. But, to her relief, in no time at all another man had cut in.

The relief was short-lived. As the music became louder, steamier, her latest partner jerked her against his chest and dropped his left hand down below her waist. Where it had no business to be – certainly no business to be doing what it was. Isabella opened her mouth to tell him to remove it. But before she could get the words out she felt familiar hands on her waist, and within seconds she had been dragged out of the groper's arms and into Brand's.

'Thank you,' she murmured quickly to her husband, in case he felt inclined to provoke a scene. 'But I think he was only trying to – '

'I know what he was trying to.' Brand's voice was soft and dangerous. 'And, in all honesty, I can't say I blame him.'

Isabella gasped as he slipped his hand over the same forbidden zone. But this time she felt no urge to tell him to remove it. When she swayed her hips voluptuously beneath his touch, she heard him draw in his breath.

Now there was no question of dancing at a civilized distance, and the morning papers were conveniently forgotten. As the music swirled around them, and the other dancers receded into the background, they moved as one, gliding in the direction of the big double doors.

When they reached the vestibule Brand paused with his hand on her hip. 'We're leaving,' he said. His eyes were fixed on hers with such sensuous certainty that she felt as if he'd peeled off all her clothes.

It wasn't a question, but she knew he was waiting

for an answer. 'Yes.' She gave him a quick, almost shy smile.

He inclined his head. 'Fetch your wrap. I'll make our apologies.'

Later, in the limousine, with all her senses still spinning, Isabella asked him faintly, 'What did you tell them? That I had a headache?'

'No. I told the truth. I said I was taking you home to bed.'

'You didn't! Oh, Brand . . .'

'I did, you know. But don't worry.' He patted the handiest part of her, which happened to be her thigh. 'They're under the impression you're pregnant.'

'Oh! How could you? You bas – ' She turned towards him with her hand automatically raised to strike, but he caught it and held it at her side.

'Hold it. Your pregnancy wasn't my idea. I believe the chairman's wife had a lot to do with the rumour. It started the moment she heard you were back in town. Apparently I've been keeping you on ice waiting for just the right moment to produce you.'

'Like a rabbit out of a hat?' Isabella asked disbelievingly.

'A frozen one, presumably.' Brand cast an appreciative eye over her soft curves. 'I'll have to fix that.' He relapsed into a contemplative silence, and when he spoke again again his voice was deeper, husky with meaning. 'I *was* telling the truth, wasn't I? I *am* taking you home to bed.'

Again, it wasn't a question, but again he seemed to expect an answer. And with the part of her brain that still contained the rudiments of sanity she wanted to say, No. No, you're not, Brand. Because if you do, you will surely break my heart. But she said nothing, and when he put both arms around her waist she gave a little cry and leaned towards him.

He laughed softly, opened his coat and drew her up against his chest.

It wasn't until the limo pulled into the driveway at Marshlands that Isabella realized that 'home', to Brand, did not mean her own small apartment.

'Brand, this is Marshlands,' she exclaimed.

'I know. Where did you think we were going?'

'Home. My home. Brand, what about Connie . . .?'

'I've already called Edwina. She's quite happy to keep her for the night. In fact she heartily approves. Unlike my wife . . .' he paused to lift an eloquent black eyebrow '. . . *she* believes married couples should sleep in the same bed. On a regular basis. Come on, out you get.' He eased himself onto the gravel and held out an authoritative hand.

'But . . .'

Brand gave her arm a swift tug and hauled her out of the limo. Then, as she stood nervous and indecisive before him, he curved his fingers round the back of her neck and drew her slowly towards him. When his lips were a bare inch away from hers he moved his

310

free hand around her waist and began, very lightly, to stroke her rear. 'But what?' he whispered against her mouth.

'Nothing.' Her voice was a soft moan in the night. 'Brand, please . . .'

'Yes,' said Brand, and scooped her up in his arms. Isabella didn't hear the limo purr off into the night, didn't hear the frogs in the marsh or the hoot of an owl on the hunt. She was conscious only of the heat of Brand's body, of the feel of his arms holding her tight and of the warm male scent of his desire. Then, a little later, when he dropped her none too gently onto the black quilt covering his bed, she was conscious of a sharp sense of loss. She held out her arms, and Brand, after tossing his jacket over a chair, fell on top of her with a sound that was pure primitive passion. The passion of a man who has waited too long for his woman.

With a glad cry Isabella tangled her fingers in his hair. His mouth moved over her face, across her neck, down to the deep vee between her breasts, making every inch of her come alive.

'Brand,' she gasped, digging her fingers into his back. 'Brand, yes . . .'

'No,' he rasped, and she could feel him fighting for control. 'No, Belleza. This time it has to be for you.' Gently he removed the carnation from her hair.

'But it's all right . . .'

Brand wasn't listening. With steady, exquisite

competence he was stripping off the flame-red dress and then the lacy underclothes that since the day she left him had remained her one self-indulgence. When at last she lay naked beneath him he began to run his fingers over her arching body, as if he were familiar with every inch of it and knew exactly where and how to drive her wild. It was only when he paused briefly to throw off his shirt and trousers that she remembered he hardly knew her at all.

It didn't matter. In moments she was crying out for him to take her, and, with a groan of despairing acquiescence, he did.

Their coming together was not slow and gentle as Brand had planned, bringing Isabella to the peak of a rapture he believed he had denied her in the past. It was wild, savage, a feast of untamed passion after a famine that had lasted five years. And when it was over they were no longer on the bed, but in a tangle of limbs and black satin on the ivory-white carpet.

Brand extricated an arm and propped himself up on one elbow. He looked into the soft warmth shining from Isabella's eyes and ran a finger gently across her cheek. It was smooth and soft and glowing with fulfilment.

'I'm sorry,' he said. 'I meant to take it slow and easy. This time I wanted to do it right.'

'You did,' said Isabella with a voluptuous sigh. 'You did it exactly right. I couldn't have waited for slow and easy.' She touched a hand to the beloved fold in his left ear.

Brand smiled, a tender smile that almost gave her hope. 'Sometimes, Mrs Ryder, you're surprisingly good for a man's ego. All the same, next time we're going to do it my way.'

In the course of the night they did do it Brand's way. Several times. And Isabella was forced to concede that he was right. Wild and crazy was good. Slow and easy was even better.

Finally, in the morning, she fell into an exhausted and deeply contented sleep, too physically sated to think of questioning the future.

When she woke, Mrs Crackitt, looking as pale as her grey dress with the collar that matched her white hair, was standing beside the bed with a tray of coffee. But the place where Brand had lain was empty, and only a faint depression in the pillow showed where he had spent the night.

'Where is Mr Ryder?' Isabella asked, feeling suddenly chilled.

'In the garden, I think. It's a beautiful, sunny morning, Mrs Ryder. You were asleep, and he said he felt restless.' It wasn't a rebuke. Mrs Crackitt was playing the part of reliable and discreet old retainer. And playing it well, in spite of her recent recovery from the flu.

Brand was restless? After last night? Isabella wasn't sure she believed it. The cold feeling spread, and sank into her bones. 'Thank you, Mrs Crackitt.' She managed a smile. 'This is very good coffee. And it was good of you to come back to work so soon.'

Mrs Crackitt left looking pleased, and Isabella leaped up and headed for the shower. The shower that she might have shared with Brand. If he had been here. When she came out of the bathroom wrapped in a towel the first thing she saw was her crumpled scarlet dress. She had no fresh clothes with her, but the dress she had worn to the reception was hardly suitable for a confrontation in the garden.

She opened Brand's walk-in cupboard, ran a swift eye over the contents and pulled a white, fleece-lined sweatshirt off its hanger. Then, after she had hung up the precious dress, she looked hopefully for something that would fit her lower limbs and came up with a pair of denim shorts, which she was able to hold in place with the aid of a safety pin she found on the dresser. Beside it lay the faded carnation. Isabella picked it up, sighed, and laid it carefully beside a pair of silver cufflinks.

After that, and feeling a bit like a discarded scarecrow, she made her way into the garden to find Brand.

She discovered him on the edge of the woods, leaning against a fir tree and looking dishevelled, unshaven and unfairly attractive. He was glaring at a circle of sun-kissed daffodils on the lawn.

'Good morning, Brand,' she said brightly. 'You're up early.'

'An astute observation.' He continued to glare at the daffodils.

Isabella's heart sank a little further. Sarcasm. A bad sign. She had suspected her hopes of last night were about to be ground into dust the moment she'd seen he wasn't in the bed. But if there was even a chance . . .

She decided to let him make the next overture, and went to prop herself against the tree next to his.

When he finally spoke, she wasn't sure the wait had been worth it.

'Where in hell did you get those clothes?' he demanded. 'You look like like yesterday's laundry.'

'From your cupboard,' she replied. 'I couldn't very well come out here in my dancing dress.'

'Hmm.' He grunted and relapsed into a silence which was only broken when a twig snapped somewhere above them and a pine cone landed on his head.

Although she didn't feel much like laughing, Isabella giggled and murmured, 'Bull's-eye,' under her breath.

Brand's head jerked up. There was a retaliatory glitter in his eye, but when their glances met the glitter faded, and his lips parted in a self-mocking grin. 'Right on target,' he agreed, pausing for a moment before adding reflectively, 'Of course, if you'd done as I suggested in the first place, and moved yourself and your belongings to Marshlands, there wouldn't have been a problem about clothes. So dare I hope you've reached the obvious conclusion?'

Isabella studied his deliberately impassive features, searching for some sign that her answer might mean more to him than the convenience of having a permanent bedmate along with a daughter who lived in his house. But his expression remained blank, and she knew he would give nothing away.

'I haven't reached any conclusions,' she said quietly. 'Has anything changed since – since – ?'

'Since we found out that we suit each other in bed? Changed in what way, Isabella?'

She closed her eyes. No, that wasn't encouraging. 'I meant – the way you feel about me. About what happened between us in the past.'

Brand took his hands out of his pockets and crossed his arms. 'I'm damned if I know how I feel about you. As for the past – it's over. Its consequences, in the shape of the daughter I'm still getting to know, are not. I won't lie to you, Isabella. I want you here, in my house and in my bed. I'm willing to look after you. But as for – '

'As for love, forgiveness or trust, you won't, or can't, commit yourself.' Isabella fixed her gaze on a pearl-grey cloud that was slowly obscuring the sun. 'I understand. I don't need looking after, Brand.

Luckily I can look after myself.'

'So you won't move to Marshlands?' His voice was a scalpel sharpening on her nerve-ends – as if *she* were the one withholding love. 'It won't work, Isabella.'

She shivered. The March sun was not, after all, as warm as it looked. 'What won't?'

'Blackmail.' The ugly word hung in the air between them, making her flinch.

Isabella scuffed the ground with her sandal, and unearthed an indignant family of bugs. Would Brand never understand that she was no longer that over-indulged young girl whose impulsive act of love mingled with fear had manoeuvred him into a marriage made in – well, not hell, exactly, but certainly a kind of purgatory? Hadn't even last night proved to him that she was very much a woman?

She stopped disturbing the bugs and raised her head. Dammit, he had no right to treat her as if she were some teenage Mata Hari bent on his destruction. He knew better than that. Or if he didn't, he ought to.

Sheer temper began to rescue her from the pit of despair that had, very briefly, threatened to claim her.

Of course she had wronged Brand by keeping his daughter's birth a secret. But his suspicions about Gary and Felix had been without foundation. And how *could* he accuse her of blackmail?

317

'Brand,' she said, not bothering to hide her resentment, 'I am not the juvenile idiot you seem to think me. I am well aware that affection, trust, love – whatever you want to call it – can't be won by blackmail or threats.'

'Good. In that case, don't ask for the impossible.'

A beetle ran over her foot. She kept her eyes on it because she couldn't bear to look at Brand. If she did, she knew she would see his mouth flattened into that familiarly adamant line. She had no wish to confirm that the bond forged between them by last night's loving had faded with the unforgiving light of morning.

'I'm not asking for anything,' she said.

She wasn't either. She would love Brand to the end of her days, but it looked as though her love had finally defeated her. Coming back had been a mistake. What she ought to do now was wind up her affairs as fast as possible and attempt to pick up the threads of the life she had left behind her in Edmonton. Maybe even go home to her family for a while.

Home. Home to her gentle mother and her autocratic father who, in a way, reminded her of Brand. Home to her busy, bustling sisters and their noisy children. Home to the family who had given her everything she needed except the right to choose her own husband . . .

All at once Isabella felt her throat close up. She swallowed, and lifted a hand to her neck. Then, feeling Brand's gaze on her, she turned her head.

He was standing with one hand pressed flat against the tree trunk. And he was frowning, as if he was puzzled as well as angry.

Well, he would certainly be angry if she left the province. Because of Connie. Perhaps . . . She caught at a branch then released it, and a shower of silver droplets spattered her hair. Perhaps he might even miss his wife, if only for her warmth in his bed. But she couldn't think of that. If – *when* she left, it would be because she couldn't stay in a marriage held together by chemistry, convenience and a child. Or stay in a city where Brand could turn up at any time to torture her with his unforgiving presence. What she could do was arrange for Connie to visit him often. In fairness to both of them, she would do so.

'Neither am I *asking* for anything.' Brand's voice came to her as if he were a long way away. It was cool, inflexible, the voice she had heard him use on the phone when dealing with inefficient employees. She shivered in the bright morning air and made herself focus on his face. He looked tough, pitiless, capable of any outrage. And he was used to taking what he wanted out of life . . .

'You can't *make* me stay with you.' Isabella took his statement as the threat she sensed it was. 'Kidnapping is a criminal offence.'

'And therefore inadvisable.' He smiled, showing

his teeth. 'But you realize there are other, more effective methods of persuasion.'

When he began to move towards her, looking as if he meant to do some persuading on the spot, Isabella took a hasty step backwards and collided with a tree.

'Your fangs are showing. Have you had breakfast?' she asked with false bravado, as he advanced on her with a further disturbing show of teeth.

'Breakfast?' He stood stock-still, as if she had just suggested a quick meal of daffodils. 'I wasn't thinking about food, Isabella. I had something rather warmer in mind.'

'Brand! You stay away from me.' Isabella edged sideways and started moving backwards towards the house. 'Don't you even think – ' She broke off, gulping, as a white furry puffball darted across the lawn and threw itself enthusiastically at Brand's knees.

'Saved by a hair,' he muttered to Isabella. 'OK, persuasion postponed. Temporarily. Good morning, Fluffy.' He bent down to pick up the little dog, who wriggled delightedly in his arms and ran a wet pink tongue down his nose.

Isabella felt her muscles relax. She didn't know what form Brand's persuasion might have taken – and right now she wasn't sure if she had been frightened, angry or just plain overwhelmed – but slowly, unavoidably, it was being borne in on her that very soon she would have no choice but to leave him. For good.

The knowledge was almost unendurable.

At that moment Fluffy chose to stick his tongue in Brand's ear. Watching the astonished expression on her husband's face, and in the midst of the most mind-numbing unhappiness she had ever known, Isabella found herself smiling. Even that ridiculous white mop had fallen a willing victim to Brand's charisma.

Brand saw the smile and said caustically, 'Your daughter and her dog have the sense to appreciate the life I can give them, Mrs Ryder. Even if you don't. Now, let's go eat Mrs O'Brien's breakfast.'

Isabella nodded doubtfully. Had Brand actually accepted that she couldn't stay with him? She hoped he had. But it wasn't like him to give up without a battle. Nor was it like him to lose any battle he took the trouble to engage in. He expected to win – and usually did.

He didn't take her hand as they made their way back to the house. Instead he concentrated his attention on Fluffy, leaving Isabella to the troubled reflection that he'd made a good point. It *would* be hard to convince Connie that a return to Edmonton was in their best interests. All the same, it would have to be done.

She swallowed hard, several times, and resolved that no matter what she would get through breakfast without crying.

It wasn't easy, but she managed it – in spite of tear-ducts that kept filling up as she watched Brand calmly butter toast and read the paper. Once or twice, when their eyes met, she even produced a smile, just as if there wasn't a leaden lump weighing down her chest.

After breakfast she announced that she was leaving.

'Like that?' asked Brand, gesturing at the white sweatshirt hanging sack-like over his denim shorts.

'Yes, if you don't mind. I'll wash them and see you get them back.'

'Thank you.' He inclined his head gravely and returned to the morning paper. 'When you're ready, let me know. I'll drive you home.'

'No need. I'll call a taxi.'

He laid the paper carefully back beside his plate. 'I said I'd drive you. No wife of mine is getting into a taxi looking like salvage from the scrapyard.' When her small jaw set obstinately, he added, 'Besides, I want to see Connie.'

He's providing me with an excuse to give in, she thought, with a mixture of gratitude, surprise and chagrin. And how well he knows me. 'All right,' she agreed. 'Thank you. I'll be ready in about half an hour.'

Brand raised an eyebrow and went on reading the paper.

An hour later, when the Jaguar pulled up in front of the apartment in Point Grey, Isabella was taken aback to see a man standing in front of the door with his finger pressed firmly to the bell.

'You have a visitor,' Brand said without inflection.

'Yes. I wasn't expecting – ' She stopped, choking on her words.

The man on her doorstep was Felix.

CHAPTER 14

Isabella put a hand to her mouth – and discovered she was biting her knuckles. 'I – it's . . .' she began.

'Yes. Your old flame. I guess he didn't give up on you after all. In his place, I wouldn't either.'

She wondered if she was only imagining Brand's stress on the word 'old'. Beyond that he spoke without emphasis, as if Felix's presence was a matter of indifference.

'I don't understand,' she said.

'Seems simple enough to me. He's come back to pick up where he left off.'

'But he couldn't have. I haven't heard from him at all since – ' She stopped, then began again, choosing her words with care. 'Felix didn't leave off anywhere. I told you, nothing happened between us. Ever.' Hadn't she played this scene and spoken those same words to him before? Several times?

'So you did.' Still that neutral lack of interest. There was no way of telling what he really thought, but a small muscle was dancing a jitterbug just below his left eye.

324

'I'll have to talk to him, Brand.' It wasn't an apology, but she was afraid it sounded like one. As she reached for the door Brand's hand closed over her wrist.

Isabella looked round. What now? His jaw was stiff, his mouth as straight as a ruler, and his eyes were as darkly intent as she had ever seen them. She waited tensely for him to speak. When he didn't she pushed the handle of the door.

Brand made an odd sound through his nose, and let her go.

Without looking back, Isabella eased herself out of the car and walked slowly across the pavement to meet Felix.

Behind her an engine roared to life. She did look back then, reluctantly, but the Jaguar was already out of sight.

Felix cleared his throat, and Isabella braced herself for whatever was coming next.

'Hi, Belle.' He squinted at Brand's sweatshirt and shorts. 'Sorry if I picked a bad time.'

A bad time? Yes, perhaps it was that. More likely it made no difference. Brand had already made it clear that his feelings towards her wouldn't change.

'It doesn't matter,' she said wearily. 'Why did you come?'

'Happened to be in town. Business this time. I came to apologize.'

'Apologize?'

'Yup. For behaving the way I did when you turned me down. Wasn't your fault; I could see that. But I guess when the Cro – when your husband turned up, I didn't know just how to handle it.'

Not the way you did, Isabella thought with a feeling of hopelessness.

She couldn't hold it against Felix, though. When she'd left Edmonton she had more or less told him she expected her reunion with Brand to result in the start of divorce proceedings.

Of course he felt cheated. And Brand's behaviour hadn't helped matters either.

'Please don't worry,' she said. 'It's not important.'

'It is to me, Belle.'

But not to me, Isabella thought. She had enough troubles of her own without the added burden of coping with Felix's sudden attack of conscience.

'Would you like to come in?' she asked, hoping devoutly that he wouldn't.

'If you don't mind. Just for a minute.'

Suppressing an impulse to tell him that she did mind, Isabella put her key in the lock and waved him into the apartment.

'Coffee?' she asked. The habit of hospitality, ingrained in her since childhood, brought the offer automatically to her lips.

Felix shook his head. 'No, thanks. Um – thing is, Annie's waiting for me back at the hotel. We're – harrumph – going to get married.'

Isabella moved across to the counter to escape the faint smell of beer, and put down the black satin bag she had carried to the dance. 'Already? But . . .'

'I know.' Felix smiled sheepishly. 'Couldn't believe it myself. You did me a favour there, Belle. Annie's a great little woman.'

'A great little . . .?' Isabella gulped. Annie was charming and efficient. She was also nearly six feet tall and well-upholstered. 'I'm glad you're both happy,' she said, recovering her poise just in time. When Felix continued to stand by the door, as if he expected something more from her, she said, 'Thank you for coming,' very firmly, and waited for him to leave.

'Belle,' he murmured. 'Sweet little Belle.'

She went on waiting. Faintly, through the open window, came the sound of someone singing 'Greensleeves' off-key. Felix glanced sideways. Isabella stroked the smooth satin of her bag and was about to say goodbye again, even more firmly, when, to her astonishment, he swaggered across the floor and seized her hand.

She tried to pull away, but her elbow slammed against the counter and sent the satin bag spinning to the floor, along with a sheet of lined yellow paper,

'Ouch!' she exclaimed. And then, recognizing the spiky writing on the paper, 'Oh. That may be a note from my babysitter. Please . . .'

Felix dipped his head and, with clumsy gallantry,

delivered a damp and unprofessional kiss to her taut knuckles. Then he bent to pick up the bag and the yellow paper.

Watching him, Isabella thought how much more appealing Brand would have looked from that particular angle. Had she really considered marrying this man?

He straightened stiffly, replaced the bag on the counter and handed her the crumpled note with a bow. Isabella unfolded it.

'Connie and Edwina have gone to the beach,' she said, after scanning it quickly. 'They should be back any minute . . .' She waited for Felix to take the hint.

But, instead of leaving, he sat down heavily in the tweed wing-back, crossed his ankles and linked his hands under the beginnings of a paunch. An expanse of pale white flesh was exposed between the tops of his socks and his trousers.

'I owe you an explanation, Belle,' he said.

Isabella didn't want an explanation. She wanted him to leave.

'No, it's all right,' she said. 'I understand. Really, I do.'

Felix pretended not to hear. 'The thing is,' he said, 'it was kind of lonely after you left town. So when I ran into Annie Belinda at one of those government receptions – well, you know how it is. We talked, and then we went for a drink. Just a friendly one, you know.'

'And one thing led to another?' suggested Isabella, attempting to hurry him along.

'No, no. Nothing happened. That is . . .' He cleared his throat busily. 'Nothing happened until after you turned me down. I wasn't quite telling you – I mean, when I told you Annie would be glad to have me back, I wasn't sure she would be.' He sat back in the chair and placed his hands flat on his stomach, as if he expected this revelation to astonish her.

'Of course. I said I understand.' Surely *now* he would go and leave her in peace.

'Thanks, Belle. I hoped you would. Wouldn't want there to be any hard feelings.'

'None at all.' Isabella began to move discreetly in the direction of the door.

'Good. Good.' He made a noise like an engine that didn't want to start and levered himself slowly to his feet.

Isabella edged round the arm of the sofa, but suddenly Felix stepped in front of her. 'It's been a pleasure, Belle,' he said in a throaty whisper.

'Yes. Goodbye.' She stood to one side, giving him clear access to the door.

'Just for old times' sake,' he said.

'What?' She caught his intention just a second too late. As she started back Felix grabbed her by the shoulders, pulled her towards him and planted a damp kiss on her indignantly closed lips.

Isabella drew away from him at once. But already something in the atmosphere had changed. The air was cooler and – and someone who wasn't Felix had just hiccupped. At least it had sounded like a hiccup. She wiped the back of her wrist across lips that tasted of beer.

Soon she would have to turn her head towards the door. She didn't want to, because she already knew what she would see. Why, oh, why had she given Edwina that extra key?

Cold air curled around her ankles, and Isabella gave up pretending she could ignore it. Very slowly she turned her eyes in the direction of its source.

Connie, with Edwina beside her, stood framed in the doorway against a backdrop of the squat grey buildings across the street. The wind had come up and it was blowing the little girl's hair around her face. At first Isabella could see only a small, sandy fist pressed to her daughter's mouth. Then Edwina closed the door and she realized that Connie's eyes were filled with tears.

Edwina, her white handbag clasped against her stomach, was gently patting Connie's shoulder.

Felix, seeing Isabella's skin assume the cast of bleached marble, belatedly lumbered round to find out what was wrong.

'Connie!' he exclaimed, all at once jovial and avuncular. 'How's my girl, then? I swear you've grown another six inches.'

'No, I haven't.' Connie's lower lip was trembling. 'And I'm not your girl. I'm my daddy's.'

'Well, of course you are. But you and I are still friends, aren't we?'

Connie shook her head. 'You were kissing Mommy,' she accused.

'Your mommy and I are good friends,' Felix blustered. He glanced at Isabella for support.

Dazed, she tugged at the bottom of Brand's sweatshirt. Somehow she had to pull herself together. Connie needed reassurance – and she needed it fast.

'Uncle Felix was giving me a goodbye kiss,' she explained. 'Friends do that sometimes.'

'Not on the lips.' Connie, as usual, went straight for the jugular.

Isabella knew better than to labour the point. 'Sometimes they do,' she said briskly. 'Now, then, you'd better go and wash off some of that sand. Edwina, won't you sit down?'

Edwina shook her head. 'No, no. I can see you have your hands full.'

That was one way of putting it. 'Yes, I suppose I have,' Isabella agreed. 'I'll call you later, then.'

'You do that, dear. Let me know if I can be of any help.'

Isabella nodded. 'Thank you. I will.' She could see from Edwina's worried smile that the older woman had a fair idea of what had taken place and was inclined to sympathize. Thank heaven somebody was. Connie, who had departed resentfully for the bathroom, was likely to be harder to placate.

'I'll be off too, then,' said Felix, after Edwina had clumped off up the stairs. 'Sorry about that,' he added, turning to face her when he reached the top step. 'You'll explain it to young Connie, won't you? Didn't mean to upset her.'

Isabella sighed. 'I know you didn't. It's all right. Please give my good wishes to Annie.'

'Sure.' Felix, beaming his relief at the absolution, shook her hand and walked jauntily down the steps to a grey Buick parked by the corner.

'Lucky Felix,' muttered Isabella as she closed the door. 'Duty done, conscience eased. At least his problems are solved.'

When she turned round Connie was curled up in a corner of the sofa with her face pressed into a fat brown cushion. Isabella sat down beside her and pulled her onto her lap.

Connie squirmed back to her cushion.

'Don't cry, darling,' said Isabella, stroking her daughter's soft hair. 'Please don't cry. Uncle Felix was only trying to be kind.'

'Are we going to live at Marshlands, then?' Connie, obviously pressing what she perceived as an advantage, sat up at once and fixed her mother with an uncompromising eye.

'I don't think so.' Isabella shook her head. There was no point in raising the child's hopes.

'But I want to. I want to stay with Daddy.'

'You'll see him even if we don't live at Marshlands.'

'But it's not the same. I want – '

'I know you do.' For Connie's sake she had to hang onto her patience. 'But your father and I have to do what we think is best. For all of us. When we've decided just what that is, we'll talk about it. OK?'

'It's best for us to go live at Marshlands. With Fluffy.' Connie had a single-track mind.

'Yes, well . . .' Isabella rubbed a hand across her forehead. She could feel a headache coming on. 'We'll see,' she said.

Connie, ever the optimist, took that as acquiescence and bounced off the sofa. 'I'm going to draw a picture of Fluffy,' she announced.

Isabella, watching her head into the bedroom in pursuit of paper and crayons, wished she had half her child's resilience.

That night, after Connie had gone to bed, she collapsed into her chair and gazed vacantly into the square face of the TV. She didn't switch it on. Tonight she needed a clear head and no distractions.

The events of the past two days had shown her, with a terrible clarity, that she could indulge her indecisiveness no longer.

But, oh, it wasn't going to be easy. Like Connie, she wanted so much to stay, to be near Brand even if she couldn't be his wife . . .

She thought about that for a long time, remembering how, only last night, she had slept in his arms believing everything had come right at last. Then she remembered his eyes when he had seen Felix waiting by the door.

What would her life be like if she allowed herself to give in to the impulse to stay? Could she live with a permanent lack of trust? With doubt and suspicion, and memories that wouldn't go away?

Isabella didn't sleep well that night. But by the time morning came she had her answer.

'Daddy, Daddy, you mustn't let Mommy take me away.'

'What? Wait a minute, sweetheart, what is this?'

Six days had passed since the morning Brand had allowed Isabella to walk away from his car because he'd known that if he didn't he was likely to cause a scene he would regret. A scene that would definitely involve blood and broken teeth. Not that he believed he had any real excuse to hit Felix. It was just something he knew he would have done.

During those six days he had phoned his daughter three times and his wife once – to make an arrangement to take Connie to Stanley Park. Oh, he was well aware that he had been abrupt with Isabella far beyond the point of rudeness. But at the time he had felt as if he were struggling to keep his head out of a swamp that threatened with every second to suck him under. And if her ladyship didn't like his manners, that was too bad. His need for her was as strong as it had ever been. But he couldn't give her what she wanted.

Once, perhaps, there might have been a chance. But not since he had learned about Connie.

Now it was Saturday, and he had come to collect the child who, with a face like a crumpled sponge, had just hurled herself at his knees and let out a noisy wail of protest.

'Mommy says we have to leave. I don't want to leave. I hate Edmonton. I want to stay with you and Fluffy. Daddy, don't let her make me go. It's not fair. I don't want – '

'Hush, now, hold it just a minute, sweetheart.' Brand lifted her into his arms. 'What's all this about? Mommy's not going – '

'She is. She *is*. And she says I have to go too. I *won't*. I won't go to Edmonton. Daddy, tell her I don't have to go.'

Brand looked over the top of Connie's head, his eyes swiftly scanning the room. Two of the cupboards in the kitchen alcove hung open. They were almost empty. On the sofa a battered brown suitcase bulged with a hodge-podge of clothes. Then Isabella came out of the bedroom carrying an armful of linen.

'What's going on?' Brand demanded. He wanted to shout, but forced himself to keep cool. 'Planning a holiday?'

'It's *not* a holiday.' Connie interrupted before her mother had a chance to speak. 'And it's all 'cos of Uncle Felix. I know it is.'

'Of course it isn't,' Isabella said.

'It is – it *is*. You were *kissing* him.'

Oh. Shock hit Brand with the force of a hammer blow to the brain. He turned to his wife, forcing his hands into his pockets to keep them off her. She met his gaze with a look of frozen guilt.

It was true, then. She had lied to him again.

These last six days had been hell. He had stayed away from Isabella because he knew he had to. Yet when he had woken this morning, knowing he would see her again, he hadn't been able to keep himself from grinning at Mrs Crackitt when she brought his coffee and telling her it was going to be a rare and beautiful day.

'You look like you just won a million,' Mrs Crackitt had said.

He had been obliged to admit, if only to himself, that although he didn't need another million, that was pretty much the way he felt.

Not any more. His mouth tasted of vinegar, and pressure was building up behind his eyes.

'So,' he said to Isabella, 'We have your ageing Romeo to thank for all this.' He waved a hand at the bulging suitcase. 'I see you're planning to join him after all.'

Isabella shook her head, and a lock of dark hair fell

forward over her shoulders. Her heart-shaped face was suddenly all eyes. 'No. I wasn't kissing Felix. What Connie saw was Felix kissing *me*. It was his way of saying goodbye. He's going to marry Annie Belinda.'

'You expect me to believe that?' Brand sounded amazingly detached, even to himself.

'Why not? It's the truth.' Her arms tightened around the linen.

'Is it?'

'Yes. Felix only came to apologize.'

Connie, who was still clinging to him like a small and determined squid, chose that moment to run her fingers across his forehead. 'You're all sweaty, Daddy,' she said.

Her hand was so small. And warm. Brand gave her a quick hug. 'I expect I am,' he agreed. He didn't add that the sweat wasn't caused by the heat in the room.

Isabella started to speak, but she didn't seem able to get the words out. He waited, and after a while she tried again. 'It's nothing to do with Felix,' she said, in a voice so low he could hardly hear it. 'But – I'm sorry, Brand – Connie and I *are* leaving Vancouver.'

Oh, no, you're not! Brand felt a great white rage shouting inside his head. Oh, no, my lovely Isabella-without-a-heart. You got away with it once, but you are not going to get away with it again. And if I have to use force to stop you, you had better believe I'm willing to do it.

'No,' he said, with such quiet and chilling authority that he saw her flinch. 'You are not leaving, Isabella. Not this time. And certainly not with my daughter. Start unpacking.'

Isabella, unprepared for either his arrival or his icy outrage, staggered and almost dropped her burden on the floor.

She had only seen Brand this angry once before. It wasn't an obvious anger. His voice was level, the planes of his face strictly controlled. But rage, white-hot and seething, blazed at her out of his eyes.

She edged round the back of the sofa, bracing herself against the wall, and the two of them faced each other across the room. Brand still held Connie in his arms and Isabella hung on to her pile of linen as if it were a shield against assault.

'No,' she said steadily. 'I'm sorry, Brand. Sorry about Connie. I'll make sure she visits you often – '

'You are not leaving Vancouver, Isabella. At least not with Connie.'

Oh, heaven and all the saints! He wasn't going to see reason. The last time he had been this angry was the night . . . She swallowed, and had to make herself finish the thought. The last time he had been this angry was the night when Connie had been conceived. The best and the worst night of her life. But the outcome hadn't been so bad . . .

'Brand, truly I don't want to hurt you. But you can't make me stay,' she said quietly.

338

'Can't I?' His smile sent a shiver rippling down her spine. 'Tell me, Isabella, were you planning to run off like you did the last time? Without so much as a word to your devoted husband?'

'No! No, of course I wasn't.' Isabella dug her fingers into a pale yellow pillowcase. 'I still have to arrange for a reliable caterer to take over my business. I can't let my customers down. And I haven't nearly finished packing, so we won't be going for a while. I – um – I thought you said you had a meeting this morning. I planned to tell you when you came this afternoon.'

'Did you? By which time, I suppose, all signs of packing would have vanished and you'd have been able to break it to me gently. Was that the idea? Unfortunately for you, I finished my business earlier than expected.'

Connie nuzzled her nose into Brand's neck. 'I'm glad you came early, Daddy,' she murmured, tightening her grip on his shoulders. 'Now we won't have to go to Edmonton, will we?'

'Of course not.' Brand unclasped her arms and lowered her gently to the floor.

'Brand, you have no right to raise her hopes like that,' Isabella snapped. 'Connie, I'm sorry, darling, but it really isn't up to your father. You liked Edmonton before. You were happy there – '

'That was then. I didn't have Fluffy. Or my daddy.' Connie stuck out her lower lip and kicked mulishly at a worn patch on the carpet.

Brand put his hand on the top of his daughter's head. 'Listen, sweetheart,' he said, in a voice that Isabella could tell he was having trouble keeping even. 'Your mother and I need to talk this over on our own . . .'

'And you want me to go see Edwina,' Connie finished for him with a sigh.

Brand's mouth twisted, and he touched her lightly on the nose. 'That's right, I'm afraid I do.'

Connie gave the carpet one last kick. 'All right,' she agreed. 'I will. But only if you promise not to let Mommy make us move to Edmonton. I want to stay here with you.'

'I promise,' Brand said grimly.

Connie nodded. 'OK. Then I'll go.'

'Just a minute.' Isabella flashed her a brief smile, trying to hide her anguish from the child. 'First we'll have to make sure Edwina is able to have you.' She picked up the phone.

Edwina was available and willing, and within moments Brand had hoisted Connie onto his shoulders and was carrying her briskly outside and up the stairs. Isabella heard them laughing together, and felt an unexpected swelling in her throat. By the time Brand came back she had relinquished the linen and was sitting on the sofa, with her knees crossed and her arms wrapped protectively around her chest.

'Very affecting,' Brand said, leaning against the door and snapping it shut. 'The lost-little-girl look.

I've seen it before, Isabella, and I'm afraid it leaves me totally cold.'

With an effort, Isabella loosened her arms and folded her hands in her lap. She wished she could say that his overpowering figure in jeans and a dark blue sweater left *her* totally cold. But it didn't. In spite of the anger she could feel pulsing across the room at her in waves, she longed, as always, to throw herself into his arms.

'Why, Isabella?' he demanded. 'Is it just that you get off on disrupting other people's lives – in this case, mine and my daughter's – or do you have some other, more devious plan in mind? Felix, for instance.'

She closed her hands into fists. There was no point in letting him see that she was wounded. Nor was there any point in lying to him for the sake of saving her pride. What did pride matter compared to the tearing pain of being forced to live the rest of her life with the knowledge that the man she loved would never love her back?

'I already told you, Felix is going to marry Annie,' she said quietly. 'And the only purpose I have in mind is to put as many miles as possible between myself and any further hurt.'

'Hurt?' Brand's lips curled unpleasantly. '*You* talk about hurt? What about Connie? It's obvious she doesn't want to leave. Don't her feelings matter to you at all?'

'More than anything else. But she's only a little girl, Brand, and she wants her parents to be just like other parents. A family. We can't be that, can we? So most of all she needs her mother – '

'*And* her father. Not to mention her dog. If you insist on leaving, that's your business. Connie is mine, and I'm not about to let you drag her off to another dreary apartment where she'll have to get used to a new school and a new sitter while you're off catering your parties every night – '

'Is that so? And I suppose she'd be better off drifting around that mansion of yours with only Mrs Crackitt to watch out for her while you fly off to God knows where and – '

'Yes. As a matter of fact, she would. For one thing, if I were responsible for Connie, I'd make sure I didn't "fly off" any more than I had to. For another, my mother would move in.' Brand folded his arms and looked down at her, as if daring her to find an answer to that.

Isabella crossed and recrossed her legs. 'Mairead? But she has a home of her own – '

'Which she is now in the process of selling. She wants to move closer to her granddaughter. Another reason I have no intention of letting you take Connie away.'

Isabella began to feel as if she were being backed into a corner by forces beyond her control. No. Not forces. Force. Brand, with his mind made up, had always been immovable as rock. And she didn't want to hurt Mairead – didn't want to hurt anyone. But she wouldn't, *couldn't* stay in Vancouver knowing Brand was only a few miles away, free to arrive on her doorstep at any moment to disrupt her life and break her heart afresh.

She studied him, standing with his legs apart and his head thrown back against the door, looking for all the world like a warrior who had just defeated a mortal enemy in battle. Any moment now, she thought, he would put his foot on her throat and let out a primitive roar.

For a second she was tempted to give in. It would be easier to stay, to do exactly as Brand wanted . . .

No! She stiffened her back against the sofa. She must be crazy. If she wasn't already, she soon would be if she gave in.

'It's no use, Brand.' Isabella fixed her gaze on the gold band she still wore around her finger. 'I do have to leave – whether you like it or not.'

He said nothing as she twisted the ring round and round, watching the dull gold catch the light, not looking at her husband. When the silence became so highly charged that she could bear it no longer she raised her eyes.

Brand's head was bent forward, his jaw thrust out, hard and belligerent, and the big hands clenched at his thighs seemed poised to smash the first object they encountered. When, suddenly, he moved across the room to grasp her forearms, she was unable to suppress a small scream. He ignored it and pulled her to her feet.

'Did you think I meant to hit you?' he asked. 'No, Isabella, not even you can reduce me to that. For all it might . . . Never mind. All I have to say to you right now is that I'll fight you every inch of the way. If you try to take Connie – '

'I *am* taking Connie.'

'No. You will do what is best for our daughter.'

Our daughter? He hadn't said 'my' daughter this time. 'Yes,' she agreed. 'I will. I'm sorry, Brand – '

Brand shook his head. 'Sorry? Yes, you will be. I promise you, Isabella, this is one battle I don't mean to lose.' Abruptly he released her wrists, and she fell against the arm of the sofa. By the time she had regained her balance he was already outside the door.

All at once Isabella was overtaken by a burning desire to shake some understanding into this man she loved more than her life – this man who wanted to take her daughter from her.

As he started down the steps she ran after him and stood in the entrance. 'You will lose,' she shouted. 'This time, Brand, it looks as though we're both going to lose.'

He paused to look up at her, and for a few seconds she thought she saw pain as well as confusion and a certain hard wariness in his eyes. Then his mouth turned down, and he shrugged. 'Tell Connie I'll be back this afternoon,' he said, and continued on his way down the steps.

Isabella, shoulders drooping, stumbled back into the apartment and shut the door. For a moment she leaned against it, staring at nothing, then she moved to the sofa and closed her eyes.

Brand had been so angry. Angry because he loved Connie and didn't want to lose her. Angry, too, because he thought his wife was deliberately setting out to torment him. As if she would ever choose to hurt Brand if she could think of any conceivable way out.

Was it possible – could she, for Connie's sake, endure Brand's continual presence in her life? Could she live with him again without his love? She pressed her knuckles to her eyelids. Connie was a perceptive little girl. Most children were. Surely life in a loveless household couldn't be good for any child. Sooner or later, wouldn't she sense that something was wrong between her parents? In the long run, wouldn't she be more hurt by that than by a clean, quick break and another move?

With a sigh of indecision, Isabella heaved herself upright. A solution to her dilemma seemed no closer, but that didn't mean she could leave Connie with Edwina for the remainder of the day. The little girl was expecting to go to Stanley Park with her father, and once Brand had a grip on his temper he'd be back.

Reluctantly, Isabella made her way up the stairs.

Edwina opened her door with a welcoming smile that turned rapidly into a frown. 'Is something wrong?' she asked, after one look at her visitor's haggard face. 'We thought we heard shouting, but Connie said it was just her father, and that he was going to make everything all right.'

'Connie has always been an optimist,' Isabella said, trying to return Edwina's smile. 'And I'm afraid most of the shouting was me.' She explained what had happened.

Edwina shook her head disapprovingly. 'You modern young people,' she muttered. 'In my day when things went wrong we didn't just up and leave our husbands and go running off to strange cities – '

'Yes, but Edmonton isn't at all strange,' Isabella interrupted. She was in no mood to listen to a grandmotherly dissertation on the responsibility of flighty young wives to stay with difficult husbands who didn't love them. 'Where *is* Connie, Edwina?'

'In the bathroom. She's making soap bubbles. I'll tell her you're here.'

'I'll go. Thanks, Edwina.' Isabella wound her way through a clutter of overstuffed furniture and came to a stop at the open bathroom door. 'Connie?' she called. 'Connie, it's time to – ' She broke off abruptly.

The floor was wet, the mirror covered in a thin film of soap. But of Connie there wasn't a sign.

Isabella glanced doubtfully at Edwina, who was peering over her shoulder.

'She must have slipped out while while I was filling the kettle,' said Edwina. She raised her voice. 'Connie? Connie, where are you?'

When that brought no response they checked the bedroom, the kitchen, three closets and the living room. Then the bathroom again. It didn't take long. And Connie was definitely not in the apartment.

'I expect she's gone home,' said Isabella, with more assurance than she felt. 'I'll go and check.'

But Connie hadn't gone home. Or if she had, it had only been to fetch her pink hippotamus. He was missing too.

'Perhaps she's visiting one of the other suites,' Edwina suggested.

'Yes, of course. That must be it.'

There were only eight suites in the building. Three of them failed to answer Isabella's insistent knock. The people in the other three had not seen Connie, and weren't at all sure who she was.

With rising panic, Isabella hurried out onto the street. A bus was just rounding the corner, but no dark-haired child was playing on the pavement or hiding in the bushes by the door.

'You take this side of the road, I'll take the other,' Isabella called to a dithering Edwina. 'She can't have got far.' She couldn't, could she? Connie was only four years old.

'Connie!' she cried, rounding a corner and catching sight of two small, giggling figures running up a long flight of steps.

But the two heads that turned to stare at her belonged to a freckle-faced boy and a little girl with blue eyes.

Isabella's heart returned to its place in the pit of her stomach. Connie *couldn't* be lost. She couldn't. Ah! Surely that was her daughter's high-pitched laughter coming through the window of the store where they always bought their milk . . .

She hurried to the door. But the only customer in the store was a gangly teenager trying to persuade the man behind the counter to sell her cigarettes. Neither of them was laughing.

Isabella looked at her watch. Connie had been missing for over half an hour. Unless . . .

Of course. By now she was probably home again, being fussed over by a thankful Edwina. Yes, *that* had to be it. She had been wasting her time searching in all the wrong places.

Isabella spun round and began to run.

By the time she met up with Edwina, hurrying from the opposite direction, both of them were panting and Isabella had a painful stitch in her side.

Connie was still missing. They compared notes and started out again.

Three quarters of an hour later they had scoured

all the neighbouring streets, twice, and Isabella had even tried the beach.

'But where could she have gone?' she cried. 'Oh, Edwina, you don't think – I mean, she's so little. Anything could have happened.'

There had been so many awful incidents in the paper lately. And just last week that poor child . . . *Madre de Dios!* No. She put a hand up to her mouth to stop herself from screaming.

Edwina shook her head, her pudgy face wrinkled with guilt and distress. 'I am so sorry, Isabella. She was right there. In the bathroom. I had no idea – '

'It's not your fault.' Isabella hadn't time to worry about Edwina's sensibilities, and she knew all too well that it could take only a few seconds for a child bent on eluding adult detection to disappear. 'Did she say anything – anything at all that might give us a clue – ?'

'I don't think – why, yes.' Edwina's eyes brightened, then turned anxious again. 'Yes, now that you mention it, she *did* say something about giving her father a nice surprise and showing her mother she's a big, grown-up girl. She said big girls get to live wherever they like.'

'Oh, no! She didn't.' Isabella slumped against the stucco. She could feel its roughness through her blouse. 'Did she seem worried? Or upset? Her father – '

'No, I don't think so. Well . . . perhaps a little. But

she seemed quite sure her daddy wouldn't let anything bad happen. Hadn't – hadn't you perhaps better phone him?' Edwina sounded as if she might burst into tears at any moment.

Isabella blinked at her. 'Phone Brand?' she repeated dazedly. 'Yes. Yes, of course. You're quite right.'

She stumbled into the apartment, but her hands were shaking so badly that she dialled the wrong number. She tried again, without success. Then Edwina came up behind her, removed the instrument gently from her hand and dialled for her.

Mrs Crackitt answered. 'Yes, Mr Ryder just came in,' she admitted. 'But I don't think he's taking calls at present – '

'He'll take this one,' Isabella said.

'Oh. Oh, well, just a moment.' Mrs Crackitt was flustered. She put down the phone with a clatter, and a minute later Brand came on the line.

'Yes,' he snapped.

'Brand. It's Isabella – '

'So Mrs Crackitt said. What is it?'

She wiped a thin film of moisture off her upper lip. 'It's Connie,' she whispered. 'Brand, she's disappeared.'

'What? What did you say? You'll have to speak up.'

'I said it's Connie.' Isabella was shouting now. 'She's disappeared.'

'Dis – What do you mean, disappeared?' He sounded more impatient than worried.

Isabella explained. There was silence for a moment, and she felt as if she could actually hear him checking options and making snap decisions. Recriminations, she knew, would come later.

'Right,' he said brusquely. 'You stay right where you are. In case she comes back. Have you called the police?'

'Not yet. I – '

'Then do it. And tell Edwina and anyone else who can help to keep on searching. I'll join them as soon as I can get there.

Brand was brisk, efficient and to the point. Isabella had no idea what he was feeling. Then he hung up.

She passed the message to Edwina, who nodded, and left at once to get help. Then she picked up the phone to call the police, willing her hands to remain steady.

The woman who took her call was brisk and reassuring. Isabella got the impression that she was used to dealing with overwrought and overprotective mothers and thought she was just another one of those. But she took down the details of Connie's disappearance and said an officer would call as soon as possible.

After that there was nothing to do. Isabella began to pace back and forth across the floor. She felt cold, frozen to the bone, but she made no attempt to look

351

for an extra sweater. Every few seconds she stopped pacing long enough to run to the window and gaze frantically up and down the street.

There were plenty of people about, but no little girl in a pink tracksuit.

Twenty-two minutes from the moment he had hung up the phone, Brand's Jaguar roared to a stop at the kerb.

'Any word?' he demanded, striding into the apartment as if he were taking over a command post.

'No.' Isabella shook her head. 'Edwina and some of our neighbours are out looking – '

'Good. Have the police come?'

'Not yet. They'll be here.'

'All right. Tell me exactly what happened.' His face was a mask – flat, hard and unrevealing.

Isabella made herself stop pacing as she repeated, in more detail, the story she had told him over the phone.

Brand slapped a hand against his thigh. 'I see.' He stared over her head as if she wasn't there.

Isabella felt a tear forming in the corner of her eye. She lifted a hand to brush it away and was surprised to feel Brand's fingers on her elbow. He guided her over to the wingback chair. 'Sit down,' he ordered, quite gently. 'Don't worry. We'll find her.'

'Where are you going?' she asked, because he was already halfway out the door.

'To find my daughter.'

'I'll come too. I've *got* to do something.'

'No. You'll stay right here and wait for the police. If you want to do something, make coffee.'

She nodded. An extraordinary numbness was creeping into every corner of her body, turning the blood in her veins to ice and emptying her mind of rational thought. This was all a dream. It couldn't be real. Connie wasn't lost. Not her little girl with the laughing eyes. It had to be a mistake. Connie was only upstairs. She'd be back any minute . . .

'Isabella? Did you understand what I said?' Brand was abrupt to the point of harshness, and for the first time she thought she heard a break in his voice.

It brought her out of her trance. 'Yes,' she said. 'Yes, I understand. Brand . . .?'

'What?' He turned back impatiently.

'I – I – nothing.'

He muttered something under his breath, and started to pull the door closed. But just as he did so the phone rang. Before Isabella could move he was across the room and into her office-bedroom. She turned in her chair, watching his face as he seized the receiver.

Fear pricked at her skin.

'Yes,' she heard him say. 'Yes. Yes, I see. Thank you, officer. We'll be right there.'

He put the phone down and came back into the

living room. 'They've found her,' he said. His voice was devoid of emotion.

Isabella gulped. 'Is she – ? Is she – ?'

She couldn't get the words out, and all of a sudden Brand's features were slashed by the widest, whitest grin she had ever seen. 'She's fine,' he assured her. 'She climbed on a bus. With her pink hippopotamus and a bubble pipe. The driver got suspicious and called the police. They have her down at the station. It seems she told them she was on her way to Marshlands.'

Relief, cleansing and cathartic, swept over Isabella and made her laugh.

'Thank God. Is she – is she very upset?'

'Apparently not,' Brand said drily. 'She's bragging to anyone who will listen that she caught the bus all by herself because she wanted to give her daddy a big surprise. She also told them Marshlands is where she and her mommy are going to live.' He smoothed a hand over his jaw. 'Our daughter has a touching faith in my powers of persuasion.'

'Oh.' Isabella felt her body go limp. She slumped down into the chair as the thankfulness that had welled up like loud music and burst over her in great waves of relief turned slowly into a furious need to strike out at whoever or whatever had put her through this agonizing nightmare. She felt dizzy, disorientated, out of touch with reality. And Brand's powers of persuasion weren't nearly as infallible as Connie thought.

Without thinking, she jumped to her feet. 'Let's go,' she snapped. 'And when I get my hands on that young lady, I'm going to give her – '

'No.' Brand's voice was cold. 'You are not going to give her anything except a smile and a hug and the assurance that you love her a lot. You do, don't you?'

Isabella dropped her eyes. The carpet was even more threadbare than she'd thought. She twisted a button on the red shirt she was wearing with her jeans.

Brand was right. What had she been thinking of? Of course she was going to give Connie a smile and a hug. They had found her. That was all that mattered.

And Brand had been the one to see it. Not her. Not the mother who had loved her and cared for her all her life.

She looked up, no longer caring that there were tears in her eyes. 'Yes,' she said. 'Of course you're right. I'm sorry. Shall we go and fetch her now?'

Brand didn't answer, but through a mist she saw him extend his arm. Then it was around her waist and he was turning her towards the door and saying, 'Don't blame yourself too much, Belleza. You have had one hell of a day.'

Belleza. He had called her Belleza again. She sagged against him, glad of his strength, grateful for his support, and unable to think beyond the moment.

As they walked out to the car together Edwina came panting up beside them.

'They've found her. She's all right,' said Isabella.

Edwina's face lit up and her mouth split into a huge, beaming smile. 'They've found her?' she repeated. 'Thank the Lord. Oh, my dear children.' Only after she had flung her arms first around Isabella and then around a mildly startled Brand did she pause to ask, 'Where was she?'

They told her, and the elderly babysitter let out such a whoop of laughing relief that Brand and Isabella winced.

'Imagine that little imp thinking she could make it all the way to Richmond by herself,' she marvelled.

'She would have made it too, if the bus driver hadn't checked on her,' said Brand, with what Isabella suspected was fatherly pride – now that his daughter was safely in the hands of the police.

'Maybe,' she said dampeningly.

'Oh, very likely,' Edwina said. 'And now, if you don't mind, I'd better tell the rest of them she's been found. They've all been so worried.'

They watched her puff her way back down the block, shouting the glad tidings of Connie's safe return to the whole neighbourhood.

As Brand helped Isabella into the Jaguar a little cluster of cheering well-wishers gathered on the corner to wave them off.

Long before they arrived at the police station, her

head had fallen onto his shoulder. She closed her eyes, worn out with the strain of the past hours.

Brand glanced down at the long hair trailing across his chest, sighed, and draped his arm around her.

He drove the rest of the way to the station with one hand.

CHAPTER 15

Isabella sat on a log at Jericho Beach and watched the waves streaming up the sand. It was a grey, blustery morning, and she could hear the leaves on the trees behind her whispering a sibilant protest at the wind.

She wanted to scream in protest herself.

Yesterday Brand had driven her and Connie back to Marshlands. There had been no question of any other destination. Nor had there been any question, when evening came, about where Connie was to spend the night. The little girl had been tired and – belatedly – uncertain of her parents' reaction to her escapade. But she had brightened up when Brand had told her that nothing dreadful was going to happen to her as long as she kept her promise never to run away again. A joyful reunion with Fluffy had followed, and in the end Connie had fallen asleep in Brand's arms.

Isabella had said nothing when, with a tenderness that had nearly broken her heart, he'd carried his daughter upstairs and laid her on the pink and white bed. Connie hadn't even woke when they took her clothes off.

After that, and with his mouth only slightly flatter than usual, Brand had asked Isabella if she wished to make use of his spare bedroom.

'The spare bedroom?' When her voice came out like the squawk of a disappointed parrot she put her hand self-consciously to her mouth.

'You have somewhere else in mind?'

Brand's tone was politely enquiring. Anyone hearing it would never have guessed that the two of them had recently shared a night of passion so explosive it could have put the eruption of Mount St Helens in the shade.

Isabella searched his face for some sign of affection, for any indication that it mattered to him where she spent the night. When she didn't find it she said stoically, 'No. No, of course not. If you don't mind, I'd rather go home.'

'As you wish.' Brand inclined his head and left the room abruptly. By the time Isabella caught up with him he already had his car keys in his hand and was waiting impassively in the hall.

'I can call a taxi . . .' she began.

'No,' Brand said. 'You can't. We've been through this before, Isabella, and you're exhausted. I won't have you waiting around for a taxi that may never turn up. So, either you accept a bed in my spare room or you accept my offer to drive you. Understood?'

'Understood.' Defeated, Isabella gave in to him quietly. He was right that she was exhausted. She hadn't the heart for an argument.

They didn't speak on the drive back to Point Grey. Brand's uncommunicative profile didn't invite conversation, and even if it had, Isabella had nothing to say to him.

When he escorted her to her door all she could manage was a chilly, 'Thank you.'

Brand nodded, but instead of leaving for a few seconds he stood motionless, watching her as she groped in her purse for her key. Then, as Isabella felt a coldness begin to creep into her veins, he reached out and took her in his arms.

She made no attempt to pull away. Nor, when he bent to kiss her, softly but with infinite expertise, did she respond. But when his kiss deepened, and the paralysis that had gripped her from the moment he put his hands on her at last began to wear off, she put her arms around his neck and kissed him back.

It was a long kiss, more sensitive than sensual, but eventually, and as if by mutual consent, they drew apart. 'Why, Brand? What was that for?' Isabella asked shakily.

He rested his shoulders against the doorjamb. 'Is there some reason I shouldn't kiss my wife?'

Somewhere in the night a cat howled. 'Yes,' said Isabella. 'There is. Because some time soon I won't be your wife any more.'

'You're sure of that?' He spoke as though he was asking her if she was sure she had remembered to put the dog out.

She nodded.

'And what about Connie?'

His eyes beneath the streetlight seemed to gleam. To Isabella he was suddenly a creature of the night, wary, predatory and certain of what he wanted. He frightened her a little.

'What *about* Connie?' she said.

'Hasn't today's episode given you the answer to that?'

Isabella shook her head helplessly. 'It's taught me that my daughter can be as determinedly pig-headed as her father.'

'That's all?'

She knew what he was getting at. She also knew that he would fight her to the bitter end for Connie, and that there was a very good chance he would win. It was a risk that for the sake of her sanity and Connie's well-being she must take. No child should have to live in a house where there wasn't love. One-sided love could never be enough.

'Yes,' she said. 'That's all. Goodnight, Brand.'

He didn't answer, but she thought she saw him frown in the dim light. Then suddenly he put his hand on the back of her head and drew her to him, crushing her lips briefly and thoroughly before he let her go. Isabella knew, with an instinct that had rarely let her down, that this was Brand's way of telling her goodbye.

'Goodnight, Isabella,' he said, as if it were any normal night. 'Sleep well.'

Isabella was too worn out and too devastated to do anything but nod. Because it wasn't any night. It was the last time Brand would hold her in his arms.

A branch snapped in the wind and came crashing to the ground behind her. Isabella jumped. She was on the beach, not leaning alone and empty in her doorway watching Brand drive off into the night.

Oh, Mother of God! Had she made a terrible mistake? Were the wind and the waves trying to tell her something? She watched as two seagulls battled the up-draughts to descend onto a patch of seaweed draped over a small mound of pebbles. The moment they landed the gulls began to fight over the decaying remains of something raw and bloody that up until now had been hidden by the weeds. Isabella shuddered and closed her eyes.

When she opened them again another seagull was swooping towards the combatants. So engrossed were they in their battle that they didn't notice the newcomer until he landed beside them and snatched the disputed delicacy from between their beaks. As he flew off on the wind the other two squawked indignantly and took off in futile pursuit of their booty.

'Stupid things,' muttered Isabella. 'If they had just been willing to share . . .'

She didn't much like the direction of that thought, so she got up and began to throw pebbles into the foam.

Behind her, a childish voice shouted, 'Mommy, Daddy, look. I found a shell.'

'I saw it first,' screamed another voice.

Isabella turned to look as two small figures in bulky jackets and red hoods tumbled onto the sand and began to wrestle. When they stood up each of them held a broken half of a delicate white shell.

'Now you see what happens when you don't share nicely like I told you,' crowed a preachy adult voice.

Isabella groaned and went back to her log. Sharing. Was that what life was all about? Surely somebody, something was on her side. It *couldn't* be right to live with a man who didn't love you. Yet nature seemed to be conspiring to point her towards a decision she didn't want to make. One that would, perhaps, be different from the conclusion that had seemed so sane and sensible – was it only last week?

But that had been before her daughter ran away.

Was it possible? For Connie's sake, *could* she move to Marshlands and live a lie? Surely it was too much to ask of any woman . . .

But she wasn't any woman. She was Isabella Sanchez Ryder, who, in her twenty-three years, and without meaning to in the least, had brought more chaos into the life of an honourable man than he could reasonably have been expected to put up with.

Yet he had put up with it. Isabella picked up a handful of damp sand and thought of the very beginning, when without hesitation Brand had offered a frightened young girl his protection. She remembered the good times as well as the bad – and as the unseen sun rose higher in the sky, and the cresting waves foamed almost to her feet, she tried to imagine what her life would be like without the man she loved.

Empty. It would be empty. A pair of seagulls, the same two, perhaps, flew squawking overhead. Their wild cries startled her. The past, they seemed to be saying, was gone for ever. It couldn't be altered. But she could make a choice this morning that might, in some measure, make up for the pain she had caused. A choice that might be desperately hard to bear but which would, if she could keep faith with herself and hide her hurt, be fairer to the two people she loved the most.

However much it cost her, she had to do what was best for her daughter. And maybe, just maybe, for Brand.

Slowly, her movements unusually lethargic, Isabella dragged herself up from the log. When she reached the road it began to rain, and the rain mingled with the tears cascading unashamedly down her face.

It wasn't until twenty minutes later, while she was

dropping her saturated clothing into the bath, that she paused to wonder why she was smiling through her tears.

'Thank you, Mrs Crackitt. Just put it on the desk, will you?'

Brand barely glanced at the tray of coffee the bustling housekeeper was setting down amidst the clutter of files and books in the small library he used as a study. He would have preferred something stronger than coffee, but it was only two o'clock – not much of an example for Connie, who was playing quietly in the corner with Fluffy.

'You'd better have a cup, Mr Ryder. You look all done in.' Mrs Crackitt had a habit of noticing when people didn't respond to her faultless service. In that, Brand thought, she wasn't much different from Veronica.

'Yes. Yes, I'll have some in a minute. Thank you.' He waited until she had backed, frowning, into the corridor, then went back to staring out of the window at the rain.

His computer was switched on and, in theory at least, he was looking over the latest budget figures for Ryder Airlines. In fact, when he wasn't glaring at the rain billowing in a relentless grey curtain across the garden, he was watching Connie.

She was sprawled on the Arabian carpet with her feet on the ground and her knees pointed up in the air. Fluffy lay half-on and half-off her chest, with his tongue hanging out and his black nose resting on her chin.

Brand's features softened as, from the corner of his eye, he saw Fluffy roll over onto his back and Connie obligingly begin to rub his tummy. He started to smile, but at once the ache that had been pounding at his temples all day grew more intense. The top of his head felt as if it were ready to explode. He pressed his fingertips to his forehead and reflected wryly that Connie's presence usually made headaches go away.

Not today.

In the few weeks he had known his little daughter, he had come to love her with a deep, unconditional devotion.

And he was going to lose her.

Until yesterday he would have moved heaven and earth to keep her in Vancouver, whether or not Isabella agreed to stay. But that had been before Connie had taken it into her head to pull her vanishing act and he had seen the fear and desolation in her mother's eyes.

Isabella, his beautiful, once self-absorbed young wife, had changed far more than he had been willing to admit. Her courage he had always acknowledged, even as he'd contemplated wringing her pretty neck, but that she should be capable of giving so much of herself to her child – that was something he had never expected.

He knew now that no matter what she had done in the past he couldn't, and wouldn't, try to separate Isabella from her daughter.

He propped his elbows on the desk and dropped his head onto his hands. God, he would miss them. Both of them. He hadn't known it was possible . . .

'Mr Ryder? Mrs Ryder's here. Shall I show her in?'

Brand looked up quickly. Mrs Crackitt's mottled grey head was poking round the edge of the door. She looked vaguely uneasy.

'Think of the devil,' he muttered. And then, when he saw from his housekeeper's face that he'd spoken out loud, said hastily, 'Yes. Yes, of course, show her in.'

Isabella must have been waiting outside, because she was in the room almost at once. She was carrying a heavy black shoulder-bag and wearing a black fitted skirt and a baggy red sweater several sizes too large for her small frame. She looked lost in it, a pathetic waif from the storm that was raging outside. He wondered if the pose was deliberate.

After one glance at her face, Brand stood up.

'What is it?' he demanded, cursing the sudden tightness in his chest. 'Has something happened? You're crying . . .'

Isabella, catching sight of Connie in the corner, gave a determined sniff and made an attempt to smile. 'No, I'm not,' she said quickly. 'It's just that the wind made my eyes smart. Connie, darling – '

'I know.' Connie heaved a martyred sigh. 'You want me to go and see Mrs 'Brine.' She put her hands on her hips. 'I like Mrs 'Brine. *And* Crackitt and Fluffy. And I'm not going to Edmonton, Mommy.'

'Connie – ' began Brand.

'It's all right.' Isabella smiled with more assurance. 'No, darling, you're not. We're both going to stay here with your daddy.'

Connie's face lit up as if the lights had come on after a power-cut. 'Oh, Mommy, I do love you. And I knew Daddy would make it all right.' She ran to throw her arms around her mother's waist. Then, before Isabella could speak, she was skidding out the door, pursued by a barking and over-excited Fluffy. They listened to his paws scrabbling a staccato beat on Mrs Crackitt's highly polished floors.

'Mrs 'Brine! Mrs 'Brine!' Connie shouted at the top of her lungs. 'Crackitt! Crackitt! It's 'ficial. I'm going to stay here with you.'

Brand closed the door deliberately behind her and turned to face Isabella. She had laid her black bag on his desk and was standing in the centre of the carpet with her hands behind her back, like a child who expected to be scolded.

'Does this mean you accept my proposal?' he asked.

Isabella tried not to flinch. His voice was gruff. Not the voice of a man who had just been given a reprieve. And yet there was a sensuous fullness about his mouth, a tension in the deep lines grooved between his nose and lips that, for a few seconds, almost gave her hope. Then she remembered what he had said to her in the garden, and knew that any relief he might be feeling was about Connie. Not about the wife who was the mother of his child and, occasionally, a convenient object for his passion.

'Yes,' she said quietly, meeting his dark gaze with resolution. 'I do accept. I've decided I really have no choice. Because it's true what you said. I do have to do what's best for Connie. And – and for you. I know you love her, Brand.' Her voice cracked a little before she was able to go on. 'It was just that I didn't see how I'd be able to bear living with you again. Not the way I know it will have to be from now on.'

She drew a quick breath as Connie's laughter drifted from somewhere down the hall, then continued hurriedly, 'But of course you were right when you said it would be hard for Connie to adjust to a new school and new sitters just when she's got used to Vancouver. And quite probably I *would* have been out a lot at first. So, yes, I'm accepting your offer. And I'll *have* to bear it.'

She hesitated, then added with a certain reluctance, 'Brand . . . Connie is a bright little girl. I'm afraid that means – well, it means we'll have to behave as if we at least *like* each other – most of the time anyway.'

369

Brand started to say something, and she hurried on before he could interrupt. 'I know it won't be easy. But I believe children are only better off with two parents if those parents aren't estranged from each other. It's not enough that Connie will have that ridiculous dog. She needs a – a loving family.'

Brand said nothing. His eyes, deeper than midnight on a moonless night, gave her no clue to his thoughts. After a while she couldn't stand to look at him any more, so she attempted a mockery of a smile and pretended to study the intricate eastern pattern of the carpet.

'So *that's* why you were crying.' His voice seemed to come from far off, and there was an unusual hoarseness about it that made her lift her head.

His brows were a thick black line, but she saw at once that he wasn't angry. Instead he seemed almost incredulous, as if he'd been granted a revelation. As she watched incredulity was replaced by the dawning of – what? Guilt? Regret? Sorrow? No, surely not any of those . . .

She closed her eyes, opened them again. Now Brand looked as if he were waking from a very bad dream.

'Yes,' she said, swallowing, trying not to sound like one of the frogs from the marsh. 'But I didn't want Connie to see. In case she worried.'

'Let me get this straight,' Brand said slowly. 'You have just agreed to live with me as my wife. For the

370

sake of our daughter. And you're crying because you find the prospect just about – intolerable. Is that it?'

Isabella, still with her hands behind her back, fixed her gaze on the top button of his cream-coloured shirt. 'No. Not intolerable. Just – painful. But I'll be all right. I promise I won't go around blowing my nose all the time. And I know I've done a lot of things wrong, but I'll try to do everything right from now on – try to make up for not having told you about Connie.'

She was blinking very fast to dissolve the mist that kept forming over her eyes, so she was startled when she felt Brand's fingers beneath her chin. The shock of his touch made her gasp.

'Isabella? Are you telling me you're making this . . . sacrifice . . . not just for Connie, but for me?' He tilted her head up. His face was so close she could see the pores in his skin and feel the warmth of his breath in her hair.

She tried to smile at him and very nearly succeeded. 'It's hardly a sacrifice, is it? A handsome husband. A father for my daughter. A beautiful house. Considering I've just about closed down my business, and find myself currently unemployed, a lot of people would say I should be grateful.'

'But you're not.' He let go of her chin abruptly and moved back. 'Isabella, is there someone you'd rather be with?'

371

'What?' She stared at him in amazement. 'No, of course there isn't. You can't seriously believe – '

'All right.' He held up a hand that wasn't quite steady. 'I accept that. Which means it's me. I'm the problem.'

'I – yes. In a way. But you see – ' She broke off, unable to find the words to make him see that she understood he couldn't manufacture love where no love existed.

Fluffy started to bark outside the closed door and they heard Connie tell him to be quiet. Brand still had that strange, haunted look about him. If she hadn't known better Isabella might have described it as remorse.

'Yes,' he said. 'I think I do see. You told me once you wanted the whole bit. Not just a house and a husband, but that other essential ingredient for a happy marriage.'

So he did understand. She nodded, hoping the lump in her throat wouldn't swell up and choke her. 'Yes. But I know it's too much to ask.'

Brand was shaking his head back and forth as if she'd hit it with her black shoulder-bag. And for the first time since the night of the dance he seemed to be making no attempt to hide his feelings. Pain and self-condemnation were etched into every line of his face.

'And I didn't believe you. Didn't believe I could trust you,' he groaned softly. 'Can you ever forgive me, Belleza?'

'Forgive you?' She was bewildered now. 'But – Brand, I have nothing to forgive.'

His mouth twisted. 'A week ago I might have agreed. A week ago I believed you were still the little man-eater I married in a fit of remorse, found myself falling in love with and then drove away one cold December night . . .' He started to reach for her, then his eyes narrowed and he let his hand drop back against his side. 'You're wearing my bracelet,' he said.

Isabella felt the blood leave her face. Her heart was beating like the wings of a butterfly caught in a net. She took a step backwards and groped blindly for Brand's tall leather desk-chair. It had to be somewhere behind her.

'What did you say?' she whispered, finding the chair and sinking into it.

'I said, you're wearing my bracelet.'

'Oh. Yes. It seemed – right.'

'It is right. I want you to wear it.'

She smiled slightly. 'I'm glad. I want to wear it too. But I meant before that. Did – did I hear you say you found yourself falling in love? With me? I thought – '

'So did I.' Brand's voice was sandpaper on gravel. 'I thought I must be losing my mind. Because I believed you had used me as nothing more than a plane ticket out of a country whose culture was forcing you into a marriage you didn't want. I assumed you saw me as a vast improvement on the man your father had picked out for you – but only because I came from a place where, no doubt, you imagined women had the freedom to do whatever they liked.'

Gradually Isabella felt the blood coming back into her cheeks. Brand was staring at her with such intensity, such bitter regret, that she felt compelled to admit reluctantly, 'If that's what you thought . . . you were partly right. From the moment I first saw you with Mary I did have visions of a new and different life. You see, I'd been brought up to believe love was for storytellers and dreamers. That's what my father said. But there was something in the way you looked at Mary that made me restless, made me want what I'd been told didn't exist in the practical world of property rights, and power based on money and land.'

She dropped her eyes, ran a finger along the edge of his desk. 'When I saw you again on the street I was certain our meeting must be fate. That you and I were destined to be together. Girlish fantasy, of course. Although later on – '

'I know,' Brand interrupted roughly. 'Later on all that changed. Didn't it? Oh, yes, you were still a child in many ways. But, thinking back on it, I should have seen you were beginning to grow up.'

'Loving you wasn't easy.' Isabella glanced up at him with the beginnings of a smile. 'It did have an ageing effect.'

Brand groaned. 'Was I that bad?'

'No. Not really. Most of the time you tried to be a responsible husband. Or what you thought of as a responsible husband. But you were still so in love with Mary that you couldn't take me seriously as a wife.' She hesitated, but made herself add honestly, 'That's why I tried to use Gary to make you jealous.'

Brand stared at her, then shoved his hands deep into his pockets. Isabella met his stare without flinching, and after a moment he spun round and went to stare out of the window. The rain was as relentless as ever. 'I still have the occasional urge to throttle that young man,' he growled at her over his shoulder.

'Do you?' Was that good news or bad?

'Oh, yes. On the other hand – it worked.' Brand turned his back on the weather and gave her a straightforward look. 'Your little intrigue with Gary was what woke me up to the fact that Mary had become no more to me than a bittersweet memory of first love – and the fact that I was married to a real live woman I wanted very much.'

He lowered his head and seemed to be examining his shoes. 'The trouble was, I couldn't bring myself to tell you how I felt – partly, I suppose, because I couldn't accept it myself; partly because you were so damned young. So I kept my hands off you, knowing that if I didn't I would either murder you or make love to you most thoroughly.' He gave her a brief smile, and hitched his hip on the window-sill.

'I think I like the second one better.' Isabella's smile was a lot less ambiguous than his.

The corner of Brand's mouth edged up again. 'Mmm. But I couldn't see myself going to bed with – or to gaol for – a flighty young woman who started out flirting with my neighbour and ended up swooning in his arms.'

'I didn't swoon. And in the end you did go to bed with me.' Isabella pulled at the sleeve of her red sweater.

'Yes. And I was desperately ashamed of myself. As I had every reason to be.' He shook his head, as if he still found it hard to accept what he had done. 'Hell, I was nearly ten years older than you, Isabella. I had to give you a chance to grow up, to make up your mind what you really wanted once you were no longer driven by fear, the need for protection and . . .' His lips tipped up unexpectedly. 'And, I suspect, the desire to get the better of your father.'

'Oh. I thought you didn't want me. Because of Mary.' His long body, draped with easy elegance against the rain-washed glass, was so achingly desirable that she had to grip the arms of the chair to stop herself from rushing into his arms.

'Didn't want . . .' Brand folded his arms on his chest. 'I am a man, Isabella. Of course I hadn't forgotten Mary. But that didn't mean I wasn't aware that I had an incredibly sexy young wife.'

Isabella discovered that her mouth had turned

unusually dry. Still grasping the arms of the chair, she pushed herself onto her feet. 'Are you telling me that all those months we lived together – ?'

Brand detached himself from the window, and as he moved towards her she saw evidence of weeks of strain reflected in his eyes. 'The last few of those months were pure hell,' he said. 'I had made love to you precisely once, and I was nearly crazy with wanting to do it again. But there was no way I could reconcile that wanting with what I perceived as my responsibility to my very young bride.' He smiled ruefully. 'Pride came into it as well. The question of will-power. As you may have noticed, Isabella Belleza, I *do* have my fair share of pride.'

Oh, yes, she had noticed. It was part of the reason she loved him. And watching him now, seeing the regret for what might have been, hearing the bleak, husky rasp of his voice, she longed to go to him – to smooth the lines of care very gently from his face.

Yet she hesitated. Did his words mean what she hoped they meant? Or would he reject her yet again? She couldn't afford to make a mistake now.

Brand was moving closer. It was as if he were walking in his sleep and couldn't stop himself. Or didn't want to. Isabella took a step towards him. Then there was no more space between them – no great chasm that couldn't be bridged – and she was being crushed so tightly in his arms that she barely had breath to lift her face. But when she did, and their lips met in the kiss she had waited five years for, the kiss that was a statement of Brand's love, she knew that at last and for evermore, and whatever the future might bring, the two of them would face it together.

Brand never did drink Mrs Crackitt's coffee. But his headache was gone.

'Brand,' said Isabella some hours later, as they walked hand in hand through the rain-soaked woods behind the house. 'Brand, can you truly forgive me? For not telling you about Connie? Because if I can make it up to you in any way – '

'You have,' he said. 'You've come back to me, Belleza.' He touched the damp fronds of an evergreen and a shower of raindrops sparkled to the ground. 'How can I hold what you did against you?'

'You did,' said Isabella. 'For a long time.'

'Yes. And maybe some part of me always will. In the middle of the night when I can't sleep, or when problems at work get on top of me. But I want you to know something – this afternoon, before you came back, I had made up my mind I could never take Connie away from you. I couldn't hurt you like that.'

'Thank you,' she said simply, as the last whisper of doubt drifted away and peace, and the certainty that went with it, filled her heart. Brand loved her enough to relinquish his claim to his daughter.

'I couldn't take her from you either,' she admitted

softly. 'I thought I could, but I couldn't. What a pair of fools we've been, Brand.'

'Speak for yourself,' Brand said, dropping a kiss onto her hair.

Isabella laughed. She wanted to sing like the wild canary perched in the willow tree by the pond. She wanted, like the little bird, to give thanks to the sun for emerging in all its golden glory from behind the clouds. But before she gave way to that impulse there was something she needed to be sure of.

'Brand, are you quite certain?' she asked.

'Certain?'

'Yes. That you trust me. And if you do – '

'Oh, I do.' Brand put his hands on her waist and swung her into the air. His lips parted in a wry white grin. 'You know, I think perhaps I guessed that you were no longer my dizzy, thoughtless little bride from the moment you came into my dining room last Christmas wearing that grimly sensible black dress. You didn't look anything like the frivolous young woman who had stolen away from my bed five years before. I was surprised, fascinated and mystified. As well as angry.'

'Were you? Really?'

'Of course. Why do you think I came looking for you?'

She smiled. 'I wasn't sure. You looked so stern and unforgiving I thought you might have come to take revenge.'

'It crossed my mind when I saw Connie's ears,' he said drily. 'But, no. I came because I couldn't stay away.'

'Oh, Brand.' Isabella dropped her forehead onto his shoulder. 'I always knew all that high-powered bossiness hid a marshmallow heart.'

'Marshmallow! I'll give you marshmallow, Mrs Ryder. There was a time when I was ready to send you express delivery to the moon.'

She lifted her head. 'I know. When you realized Connie was your daughter.'

Brand nodded, and closed his eyes briefly. 'That *was* hard to take. I felt as if I'd been hired to do a job for you, that I was merely a stud to be taken advantage of as the need arose – '

'Brand!' Isabella sprang back indignantly. 'Didn't it occur to you that you're not the sort of person people take advantage of? That is . . .' She hunched her shoulders. 'Except that once, when I got you in a weak moment.'

Just for a second Brand looked startled. Then he grinned, a wolfish, determined grin that made her stomach turn over and over. He ran a firm, flat hand down her spine. 'I plan to have a lot more weak moments, Mrs Ryder,' he assured her. 'Almost immediately.' His fingers played a gentle tattoo on the fabric of her skirt, and Isabella wriggled voluptuously.

'Good,' she said.

Brand planted a kiss on her nose. 'How could I not have seen the truth?' he muttered, as if he were talking to himself.

She gave him a puzzled frown. 'And what *was* the truth?'

Brand took her hands and held her at arm's length. 'That you loved me, unselfishly and with your whole heart. At first I thought it was all for Connie's sake. Then I looked into your eyes and saw what I should have seen from the beginning.'

Love and tenderness shone from his face, bathing her in a warm, dreamy glow. And when he bent to kiss her again she was certain her heart would explode with the pure joy of loving.

Brand lifted his head and tangled his fingers in her hair. 'Beautiful Isabella,' he murmured, half to himself. 'However did I survive all those lost and lonely years without you?'

'Badly, according to your mother.' Isabella laughed up at him. 'She told me you were in sore need of a good boot in a soft place.'

'Is that so?' Brand gave her a severe look and pulled her to him. 'Speaking of soft places . . .' He ran a provocative hand over her rear. 'Did I mention that seeing you burst into tears at the prospect of spending your life with me isn't the sort of thing that does a whole lot for a man's ego? I hope we won't have any more of it.'

Isabella's answer was to press her body up against

him, moving her hips until she heard him groan. After that he gave her a look so deliberately, purposefully seductive that she longed to wrap her arms around his neck and pull him down with her onto the pine needles and moss. There, under the bright spring green of the leaves and the filtering sunlight, she would make love to him until the sky was painted orange and all the shadows of the past were washed away . . .

But it was not to be. Not now, at any rate, because Connie and Fluffy were fast approaching across the lawn.

Isabella gave a small sigh, and contented herself with resting both hands on her husband's chest and murmuring a little breathlessly, 'As long as I'm with you, Brand, I don't think I'll ever cry again. Is *that* the sort of thing your ego needs?'

'It'll do for a beginning,' Brand said. He draped an arm around her waist and bent to whisper in her ear.

Connie came running up to them seconds later, and was enormously entertained to see her mother's face turning a bright, geranium-red.

EPILOGUE

A week before Christmas, on the anniversary of the day two years earlier when Isabella Sanchez had driven to Marshlands to cater a dinner for Brandon Ryder, Brandon Ryder the Second was about to make his noisy entrance into the world.

Brand drove Isabella to the hospital with one eye on the road and the other on his wife. How could a woman who had doubled in size over the past nine months still manage to look as delicately perfect as an orchid? he asked himself. He gripped the wheel and pressed his foot down hard on the accelerator.

Later, as he sat beside her bed holding her hands and feeling utterly helpless in the face of the miracle taking place in front of his eyes, he heard the doctor say the baby's crown was showing.

The muscles in his chest contracted, and for a few seconds he couldn't seem to breathe. Then he looked down at Isabella's face on the pillow. It was white, almost translucent in the glare of the artificial lighting. A light veil of sweat covered her forehead.

'Isabella . . .?' He was afraid to break her concentration, afraid, in this most sacred of moments, that something, even now, would go wrong. He had to tell her one more time.

'Isabella, I love you. Thank you – thank you for being my wife. And the mother of my daughter . . .'

She started to smile, but the smile twisted into a scream.

Brand grasped her hands, so small and fragile compared to his, and for the first time in years he began to pray. 'Take care of her, Lord, keep her safe . . .'

It was as far as he got. Isabella gave a long drawn-out groan, and he heard the doctor's voice saying, 'The head's turning.' And then, 'It's a boy.'

'Thank you,' Brand said, raising his eyes to the antiseptic ceiling.

When he bent his head again, to gaze with love and adoration at the woman lying on the bed, he saw that her long hair was soaked with perspiration. She looked even more ethereal than she had before the birth. Yet there was a glow about her that made Brand catch his breath.

He thought she had never looked so lovely.

'Thank you,' he said again. 'For being the mother of my daughter and . . .' He paused to swallow an unaccustomed fullness in his throat. 'And of my son.'

Isabella started to say something, but at that moment Brandon Ryder the Second decided he'd been ignored long enough.

Listening to the lusty wail of his firstborn son, Brand brushed the moisture from his eyes and started to laugh.

Isabella smiled sleepily. 'It's obvious he has the Ryder lungs,' she said.

The next day Brand stood beside her bed, holding a wide-eyed Connie by the hand. His heart swelled with pride as he gazed with a certain awe at the soft, sleeping face of his tiny son. When he turned to his wife there was a world of love and gratitude in his eyes.

'Isn't he beautiful?' Isabella said dreamily. She smoothed a hand over the baby's dark head. 'He looks just like you, Brand.'

'*I* think he looks like a wrinkly Christmas orange with black hair,' Connie announced. She tilted her head to one side. 'But he's kinda cute if you look at him sideways.'

'Thank you, Connie.' Brand brushed a hand across his mouth. 'I'm pleased to see you have your mother's talent for boosting a man's ego.' He laid an affectionate hand on her head. 'But oranges, even ones with black hair, hardly ever come with the Ryder ears.'

'What's that about the Ryder ears?'

A dazzling sunburst of yellow billowed briefly in

the doorway, then floated into the room like a miniature schooner in full sail.

Brand blinked. 'Hello, Mother. You're looking very – um – colourful today.'

'I'm always colourful,' said Mairead. 'Only the young can wear black and get away with it. And I refuse to be laid out on a slab before my time by anyone.'

Brand choked into the red roses he had brought for Isabella. 'And I pity the man or woman who tries,' he murmured, endeavouring to suppress a delicious vision of his mother rising up like an imperious elderly rainbow to flatten a flabbergasted mortician with a look from her button-black eyes.

'So do I,' Mairead agreed with aplomb. She turned towards the bed and stared down at her fuzzy-haired grandson. 'So this is the newest Ryder. Ears and all. I wish you good luck, Isabella.'

'Thank you,' said Isabella, slanting a glance towards Brand. 'Do you think I'll need it?'

'In spades,' replied her mother-in-law with feeling.

'Spades? I don't see any spades,' Connie put in. 'Grandma – '

'Neither do I,' admitted Mairead. She cast a shrewd look at the unusually soft expression on her son's face. 'Connie, I think you and I ought to go for a – for whatever unpleasant concoction you young people are eating these days.'

'Ice cream, toffee and chips,' said Connie, quickly turning her back on her mother.

Isabella wasn't even listening. Her eyes were fixed on Brand, who was looking down at her as if, to him, she was the only person in the room.

'Don't worry,' Mairead said to Connie. 'They'll return to normal with a bump once they get that little demon home.' She nodded at her new grandson. 'I should know. He has his father's eyes – even if they are blue at the moment.' She hoisted the strap of a big straw bag onto her shoulder. 'And I say it's a good thing your other grandparents are arriving tomorrow. It's going to take teamwork to keep that one in order. How long are they staying?'

'Until they get tired of us,' said Brand. 'Or until the rainy season is over back home. Whichever comes first.'

Connie giggled, and Brandon Ryder the Second chose that moment to open his mouth and demand supper.

'You see what I mean,' said Mairead. 'Come on, Connie. This is our cue to get our . . .' She cleared her throat vigorously. 'To get out of here.' She took Connie's hand and the two of them left the room together, without so much as a second glance at Brandon the Second – who let out another wail of protest.

'I said he was just like you, Brand,' said Isabella, smiling up at him. 'He expects immediate attention to his needs.'

'And he's had the good sense to hire the very best catering service in town,' Brand observed with a grin. 'I have to admit I've found it quite satisfactory myself.'

'Only satisfactory?' she asked, pulling a face at him.

'All right. Impressive.'

'Impressive?'

'Excellent. Sublime,' he amended, bending down to touch his lips to her forehead.

'That's better.' Isabella favoured him with the soft, sweet smile that, eight years ago, had changed his life for ever. 'Kiss me, stranger,' she whispered.

Brand shook his head and gave her a mock-ferocious scowl. 'Watch it,' he ordered. 'Remember what kissing strangers got you last time.'

But Isabella only laughed. 'It got me you,' she said simply. 'And Connie and our son. What more could I possibly ask?'

So Brand kissed her again, tenderly, slowly and with love. His heart was too full for mere words.

And what else was there to do?

THE EXCITING NEW NAME IN WOMEN'S FICTION!

PLEASE HELP ME TO HELP YOU!

Dear *Scarlet* Reader,

As Editor of *Scarlet* Books I want to make sure that the books I offer you every month are up to the high standards *Scarlet* readers expect. And to do that I need to know a little more about you and your reading likes and dislikes. So please spare a few minutes to fill in the short questionnaire on the following pages and send it to me. I'll send *you* a surprise gift as a thank you!

Looking forward to hearing from you,

Sally Cooper

Editor-in-Chief, *Scarlet*

QUESTIONNAIRE

Please tick the appropriate boxes to indicate your answers

1 Where did you get this Scarlet title?
Bought in Supermarket ☐
Bought at W H Smith or other High St bookshop ☐
Bought at book exchange or second-hand shop ☐
Borrowed from a friend ☐
Other _____

2 Did you enjoy reading it?
A lot ☐   A little ☐   Not at all ☐

3 What did you particularly like about this book?
Believable characters ☐   Easy to read ☐
Good value for money ☐   Enjoyable locations ☐
Interesting story ☐   Modern setting ☐
Other _____

4 What did you particularly dislike about this book?
_____

5 Would you buy another Scarlet book?
Yes ☐   No ☐

6 What other kinds of book do you enjoy reading?
Horror ☐   Puzzle books ☐   Historical fiction ☐
General fiction ☐   Crime/Detective ☐   Cookery ☐
Other _____

7 Which magazines do you enjoy most?
Bella ☐   Best ☐   Woman's Weekly ☐
Woman and Home ☐   Hello ☐   Cosmopolitan ☐
Good Housekeeping ☐
Other _____

cont.

And now a little about you –

8 How old are you?

Under 25 ☐ 25–34 ☐ 35–44 ☐
45–54 ☐ 55–64 ☐ over 65 ☐

9 What is your marital status?

Single ☐ Married/living with partner ☐
Widowed ☐ Separated/divorced ☐

10 What is your current occupation?

Employed full-time ☐ Employed part-time ☐
Student ☐ Housewife full-time ☐
Unemployed ☐ Retired ☐

11 Do you have children? If so, how many and how old are they?

_____

_____

12 What is your annual household income?

under £10,000 ☐ £10–20,000 ☐ £20–30,000 ☐
£30–40,000 ☐ over £40,000 ☐

Miss/Mrs/Ms _____

Address _____

_____

_____

_____

Thank you for completing this questionnaire. Now tear it out – put it in an envelope and send it before 31 January 1997, to:

Sally Cooper, Editor-in-Chief

SCARLET
FREEPOST LON 3335
LONDON W8 4BR
Please use block capitals for address.
No stamp is required!

MASTR/7/96

Scarlet **titles coming next month:**

RENTON'S ROYAL Nina Tinsley
Sarah Renton is troubled. **Renton's Royal,** her one abiding passion, is under threat. Her rivals for power and success are other Renton women – who each have their own reasons for wanting to take over from Sarah. What these women all discover, in their search for success, is that passion and power make dangerous bedfellows . . .

DARK LEGACY Clare Benedict
Greg Randall haunted Bethany Lyall's dreams . . . and her every waking moment too. Before Bethany could follow her heart, though, she had to conquer the demons from the past and face the dangers in the present. Of the *three* men in her life, only Bethany could decide who was her friend, who was her enemy and who would be her lover!

WILD JUSTICE Liz Fielding
Book One of **The Beaumont Brides trilogy**:
Fizz Beaumont hates Luke Devlin before she even meets him! So Luke Devlin in the flesh is a total shock to her, particularly when he decides to take over her life. Fizz is so sure she can resist him, but then he kisses her – and her resistance melts away . . .

NO DARKER HEAVEN Stella Whitelaw
Jeth *wants* Lyssa. Lyssa wants marriage without romance. Jeth offers excitement and passion, but his son, Matt, offers uncomplicated commitment. Against her will, Lyssa is caught up in an eternal triangle of passion.